PRIMAL Renegade

JACK SILKSTONE

The characters and events portrayed in this book are fictitious. Any similarity to real persons, living or dead, is coincidental and not intended by the author.

Published by Jack Silkstone

www.primalunleashed.com

ISBN-13: 978-1533629265
ISBN-10: 1533629269

BOOKS BY JACK SILKSTONE

PRIMAL Inception
PRIMAL Mirza
PRIMAL Origin
PRIMAL Unleashed
PRIMAL Vengeance
PRIMAL Fury
PRIMAL Reckoning
PRIMAL Nemesis
PRIMAL Redemption
PRIMAL Compendium
PRIMAL Renegade
SEAL of Approval

Human greed is the most significant threat to our planet. It is driving species after species into extinction as poachers scrabble for a quick buck at the expense of all that is pure in the world. Fortunately there are people who are willing to stand against this greed. They stand ready to put their lives on the line to protect wildlife and ensure that our children's children will inherit an earth still populated by amazing creatures such as rhinos and elephants. This book is dedicated to the men and women who choose to stand and fight against greed.

Your fight is just. You are PRIMAL.

PROLOGUE

NORTH LUANGWA NATIONAL PARK, ZAMBIA

The black rhino stood with her calf in the shade cast by a camel thorn tree. The film crew that watched from less than a hundred yards away didn't in the least bit bother the majestic grey beast. She was familiar with the humans and their vehicles. As long as they kept their distance they caused her no concern.

Two cut-down safari trucks were parked to take advantage of the soft morning light. A cameraman and a sound technician stood in the back of one with a journalist in the other. Uniformed park rangers sat behind the wheel of each vehicle, ready to beat a hasty retreat if the rhino decided they had overstayed their welcome. The black rhino, unlike their cousins the white, were renowned for having a short temper, especially the mothers.

It was an instinct Afsaneh Ebadi could relate to. Four months pregnant, Saneh was already fiercely protective of the tiny life growing inside her. Although, not as protective as her partner. It had taken all her charms to convince Aden Bishop that she would be perfectly safe with the film crew and their ranger escort. A former Australian soldier, he wanted to wrap her in cotton wool and reinforce it with Kevlar.

The striking former Iranian intelligence operative had joined the group that morning, not willing to miss an opportunity to see the rhino calf. She sat in the front passenger seat of the truck that carried the journalist, dressed in the same khaki work shirt and shorts as the rangers.

In the opposite vehicle, Christina Munoz, a photographer and her close friend, shot stills of the rhino and film crew. She caught the eye of the petite brunette and flashed a grin. Christina smiled back and turned the camera on her.

Saneh tossed her long hair and pouted pretending it was a fashion shoot. With her Persian features, full lips, and mane of dark glossy hair, she was a natural in front of the camera. The photographer giggled and Saneh pressed a finger to her lips reminding her that they were still filming.

Christina poked out her tongue and directed her attention back to the rhinos.

She smiled contentedly. Luangwa National Park was a paradise for her. Almost completely untouched by tourism and protected from poaching it was one of Africa's few pristine wildlife reserves. She tipped her head to one side as she watched the rhino and her calf, listening to the words of the journalist.

"Behind me is Kitana the black rhino and her calf. This particular animal is important because she is one of only a handful of breeding females left in Zambia." The journalist was from the BBC and had a crisp British accent that reminded her of David Attenborough. "Reintroduced to the Luangwa National Park in 2003, the black rhinos are making a slow comeback. This young calf is the third to be born in as many years. She lives here under the watchful eye of the Luangwa Rangers, a local force trained by volunteers. But, while this is a good-news story for the future of black rhinos here in Luangwa, the same cannot be said across Africa. With less than four thousand animals remaining and a ferocious appetite on the black market for their horns, the rangers are fighting a losing battle. They simply do not have the resources to protect them all. So far this year, Kruger National Park in South Africa, only a thousand miles away, has lost a dozen rhinos to poachers. If this continues we can expect the black rhino to be extinct in less than ten years."

Saneh watched the noble beast and her calf with a heavy heart. The mother had two horns; the one at the end of her snout was long and curved, a lethal weapon with which to defend her offspring against lions and hyenas. Unfortunately it offered her no protection from poachers. The British journalist was on the money; her partner, Bishop, and the other volunteers were fighting a rearguard action. Every day endangered animals across Africa were slain for their horns or tusks. Why? So ignorant superstitious assholes in China and Vietnam could adorn their desks with carvings and pop pills containing the same chemical compound as their fingernails. The mere thought filled her with rage. She took a deep breath and tried to relax as the journalist wrapped up his monologue.

A faint noise caught her attention and she looked up. She spotted an electric drone circling above them and gave it a wave. Bishop was keeping an eye on her.

The PRIMAL operatives had been in Zambia for a little over a week. They'd flown in from Spain where builders were turning their tiny cottage into a family home. With PRIMAL off-line they had chosen to spend a few months working with Christina and her boyfriend Dominic Marks at the recently established Luangwa Anti-Poaching Academy.

Saneh and Bishop had met Dom only a few weeks earlier. They'd been visiting Christina at Kruger National Park and saved her from an attempted kidnapping. It was there that the Africa bug had bitten them both. Now they couldn't get enough of the exotic wildlife roaming the rolling savannah and lush floodplains.

"That's a wrap, people," announced the journalist. "Let's get back to camp for breakfast and a cup of tea."

Saneh gave the rhinos one last glance as the drivers started the vehicles. When the BBC team was ready they drove back to the track that led to base camp.

"So when will you broadcast your piece?" Saneh asked the journalist a mile into the journey.

"The crew will edit it and send it back to London tonight. Should be hitting the airwaves tomorrow morning."

"That soon?"

"The joys of technology. So how do you fit in here? Your partner works with Dom doesn't he?"

"Yes, we're friends of Christina. Taking the opportunity to see a bit of Africa while we can."

"I understand that. I can't get enough of the place."

"Yes, it does have that effect." She turned and took in the surroundings as they covered the last few miles through the bush.

As they pulled into the camp she spotted Bishop standing in front of the low-slung building that served as a training facility and headquarters. He was an unremarkable looking man. Medium height with an athletic build, he wore camouflage pants cut off at the knee, battered hiking boots, a short-sleeved khaki shirt, and a faded blue Yankees cap. The hat covered a mop of shaggy hair that matched the stubble on his face. Intelligent brown eyes and a lopsided grin greeted her as she jumped out of the truck, walked across, and flung her arms around him. "How are your little spy planes going?"

"Not great, we're getting some kind of interference on the signal. How was the trip out to see Kitana?"

"It was lovely. But, now I'm hungry."

Bishop touched her growing belly and kissed her. "You never stop eating. Come on then, let's find you something."

"Steak, Aden, I want a steak," she said as they walked to the camp kitchen.

"That kid's got to be a boy with the amount of red meat you've been craving. Oh, by the way, Kruger is heading up in the next few days. He's going to help us out for a week with some training." He referred to a South African former Recce operator who was one of PRIMAL's most capable warriors.

"How's he doing?" asked Saneh as she opened the refrigerator.

"He sounds a little bored."

She found a steak on a plate and pulled it out. "That's the biggest issue facing Vance and Chua. When they shut down operations they released an army of adrenaline junkies on the world." She referred to the leaders of PRIMAL, the vigilante organization that she and Bishop were part of.

Bishop took the plate and lit the grill. "Hey, some of us are doing just fine."

"Sure you are." She kissed him on the cheek.

***

SHANGHAI, CHINA

Wang Hejun's apartment was perched on the top floor of a residential tower overlooking Shanghai's business district. The beverage baron was one of the wealthiest men in China. With a net worth estimated at close to twelve billion dollars only a small number of Internet entrepreneurs sat higher on the Forbes China Rich List.

The apartment encompassed the entire penthouse level. Originally three separate residences, he had combined them into a single high-rise mansion. His study, formerly one of the master bedrooms, was where he spent most of his time now he was retired. Decorated in a garish interpretation of Italian baroque that included gilded mirrors and intricately carved furniture, it was where he hoarded his most prized possessions. Jade carvings, fine porcelain, and other works of art were displayed on either side of the room. In the far corner stood an illuminated glass cabinet with his prized collection of ivory, bone, and horn carvings. They represented trophies of exotic animals, with thousands of hours of work by master carvers to craft them into precious artifacts.

Hejun sat at his desk in a silk robe nursing a glass of Maotai as he stared at the gilded television on the wall. On screen a black rhino and her calf were standing in the shade of a tree. He didn't understand the journalist; he had never learned English. No doubt wailing about the animals' dwindling numbers or some such rhetoric, he thought. That was a weakness of the West. They did not seem to comprehend that nature was a resource to be exploited for the betterment of man.

His eyes never left the magnificent curved horn that adorned the beast's snout. The black rhino was one animal missing from his extensive collection. The Chinese government's ban on rhino horn had made it increasingly difficult and expensive to procure. Black rhino horn had become impossible to find. But here, on his television, was one of the finest examples he had ever seen. He hit a buzzer on the desk and a moment later the door opened and his assistant appeared.

"Yes, Mr. Wang." Fan Wei was in her mid-thirties with an attractive round face and high cheekbones. A tailored skirt and suit jacket emphasized her slender build.

He pointed to the screen where the journalist was still talking. "I want you to get me that horn," he croaked.

"Of course." Fluent in English, Fan read the tagline across the bottom of the screen. She committed the location of the animal to memory.

"Do you want it sent to a carver?"

He shook his head. "No, I want to see it first. Then I will decide what to do with it."

She bowed. "Very good, sir. Will that be all?"

"I want it now. Cost does not matter."

"I will contact our supplier immediately." She turned and left the room.

He continued watching the television until the segment about the rhino had finished. Then he turned it off, left the desk, and walked across to the ornate glass cabinet in the corner. The interior was lit showcasing the intricately carved horns and ivory inside. Opening it, he took out one of the horns and inspected it lovingly. The artwork was finely detailed; it would have taken a skilled artisan thousands of hours to work the delicate scrolls into the horn. The carvings represented power, longevity, and health, things he craved more than all else. This collection, along with his business empire, would be handed down for generations to come. It would be his legacy.

***

Fan had been to the Shanghai Greater Exports office on a number of occasions to collect packages for her master. Tucked away in the sprawling Shanghai docks, the office gave the impression of a legitimate business. Run by gangsters, it was a one-stop shop for anyone looking for access to the Chinese underground trafficking market. Illicit goods including endangered animals, military hardware, even slaves, were available for the right price.

She parked Hejun's Mercedes outside the office and introduced herself to the middle-aged woman behind the front desk. She was ushered through to see the man who controlled the gateway to illicit goods, Zhou. She didn't know the Triad's last name nor did she feel it necessary to enquire. She cared only that he could deliver the black rhino horn her master desired.

"Ah the pretty Fan Wei, back again to do the bidding of her wrinkled master." Zhou sat behind a large desk on which lay no less than a dozen cell phones, the tools of his trade.

She fought the urge to vomit as the gangster's eyes lingered on her. The man had a habit of licking his lips every few seconds. He reminded her of a bloated lizard she once saw at the Shanghai zoo. "Hejun would like you to procure something for him, something of great rarity."

"Of course, he desires only the finest ivory."

"He wants a black rhino horn."

Zhou sneered, "Of course he does but there are none to be had."

"There is one in Zambia, North Luangwa National Park."

He locked eyes with her. "How much is he willing to pay?"

"Whatever it costs."

Zhou's tongue circled his lips. "I'll see what can be done."

"He wants it as soon as possible."

"Then I will have an answer for you today."

"I will wait here."

"That is not necessary. I'll call you and confirm the price. Unless you wanted to stay for a different reason?" He licked his lips again and watched her stride out of the office. Maybe he would offer Hejun a discount for a night with her, he thought. He smirked; the old dog had probably already had his way with her. He reached for one of his phones and dialed a number. As it rang he imagined what Fan Wei would look like naked, bouncing on his lap.

***

MOMBASA, KENYA

Six thousand miles away in a rusted warehouse a battered phone rang. David 'Mamba' Mboya scowled from the stack of crates he was perched on. The leader of the poaching gang drank from a bottle of beer and let the phone ring a half-dozen more times before it finally got the better of him. He tossed the bottle and it shattered against the sheet iron wall. "Kogo, answer the damn phone!"

A moment later Julias Kogo appeared; lighter-skinned, slight of build, and with a shaved head. Kogo was Mamba's right hand man and errand boy. "Yes, Mamba." He used the former Ugandan paratrooper's nickname, a reference to the African snake renowned for its ferocity and speed. Grabbing the phone off the cradle he pressed it to his ear and listened before turning to his boss. "It's Zhou, says he has another job for us."

Mamba climbed off the crates, uncoiling his wiry frame to its full six-foot-five. Without a hint of fat, the ebony-skinned Ugandan was an imposing sight. His hair was clipped short, a testament to his time in the military. He wore a faded check shirt left unbuttoned, revealing a lean torso covered in scars. "I don't want to talk to that piece of shit. He ripped us off on the last shipment of tusks. Tell him I'm going to find a new buyer for this batch."

Kogo relayed the response to the Chinese gangster on the other end of the line. "He says he has something big this time."

"He always does." Mamba opened the refrigerator and pulled out another bottle of beer. He twisted the lid off using the crook of his bicep and downed half of it. "Give me the phone." Grabbing the handset he raised it to his ear. "Zhou, you crooked Chinese hyena, do you have the money you owe me?"

"I paid you the agreed amount."

"Yes, but then you doubled the price you sold it for."

"That's not true."

"I saw it on the internet, Zhou. You might think we're all monkeys you yellow bastard but we're smarter than that."

The gangster paused. "I will make it up to you on this next consignment."

"Tell me more."

"I have a buyer for a black rhino horn."

"That's great, Zhou, but I don't have a fucking death wish."

"You can name the price."

He took a swig from the beer.

"I'm talking big numbers, Mamba, two, three hundred thousand."

He smacked his lips. "Make it five." He could hear Zhou hissing through his teeth. "The black rhinos are protected by armed rangers. Not the usual deadbeats, I'm talking ex-military and police. I'll need men who are willing to take the risk and I'm going to have to find a rhino with a big enough horn. None of that comes cheap."

"Do you know North Luangwa National Park?"

"Do you know The Great Wall of China? Of course I know it, you idiot, it's in Zambia."

"There's a black rhino there."

"There are also rangers. Your number just became six hundred."

"Fine, but I am not paying you extra money for the elephant horns."

"They're called tusks and I've spent two weeks assembling the weight you ordered. I will include the black rhino horn for a total of eight hundred thousand, American dollars."

He could hear Zhou typing on the other end. "I have a ship due in at Mombasa on Friday. Can you have the entire shipment ready by then?"

Mamba drained the last of his beer. "Transfer a hundred grand into my account now and we'll go to work."

"You've never needed money up front before."

Mamba lobbed the bottle at the back of the warehouse where it shattered. "You haven't asked for a black rhino horn before, Zhou. Make it happen." He passed the phone back to Kogo who returned it to the cradle. "We're going to need at least five men."

"Any preference?"

"For this job, only the best, and I want one who knows Luangwa."

"OK, boss."

Mamba pulled another beer from the refrigerator. "And Kogo, make sure they're killers."

CHAPTER 1

NORTH LUANGWA NATIONAL PARK, ZAMBIA

Aden Bishop stood on the verandah of the raised bungalow he shared with Saneh, staring out at the rolling savannah. He ate from a bowl of oatmeal as he watched a family of warthogs foraging in the dry grass. PRIMAL seemed like a distant memory as he watched the sow and her two piglets digging for roots. There was something about Africa that soothed the soul. It was a harsh land with an underlying beauty that took your breath away.

"Good morning, handsome," Saneh purred from behind him. She wrapped her arms around his waist and he could feel the slight bulge of her belly against his back. Her pregnancy was beginning to show.

Bishop smiled as he spooned more oatmeal into his mouth. In a couple more months they would head to Sydney, Australia, to have the baby in his hometown. Then, after a few weeks, it would be back to their newly renovated home in Spain. That reminded him, he needed to check in with the builder.

Saneh rested her chin on his shoulder and spotted the hogs. "They're so cute."

"They have a certain repugnant appeal."

"You've got something in common." She laughed. "Hey, we got an update from Vance."

"Yeah, and how is the team doing?"

"Remarkably busy considering we're supposed to have stood down. Mitch is in Israel building spare parts for Ice, Mirza is working with Tariq delivering humanitarian aid, and the headquarters staff are still working the intel piece from Abu Dhabi. They're calling the new safe house the Sandpit."

"I knew they wouldn't be able to stay away from work. What games are they playing in their new play pen?"

“The usual, keeping an eye on things. Making sure the CIA isn't still trying to find PRIMAL.” She kissed his neck. “Oh, and they're running a sweepstake.”

“Yeah, and what are the odds?”

“Twenty to one.”

“Let me guess, they’re all betting we're going to have a girl.”

“How did you know that?” She feigned surprise.

He chuckled. “Because, they all think I deserve a daughter.”

“Come on, it wouldn't be so bad, would it? I mean, I've wrapped you around my little finger. Imagine what it would be like with two of us.”

He shook his head. “That’s not something I want to contemplate.”

“So, what have you got planned for today?”

“I'm going to help Dom train the new guys in apprehension techniques.”

“Sounds exciting.”

“Hardly, but it's necessary.”

“Christina is heading out this afternoon to take photos of one of the black rhinos.”

“The one with the calf?” He took another mouthful of his breakfast.

“Yes, I want to go with her. Two of the rangers will accompany us, it will be perfectly safe.”

Bishop put down his bowl and turned to face her. “I'm allowed to be a little protective of the woman I love and our unborn child.”

She smiled. “Of course you are. But, nothing’s going to happen. You know there hasn't been a poaching incident here in years.”

“It's not the poachers I'm worried about. Those black rhinos are grumpy mothers.”

“Oh please, Kitana is not aggressive at all. Plus, I won't leave the truck.”

“I don't know why you're asking when you've already made up your mind. I'll see you later today. I’ve got to run, Dom’s waiting for me.” He kissed her on the forehead and entered the bungalow. As he dropped his bowl into the sink his phone rang. He glanced at the screen. It was Kruger, the South African PRIMAL operative. "Hey, brother, what's up?"

"I'm fucking bored, *ja*. What are you doing?"

Bishop laughed as he left the bungalow and walked across a dusty clearing to the training hall. "I'm still up at Luangwa. I thought you were going to drop in, plenty of work here to keep you busy. Where are you?"

"I'm in Zimbabwe, just north of Harare. Been spending some time with an old Recce mate. He's a family man now so he has to go to work and all that."

"You're not far away. Come on up, we're at the ranger school. I'll flick you the coordinates."

"Maybe tomorrow, *ja*."

Bishop could hear a dog barking in the background.

"Hey, I've got to go but I'll give you a call before I head up, OK?"

"Sounds good, mate."

Bishop ended the call as he entered the training room. Dom was standing in front of a bench lined with flexicuffs and lengths of rope.

"You running a detention lesson or an S and M workshop?"

Dom chuckled. "Morning, Aden, you ready to get started?"

"Yeah, how long do you have the lesson scheduled for?"

"An hour. What's up? You got a hot date with Saneh, bro?"

"No, I'm keen to work through the bugs in the drone and get it up again tonight." Bishop spotted the first of the rangers filing into the shed for the lesson.

"I've got nothing else planned for the day. We can mess about with the drones all afternoon." He grinned. "Use it to keep an eye on the girls."

"Sounds like a plan."

***

Mamba pulled a cold beer from the cooler in the back of his four-wheel drive and twisted the lid off on his bicep. It was midday and the sun beat down relentlessly on the Zambian bush. "Kogo, where the fuck is your boy, hey?" He glared at his second-in-command who was sitting in the shade of a tree with the other three members of the hunting party. They had waited for twenty minutes for the guide Kogo had arranged.

Less the absent guide, they were all poachers that Mamba trusted. The two black Ugandans were brothers recruited from his old Army unit. Reconnaissance specialists, they were the finest trackers in the business. The older white Zimbabwean, Colin, was a professional poacher who shot his first elephant when his country was still called Rhodesia. He was their shooter. Mamba had witnessed the grey-haired hunter drop a bull with a single bullet from over five hundred yards.

"He'll be here," Kogo said peering down the track.

Mamba took a swig from the beer. "He better."

The five men were armed with assault rifles and carried an assortment of backpacks. They wore a mixture of faded camouflage pants, khakis, and long-sleeved bush shirts. All except Mamba, who wore a black T-shirt with the sleeves torn off under a tan South African-style assault vest. The handle of a machete protruded from a scabbard secured to the back pouch between his broad shoulder blades.

The splutter of a motorcycle caught the poaching boss's attention and he turned to spot a scooter struggling along the sandy track. As it pulled up alongside them he scowled. Kogo's guide was a scrawny kid who didn't look a day over sixteen. "What the fuck is this?"

The barrel of the AK-47 slung over the teenager's bony shoulder stuck up above his head like a radio antenna.

"He was a ranger here," said Kogo as the youth parked his battered scooter under a bush by the side of the road.

"Why isn't he anymore?"

"Because he stole from his comrades."

"He's a fucking thief?"

Kogo shrugged. "Aren't we all?"

The youth eyed the five men suspiciously as he unslung his AK and held it across his body. "Who is Kogo?"

"That's me."

He held out his hand. "I want my money."

Mamba stepped forward, towering over the boy. "You'll have your money when I have my horn."

The youth made to reply but Mamba continued, "Now, are you going to lead us to the animal or are you wasting my time?"

The kid swallowed but looked up defiantly. "We have to leave the car here. We walk east to the Mwaleshi river. That is where the rhino will be. It is a hard walk but if we go now we will be there by nighttime."

"Why can't we drive in, eh?" asked Colin. "There's probably plenty of tracks through the park."

"No, the rangers patrol the tracks and there are tour operators. Between here and the river it is bush, no one goes there much. We will not be seen."

"Are there many camps near where the rhino is?" asked Mamba.

The former ranger nodded.

Mamba turned to Colin. "Needs to be a silent kill."

"I'll take the dart gun. More than enough cyanide to drop a big female. We'll take off her horn with machetes." He made a chopping gesture with his hand. "Real sharp, real quiet, then we get the fuck out of there."

Mamba nodded. "We're gone by the time they find the carcass." He raised his voice. "OK, get your gear ready. We're leaving in five." He turned to the teenager. "You'd better lead us to the rhino, boy." He finished his beer and tossed it into the bushes. "Because if we don't find her I'm going to hang you from a boab and skin you like an antelope." He laughed as he took a folding-stock AK assault rifle out of the four-wheel drive and cocked it.

***

Saneh found the men in the clearing behind the training hall. They had set up a table in the shade of a tree and were working on the delta-winged electric drone. There were laptops, a toolbox, and components strewn across the bench. "Have you boys eaten any dinner?" she asked as she approached.

"Huh?" Bishop glanced up from where he was inspecting the aircraft. "Yeah, we grabbed some sandwiches from the kitchen."

"Hi Saneh." Dom shot her a smile. "You and Chris off soon?"

"In a few minutes. How's the drone going?"

"Ask Aden, this stuff's all alien to me."

Saneh laughed. "I can see you're very busy. OK, boys, we'll see you when we get back." She gestured to the drone. "Or, if you ever get that thing working again, you'll see us out there."

"OK, babe, have fun."

Saneh shook her head as she walked back. "Boys and their toys." As she entered the lecture room she spotted Christina crouched over a backpack. "You all good?"

The photographer gave a smile. "Yep, the guys are already loaded and out the front." She zipped up the bag and hefted it over her shoulders. Loaded with camera gear, it was almost larger than her petite frame. "Let's go."

One of the stripped-down Land Cruisers was parked in front of the building with two rangers in the front seats. They greeted Saneh and Christina with broad smiles as the women climbed into the back.

"All right, boys, do we know where Kitana is?" asked Christina as she buckled in.

"One of the patrols spotted her up north," said Francis, the driver. "Near the Mwaleshi falls."

"Well, let's head up there and have a look. We've got about thirty minutes till sunset so we need to find her quickly." Christina unzipped her backpack and withdrew a camera with a telephoto lens. She slung it around her neck and cradled the body in her lap.

Francis started the engine with a clatter. "We'll find her. Kitana doesn't like to walk far with the baby."

"Who could blame her?" Saneh chuckled.

"Do rhinos get morning sickness?" asked Christina as they left the camp.

"I hope not, I wouldn't wish it on anyone."

They continued their banter as the Land Cruiser negotiated a sandy track through the bush. It followed the Mwaleshi River for five miles before they turned off and skidded down a steep bank. Francis slowed as they negotiated a rocky riverbed pock-marked with bath-sized pools of slimy green water.

"Is it this low all year round?" asked Saneh as they splashed through a stagnant pond.

"No, when the wet comes the river becomes a torrent. It's only really low during the dry months. Look, it's deeper over there," Christina said as she raised her camera. She aimed it at a group of hippos half-submerged in a lagoon on the opposite side of the river.

Saneh smiled as one of the massive beasts yawned opening its mouth to reveal a lethal array of yellow teeth. Behind them, on the bank, a herd of impala were making their way down to the river to drink.

Christina snapped a few shots. "They're smart, they know if there are hippos there won't be any crocodiles."

Francis stopped and waited for Christina to finish taking photos before continuing. "If we don't hurry, Miss Munoz, you will miss the light."

Christina laughed. "You're all over it, aren't you, Francis."

The two rangers in the front chatted in their native language as they drove through a shallow rivulet and back up the sandy bank. They continued to follow the river as it wound its way toward the falls.

"This is the best time to be out," said Christina as she snapped a photo of a giraffe and her calf drinking. The mother eyed them warily as they drove slowly past. "So many mothers out with their babies." She shot Saneh a smile. "That'll be you soon."

"I might avoid hippo and crocodile-infested waters. Aden wasn't exactly happy with me being out tonight." She glanced at the pump-action shotguns mounted between the front seats.

Even though there had not been a poaching incident in nearly three years Dom insisted every patrol was armed.

"I've been meaning to ask," said Christina as they turned onto another track. "How did you two meet?"

"He caught my eye in a restaurant." Saneh wasn't about to explain that she had first crossed paths with Bishop when she was a covert operative in the Iranian intelligence service. Nor did Christina need to know that she had saved Bishop's life on the streets of Kiev while dressed in heels and a particularly revealing cocktail dress. It all seemed so long ago. A tear formed in the corner of her eye as she remembered her friend and former comrade, Aleks. She had met him the same day she met Bishop, but now he was dead.

"Are you OK?"

Christina's voice snapped her back to reality. "I'm fine."

"We're nearly there," interrupted Francis from the front of the truck. "One of the rangers saw Kitana around the next bend earlier today."

"Excellent, can we go slow so we don't spook her?" Christina asked before turning to Saneh. "The two of you are a great couple. He's going to make an awesome father."

She shook her head. "Yes, I know Aden's going to be a great dad. I just, well... Something reminded me of an old friend. Someone I cared about very much who passed away, that's all."

"Oh, I'm sorry." Christina reached inside her backpack, pulled out binoculars, and handed them to her. "But hey, I need your eyes tear-free and ready to spot a two thousand pound momma and her four hundred pound bubba."

"God, I hope I don't get that heavy." Saneh managed a smile as she hung the binoculars around her neck.

***

Mamba sat against a tree cradling his AK assault rifle. He sipped from a canteen as he watched the remaining members of his hunting party resting in the shade. They had walked for a half a day to reach the banks of the river. All were seasoned bushmen but the heat had made it hard going. The walk back in the cool of the night would be easier. He squinted and scanned the scrub for any sign of their young guide and one of the trackers. The pair had been sent forward to locate the rhino and check for rangers. "Kogo, where the hell is that little thief? He better not have sold us out."

Kogo lay in the shade half asleep. "He'll be back. The rangers can't pay him what we can."

"Maybe, but I still don't trust him. You know what they say, you can't buy a Zambian, you rent them."

Colin, the grizzled Rhodesian, laughed from where he was assembling his dart gun. The weapon resembled a hunting rifle complete with a scope and long barrel. In place of gunpowder it used compressed gas to propel a poisoned projectile out to a range of seventy yards. That meant the hunter had to stalk very close to the target and a rhino was not an animal you wanted to anger. It was a job requiring steely nerves and a crack shot; Colin was both.

A rustle in the bushes alerted the men. Safety catches clicked to fire. The thick grass parted and the young former ranger appeared with the tracker. Both were sweating heavily as they dropped in the shade.

"Well?" demanded Mamba.

"We found her," reported the tracker. "She and the calf are not far from here. They're sleeping in the shade of a big thorn tree."

"Good, we'll make the kill now and recover the horn." He glanced up at the darkening sky. "By the time we finish it will be nightfall."

"Solid plan." Colin slid a dart the size of a cigar tube into the gun and closed the bolt. "Ready when you are." The projectile contained nearly an ounce of pure cyanide, more than enough to kill a full-grown rhino. He had three more like it secured in his hunting vest.

Mamba tucked his water bottle back into a pouch. "Lead the way, little ranger boy."

The youth scowled and set off back into the bush with the others in tow. They followed a game trail along the riverbank to a thicket of saplings. The teenager held up his hand then pointed. Mamba knelt and peered through the branches. It took him a second to spot the massive animal. She resembled a granite boulder in the fading light.

"She's a big one, eh," whispered Colin as he cradled the dart gun. "Good thing I brought extra darts. Might not go down with just one."

"Just get it done."

Colin slid forward on his chest, tucked the weapon against his shoulder, and aimed through the scope.

Mamba crouched behind him watching the massive beast as she rested on her belly. He couldn't see the head but he had no doubt the horn was impressive.

The gun emitted a pop not unlike an air rifle and the dart struck the thick hide with a thud. A loud bellow reverberated as the rhino struggled to her feet and turned toward them, nostrils flaring.

Now Mamba could see the long curved horn as well as the sheer size of the fully-grown rhino. She bellowed again and he caught a glimpse of the calf cowering behind its mother. Mamba shouldered his assault rifle as the one-ton animal lowered her horn. He swore it was staring directly at him.

Colin had already reloaded the dart gun and fired once more hitting her square in the chest.

"Jesus Christ!" Mamba yelled as the rhino charged.

She halved the distance between them in under a second. As she was about to plough into the thicket where they hid she skidded to a halt and stood panting not a dozen feet away. Mamba raised his AK and aimed at her head.

"Steady." Colin pushed the barrel of the assault rifle down. "She's done."

The rhino wheezed and convulsed. Her eyes grew wide as her front legs crumpled and she dropped to her knees. It took mere seconds for the huge dose of cyanide to cripple her respiratory system. Her powerful heart was the next to go. It beat slower and slower before finally, as the flow of oxygen ceased, it stopped and she toppled over.

"Good work." Mamba pushed through the thicket and approached tentatively. He ran his hand over the horn. It was impressive measuring as long as his forearm. The animal lifted her head and gave one last bellow. The forlorn cry for help startled Mamba and he fell backward in the long grass.

"She was a beautiful animal," Colin said staring with sad eyes.

"Don't get all soppy on me, old man. You've killed more than most." Mamba scrambled to his feet and pulled the razor sharp machete from its scabbard. With deft blows he hacked at the flesh around the horn. A pathetic bleating sound interrupted his butchering and he turned to see the rhino calf standing a few yards away. It was as big as a large dog with a tiny horn the size of a golf ball.

"Can I shoot it?" asked the ex-ranger.

"No, you idiot. It will grow and then we come back for the horn."

As Mamba worked to hack the horn free the other men faced outward with their guns. The teenager, sulking, moved down to the riverbank.

Mamba sweated as he worked. His preferred method of removing horns and tusks was a chainsaw. However, with the threat of rangers he couldn't risk the noise. As he continued to hack at the base of the horn the kid called out.

"Hey, hey, can you hear that?" The teen scrambled through the tall grass back to the carcass.

He paused and listened. Over the bleating of the calf he could hear a faint noise. It took him a moment to identify it as the clatter of a diesel engine. "Fucking hell." He handed the machete to Kogo. "Finish this."

He gestured to the others as he unslung his AK. "We'll check it out." With the rifle held at the ready he patrolled through the thick grass until he could see down into the riverbed and across to the other bank.

A cut-down safari truck appeared a few hundred yards downstream on the opposite bank. He knelt and watched as it crept toward them. Whoever was in it was searching for something, probably the rhino and her calf. Mamba took a compact monocular from his vest and focused it on the vehicle. There were two green-uniformed rangers in the front seats. Shifting his focus he spotted two women in the back. One of them was holding a long-lensed camera. The other, a strikingly attractive brunette, had a pair of binoculars slung around her neck.

"What are we going to do?" the youth whispered as he caught up.

"Nothing, unless they see us," Mamba said as he flicked the safety off his AK.

***

The Land Cruiser slowed and came to a halt at the river. It gave the occupants a clear view of both the rocky riverbed and the opposite side.

Saneh looked up, searching the sky for Bishop's drone. Maybe he would spot the rhinos first, she thought.

"Was this where she was last seen?" asked Christina.

"Yes, it was a hot one today. She will stay close to water," replied Francis as he switched off the engine.

Saneh scanned the far bank with her binoculars. Searching the thick grass she caught a glimpse of what looked like a man crouched behind a clump of foliage. Beyond the figure a flash of movement caught her eye and a heart-wrenching bleat filled the air. "Oh my god, it's Kitana's calf."

The bark of an AK-47 sounded in the still air jolting her into action. "Get down!" She shoved Christina out of the vehicle and leaped after her. They landed in a heap as bullets thudded against the vehicle.

Her training kicked in and she assessed the situation. Realizing the only weapons were in the front of the vehicle she wrenched the driver's door open. Francis rolled out into the dust. His shirt was covered in blood, his face pale, eyes wide.

She fought the urge to check him for wounds. The only aid in a gunfight is self-aid, she reminded herself as she grabbed a pump-action shotgun from between the front seats. A quick glance told her the other ranger had been hit. He was slumped forward against the dash. Bullets slapped the bonnet of the truck as she pulled the weapon free and took cover with Christina.

"Are they poachers?" asked Christina.

"Yes, there are three shooters," Saneh said as she pumped the fore grip of the shotgun. "I need you to check Francis."

Christina was staring at her with her mouth open. "What… how?"

"Chris, focus. If we're going to get out of here we need to work together. I'm going to try to buy us some space. You need to look after Francis."

"I'm OK," the driver stammered from where he lay in the dust. "I think Melon is dead."

Saneh crab-walked to the front of the truck and peeked around the bumper. Spotting a muzzle flash she pulled back and took a deep breath. She knelt, grasped the shotgun firmly and leaned out sideways. The 12-gauge bucked in her shoulder as she fired two rounds where she had seen the flash. She heard a scream as she pulled back. "One down. Chris can you get to the radio?"

The bursts of gunfire intensified as she shuffled backward. Popping up over the front of the truck she searched for another target. Darkness was closing in and she could barely make out the opposite bank. She snapped off a single shot. The scrub exploded with muzzle flashes. Bullets snapped through the air and slammed into the side of the Land Cruiser. Saneh kept firing the shotgun until, as the trigger clicked on an empty chamber, she registered a flash of pain and felt herself falling. As she collapsed she realized her life was not the only one that could be lost. "I'm sorry, Aden," she whispered as she slipped into a black pool of nothingness. "I'm sorry."

***

Bishop swatted an insect the size of a fist away from his face as he squinted at the laptop screen. The sun had long dropped behind the horizon and the bugs were going nuts over the glow of his equipment.

"Aden, might be time to call it quits." Dom offered him a cold beer.

He glanced up and took the bottle. "Thanks, you might be right. I can't get the damn ground station to sync with the updated autopilot software. Keep getting the same error message." He slammed the laptop shut in frustration and took a swig from the beer.

"All good, we'll have another look tomorrow."

He nodded. "I know someone I can call. He's all over this sort of stuff."

"You've got a lot of interesting friends."

"Wait till you meet Kruger."

"The guy that's coming up tomorrow?"

"Yeah, former South African Recce. You two will get along just fine. Hell, you might be able to convince him to stay and help out."

"Could definitely use another hand."

Bishop packed the laptop and the compact drone inside a purpose-built case.

"Can you hear that?" Dom asked.

He tipped his head. There was a slight breeze that carried the sounds of the river. Faintly, in the background, he thought he could hear the sound of a car horn.

"Someone's in a hurry," added Dom.

The horn got louder and soon it blended with the roar of an engine.

"Yeah, sounds like one of our Land Cruisers." Dom placed his beer down and ran toward the lecture rooms.

Bishop's heart was pounding before he even started sprinting. He passed the New Zealander, dashed through the building and out to the track. The safari truck roared toward him with the horn still blaring. He spotted Christina at the wheel as it skidded to a halt in a cloud of dust. Francis, the driver, was in the back cradling someone in his arms. It was Saneh. Bishop fought the panic welling up inside him. "Dom, we need a medevac."

"Already on it."

He took Saneh's limp body from the truck and laid her gently on the ground. As he frantically checked her vitals Dom appeared with a medical kit and stretcher. She had a weak pulse. He tipped his ear to her mouth; she was breathing.

"Her head, her head, they shot her in the head," Francis blurted.

A quick check found the wound above her right ear, beneath hair matted with blood. A bullet had creased her skull leaving a half-inch groove. "I need a bandage," he yelled at Dom.

Bishop bound the wound and they transferred her to the stretcher wrapping a space blanket around her body. "Who did this?" he asked as he monitored her vitals.

Christina sobbed hysterically. "It was poachers. They shot the radio, we couldn't call through."

"They killed Melo," added Francis.

Bishop clenched his jaw. "How long till the medevac arrives?"

"Thirty minutes," said Dom.

He clutched Saneh's hand. "Hang in there, babe."

CHAPTER 2

NORTH LUANGWA NATIONAL PARK, ZAMBIA

The hacking laugh of a hyena sent a ripple of fear down Mamba's spine. He knew the predators posed no immediate threat but still aimed his AK at the dark shapes that lingered at the edge of his vision. The pack had been tailing them through the bush for the last few hours. He knew they sensed a meal was coming. They could smell death and it excited them.

"How much further?" he asked the younger of the brothers.

"At least eight miles, we're moving very slowly."

"No shit." He glanced back at the two men carrying the makeshift stretcher; it was what had attracted the hyenas. Their guide, the young thief, had taken a shotgun blast to the stomach. Mamba wanted to ditch the casualty but Colin had convinced him otherwise and volunteered to help carry the boy. A body was evidence he'd argued; sign on a trail that might lead the authorities to his door.

The two stretcher-bearers, Colin and the other tracker, lowered the wounded boy to the ground as Mamba strode toward them. There was a half moon in the clear night sky and he could see the shine of sweat on their faces. "We're moving too slow."

"We're going as fast as we can," Colin said between catching his breath. He pulled a water bottle from his pack and took few measured sips.

"The thief is as good as dead. We'll leave him for the hyenas."

"The boy will live if we get him to help."

"And I suppose you'll drive him to the hospital?" Mamba hissed.

Colin nodded as he stowed the bottle. "If need be, he did his job. I won't leave him to die."

Mamba slid his finger to the trigger of his AK as he glared at the wounded teenager. It might be easier to put a bullet in both the boy and the old man. He thought better of it. Professional poachers were a tight-knit community and word would spread that he had killed one of their own. What's more, the Rhodesian was one of the best hunters in the business and quality ivory was getting harder and harder to find.

"Fine, but if we're not out of the park by dawn I'm going to leave you both here." Mamba turned and re-joined the tracker who was conversing with Kogo. "Let's get going."

The man glanced back at his brother and Colin. "What about them?"

"If they can't keep up we're going to leave the thief."

"OK, boss." The tracker rose and started off into the bush, his weapon held ready.

"We should leave the boy now. Save us some money," said Kogo.

"Do as you're fucking told."

Kogo shrugged and followed the tracker.

Mamba waited for the stretcher-bearers to pass him. Then he turned and peered into the darkness behind them. Despite the gunfight and the rangers escaping it looked like they were in the clear. No one but hyenas followed them.

***

CURE HOSPITAL, LUSAKA

The Special Emergency Services helicopter touched down at the CURE Hospital on the outskirts of Lusaka, the capital of Zambia. The crew rapidly offloaded the gurney carrying Saneh and pushed it across the helipad and inside the hospital. Funded by US and UK charities, the hospital was a beacon of professionalism in a region starved of medical services. Bishop followed the stretcher as far as the swinging doors to the emergency ward where a grandmotherly nurse stopped him.

"You can't go any further, dear. Come with me, I'll show you to the waiting room," she said guiding him through a separate door.

Bishop took a seat in the empty waiting area. There had been limited room on the helicopter; he was the only one who had accompanied Saneh. He stared at the wall, trying to contain his emotions. There was a war waging inside him, a battle between grief, rage, and guilt that left him numb. If he lost Saneh he... The truth was he didn't know what would happen if he lost her or their child. He didn't want to contemplate it. What he needed to do was get her the best medical attention possible.

He pulled out his phone and dialed a number.

"Hello," said the automated voice. "You've reached Telemetry Transport please enter your tracking number for an update on the progress of your shipment."

He punched in a five-digit code.

"Bish, that you?" The voice belonged to Frank, a member of PRIMAL, the vigilante organization that Saneh and Bishop were part of. His call had connected to their makeshift headquarters in Abu Dhabi where a bare-bones team was monitoring intelligence sources for any sign the organization had been compromised.

"Yeah, it's me. Is Vance there?"

"Sure is, I'll grab him."

A moment later the PRIMAL director's deep voice replaced Frank's. "Bish, what's up, buddy?"

"There's been an accident. Saneh has been shot. She's at the CURE hospital in Lusaka. I need you to coordinate a medical evacuation to Abu Dhabi so she can receive appropriate treatment."

"What?"

"Poachers ambushed her."

"Jesus Christ, OK, OK, we'll organize a medical evacuation for both of you. Tariq's people can arrange care here... Listen, buddy, are you OK?"

"I'm fine, just get Saneh the hell out of here." He terminated the call and glanced back at the nurse who was now manning the counter. Her friendly smile had turned into a frown.

"I'm sorry," said Bishop. "It's a lovely hospital."

"It's fine, dear. I know you must be very worried about your girlfriend but she's in good hands. Now, can I get you a cup of tea? It will make you feel better."

Bishop managed a nod as he slumped back into his chair. "She's in good hands," he murmured to himself. Panic welled up inside him and he fought the urge to scream.

"Here you are." The nurse appeared with a mug of tea.

"Thanks." Bishop took a sip of the hot, sweet liquid.

"Doctor Anderson is very good," she said once she'd returned to the counter. "He trained in America and is very experienced in trauma surgery."

Her words did little to comfort Bishop. However, as he sipped the tea reality dawned on him. There was nothing more he could do to help Saneh. He had taken her to the hospital and now her life was in the hands of the doctor. His skills were better applied at bringing justice to the men who had hurt her. Placing the tea down he reached in his pocket for his phone and made a call. "Kruger, it's Bishop. How far are you from Lusaka?"

***

It seemed like an eternity before Doctor Anderson finally reappeared through the swinging doors guarding the emergency ward. Bishop's heart lurched as he spotted the grim expression on the man's face. "Is she OK?" he asked softly when the doctor sat next to him.

"She's in a coma."

"And the baby?"

"At this stage the baby is fine."

Bishop's throat was dry and he fought the urge to cry. "Will she wake up?"

"It's hard to say. The bullet damaged part of her skull causing trauma to the brain. The bleeding has stopped but she is going to need additional surgery to remove fragments and check for damage. I'm not going to lie, the prognosis is not great. I've seen people recover from injuries like this but I've also had patients who simply never regain consciousness."

Tears welled in Bishop's eyes and the doctor put a hand on his shoulder. "Your friends have been in touch. There's a private jet flying in. We'll help prepare for her transfer tomorrow morning. She is going to have the best care available."

The words did little to comfort him. He put his head in his hands, closed his eyes, and attempted to bring his emotions under control.

"There's nothing more you can do here, Mr. Barnes," the doctor said using the name he had given. "You should get some rest. If you like, the duty nurse can organize a hotel and transport."

Bishop rose. "No thanks." He felt like a zombie as he walked out of the hospital into the crisp evening air. Glancing at his watch he calculated that only two hours had passed since Christina had driven the shot-up truck into the camp. Kruger was due to arrive at any moment and if they moved fast there was a chance they could track down the men who had shot her.

The clatter of a diesel engine caught his attention and he squinted as headlights swung into the parking lot.

A Nissan truck pulled up alongside him. "Get in," yelled an Afrikaans-accented voice.

He opened the door and climbed inside. The man at the wheel was what was commonly referred to in the military as a 'unit'. Kruger's spiked brown hair touched the roof of the shabby interior of the truck and his broad shoulders filled the cab.

"OK, here's the plan." Kruger wasn't one to mince words. "Old mate of mine has a light aircraft waiting at a strip nearby. He's got us weapons and transport to Luangwa and there's enough room for Princess."

"Who is Princess?"

Kruger turned to him with a frown. "Princess is a Rhodesian-Mastiff cross. She's the best hunting dog on the continent." He jerked his head over his shoulder. "They've got a bit of a head start but if you're keen we can track them down."

Bishop turned in his seat and spotted a pair of brown eyes and a wet black nose. "I want these bastards dead."

Kruger drove the truck out of the parking lot and accelerated down the dark road. "Dead we can do."

***

NORTH LUANGWA NATIONAL PARK, ZAMBIA

Thirty minutes later a Cessna Caravan touched down at the dark airstrip behind the ranger camp at Luangwa. Bishop jumped out of the cabin wearing a South African-style chest rig, carrying a worn R5 carbine. He strode across to the waiting Land Cruiser and climbed in the passenger side.

"Is she OK?" asked Dom from the driver's seat. He glanced at their weapons.

"No, she's in a coma."

"I'm so sorry, Aden."

Kruger climbed into the back of the vehicle and Princess followed, leaping in beside him. He was similarly equipped as Bishop but carried a heavier R1 rifle.

"Dom, this is Kruger."

The massive South African leant forward and shook the New Zealander's hand.

Dom drove at high speed away from the airfield, through the camp, and out onto the track north toward Mwaleshi Falls.

"How is Christina?" yelled Bishop over the engine.

"Pretty shook up. They took her by ambulance to Lusaka." Dom weaved the two-ton truck through a thicket of trees with the finesse of a rally driver. "Look, I can't send my rangers with you. They're not trained or equipped to deal with people like this."

"That's OK. We've got it."

"I don't think you understand. We're talking military training and weapons. These guys are hard-core criminals. They'll gun you down in cold blood."

"Not if we get the drop on them," said Kruger.

"You're seriously going after them?"

"Yep," replied Bishop.

"Then I should come with you, you'll need an extra shooter."

Bishop shook his head. "Negative, we'll take care of it."

They drove in silence before he caught a glimpse of lights through the scrub. As they got closer he could see there were vehicles parked beside the riverbank.

"OK, we're here," said Dom as he skidded the truck to a halt.

"Princess, let's go." Kruger and the dog leaped out of the cab. The South African surveyed the scene with his weapon at the ready.

"They killed a black rhino on the other side of the river," said Dom. "Left her calf." He gestured to the four-wheel drives parked in the long grass. A team of rangers were clustered around the baby rhino, illuminated by the headlights of the vehicles. "Poor little bugger was hysterical. We're lucky we found him before the hyenas or the lions got to him."

"You said there were at least four, with one possible casualty?"

"Correct. And they've got at least an eight hour stomp before they're clear of the park."

"Alright, you stay and take care of Christina and the calf. Kruger and I will run with this." He stepped out of the truck and skidded down the riverbank into the water. It reached his knees as he waded across. Princess and Kruger were already on the other side. He scrambled up the bank pushing his way through the long grass. A flashlight flicked on and he could hear Kruger talking to the dog.

"What have you got?" Bishop asked as he caught up.

The light revealed the corpse of the rhino. Its head was drenched in blood. A hole had been hacked in its snout where the horn once was.

"Fucking bastards," Bishop said as he stared at the macabre remains.

There was a snuffle from the bushes and Kruger aimed the flashlight. Princess had her nose to the ground and was moving in circles sniffing frantically. "Find them, girl."

The stocky hound gave a loud snort and bounded off into the bush.

"She's got them. You ready to run all night?" Kruger said switching off the light.

"I'll chase them to the gates of hell if I have to."

"Well, that's exactly where we're going to send these pricks." Kruger slapped him on the shoulder. "Half moon, plenty of light. Let's hope we don't run up against anything that wants to eat us." He laughed heartily as he trotted off into the bush after his baying hound.

Bishop paused for a second, glanced up at the stars, and said a quick prayer for Saneh. Then he grasped the R5 with both hands and held it close to his chest as he ran after Kruger.

***

ABU DHABI INTERNATIONAL AIRPORT

The G450 Gulfstream was powered up and waiting on the tarmac when Vance strode out from the airport's VIP terminal. Bathed in floodlights, the green cross emblazoned on the aircraft was a poignant reminder of the mission at hand. He made a beeline to where a lone figure stood at the stairs of the jet.

Dressed in one of his signature Savile Row suits Tariq Ahmed waited with a grim expression. "Do we know any more?" he asked as he shook Vance's hand. Tariq, who was

PRIMAL's benefactor, had pulled out all stops to organize Saneh's evacuation. As the owner of Lascar Logistics, an airfreight company with a fleet of aircraft, sourcing the aeromedical jet had not been difficult. However his staff had also arranged the best neurosurgeon they could find to accompany Saneh, and had also convinced the world's foremost expert on coma treatment to fly in from the UK.

"There has been no change to her situation. She's stable but no sign of waking."

"And the child?"

Vance frowned. "How did you know she was pregnant? It was supposed to be a secret."

"Please, you think Mirza can keep a secret?"

"I would hope so, all things considered." Mirza Mansoor, Bishop's operational partner, was currently working for Tariq helping to coordinate humanitarian relief flights.

"Does he know about Saneh?"

Tariq shook his head. "No, I didn't want to tell him until he gets back. He's got enough on his plate for the moment. I take it you're not recalling everyone?"

"That's right. We're keeping this low key. Chua and I are concerned that if we spread the word the team is going to converge on Abu Dhabi. We can't afford that sort of visibility at the moment. It seems harsh but I think it's for the best."

A voice from the top of the stairs drew their attention. "Gentlemen, we'll be ready to go in a minute."

Vance gave the green-uniformed crewmember a nod and turned back to Tariq. "Thanks for pulling this all together."

"We're a family, Vance, and families take care of each other. Now go get our girl. I've got a coma specialist flying in from London and everything will be ready when you return." He gave Vance's hand a firm shake and walked toward the terminal.

Vance climbed the stairs into the sleek white interior of the jet. Along one side were two stretchers with a bank of state-of-the-art medical equipment attached to the wall. At the front of the cabin the medical team was already strapped into their seats. He took his place next to one of them as the door closed and the engines spooled up.

"Are you the father?" asked the middle-aged woman next to him.

He pulled his safety belt tight and gave her a grim smile. "Yeah, I guess you could say that."

"My name's Lynne. We'll get your daughter home safe and sound."

"Thanks." Vance glanced out the window as the jet rolled forward. While getting Saneh back to Abu Dhabi and world-class medical attention was his focus it wasn't the only thing weighing on his mind. Another concern was how badly Bishop was going to react to the situation. The PRIMAL operative already carried the weight of his parent's death along with dozens of innocent lives that he held himself responsible for. Saneh was his rock, his beacon of light in a very dark existence. With her life hanging by a thread it was possible he would go completely off the reservation. His only hope, that Kruger could talk some sense into him before he turned renegade.

***

NORTH LUANGWA NATIONAL PARK, ZAMBIA

Despite the cool night air Bishop's shirt was damp under his chest rig and his hair was matted with perspiration. He caught up with Kruger as the South African paused to inspect the ground with his flashlight.

"They're moving slowly." Kruger shone the light on an area of crushed grass. Ignoring the stiffness in his legs Bishop knelt and took a closer look.

"Stretcher?" he asked.

"*Ja*. You can see where they placed it down. Saneh definitely wounded one of them." The light revealed a patch of bloodstained grass. "Badly!"

He touched the grass; the blood was dry.

Kruger moved the beam behind the stretcher. There were fresh paw prints in the sand. “Princess isn't the only one following them.”

“They're not her tracks?”

“No, hyenas. They can smell the blood.”

A single bark penetrated the darkness reminding them Kruger's hound was still hot on the poachers’ scent.

“Will they attack her?”

“Yes, we need to catch up. You good?”

His knees cracked as rose. “Yeah.” He cradled his R5 as Kruger secured his flashlight in a pouch and took a quick sip of water. The big man reminded Bishop of a lion stalking its prey through the dark savannah; alert, poised, and lethal.

“Let's go.”

Princess barked again and they set off jogging in her direction.

***

Barely a mile away Mamba tilted his head and listened. He was moving at the rear of the column pushing the stretcher crew to move faster. Noise travelled far in the cool night air and he clearly heard the bark of a dog. The noise troubled him more than any hyena. It meant someone was hunting them. “Fuck!” He grabbed Colin by the shoulder. “We need to dump the kid.”

The lack of a rebuke confirmed that Colin also heard the dog. The stretcher was lowered and he unslung his rifle. “The kid will have to take his chances with the rangers.”

“No, he'll talk.” Mamba slid the machete from the sheath between his shoulder blades.

“He won't,” Colin said half-heartedly.

“You want to risk spending the rest of your life in a Zambian prison? You wouldn't last a week, old man.”

The boy mumbled something from the stretcher. The sweat glazed across his face shone in the starlight.

“He's almost dead. I'm doing him a favor.”

"You're a bloody animal, Mamba," Colin said as he turned and walked away.

Mamba knelt down and whispered in the boy's ear. "Nobody likes a thief."

The rhino's thick hide and horn had dulled the machete's edge. It smashed rather than sliced through the windpipe. A gurgling emitted from the boy's mouth and he feebly tried to raise his hands. Mamba drew back and swung harder. This time the blow almost severed the slight neck and blood sprayed. In a few seconds the gurgling ceased and the thief lay silent.

He wiped the blade on the dead youth's pants before returning it to the sheath. A hasty inspection of the corpse's pockets revealed a wallet and mobile phone. The hyenas would consume the rest leaving nothing to identify, he thought as he joined the other men.

"Now we move fast. If we're not at the trucks by dawn you all lose half."

"Boss, that's not—" whined Kogo.

"Shut up and run."

They ran through the scrub with the trackers in the lead and Colin bringing up the rear. Behind them the dog barked again, this time louder. Mamba's lip turned up in a snarl, which transitioned to a smile as he remembered the hyenas. Feasting on the corpse the savage predators would hopefully make short work of the dog. Without the hound there was no way the rangers could catch them.

CHAPTER 3

NORTH LUANGWA NATIONAL PARK, ZAMBIA

Bishop struggled to keep pace with the tall South African as he ran over the rugged terrain. The sandy soil had been replaced by loose rock that shifted under foot and thick patches of thorn-covered bushes. His legs were burning and his lungs screamed but the thought that the men who had attacked Saneh and Christina could get away drove him on.

He was falling behind when Kruger skidded to a halt alongside Princess. The dog's hackles were raised and she emitted a low, savage growl, sending a shiver up Bishop's spine. In the darkness ahead he spotted half a dozen canine-like shapes clustered around something on the ground. Moonlight reflected off white teeth and yellow eyes as the hyenas shifted their attention toward the dog.

"Fucking hyenas," said Kruger as he drew a suppressed pistol and fired a round at the ground in front of the animals.

With their hunched backs, flashing teeth, and a hackling snarl, the creatures reminded Bishop of something from a horror movie. He flicked off the safety on his R5 and prepared to follow Kruger's lead.

Princess stalked forward, her growl increasing in intensity.

"Hold." Kruger fired another round. "Get the fuck out of here!"

The hyenas were unwilling to give up their meal. The largest of the pack, the alpha, lunged forward snapping and snarling. Kruger shot it neatly through the head and it dropped to the ground.

Spurred on by her master's actions the Rhodesian-Mastiff cross leaped forward and the remainder of the Hyenas turned tail and fled.

He exhaled, releasing a breath he didn't realize he held.

"Didn't want to have to kill one, but they might have hurt Princess." Kruger strode past the dead pack leader and shone his flashlight at the object they had been feeding on. It was a body. "Christ."

Bishop grimaced as he inspected the mangled corpse. It was barely identifiable as human. Most of the clothing had been ripped off and the torso torn apart exposing the bloodied organs contained within. Most of the stomach, intestines, groin, and a leg were missing.

"This must be the one Saneh wounded, *ja*. He looks young."

"They left him for the hyenas?" Bishop said in disbelief.

Kruger aimed his light at the body's neck. It was almost fully severed. "They cut his throat first."

The chuckle of a hyena sounded from the bush and Princess growled. Standing a few yards away she stared into the darkness intently, teeth bared.

"The body's still warm," said Kruger drawing Bishop's attention to the steam rising off the gaping abdomen cavity. "They're not far away." He snapped an order in Afrikaans to the hound and she focused her attention back to their direction of travel.

Bishop spotted a glint of metal and bent down to find the corpse had a cord around what was left of its neck. Underneath the tattered and blood-soaked shirt hung a key. He ripped it off and stuffed it into his pocket.

"We'll catch these fuckers within an hour." Kruger switched off the flashlight.

Bishop's eyes adjusted back to the darkness as they stepped off after the dog. They weren't more than a dozen yards from the body when he heard it being ripped apart by the hyenas. He felt no compassion for the poacher; there was every chance he could be the one who shot Saneh. Before long he would be joined in hell by the rest of his gang.

***

Every poacher heard the excited bark of the dog when it rang through the night air. By Mamba's estimates it was only a few hundred yards away and gaining fast. He swore; they might not cover the final few miles before the rangers were on them. Fatigue was taking a toll and Kogo and Colin were lagging behind. Waiting till they reached a clearing he called out to halt. Once the men had gathered he spoke. "They're going to catch us. We need to ambush them."

"That's risky," Kogo managed to say between breaths. "We don't know how many there are."

"They're moving too fast to be a large team," said Colin. "One dog and three or four men at most. They'll be gathering a bigger party to come out at dawn."

"We can handle them," said the younger of the trackers.

He addressed the Ugandan brothers. "Both of you take care of it and I'll give you the thief's share right now."

The trackers glanced at each other and nodded. Mamba had appealed to the strongest of their desires, greed. "It's a deal."

Mamba reached into a pocket, took out a thick wad of bills, and handed half to each man.

"I'll stay as well," said Colin.

The elder of the brothers shook his head. "No, white man, we can handle this. You go with them to the trucks. Up ahead there's open ground and a ridge. We'll kill them there."

Mamba smiled. "Let's do this." He followed the two trackers into the bush. Both of them were experienced fighters as well as poachers. Recruited from his old Army unit they were experienced bush warriors that would make short work of the park rangers following them.

Less than a hundred yards further they reached a dry sandy riverbed. To one side a rocky outcrop of boulders offered excellent cover for an ambush.

"Follow this river all the way to the road," said the tracker.

"Yes, I remember," said Mamba.

The two brothers left them in the riverbed and climbed up to the rocky outcrop. A moment later they were hidden among the boulders. Mamba gave the exposed killing area one last scan then led Colin and Kogo along the dried waterway. The men following them would soon be dead. Even if they weren't the ambush would slow them enough for him to reach the vehicles and escape.

***

Bishop sensed something was wrong when Kruger slowed to a walk then paused behind a thorn bush. Following suit he peered through the branches at the dry riverbed illuminated by the soft glow from the half moon. He spotted Princess at the edge of the clearing. She was crouched low with her head canted in the direction of a rocky outcrop.

"They've doubled back and laid an ambush," whispered Kruger.

"How the hell do you know that?"

"Princess told me."

Bishop shook his head. He'd seen Military Working Dogs in action but never witnessed the level of communication Kruger shared with his hunting dog; it was uncanny.

"They're up there in the rocks." Kruger gestured with a gloved hand. "They expect the dog to follow the scent up the river but she's too smart for that shit, fucking amateurs. We're going to hit them from the flank."

"Got it." The adrenaline had already started to pump as Bishop eased the safety off on his R5 and they stalked into the darkness. When they reached the edge of the rocky outcrop Kruger gestured for him to move up alongside. They shouldered their weapons, Kruger gave a low whistle, and Princess started barking. Both men caught the slight movement ahead in the rocks and opened fire, their muzzle flashes lighting up the bush.

"Covering!" yelled Bishop as he took a knee and continued to shoot in the direction of the movement.

Kruger moved forward his weapon held ready. He dropped to a knee and they repeated the sequence. "Covering!"

The stench of cordite filled Bishop's nostrils as he flicked the empty magazine out of his rifle and inserted a fresh one. He kept one eye closed, only opening it between shots, an old trick an instructor had taught him to preserve his night vision. He spotted the flash of a muzzle as he dashed forward. A bullet ricocheted off a rock and Kruger retaliated with a half dozen well-aimed shots. One of the ambushers cried out and the firing ceased.

When Bishop reached the position they had seen movement he spotted a crumpled body. He felt zero remorse as he fired two rounds into the poacher then continued to scan ahead. Spotting a figure dash toward the creek he fired again. His bullets went wide as the man disappeared from view.

"Princess, hunt!" bellowed Kruger as he and the dog gave chase.

Bishop took a split-second to check the first poacher was dead before running in the direction of Princess's frantic barking. Stumbling on the loose rocks he slipped down the bank into the sandy riverbed.

"Son of a bitch."

Climbing to his feet he realized he'd rolled his ankle. The pain was sharp but bearable. He ignored it as he limped up the riverbed. As he rounded a bend a horrific scream reverberated through the air. Bishop forgot his ankle as he as he caught up with the others.

The poacher writhed on the ground screaming as he held an arm across his chest. Kruger stood over him, the long-barreled R1 aimed at the man's face. Princess crouched to one side, her teeth glinting in the moonlight as she emitted a savage growl.

Bishop knelt by poacher's head. "Do you speak English?" He took a glow stick from one of his pouches and cracked it. In the soft orange glow he inspected their captive.

The poacher looked young, mid-twenties, his face a mask of agony and his shirt drenched in blood. Princess had de-gloved the right arm from midway up his forearm. The skin had peeled back to his knuckles exposing bloodied muscle fibers and bone. He sucked air loudly through gritted teeth.

"Answer the man. Do you speak English?" Kruger barked.

"Yes, yes I speak English. Please, please keep that dog off me. I didn't shoot the rhino, I didn't shoot it."

"How many men were with you?" Bishop asked.

"Six, there were six."

Bishop glanced up at Kruger who nodded. They still had three more to hunt down. "Who's in charge? Who organized the job?"

"Mamba, Mamba Mboya. He's the boss man poacher in Kenya. If you go fast you can catch him."

"One more question," he hissed. "Did you fire at the women in the truck?"

The wounded man's pause was all the confirmation Bishop needed. He rose to his feet and held out his hand to Kruger. The South African passed him his suppressed pistol.

"I didn't shoot. I didn't, it was Mamba."

The snap of the pistol ended his cries as Bishop shot him through the face. He felt nothing as he handed the weapon back and started up the creek. "You heard him, we can still catch them."

"Princess, hunt," commanded Kruger and the dog raced off down the riverbed.

Bishop glanced up at the horizon to the east; already the stars had disappeared, replaced with the soft orange glow of a rapidly approaching dawn. He ignored the pain in his swollen ankle and started jogging. If he had his way the men who shot Saneh were not going to see another sunrise. The poacher known as Mamba Mboya was going to die badly.

***

"Come on, you slow shit." Mamba shoved Kogo in the back as the smaller man struggled to climb the riverbank. He pushed him over the ledge then scrambled up after him to where Colin waited. As he paused to catch his breath he heard the dog bark again. He had assumed the volley of gunfire had killed the rangers and their hound. Clearly he was wrong. "Those fucking idiots."

"They're dead now," grunted Colin.

"And we will be too if we don't run." Mamba pushed past the white poacher and sprinted through the bush. The dog would catch them before they reached the vehicles and he didn't want to be last. Kogo or Colin could battle it out with the rangers; they could be replaced. He managed a smile as he reached the track. His costs for the mission had been cut significantly.

In the soft pre-dawn glow he spotted the trucks a hundred yards away parked off the dirt road. Breathing hard he stumbled in the soft sand at the edge of the track. Behind him the dog barked excitedly. He glanced over his shoulder and saw Kogo and Colin hot on his heels. Grasping his rifle he turned and sprinted for his vehicle.

The dog was louder now, a deep angry bark that shook him as he reached the four-wheel drive. Wrenching open the driver's door he jumped in and tossed the AK on the passenger's seat. He pulled the keys from his vest and turned the ignition. It coughed once as the passenger door sprung open and Kogo scrambled in screaming. "The dog, the dog, go, go, go!"

The engine spluttered again. The rear door opened. A savage snarl filled the air and Colin cried out as he dove inside. Mamba glanced over his shoulder as he pumped the accelerator and turned the key again. A massive bull-headed mastiff had one of the poacher's legs clenched firmly in its mouth.

"Drive, drive!" screamed Colin as the engine finally kicked over.

Mamba jammed the truck into gear and stomped on the accelerator. Checking the wing mirror he spotted two figures crash out of the bush. They were silhouetted by the first fingernail of the orange sunrise. "Get down!"

Bullets smashed through the back window and out through the windshield showering Mamba in glass.

"Jesus Christ!" screamed Kogo as they accelerated up the dirt track.

He held the wheel steady as more rounds slammed against the four-wheel drive. They rocketed along the road until the gunfire ceased. He glanced up at the mirror; a cloud of dust obscured them from the attackers. There was no sign of the dog.

"Mamba, Mamba!" Kogo screamed from the passenger seat.

"Shut the hell up." He peered through what remained of the windshield as he drove the vehicle around a bend in the road.

"Colin's dead."

He glanced over his shoulder at the crumpled body. A bullet had punched through the old Rhodesian's skull and blood and gore was spread across the back seat.

Mamba grinned manically. "Do you want to split his share?"

***

Bishop lowered his rifle as the four-wheel drive disappeared in a cloud of thick dust. Searching frantically he spotted another truck parked among the bushes. Sprinting to the other vehicle he reached for the key he'd taken from the dead poacher. It didn't fit. "Fuck!" Then he saw the scooter dumped alongside the road. The key worked and the tiny engine spluttered to life. Twisting the throttle he lurched into the dust cloud behind the escaping vehicle.

The little bike hiccupped and coughed like a drunken smoker as it ploughed through the soft sand. He squinted, struggling to maintain visual on the escaping truck. Dust stung his eyes and as the road turned his front tire slid. The bike was dumped on its side throwing him over the handlebars. Rolling in the dirt he leaped to his feet and shouldered his weapon. Dust filled the air blocking his view. He lowered the weapon. Mamba was gone and he had failed Saneh.

Princess appeared out of the haze. She walked slowly toward him with her tail between her legs.

"I know the feeling, girl." Bishop reached out and patted the dog's head.

Kruger jogged up behind him. "I'm sorry, Bish. I really thought we had them."

"Me too. But, we're not done yet. We're going to find Mr. Mamba Mboya and I'm going to kill him."

Kruger nodded as he took a satellite phone from his chest rig. "First we have to get out of here. You need to call Dom."

CHAPTER 4

NORTH LUANGWA NATIONAL PARK, ZAMBIA

Bishop handed Kruger back his satellite phone before collapsing against a tree. "It's going to be a few hours before they get here."

"*Ja*, best get some rest then." Kruger had removed his boots and lay in the grass using his assault vest as a pillow. Princess was sitting under a tree panting, having drunk her fill from water sloshed into the South African's bush hat.

He unlaced his boots, wincing as he freed his swollen ankle from the leather. The sprain wasn't severe but had already turned a dark shade of purple. He took a roll of medical tape from his vest and strapped it. Then he leant against his gear hoping to get some rest.

The adrenalin was long gone from his system but his mind still raced. He looked over at Kruger who had his damp bush hat pulled low over his eyes.

"Kruger?"

"*Ja*."

"I should've been with her when it happened."

Kruger lifted the hat from his eyes. "First poaching incident in years, right?"

"Yeah."

"You couldn't have predicted that."

He shook his head. "You don't understand. She's pregnant and I let her put our child at risk. Two rangers with shotguns and a cheap shitty drone isn't security against gunned-up poachers."

An awkward silence passed before Kruger spoke. "Look, I know a guy in Mombasa that's got his ear to the ground. We'll deal with Mamba first, then Saneh will get better, and after that we'll talk to Vance about helping Dom and his boys out."

"Thanks, brother." Bishop closed his eyes.

The morning sun had crested the trees and was shining fiercely by the time one of the rangers picked them up. Once they'd piled into the safari truck, Kruger and Princess promptly fell asleep. The hound and her owner snored heavily as they drove along the pot-holed dirt road around the perimeter of the national park.

As exhausted as he was Bishop couldn't sleep. He stared out the window at the bush but his mind wasn't on the wilderness. All he could think about was Saneh. The image of her lying unconscious in the dust was a memory he would take to his grave, but not before he put Mamba in one of his own.

As they pulled into the camp Bishop spotted Dom at the entrance to the lecture hall. The New Zealander strode across to the truck as it slowed and yanked open the door.

"Are you guys OK?"

He climbed out and stretched his legs, testing his sprained ankle. "Yeah, we got four of them. The others escaped." As he spoke Christina appeared from the building. She looked haggard with dark bags under her eyes. "How are you feeling?" he asked, managing a half smile.

"I'm OK. I just spoke to the hospital."

"Any change?"

Tears formed in her eyes as she shook her head. She stepped forward and wrapped her arms around him. "I'm so sorry, Aden," she sobbed.

"Hey, it's not your fault." Bishop fought back tears of his own as he hugged her. He felt something brush against his leg and glanced down to see Kruger's dog leaning against him. "Hey, have you met Princess?"

The dog greeted Christina with a wet lick that brought a smile to her face and a flurry of pats in return. Bishop managed a smile as he watched the savage hound reveling in the attention. He glanced up at Dom who watched with a sad expression on his face. "Hey, bud, can we talk?"

The New Zealander nodded and led him into the lecture hall. Kruger joined them as Dom opened the refrigerator and offered them each a beer.

Bishop waved it away. "Does the name Mamba Mboya mean anything to you?"

Kruger took a beer and twisted the top off. "Tall black guy," he added.

Dom nodded. "Yeah, I've heard of him. He's a poacher out of Mombasa; ex-military with access to heavy-duty hardware. You think the boys who did this were his?"

"Not think, we know. Mamba was there, we just missed him."

"Jesus, that's not good."

"I need to find him. Kruger and I are heading to Mombasa."

Dom shook his head. "Maybe it's best to let it go, Aden. These people are killers."

Kruger snorted into his beer. "We're not exactly Boy Scouts."

Bishop shot a frown at the PRIMAL operative. "Dom, we need to bring this evil piece of shit to justice. He could have killed Chris and he may have killed Saneh."

"I've got some contacts down there in the anti-poaching community. They might be able to help." He picked up his beer and led them outside. "I want you to see something."

Bishop followed him out the back across the open area to where they had tested the drone. Behind the clearing the rangers had constructed a makeshift pen. Inside lay the baby rhino. The calf rested in the shade of a tree bleating pathetically for its dead mother.

"Poor little fella," said Bishop.

"His mother was one of three breeding-age females on Luangwa. Now, without her, the program is likely to fail. I can almost guarantee the black rhino will be extinct in Zambia within five years." He took a swig from his beer.

"Once Kruger and I are done, I can guarantee Mamba will be the one who ends up extinct," said Bishop.

"Let me know if there's anything I can do to help. I can take you down to Mombasa and introduce you to my anti-poaching contacts. You're going to need an extra set of hands."

He shook his head. "No, Kruger and I will take care of this. You need to stay here with Christina, she needs you."

"Yeah, and Saneh needs you."

"I can't do anything for her here. She would want me to hunt Mamba down." He placed his hand on Dom's broad shoulder. "I'm not putting anyone else's life at risk. Can you give us a lift to Lusaka?"

"Yeah, of course."

They walked to the front of the lecture room where Christina continued lavishing Princess with attention.

"Hey Dom, can I leave the hound here with you guys?" asked Kruger. "I'll come get her when all this is done."

"Sure, Chris will be happy with that."

"I'm going to grab some gear. I'll meet you back here in five." Bishop left the two men watching Christina with the dog and made his way across to the accommodation. He hadn't been back since the accident and the single room bungalow was exactly how he and Saneh had left it the previous morning. Their clothes were still strewn on the bed, dirty dishes in the sink. On the bedside table sat the only photo she travelled with, a picture of them at the beach. Stripping off his khaki ranger shirt and camouflage shorts he dressed in jeans and a plain T-shirt. Sitting on the edge of the bed he grabbed a backpack and stuffed some other clothes inside. As he finished packing his phone rang.

It was Vance. "Hey, buddy, how you doing?"

Bishop could tell from the background noise that the PRIMAL Director of Operations was calling him from an aircraft. "Yeah, I'm OK."

"Hey, I just wanted to let you know we'll be on the ground in Lusaka at 1330 hours local. We'll transfer Saneh direct to the medevac bird and get you both back to Abu Dhabi. You at the hospital now?"

"I'm not far away. I'll be there."

"OK, see you then."

Bishop terminated the call and grabbed his bag. He left the bungalow and strode across to where Dom and Kruger were waiting next to one of the camp's hardtop Land Cruisers. "They're going to transfer Saneh at 1330," he said tossing his bag in the four-wheel drive.

"We better get a move on if we're going to be there in time," said Dom as he climbed in with one of his rangers.

"You talk to Vance?" asked Kruger when the others were out of earshot.

"Yeah."

"You tell him we're going after Mamba?"

"No. He wants me to go back with Saneh."

"Do you think he'll authorize a mission?"

"Unlikely, not with PRIMAL on lock down. We leave now and Mamba's trail goes cold."

"Fuck that. You and me can have that prick wrapped up within a few days."

Bishop slapped him on the shoulder. "Means the world to me, Kruger."

"What can I say, you and Saneh are family... and no one messes with my family."

***

CURE HOSPITAL, LUSAKA

At 1305 hours the nurse led Bishop to Saneh's room. She lay perfectly still in the hospital bed. If it wasn't for the hoses running from her mouth and nose she could have been sleeping. He swallowed back his tears, turned to the bald African American seated in the corner of the room and gave him a nod. "Thanks for coming."

Vance pried his hulking frame from the plastic chair and gathered Bishop up in a bear hug.

"Hey steady on, old man, you're going to break a rib," he wheezed.

Vance released him and glanced at the bed. "I feel so helpless seeing her like this."

"Yeah, tell me about it."

A knock at the door caught their attention. Doctor Anderson walked in. Behind him a team of green-uniformed medical staff waited with a gurney.

"Gentlemen, we need to prepare the patient for transport. If I could ask you both to move to the waiting area."

"Saneh, her name's Saneh," said Bishop.

"That's a lovely name," said the doctor as he led the team of medical professionals into the room.

He felt Vance's hand on his shoulder and let the PRIMAL chief guide him out the door.

"She's in the best hands we could find, bud."

"Yeah, thanks, I appreciate it."

Kruger sat in the waiting room and greeted Vance with a handshake. "Hey, boss."

"I'm guessing you two have some idea of who's responsible for Saneh's condition?"

Bishop met his steely gaze. "We've got a few leads to chase down."

"I know you want vengeance, Bish, but now ain't the time. Saneh needs you. We'll mount an op to deal with these shit-kickers once we've got her safe and stable in the UAE."

"You'll do that? Even with the CIA after us?"

Vance nodded. "They messed with our family."

"Kruger and I can lay the groundwork," said Bishop.

"No, this can wait till we're ready. You roll now and you're on your own with no gear and no intel. I'll get Chua and Flash to dig up all the dirt and then we'll take 'em out together."

"Yeah, I guess you're right. Kruger and I will grab our gear and meet you at the airport. Are you OK to take care of things at this end?"

"Yeah." Vance's voice softened. "Do what you need to do, buddy."

***

KENNETH KAUNDA INTERNATIONAL AIRPORT, LUSAKA

Vance watched as Doctor Anderson and his staff handed over Saneh to the medical team he had brought from Abu Dhabi. She looked so delicate and frail strapped to a gurney with medical staff swarming around her; a dark contrast to the energetic PRIMAL operative he'd known for nearly five years. He still remembered the day she had joined the team. Bishop, in typical fashion, had rescued her from certain death at the hands of her Iranian masters. Vance admitted he'd been dubious about recruiting the beautiful intelligence operative into PRIMAL. However, his doubts had been laid to rest as Saneh had proven her mettle time and time again. She had quickly won over the team of former intelligence and military operatives and become an integral part of the family.

He waited as they lifted her inside the Gulfstream. The medevac aircraft was one of the most advanced air ambulances in the world. Had Tariq not owned the jet it would have cost close to half a million dollars to charter. A price Vance would have paid personally to ensure she received the best care available. He saw Saneh as a daughter and that meant the fragile life inside her was the closest thing to a grandchild he would ever have.

Satisfied she was safely inside, Vance scanned the airport for any sign of Bishop. He checked his watch; they were scheduled to take off within a few minutes.

"Sir, we are ready to go," the steward said sticking his head out the door.

"OK, buddy, I'll be right up."

As he pulled his phone out to call Bishop it vibrated with a text message.

Enroute to Mombasa. Objective is Mamba Mboya. Will report once target is neutralized. Have Sandpit identify follow-up targets.

He tried to call but the phone rang out. This was exactly what he was afraid of. Saneh was the only thing that had been keeping Bishop from coming undone. She was his anchor, and now with her life hanging in the balance he would let his rage consume him.

As Vance climbed the stairs he tried to ring Kruger.

"Sir, you're going to have to power your device down before take off," said the steward.

"Will do." He stared at the screen as the call rang out again.

"Sir, we need to secure the door."

"OK." Vance turned off the phone and took his seat at the front of the jet. As he strapped in he glanced over his shoulder at the medical staff preparing Saneh for takeoff. "Come on, girl," he whispered. "Come back to us before that man of yours gets himself killed."

***

MOMBASA, KENYA

Mamba threw his backpack on the bench and wrenched open the refrigerator. Pulling a beer from the shelf he twisted the lid off and poured the ice-cold amber liquid down his throat. "Twenty two hours in the back of that piece of shit pickup. That cheap chink Zhou better pony up the rest of the cash." He flung the empty bottle at the corner of the warehouse where it shattered.

He and Kogo had abandoned the shot-up four-wheel drive twenty miles from Luangwa where they had set fire to it burning their weapons and Colin's body. Kogo had haggled with a local farmer and purchased a battered single-cab truck with a missing passenger seat. Somehow the dilapidated vehicle had carried them the thousand miles across pot-holed highways back to Mombasa.

"My back is stiffer than a baboon's cock," said Mamba as he reached for another beer.

"I wouldn't mind one of those."

"What, a baboon's cock?" Mamba laughed as he tossed his assistant a bottle and slammed the refrigerator door. He put his own bottle on the bench and unzipped the backpack. Inside, wrapped in plastic, was the bloodied rhino horn. "There she is, seven hundred grand's worth of horn."

"It cost four men their lives," said Kogo.

Mamba snorted. "We can always get more men. Which reminds me, we've got a shipment due out in three days and we're short. You need to find some shooters and get us more ivory."

"There's not enough time."

"If we don't make weight it's coming out of your cut." Mamba flashed him a smile and took another swig from the beer.

"I'll find the men."

"Yeah, that's more like it." He inspected the horn before placing it on the bench. "Throw it in the safe. I'm going to go sleep. Don't wake me unless the place is burning down."

"Should we let the families know?"

"What fucking families?"

"Colin and the brothers."

Mamba spat on the floor. "You're an idiot, Kogo. What are you going to tell them? That they died poaching black rhino? If they don't report us to the police they'll come after us for their share of the loot. No, they can all go to hell. They knew the risks."

"OK, I will find more poachers."

Mamba pushed open the door to his office. "And get me a new four-wheel drive."

Kogo picked up the phone on the bench. "Yes, boss."

"Something nice."

***

ZAMBIA - TANZANIA BORDER

Bishop drove up to the checkpoint and handed their passports to the border guard. Both he and Kruger waited silently while the khaki-uniformed official inspected the documents. He watched another AK-wielding guard through the windshield as the man gave the battered Mazda hatchback the once over. Dom had helped them buy the car in Lusaka before driving Kruger's truck, with their weapons, back to the National Park.

"What will you be doing in Tanzania?" the guard asked.

"We're just passing through to Kenya."

"And what will you be doing there?"

"We're heading out to the game parks to take some photos."

He peered in through the back window. "Where's your camera gear?"

"Camera gear?"

Kruger leaned across. "Our bags were stolen in Zambia, *ja*, along with our hire car. Our insurance people have arranged for replacement equipment to meet us in Mombasa."

The guard handed back the two passports and directed them to drive through. Bishop gave him a nod of thanks, started the car, and they crossed into Tanzania.

"I should have thought more about our cover," he said as they accelerated along the highway.

"You've got a bit on your mind."

"We could have borrowed some gear from Christina."

"It's all good. My man in Mombasa, he can get us anything we need."

"Guns?"

"Guns, tanks, intel, choppers, he can provide anything for the right price."

"Good, we're going to need someone who can give us access to the underbelly of the town."

"My man will get us in." Kruger fished his phone from his pocket. It was vibrating and flashing. "It's Vance again, do you want me to answer?"

Bishop shook his head. "No, he's just going to try to talk us down. I'm not turning back now.

"In for a penny, in for a pound," said Kruger as he terminated the call and switched off the handset. "We've got at least another fifteen hours of driving before we reach Mombasa. You sure you don't want me to take over?"

"I'll drive for a few more hours then we can swap."

"OK." Kruger laid his seat back and tipped his cap low. "Let me know when you want to change."

A few minutes later the South African was snoring gently. Bishop stared intently at the road as they raced along the highway toward Kenya. He doubted he could sleep if he wanted to. He was driven by a thirst for revenge, a burning desire to make Mamba Mboya pay for the pain he had inflicted.

CHAPTER 5

BAREEN HOSPITAL, ABU DHABI

Vance paced the hospital corridor as he waited for the neurosurgeon to finish his initial assessment. To say he was uneasy was an understatement. There was every chance the specialist had bad news. A combat veteran, Vance had seen hard men felled with a blow to the head far less severe than Saneh's injury. At least the hospital itself reassured him. It was one of the most advanced medical facilities in the Middle East; funded by Emirati oil and equipped with cutting-edge technology. Tariq had arranged for a team of the brightest medical professionals available. He had gone so far as to dispatch a private jet to the UK to bring in a world authority on brain trauma and coma.

Vance turned as the door to Saneh's room opened and a nurse appeared. "You can go in now, sir."

He gave her a nod and stepped inside the pristine white room. A doctor stood next to Saneh's bed checking the readout attached to the wall. He looked to be comparing the information against the tablet in his hands.

"What's her status, doc?"

Doctor Edwards turned to Vance. "I'm sorry to keep you waiting."

"Is she going to live?"

Edwards frowned. "The question is not will she live. It is whether or not she will come out of her comatose state."

"That's what I meant."

He gestured to the seat in the corner of the room. "Would you like to sit down?"

Vance shook his head. "No, give it to me straight."

"OK." He paused. "Saneh suffered a highly traumatic head injury that inflicted significant bruising to her brain. The shock is what put her in a coma. There is a chance, once the bruising subsides, she could regain consciousness on her own. However, I want to warn you. I've seen a lot of cases where people never wake up."

Vance sighed. "And the child?"

"She is perfectly safe."

His eyebrows shot up. "It's a girl?"

"Yes, we had to do a detailed ultrasound."

Tears welled in his eyes. "She wants a girl."

"I'm not going to lie. The prognosis for Saneh is not great. I give her a thirty percent chance that she will come to of her own accord."

He swallowed and wiped a tear from the corner of his eye. "We can't improve those odds?"

"Yes, it's very expensive but we can significantly improve the odds."

"Money is not an issue," said an almost regal voice from behind them.

Tariq Ahmed strode in, impeccably dressed in a navy pinstripe suit with a crisp white shirt and a red tie. He held a huge bouquet of vibrant orange gerberas in one hand and had a book tucked under his arm. With his dark features and perfectly manicured beard he looked every part the modern Arab sheik. "Hello, Vance."

Vance gave him a nod. "Tariq."

The doctor extended his hand. "Mr. Ahmed, it's a pleasure."

Tariq shook the doctor's hand. "You were about to explain how we could improve Saneh's odds."

"Yes, I've been working on a new treatment that may significantly improve her chances of recovery. There's only one issue..."

"And that is?"

"The treatment may have adverse effects on the child."

Vance frowned. "What do you mean by adverse?"

"The drugs stimulate the body. They increase cognitive function but there is a chance it could terminate the pregnancy."

"So our choice is between the baby and Saneh?"

The doctor nodded. "My team still need to conduct some more tests but we should be able to start treatment within the next twenty-four hours. After that, every day you delay the choice the chances of saving her decrease." He paused. "Gentlemen, I realize this is a heavy decision. I'm going to leave you to discuss the options. If you need me to talk through any of the details I will be in my office."

Tariq thanked the doctor as he left the room. Vance stood by the bed and gazed at Saneh.

"Have you been able to contact Bishop?" asked Tariq.

"No, he and Kruger have gone after a poacher in Mombasa and we don't have comms."

"This is not a decision I am comfortable making without his consultation."

"Yeah, this is his decision to make," said Vance.

"However, if we cannot communicate with him then he cannot make it in a timely fashion. That in turn could cost Saneh her life."

"When he checks in he can make the decision."

"And if he doesn't?" Tariq said as he laid the flowers on a side table.

"We'll cross that hurdle when we get to it."

"Have you spoken to the rest of the team?" Tariq asked as he lowered himself into a chair.

Vance shook his head. "No, I came straight here."

"You should go. They will want to know how Saneh is faring and you need to get onto Bishop." He pulled a pair of wire-framed reading glasses from his suit and donned them. Then he opened his book and began reading to Saneh.

***

PRIMAL HEADQUARTERS (THE SANDPIT), ABU DHABI

PRIMAL had started life as a small team of former intelligence and special operations operatives. Initially based out of a hangar at Abu Dhabi International Airport, it soon grew into a sizable organization enabled with customized aircraft, advanced weaponry, and intelligence assets.

It had been Tariq Ahmed who found the vigilante organization a home on an isolated island in the South West Pacific. From there Vance and his team had waged a relentless war on injustice for five long years. But, like all good things, it had come to an end. A potential compromise by an element of the CIA had forced them to abandon their island lair and shut down operations. Most of the PRIMAL operatives were now on leave until further notice. With orders to maintain a low profile and avoid compromise, they had handed in their signature equipment: iPRIMAL secure smartphones and state-of-the-art military-grade weaponry.

Now, the only part of the organization that remained active was an intelligence monitoring post based in Abu Dhabi. Vance and three others had moved to a luxury villa in an island resort for the sole purpose of making sure no one was hunting them.

Vance dropped his backpack in the tiled hall, strode through the open-plan living area and up a staircase to where two bedrooms had been converted into offices. When he opened the door to the makeshift operations center there were two men sitting at the computer terminals.

"Hey boss, how's Saneh doing?" asked Frank, a former British paratrooper and one of PRIMAL's operations officers.

"Not good, bud."

"Is there anything we can do?" asked the other man in the room. James Castle, or Ice, was one of the original founders of PRIMAL. Tall and broad-shouldered with short blonde hair and a heavily scarred face, he had only recently re-joined the team. Presumed KIA on a mission in Afghanistan, the badly injured ex-CIA operative had been captured by US forces and spent four years in captivity. PRIMAL had rescued him from a CIA black site in Alaska and he'd spent the last few months regaining his strength and adapting to life with a prosthetic forearm and lower leg.

"Yeah, it's imperative that I talk to Bishop."

Frank shrugged. "Boss, there's nothing we can do. They're not answering their phones and since they're probably in Mombasa by now they'll be using a local number. We've got to wait for one of them to contact us."

"Damn it. I'm going to see what the intel guys can do." As Vance walked out Ice rose from his chair and followed him to the corridor. He moved with ease despite the fact that his right leg, from just below the knee, was carbon fiber and titanium.

"Hey, Vance, can I have a quick word?"

They stopped outside the door to the intel room. "What's up, brother?"

"If there's a job going downrange I want in."

"Don't know if there's going to be a gig, bud. We'll let the intel team do their thing and see if there are any targets worth hitting once Bishop's done."

"Yeah, but if there is a job."

"You think you're ready?"

Ice nodded. "The gear Mitch has hooked me up with is state-of-the-art. I can shoot and move as well as I ever could."

He had to admit that Ice's recovery was impressive. The former Marine was now physically more imposing than he remembered, and with the artificial limbs he resembled something from a Terminator movie. He made a mental note to find out what supplements he was using. "I'll keep it in mind."

"Thanks, bro."

Vance left him in the corridor and stepped into the room being used by their Chief of Intelligence, Chen Chua, and his offsider, Flash.

Chua, a lightly-built Chinese American looked up from his laptop. "How's Saneh?" he asked as Vance dropped into a spare seat.

He shook his head. "Doesn't look good. There's a new treatment that might help, but we could potentially lose either her or the baby."

Chua grimaced. "You're kidding."

"No, Bishop needs to make the decision, if we can get comms with him. What's Flash up to?"

"He's working up the intel on this poaching guy, Mamba."

"What've you got so far?"

"His real name is David Mboya, a former Ugandan military officer. Smart guy, trained by the Brits, and reported to have an exemplary service record."

Vance raised his eyebrows. "Not your average dirt-bag criminal then."

"I'm sure Bish and Kruger will have no trouble dealing with him. What Flash and I are working on is the Chinese angle. We're trying to find out who Mamba supplies."

"Good, can you also have him focus on establishing comms with Bish?"

"Not a problem. Flash has already pulled data off Kruger's sat phone."

"Yeah?"

"It's currently inactive but he last used it in Zambia the night Saneh was shot."

"And?"

"Looks like he and Bish followed up the poachers. Before they met you at the hospital they'd covered over thirty miles on foot."

Vance shook his head. "Why does that not surprise me. Let's hope that goddamn crazy Aussie finishes Mamba before it's too late."

Silence filled the room as Vance stared into space, his thoughts back with Saneh at the hospital.

"You doing alright, Vance?"

He shook his head. "No, when we started PRIMAL I always knew we would lose people. But, I thought as long as we're doing good in the world it would be a sacrifice worth making. I never thought we'd face a decision like this."

"What are we going to do if we can't raise Bishop?"

He sighed. "I don't know, bud. I really don't know."

***

MOMBASA, KENYA

"Not bad," said Bishop as he stood beside Kruger in the foyer of the New Palm Tree Hotel. The building looked well maintained and hospitable. He noticed the white walls had been freshly painted and the staff were dressed in clean, pressed uniforms.

"Don't get too excited, once we dump our gear we're going to head down to Mtongwe."

"Tong what?"

"Suburb a few miles south of the harbor. Total shit hole."

As they crossed a terracotta-tiled courtyard Bishop caught a whiff of frangipani and his heart lurched. The fragrant white flower was one of Saneh's favorites.

The room was cramped but clean with two single beds, a desk, and a wardrobe. An antique box TV sat on a stand in the corner. Bishop tossed his bag on a bed. "You good to go?"

Kruger shook his head. "No. You need a shower. You stink."

"I don't care. We need to get out there and find this Mamba fucker."

"Relax, Toppie is making some discreet inquiries."

"Your dodgy mate?"

"Yeah, Mamba won't be hard to find."

"What about weapons?"

"He can hook us up with everything we need. How much cash do you have on you?"

Bishop took out his wallet and handed over some notes. "I've got more in my backpack." He emptied his clothes out of the bag and used a knife to slice open the lining. He pulled out a thick wad of US dollars and tossed it to Kruger.

"This is a good start but we're going to need more. There's a bank around the corner. I'll see to it and get us a local phone to use. Get yourself cleaned up, *ja*."

"OK, I'll sort you out later."

Kruger shrugged. "I'll get Vance to cover it." The big man tossed a room key on the bed. "I'll be half an hour at the most." He disappeared through the door leaving Bishop alone with his pile of clothes.

For the first time since Saneh had been shot he felt tired. Checking his watch he saw it was only a little past midday. Laying back on the bed he contemplated calling Vance to check on Saneh. No, he needed to stay focused on the job at hand. He would take a five-minute nap then shower. As he drifted off his thoughts turned to killing the man called Mamba Mboya.

***

As Bishop slept, the man he wanted to kill sharpened his machete not more than two miles away. "What's going on with my new poaching crew?" he asked as he tested the edge of the blade with his thumb. His eyes narrowed and he picked up his beer, took a swig, and dripped some of the amber liquid on the sharpening stone.

Kogo grimaced at the sound of the blade dragging across the stone. "I've put the word out."

"I don't want any gang-banging scum. Get me ex-military guys. The cops are cracking down on poachers. I'm not taking chances with idiots."

"That makes it harder, boss."

He stopped sharpening and fixed Kogo with a glare. "You fuck this up and–"

The shrill ring of the phone on the bench interrupted him. He picked it up and held it to his ear. "What?"

"Have you got the horn?" Zhou asked.

"Yes, but it cost us."

"How so?"

"We ran into trouble and lost four men."

"But you will still be able to make the shipment, yes?"

"We're a few tusks short." Mamba tucked the phone under his ear, picked up his assault vest from where it lay on the bench, and slid the machete back in its scabbard. "But, I have a plan. You'll get what you requested."

"I better, I have clients who will be less than impressed if we don't deliver."

"Don't threaten me, Zhou. I can find new buyers for the ivory and the horn."

"I've already paid a deposit."

"And like I said, it will all be there." Mamba slammed the phone back on the cradle. "Send that whining chink a photo of the horn." He stormed across to a battered SUV that was parked facing the warehouse doors and flung his vest on the back seat. Then he grabbed a compact chainsaw from the bench and placed it in with his equipment. "I'm heading up to Mbale for a couple of days to get more ivory. I want you to find new men and poach elephant at Tsavo."

"By myself?"

"No, you idiot. I said find new men. Take the recruits and use it as a test." He climbed in the driver's seat. "Now, open the fucking doors before I miss my flight."

Kogo slid the warehouse doors open and watched as the vehicle disappeared down the street. When the doors were shut he chained them and walked through to the office. The room was as run-down as the rest of the building. A single bare light bulb hung over a metal desk. Behind it sat an old bank safe. He unlocked it with a brass key and swung the heavy door open. Inside were two shelves, the bottom stacked with wads of US dollars. It was a mere morsel of the fortune Mamba had made poaching. On the top shelf lay the rhino horn wrapped in plastic. As he grabbed it the stench of rotting flesh made him gag.

He locked the safe and took the horn back into the warehouse. It was hard to believe someone was willing to pay hundreds of thousands of dollars for such an ugly object, he thought. Opening a drawer in the bench he took out a wire brush, scalpel, and a box knife. He'd become quite adept at removing flesh from elephant tusks and rhino horns. Not a pleasant job but it had its perks. Mamba gave him an extra hundred dollars per item. Once he'd prepared the horn he would take photos and email them to Zhou. Then he needed to find a new team and plan their mission to Tsavo.

***

SHANGHAI, CHINA

Fan Wei was overseeing the preparation of her master's dinner when the phone in her pocket vibrated. Rinsing her hands she left the chef to continue as she checked the message. Zhou had sent her photos of the horn. Walking into a tiny office she opened her email account and hit print on the photos. As the printer hummed she opened her favorite luxury goods website and checked the price on a bag she had her eye on. If the horn turned out to be exactly what Wang Hejun wanted her bonus would be significant. She might even be able to afford some new earrings as well. She collected the images from the printer, slipped them in a folder, and carried them through the penthouse apartment. At the door of Hejun's study she knocked and waited.

"Enter."

She pushed the door open and spotted the billionaire at his desk reading. "Sir, I have photos of the black rhino horn." She stepped forward and held them out.

Hejun raised his eyes from the book. "Only photos? Where is the horn?" He snatched the folder and emptied it on his desk.

"It is still in Africa. It will leave by ship on Friday and should arrive early next week."

He grunted as he adjusted his glasses and stared intently at the images. "It is a fine horn. What are we paying for it?"

"A little under 6 million yuan."

He nodded. "A fair price. When it arrives I will collect it in person."

"Very good, sir."

He pushed the photos to one side and refocused his attention on the book. "That is all." He dismissed her with a wave of his hand.

On her way back to the kitchen Fan smiled as she visualized the outfit that would match her new bag and earrings. Working for Hejun may be a chore but at least it paid well.

CHAPTER 6

KENYA

Bishop gazed out the window of the Mazda as Kruger drove them along the highway south from Mombasa. The road was lined with ramshackle tin-roofed stalls selling everything from local farm produce to nappies, plastic buckets, and flip-flops. The contrast between this area and Mombasa Island was stark. Once they had crossed on the ferry into the suburb of Likoni the hotels and resorts were replaced with a vast shantytown stretching as far as the eye could see.

Bishop spotted a sign advertising energy drinks and contemplated asking Kruger to pull over. The half-hour nap he'd inadvertently taken instead of showering had left him feeling worse for wear. What's more he still wore the same clothes and wouldn't have a chance to shower till they got back to the hotel later that evening.

"So the guy we're going to meet," Kruger said interrupting his thoughts. "Toppie, he's a bit strange, *ja.*"

"How so?"

"He worked with me in the Recces back in the day."

"An operator?"

"No, company quartermaster before they kicked him out."

"What for?"

"Making a little on the side selling equipment."

"Right, so he's an entrepreneur."

"No, Toppie's a nut job. After they booted him from the Regiment he set up here in Kenya. Hooks people up with things they need."

"Like guns?"

"Of course. He's got a thing for Soviet-era kit, but if he likes you then he can get whatever you want. Not just weapons: intel, contacts, anything…"

"And if he doesn't like you?"

"Then you're proper fucked." Kruger laughed.

"Great." Bishop turned his attention back to the roadside. Patches of bush grew between the dilapidated shacks. Within a few miles the landscape turned to savannah with scrubby bushes and long grass.

Kruger turned them off the highway and the hatchback rattled and bounced along a rutted dirt road for a mile or two more before they reached a sandy track. A few hundred yards further and he brought them to a halt.

"What the hell is this?" Bishop stared at the fortress blocking their path in disbelief. It resembled something from a Mad Max movie. Thick steel plated gates towered over them. On either side an earthen bank was topped with coils of barbed wire. In front of the banks an eight-foot deep ditch was impassable to vehicles. "This guy really doesn't like house calls."

"Like I said, he's a bit strange." Kruger stepped out of the car.

He watched as Kruger picked up an old military wire phone bolted to the gate frame, spun the handle, and spoke into the handset. The gates gave a groan and swung slowly open revealing the road beyond.

"Bat shit crazy," said Kruger as he drove them up the driveway.

"Is he some kind of apocalypse survival prepper?" Bishop spotted no less than five sandbagged fighting positions as they followed the track through the scrub. As they came around a corner they passed another earthen bank. On the far side they approached a Soviet-era vehicle graveyard.

"BRDM, BTR, T-55." Bishop rattled off the names of the armored vehicles parked in the clearing. The better part of a Russian military museum lined either side of the track. "Is that an old An-2 Colt?" He pointed at the tail of an aircraft protruding from a curved corrugated iron hangar. Behind it a dirt airstrip stretched out into the bush.

"That's Annie, his pride and joy," Kruger replied as he parked the car in front of a pile of stacked shipping containers. "Don't get out of the car yet."

It took him a moment to realize the steel boxes had been welded together to form a building. There were windows, doors, vents, and a satellite dish perched on top.

A pack of dogs exploded around the corner barking furiously. "Shit!" The animals looked like clones of Kruger's dog, Princess; massive brown hunting hounds with lean muscular bodies and huge square heads filled with razor-sharp teeth. They jumped up against the car barking loudly and rocking the little Mazda.

A shrill whistle rang out and the dogs disappeared back in the direction they had come from.

"OK, now we're good."

As they alighted from the hatchback a short figure appeared from the hangar and strode purposefully toward them. "Kruger, that you, boy?"

The man walking toward them was almost as wide as he was tall with a long grey scruffy beard reaching to his belt. He wore jeans, cowboy boots, and a leather vest that would have been at home on one of the Village People. A pistol belt topped off his outfit and Bishop identified a modern FN Five-Seven on his hip.

"*Ja,* Toppie, it's me." Kruger took the quartermaster's hand and shook it.

"How's that hound of yours?"

"Princess, she's doing good."

Toppie turned to face Bishop and he felt the grey eyes giving him the once over. "This your friend? The one with the girlfriend who's sleeping because of that scum bag Mamba?"

"That's him."

Toppie stuck out his hand and Bishop grasped it. "Any friend of Kruger's is probably a fucking asshole." He grinned showing a set of yellow teeth. "But, aren't we all?"

Bishop forced a smile.

"Now, what do you need?"

"Weapons, ammo, and everything you know about Mamba and his operations," said Bishop.

Toppie sucked his gums as he contemplated the request. "Any chance you boys have already had a crack at Mamba?"

"Maybe. Why's that?"

"Because he's got this second-in-command, a Kenyan called Kogo, and the weaselly little prick is asking around for poachers. Rumor has it they got slapped around pretty bad down in Zambia."

Bishop shot Kruger a glance and he nodded. "Any chance you can arrange an introduction?"

"Depends?"

"On what?"

Toppie grinned again. "On how much cash you got."

"Money isn't a problem."

"Then I might know a guy. Now come and have a look at this." Toppie gestured for them to follow him to the hangar. As they approached the rusted shell Bishop spotted a number of shipping containers buried under a mound of dirt. Their scruffy host unlocked one of them, wrenched the doors open, and switched on a light.

"Sweet mother of Jesus," murmured Bishop.

The walls of the container were lined with weapons. Assault rifles, sniper rifles, sub-machine guns, pistols, rocket launchers, and machine guns, Toppie had them all.

The grey-bearded quartermaster turned to face them, his yellowed teeth exposed in a broad smile. "Welcome to Toppie's cave of carnage."

Bishop took a R5 off the wall and inspected it. "You got ammo and a couple of chest rigs, Toppie?"

"Do hippos shit in the river?"

"Yes they do." Bishop took a near mint-condition Browning High-Power pistol from the wall and checked the action. "They certainly do."

***

MBALE, UGANDA

Mamba paid the pilot with a wad of cash and opened the door of the Cessna light aircraft. Grabbing his gear from behind the seat he shrugged on his assault vest as he set off across the tarmac with the chainsaw in hand. A team of camouflage-uniformed men were waiting next to a white military Bell 412 helicopter.

"David, it is good to see you." The man who greeted Mamba by his Christian name wore the rank of a full colonel on the shoulders of his fatigues.

"You too." Mamba hugged his older brother and handed him a small bag filled with diamonds. "You've saved my skin with this one."

"Anything for family, David." The colonel turned to his aircrew as he slipped the bag into his pocket and gave them the signal to start the helicopter's engines. "Let's go hunting."

"Did you bring my gun?"

The colonel flashed a smile. "Of course I did."

Twenty minutes later the helicopter thundered over Mount Elgon National Park with the side doors open. Mamba sat in one of the side seats with a headset on and a M60 machine gun resting across his knees.

"We've only got an hour's flying time," said the colonel as they swept in low over a river and followed it north.

"It's getting dark, they'll move down to drink. We stay on the river."

"OK, but if we don't find any within thirty minutes we'll have to head back."

Mamba gave his brother thumbs-up as he scanned the banks of the river. He spotted a tour group and ignored their waves. A few miles further he found what he was searching for, a small herd of elephants on the floodplain. "Down there," he transmitted over the radio.

"Roger." The pilot banked the helicopter and circled around. The elephants raised their heads and ran from the noisy intruder.

"Come in low over the top." Mamba yanked back the cocking handle on the M60. The elephants seemed to know his intent and made a beeline for the trees. He smiled and aimed at a large bull as it turned and raised its trunk in a challenge.

The M60 roared and bucked against his shoulder as he sent a line of tracer into the bull. The elephant staggered falling behind from the rest of the pack. Mamba continued to fire, pumping round after round into the wounded beast. It dropped to its knees as he emptied the last of the one hundred round belt. "Take us down," he ordered as the weapon ran dry and smoke streamed off its barrel.

The pilot brought the helicopter down to a hover as Mamba reloaded the machine gun and slung his chainsaw over his shoulder. He dropped down onto the grass and moved cautiously toward the bull.

The groan of the dying animal was music to his ears. Setting the M60 on the ground he started the chainsaw. The sharp teeth ripped through the elephant's flesh as he cut through to the base of the tusks. When he'd exposed as much ivory as possible he sliced through the tusk and let it drop to the ground. Letting the saw idle he wiped sweat from his brow.

As he ripped into the other tusk an angry bellow caught his attention. Turning toward the noise he saw a massive elephant charging through the grass. "Holy shit." The tusks were lowered and he leaped to one side. It thundered past and he dropped the saw, diving for the machine gun. "Fuck." The weapon had been crushed under the charging beast's massive feet.

He spun toward the threat; it was a female elephant. She had turned to the corpse of her mate and prodded him with her trunk. Snorting in rage she looked up and charged again. As Mamba turned to run there was a burst of gunfire. He dropped to the ground and watched as his brother emptied an entire magazine into the skull of the animal. She died with a bellow hitting the ground with a thud.

The colonel offered his hand to Mamba and pulled him to his feet. "You're getting careless, David."

He dusted off his clothes and picked up the saw. "Maybe, but at least now I've got two sets of tusks."

"Always about the bottom dollar."

"Someone has to keep your wife in all her fancy clothes."

The colonel laughed and slapped him on the shoulder. "Just hurry up, the sun will set soon."

"Still scared of the dark, big brother?" Mamba asked as he went back to work on the first elephant.

"No, I'm scared of my pilots trying to fly in the dark."

He chopped the other tusk free from the bull, dumped it next to the crushed M60, and strode across to work on the cow. "I think you're afraid of missing dinner with your wife. She's got you by the balls." He grinned as he revved the chainsaw and sliced the dead female elephant's face open.

***

MOMBASA, KENYA

"This is the address," said Kruger as he pulled the Mazda into a poorly lit gravel parking lot.

The headlights lit up a half-dozen other vehicles including a police car. Behind the parking lot a corrugated fence topped with barbed wire was strung with colored party lights. From inside the car they could hear vibrant music.

"Looks inviting," Bishop said dryly as he double-checked the Browning pistol he'd purchased from Toppie, and tucked it into the waistband of his pants.

"Hey, it's not too bad by African standards."

"I'm not sure how comfortable I am leaving all our gear in the trunk." In addition to the pistol Toppie had sold them assault rifles, ammo, and chest rigs similar to what they had left in Zambia.

"They'll be fine." Kruger parked next to the police car.

They checked the gear was concealed in bags, locked the hatchback, and entered the drinking establishment through an open gate in the iron fence. What lay beyond surprised Bishop.

The fence hid a beer garden that looked far more inviting than the exterior suggested. Long wooden benches sat on a terracotta-tiled terrace with a web of vines forming a roof above them. The party lights illuminated the customers sitting on benches devouring plates of ribs. "You sure this is the right place? Toppie gave me the impression it was a shit hole."

"This is the address. We need to ask for a guy called Steve."

"Steve?"

Kruger shrugged as he strode to the bar. Made from polished hardwood it displayed an impressive collection of spirits on softly lit glass shelves. In an adjoining dining hall there were more benches and patrons enjoying dinner.

Bishop's stomach grumbled. "How about we grab some of those ribs?"

Kruger waved over the bartender, a middle-aged woman with an apron tied around her ample waist. "Can we order a couple of beers and some ribs?"

She smiled. "Sure thing, honey."

"Can you also tell Steve that Aden and Kruger are here to see him," added Bishop.

Her smile faded and she focused on pouring them two locally brewed ales.

"Seems Steve's not real popular around here," Bishop said as they took a seat. He took a sip of the beer and sighed. "God, I needed that."

"You also need a shower." Kruger took a swig of his own beer as a waitress appeared with a massive plate of pork ribs. "That was quick."

They ate with their hands devouring the meat in a matter of minutes. When they were done the waitress reappeared with a bowl of lemon-scented water and hand towels. "Mr. Hanna will see you now." She led them around the bar through a service door. The staff paid them no attention as they walked through the kitchen and out into a corridor. "Wait here." She knocked twice on a door before leaving.

Bishop rested his hand on the pistol concealed under his T-shirt.

The door opened and a tall middle-aged Caucasian with thick dark hair waved them inside. "Sorry to keep you waiting, gentlemen. I hope you enjoyed your dinner." He had a strong South African accent.

"Top notch," replied Kruger. "I assume you are Steve."

"That's correct. Please take a seat." He sat behind his desk. "I want to apologize in advance for this meeting being short. I have a lot of business to take care of tonight before I go home to see my children. Now, I understand from Toppie you're both ex-South African military and looking for work."

"*Ja*, we've got a bit of expertise in the bush, tracking and the like."

Steve scribbled something on a notepad. "Very good, those are skills I can sell."

"We'd like to make some real money," added Bishop with a South African accent of his own. "If you get what we mean."

"Oh, I think I do. Where are you staying?"

Bishop hesitated.

Steve smiled. "No, nothing sinister, I've got someone I want you to meet."

"We're at the New Palm Tree Hotel," said Kruger.

"Ah very nice, a friend of mine owns it. Make sure you mention my name when you check out, OK?"

"Sounds good."

Steve rose, reached out, and shook their hands. "It is very nice to meet friends of Toppie. Him and I go back a long way."

"He's a good man," said Kruger.

Steve laughed. "He's a lunatic. Anyway, I hope I can help you to find something. So you know, the deal will be I take twenty percent of everything you make."

"Fifteen," said Bishop.

"Twenty is customary."

"Maybe for criminals and petty thieves. We're neither."

Steve nodded. "OK, we've got a deal, fifteen percent. Gentlemen, it has been short but still a pleasure. Feel free to enjoy more food and drink. Have as much you wish, it's on the house." He gestured to the door.

Bishop and Kruger left the office and made their way back through the kitchen to the bar. Kruger ordered two more beers and another plate of ribs. They sat in a corner away from the other customers. "What do you think?" he asked Bishop.

"A lot more professional than I expected."

"Yeah, Toppie had me thinking we were meeting with a crime boss."

"I get the feeling Toppie lives on a different planet to everyone else."

"That's true."

"Let's finish up here and get back to the hotel. I want to take a shower and get my head down."

"Might be an idea to check in with Vance, *ja*."

For the first time in the last few hours Bishop's thoughts turned to Saneh. He felt guilty that he'd lost himself in the mission and forgotten about her. "Yeah, maybe."

***

As Bishop and Kruger finished their beers Kogo ate takeout at the bench in the warehouse. His plans were not progressing well. So far he'd only recruited one new member to the team; a bush meat poacher living in the slums of Likoni. The man could hardly be called capable. His only virtue; he knew every inch of Tsavo. Two men were not enough but he was reluctant to postpone the mission. The idea of disappointing Mamba terrified him.

The phone on the bench rang, interrupting his meal. He snatched it from the cradle. "Hello."

"Kogo, is that you?"

"Yes, who is this?"

"It's Steve, I've got two men for you. Former South African military, they've got the skills you want, and they're clean."

"You sure?"

"Yes, they're not police informants. They come highly recommended from a source I trust."

"You sure?"

"The men are staying at the New Palm Tree Hotel. You can check them out for yourself. They're under the name Aden. Oh, and I get fifteen percent of whatever they make."

"You will have to discuss that with Mamba."

"I'm discussing it with you."

"Fine, if I use them you get fifteen percent."

"Deal. Let me know if you need anything else."

"A hundred pounds of ivory."

Steve laughed. "Your game, not mine." He hung up.

Kogo contemplated the offer then grabbed his keys. If these men were suitable his mission tomorrow could still go ahead.

***

Bishop struggled to stay awake as Kruger pulled the Mazda into a parking space at their hotel. He checked his watch; it was nearly midnight and they had been on the go for almost 72 hours.

"You look and smell like shit," said Kruger as he stepped out of the car. "If you don't take a shower soon I'm going to hose you down."

"Thanks mate, good to know you've got my back."

As they unloaded their bags of gear Bishop noticed a new model Toyota Land Cruiser parked nearby. The expensive truck was fully fitted out: roof racks, spare tires, jerry can holders, and spotlights. Not a common sight in Kenya.

"Aden?" someone said from the shadows.

Kruger dropped his bag and spun toward the voice with a pistol drawn. "Show yourself."

"It's OK, I'm a friend of Steve's." The man walked forward with his hands extended. Lightly built with a shaved head, his coffee-colored skin hinted at a mixed ethnicity. "Can we talk in your room?"

Kruger glanced at Bishop who nodded and they led the man from the parking lot.

"What's your name?" asked Bishop as Kruger opened the door to their room. He knew it wasn't Mamba.

"You can call me Kogo."

Kruger dumped his bags on the floor and gestured for the man to sit on a bed.

"It's late, Kogo, so feel free to get to the point," said Bishop as he pulled the door shut. "We already spoke to Mr. Hanna. Is this the second half of the job interview?"

"Yes, he vouched for you but I wanted to meet in person before I offer you work."

Bishop sat on his bed facing the poacher. "OK. So do you have any questions?"

"Have you hunted elephants before?"

"*Ja*," said Kruger. "We did some work in South Africa but things got a little hot. That's why we're here."

"There's a lot of anti-poaching organizations in South Africa," said Kogo.

"Not so many here," said Bishop. "Hey, let's talk money, we don't come cheap."

Kogo nodded. "The money is good. We'll give you a five percent cut each of the ivory."

"We, who is we?" asked Bishop.

"I work for someone, he authorizes all the details."

"And his name is?"

"You don't need that information at the moment." Kogo got up from the bed. "I will pick you up in the morning. Do you need equipment?"

"Don't bother, we don't work for people who don't have names," said Bishop.

Kogo's brow furrowed and he glanced around the room. "OK, OK, I work for a man called Mamba Mboya."

Bishop fought the urge to grab him by the throat. "Will he be coming with us?"

The poacher shook his head. "No, think of this as a trial. If you prove yourself to me then you will work with Mamba."

"Fair enough. So, we've got our own gear. Where are we going?"

"I'll give you the location in the morning." Kogo offered Bishop his hand.

"We don't work like that." Bishop ignored Kogo's attempted handshake. "You either tell us where we're going or you find someone else."

Kogo glanced nervously at Kruger then back to Bishop. "Tsavo East National Park. Are you familiar with it?"

"No, but we'll do our research. See you in the morning."

Kogo nodded. "4.30 am. I'll have another man with me who knows the park."

Bishop opened the door. "See you then." He waited for the poacher to leave before moving across to the window and watching him climb into the Land Cruiser.

"You looked like you were going to kill him," said Kruger.

"Wanted to, that slimy prick was probably at Luangwa." He left the window. "Can I use your local phone?"

"What's up?" Kruger handed him the device.

"I'm going to give Dom a call and see if he knows people at Tsavo. I for one will not be shooting any elephants."

CHAPTER 7

TSAVO EAST NATIONAL PARK, KENYA

It was a few minutes past eight in the morning when Kogo stopped the Land Cruiser and killed the engine. He glanced in the rear vision mirror and made eye contact with Bishop. "This as far as we can drive."

"Better get cracking then, *ja*." He and Kruger alighted from the four-wheel drive and joined the third man at the back. He was their tracker; a lean bush-meat poacher familiar with Tsavo who spoke very little English. Bishop shrugged on his chest rig and inserted a magazine into his R5 assault rifle. Kruger carried a R1 and had a heavy-caliber double-barreled rifle slung over his shoulder.

"The tracker will lead us to the elephants. He says they will be near the lake a few miles from here." Kogo took a compact chainsaw from the trunk and locked the vehicle. "Kruger will make the kill. I cut the tusks and we leave as fast as we can."

"Is this area heavily patrolled?" asked Bishop as he checked his pouches. The South African-style vest he'd bought off Toppie contained the essentials including water, ammo, a compact pair of binoculars, and a medical kit.

Kogo turned to the tracker and asked him in Swahili.

The man shrugged and rattled off a few sentences.

"Not really," translated Kogo. "There are volunteers patrolling the park but it's big."

"So there's a chance we could bump into a patrol out there."

"It is possible, that's why you have been hired."

"I haven't seen any money yet, champ. I'm not about to go in there and get myself shot on the off-chance your mate here can find us an elephant. How about you cough up some cash up-front?"

Kogo shook his head. "I can't do that."

"Listen, fuckbag, you've dragged us all the way out here because you're desperate. I don't know why but you need tusks and you need them fast. The way I see it you need to pay up-front or cut us in for a bigger slice." Bishop locked eyes with the poacher.

"I can't make that decision."

"You've got a sat phone, call your boss."

Kogo looked to the tracker for support but the man shrugged. He wasn't about to challenge the heavily-armed former soldiers. "OK, fine, I will make the call." He took the satellite phone from his pocket and dialed.

Bishop watched him intently as he waited for the call to pickup. Turning his back Kogo talked in Swahili.

"Do you have a map?" Bishop asked the tracker.

The man shrugged again.

"Do you speak any English?"

The only response was another shrug.

"I guess not." He took the opportunity to check the surroundings. It was a lot like Luangwa: dry red earth, scrubby bushes, and tall thorn trees with sparse cover. It reminded him of Saneh, bloodied and wounded, lying in the dust next to the safari truck. Turning back to Kogo he saw the poacher had finished his call.

"I can't pay you now but we can offer you five thousand dollars each if we return with at least two tusks."

"And if we don't?"

"Then I can pay you a thousand each for your time."

Bishop glanced at Kruger who nodded.

"You've got a deal. But, if you try to screw us you're a dead man."

Kogo swallowed.

"Have you got a map of the area?"

The poacher reached inside his vest, pulled out a folded map, and handed it over. Bishop opened it on the bonnet of the four-wheel drive. "Ask your man where the elephants are."

Kogo spoke to the tracker who leant over the map and pointed at a smudge of blue.

"The lake. It's a good start. Kruger, we need to plan our route so we avoid patrols."

Kruger pulled out a GPS and checked the map. "We're here." He stabbed a finger at the map. "We can use this creek line to minimize the risk of hitting a patrol. They'll be sticking to the vehicle tracks."

Bishop folded the map and slid it inside his shirt. "I like it. Let's get moving."

As the local tracker and Kogo led the way Kruger hung back, took out his own satellite phone, and sent a text message.

***

THE SANDPIT, ABU DHABI

"Vance, we've got a hit," Flash yelled from the top of the staircase inside PRIMAL's Abu Dhabi headquarters.

"Where is he?" Vance slammed the refrigerator shut and stormed out of the kitchen.

"Kruger just sent a text message over his sat phone. Looks like they're in Kenya."

"Do we have an open line of communications?"

"No, the phone's switched off now."

Vance climbed the stairs and followed Flash into the intel room. "What are they up to?"

Flash returned to his terminal and showed Vance the message. "Check this out. Kruger sent a grid reference to someone in vicinity of North Luangwa National Park. I bet it's the ranger Bishop was hanging out with, Dominic Marks. According to the message the boys are hunting elephants near the lake at Tsavo East National Park."

"And why would they be doing that?" asked Vance.

"It must have something to do with tracking down Mr. Mamba Mboya."

"Find out who Kruger messaged."

"Roger." Flash's fingers danced over the keyboard.

Vance glanced at his watch. "I'm going to head across to the hospital and replace Tariq." The two of them were taking turns watching over Saneh. "Keep me posted."

"Will do."

As he walked downstairs his phone vibrated with an incoming call. "Speak of the devil." It was Tariq.

"Good afternoon, Vance."

"Tariq, I'm on my way in now."

"Doctor Edwards wants to schedule a meeting with us this afternoon. We're running out of time."

Vance sighed. "OK, I'll be there within the hour." He stopped in the kitchen and contemplated pouring a scotch.

"Hey, what's up, big man?" Ice walked into the kitchen with a pistol holstered on his hip.

"I'm about to head to the hospital. How's the training going?" Ice had set up an airsoft range in one half of the villa's garage and had been spending hours practicing weapon manipulation with his robotic hand.

"Not bad, I was wondering if I could come to the hospital with you." He took off the pistol belt and placed it on the bench.

Vance shook his head. "We're trying to keep a low profile, brother. Better if you stayed here with the team."

"Yeah, OK, well if you need to talk I'm always here for you."

"For sure." Vance swallowed hard as he grabbed a set of keys from the bench and strode toward the door.

"Oh and Vance, when it comes time to pull Bishop out of the shit, I'm good to go."

"Let's hope it doesn't come to that. Knocking off a dirt-bag poacher shouldn't be too difficult for Bishop and Kruger."

"We both know what Bish is like."

He managed a smirk. "Yep, goddamn shit magnet."

***

BAREEN HOSPITAL, ABU DHABI

Vance walked slowly along the spotless white corridors as he searched for Doctor Edwards' office. He found it five doors down, exactly where a pretty young nurse had directed him. Pausing with his hand raised to knock on the door he contemplated turning and walking away; leaving the decision that needed to be made to Tariq. In all his years as a paramilitary operative then as the Director of Operations for PRIMAL he had never faced a dilemma like this. Life and death decisions were part of his day-to-day routine but that hadn't prepared him. His shoulders dropped as he knocked.

"Come in."

He pushed the door open and nodded to the man behind his desk. "Hey, Doc."

"Vance." Edwards directed him to take the seat next to Tariq.

The Arab rose and they shook hands.

"Tariq, good to see you, brother." Vance sat and placed his clenched fists on his thighs. "So what's the prognosis?" He didn't really need to ask. The grave expression on Doctor Edwards' face said it all.

"Gentlemen, Saneh's situation has begun to deteriorate. In the last twenty-four hours her brain activity has slowed. I'm afraid we're losing her."

Vance sighed. "What about the baby?"

"I've been consulting with a colleague of mine who is the hospital's leading obstetrician. We concur that as long as we keep Saneh's body alive the child could continue to develop normally. But, there will be an increased risk of complications."

"What kind of complications?" asked Tariq.

"The child could be either mentally or physically impaired. There is also an increased likelihood that Saneh's body might terminate the pregnancy."

"And the alternative?"

"We begin a revolutionary program to stimulate Saneh's brain."

"But there will be an impact on the child."

Doctor Edwards nodded. “The risk remains that, as a side effect of some of the drugs, her body will terminate the pregnancy. This is uncharted territory, I don't know of any other cases where–”

“Can't we use other drugs?” interrupted Vance.

“We can but the chance of recovery is significantly reduced.” Edwards placed his hand on a document on the desk. “These are the release papers authorizing the treatment. I'm going to give you a few minutes to discuss the options.” He rose and left Vance and Tariq in the office.

“I never thought I’d have to make a decision like this,” said Vance.

“You still haven't been able to reach Bishop?”

He shook his head. “No, he's offline still.”

“And we've run out of time.”

“Yes, we both know what needs to be done.”

Tariq's eyes were glassy as he rose from his chair. “We always knew there would be times like this.”

“Seems to be a lot of them recently, bud.”

Tariq placed a hand on his shoulder. “We’re doing the right thing.”

“I know.”

***

TSAVO EAST NATIONAL PARK, KENYA

Bishop held up his hand signaling the hunting party to halt. Crouching in a thick patch of grass he surveyed the terrain ahead.

Five hundred yards away a meager herd of elephants foraged on a floodplain next to a shallow lake. Upwind, the majestic beasts were oblivious to their presence. Bishop grimaced as he spotted the massive tusks on the bull. Kogo would want them for sure.

He took binoculars from his vest and scanned the trees beyond the floodplain. There was no sign of human activity.

"What's the plan?" asked Kruger kneeling alongside.

He continued scanning the bush. "They should be here. Dom said he would pass on our message to the Kenyan rangers."

"Well they're not, so what are we going to do?"

The grass rustled behind them and Bishop glanced over his shoulder to see Kogo approach.

"What's going on?"

"We're waiting," said Bishop.

"What for? I can see the big bull. Shoot him, we cut off the tusks, and then we go."

"You can run out there if you want." Bishop fixed him with a glare. "Or we can wait and make sure we're not the only ones watching."

The poacher swallowed and gripped his weapon tight. "No, you're right. We should take our time."

Bishop wondered if Kogo had been there the night Saneh was shot. Had he been the man who escaped in the four-wheel drive with Mamba? He imagined dragging his knife across the poacher's throat. Instead he turned his attention back to his binoculars and the floodplain. After a few minutes he turned to Kruger. "How close do you need to get?"

"At least another three hundred yards."

He looked back at Kogo. "You and the tracker wait here. Once we make the kill come forward and take the tusks. Don't move until we shoot. Got it?"

"Yes, of course."

Kruger unslung the double-barreled hunting rifle and cracked open the breech. He checked both the high-powered cartridges and snapped it shut. Tucking the weapon under his arm he slung the R1. "I'm good to go."

"OK, you're on point. I'll hang back a few yards and cover you if needed."

They left the others at the edge of the floodplain and stalked through the grass toward the elephants. "Where the hell are they?" he whispered to himself.

"What are we doing, Bish?" Kruger hissed as he crouched behind a clump of grass only a few hundred yards from the herd, well within range.

A shout sounded from their flank startling the elephants. Bishop turned and spotted figures emerging from the far tree line. There were at least a dozen green-uniformed men swarming toward them. "Right on time." He flicked off the safety and fired a burst over the men. They disappeared as they dove to the ground.

"Let's get the hell out of here. Covering!" Bishop fired off a few more shots as Kruger dashed past him. Out the corner of his eye he saw the elephants fleeing from the gunshots. "Run, run, run," he murmured as he fired again. When Kruger's weapon barked he scrambled to his feet and dashed past. They repeated the process until they reached the spot where Kogo waited.

"What the fuck is going on?" The poacher cowered in the long grass clutching his weapon.

"Where's the tracker?" Bishop asked as he slid in next to him.

Gunfire crackled through the air as Kruger joined them.

"He ran... As soon as the firing started, he ran."

"Fucking chickenshit." Kruger fired off more rounds. "There's a crap load of these guys, *ja*. We need to keep moving." He gave Bishop a nod and grabbed Kogo by the shoulder. "We'll cover you, OK?"

The poacher's eyes were wide. "Yes, of course."

"Now go."

As Kogo took off through the bush Kruger turned and fired well-aimed shots either side of him. "Run you little cocksucker."

"Go, go, go!" Bishop yelled.

They sprinted through the bush after Kogo firing their weapons into the ground as they ran. Bishop was amazed at how fast the poacher moved. They covered half a mile in a matter of minutes.

"That's far enough," yelled Bishop as they skidded down a dry streambed. He glanced around; there was still no sign of the tracker.

"Are they going to catch us?" Kogo stammered. "If they hand us over to the Kenyan Wildlife Service we'll end up in jail."

"No one's going to get us," Bishop snapped. "We're almost at the car." He turned to Kruger who covered their rear. "Let's be careful, they may be staking it out."

"Roger, you take point. I'll bring up the rear."

Bishop led them through the scrub, his eyes peeled for any of the rangers. The Land Cruiser was where they had left it, parked off the road at the edge of the park.

"Get in, let's go." As Bishop yanked open the passenger door he heard the roar of an engine. "Shit." He stepped out onto the track and spotted an olive drab truck speeding toward them. "Kruger, you've got the wheel." He aimed at the approaching vehicle. Firing low he put five shots into the engine block. Steam and smoke exploded from under the hood.

Turning he ran back and leaped in the Land Cruiser. "Let's get the hell out of here!" He slammed the door shut as Kruger launched the four-wheel drive through the bushes and out onto the sandy track. They fish-tailed down the road, the big V8 roaring.

"Thank God," said Kogo from the back seat.

Bishop glanced over his shoulder to see the poacher staring out the rear window at the smoking truck.

"You're not going to back out of the cash are you, Kogo?"

The poacher turned and shook his head vigorously. "No, you'll get your money. You saved me from prison... or worse."

"Good, make sure you let Mamba know because we need more work."

"I will."

"Guys," Kruger interrupted. "Check this out."

Bishop squinted through the windshield and spotted a dark skinny figure running along the road in front of them; it was the tracker. "You want to pick him up, Kogo?"

"No, he ran like a startled gazelle. He can keep running, we have no need for him now."

Bishop gave Kruger a slight nod and they sped past the man leaving him in a cloud of dust. "You're a ruthless bastard."

"You haven't met Mamba yet."

"When is he back in town?"

"He should be back now."

"Will he have work for us?"

"Maybe later tonight. I'll call you this afternoon with the details."

"If you hand over the cash then we're keen, *ja*." replied Bishop. "But, first we get the money, then we do the next job. We're not running a charity."

"Yes of course, I'll talk to Mamba."

"Good, I'm looking forward to meeting him."

CHAPTER 8

THE SANDPIT, ABU DHABI

As Vance climbed the staircase to the upper levels of the villa, Chen Chua, PRIMAL's intelligence chief, called him into his workspace. Both Chua and Flash looked up from behind their computers as he walked in.

"OK, team, what's up?"

"Everything alright?" asked Chua.

"Yeah."

"How's Saneh?"

"No change," he grunted. "What have you got? Established comms with Bishop?"

"Not yet, but we'll come back to that. I spoke to Dominic Marks, the ranger who Kruger was communicating with."

"And?"

"According to Marks, Bish and Kruger were with a group of poachers in Tsavo national park. What's really interesting is they tipped off the local rangers. Marks thinks they're trying to infiltrate Mamba's poaching gang."

"Makes sense. Does Marks have a number for them other than the sat phone?"

"Yes, he gave us their Kenyan number. It's only a matter of time before they're back in range of the cell towers."

"Good work, bud. Let me know when they're online." Vance turned and left the room. He was halfway down the corridor when Chua caught up with him.

"Vance, what's going on with Saneh?"

"Like I said, no change."

Chua shook his head. "I know you're lying. Look, we're all family here and we deserve to know."

He exhaled. "They gave us a choice, Chen. Either we lose Saneh and try to save the child or we try to save Saneh and possibly lose the child."

"So that's why we need to get in contact with Bishop so urgently."

"Yeah, but we ran out of time. The decision had to be made today."

"And you and Tariq made it?"

Vance nodded.

"So what now?"

He shrugged. "We keep working the intel on the poachers and hope Bishop stays out of the shit."

"When we have comms what are you going to tell him?"

"Tell him? Tell him what? That we weighed the life of his unborn child against the life of his woman? How do you tell a man that, Chen? How do you tell him that because you couldn't reach him you had to make the hardest decision of his life for him? And what happens if he doesn't agree with the decision?"

"Bishop can't judge the decision you and Tariq made when he chose to chase vengeance rather than stand by Saneh. He'll live with it and he'll be grateful he didn't have to make it himself. You're a damn good man and a brave leader, don't you ever forget it."

He fought back tears and embraced Chua in a bear hug.

"Get some sleep, Vance. We'll have comms with Bishop in a matter of hours and the hospital will take care of Saneh."

***

MOMBASA, KENYA

Mamba swallowed another mouthful of beer as he gazed at the dial on the kitchen scales. The tusk on it weighed-in at nearly fifty pounds and there were another five like it on the bench. He grinned; his Ugandan expedition had exceeded his expectations and put him overweight on Zhou's order. It also meant that whatever Kogo had managed to scrounge in Tsavo was a bonus. Thoughts of his second-in-command brought a scowl to his face. Where was the lazy shit?

Finishing the beer he glared at the warehouse door. Where the fuck was Kogo? The shipment was due out tonight and he sure as hell wasn't going to load it by himself. His assistant was supposed to be arranging extra security. The local cops had recently hiked the price for their protection and there was a risk they would try to strong-arm him again. They needed extra muscle to keep them in line.

The rattle of the lock on the warehouse door caught his attention and he grabbed his AK from where it lay on the bench. The door slid open and Kogo stepped inside. "Where the hell have you been? I tried to call you twice."

"Sorry, Mamba, the battery went dead."

He placed the weapon back on the bench and walked to the refrigerator for another beer. "So, where the fuck's the ivory?" Twisting the cap from the bottle on his bicep, he stared at the Kenyan.

"There was a problem."

"Oh, yeah? You hire some local deadshits who couldn't find an elephant in a tent?"

Kogo shook his head. "No, we ran up against the KWS. They ambushed us up by the lake."

He frowned. "You got away OK then. What about the others? The greedy white guys who wanted their cash up front."

"They're the only reason I'm alive. They're proper bad asses, Mamba. They shot the KWS up good and got us out of there fast. Saved my life."

Mamba's eyes narrowed as he took a pull of the beer. He opened the refrigerator, pulled another bottle out, and tossed it over. "So you think you can trust these guys?"

Kogo opened the beer and took a sip. "They're mercenaries. I think if we pay them then we can trust them."

"As long as no one else pays them more."

"No one has as much money as you, boss."

It was true, he thought, and if tonight's transfer went off without a hitch then he would be rich and living on a tropical island. Maybe he could run the business from there with Kogo and these mercenaries doing all the heavy lifting and taking the risks. "Bring your white mercenaries along tonight. Have them meet us at the jetty."

Kogo frowned. "You want them as well as the cops?"

"Do you trust the cops?"

He shook his head.

"But you trust these guys. So double the standard rate and get them to keep an eye on the crooked cops."

"They can help us load the boat."

"Always looking for value aren't you."

Kogo picked up one of the tusks on the bench. "You're not mad we didn't get any tusks?" he asked cautiously.

Mamba shrugged. "We have enough. But, of course your cut won't be as big." He grinned. "And I'm taking the money for the mercenaries out of your share."

The Kenyan placed the tusk down. "Yes, boss."

"So, before I get you to call up your white boys how about you tell me everything you know about them. Starting with who recommended them."

***

Bishop's stomach growled as he lay on his bed in the hotel room staring at the ceiling fan.

"You might be hungry, bro." Kruger laughed as he pulled on a clean T-shirt.

"Skipped breakfast and lunch, who would have thought?"

"There's a place I saw around the corner, looks OK."

"What level of dining does an African OK get you?" Bishop asked. "Is that the local equivalent of a Michelin Star?"

"It means you can eat there and not shit yourself within ten minutes."

"Ah, the shit-yourself scale; very popular measure of culinary standards in South East Asia." He sat up and pulled on his boots. As he tied them Kruger's local phone rang.

The South African frowned at the screen, answered the call, and listened. "It's Vance, he wants to talk to you."

Bishop's stomach lurched and his throat went dry. He swallowed and held out his hand for the device. "Hello."

"Buddy, this line is not secure so I'm going to keep this brief. Her situation hasn't improved. We needed to make a decision to authorize a new treatment that could save her."

"Of course."

"There's more, it's possible this new treatment could cause her body to terminate the pregnancy."

Bishop felt like a truck had hit him. The room spun and the phone dropped from his hand.

"Hey, you OK? Is Saneh OK?" Kruger asked as he picked up the phone.

"We could lose the baby," he murmured.

Kruger spoke into the phone but Bishop heard nothing. He collapsed back on the bed, his emotions in turmoil. Despite the gunshot wound Bishop had never doubted Saneh would recover from her injury and give birth to their child. Previously a feeling of helplessness had driven his need for revenge. In the last few seconds that had changed. Now pure rage coursed through his veins. He vowed to slaughter Mamba, Kogo, and anyone else who stood in his way.

"Vance wants us to stand down." Kruger's persistent tone snapped him out of his thoughts. "He's going to recall the CAT and send them down here to help target Mamba and his network."

Bishop sat up and shook his head. "No, I'm going to kill Mamba and I'm going to do it tonight."

"OK." Kruger relayed the information to Vance. Then he turned back to Bishop. "He wants to talk to you again."

Bishop held out his hand and took the phone. Terminating the call he tossed it back on the bed. "You in or out, Kruger?"

"I'm in."

"Good, now we wait for Kogo's call."

"You still want some food?"

Bishop pushed his emotions deep inside and vowed to leave them there. "Yeah, I prefer to kill on a full stomach."

CHAPTER 9

MOMBASA, KENYA

Bishop didn't feel like eating but he knew if he didn't he would crash. It was past eight in the evening and he hadn't eaten all day. Food was vital; he would need his energy to kill Mamba and Kogo. The bean salad he'd chosen from the menu could have been filled with flavor but to him it was bland. He shoveled a spoonful into his mouth as Kruger took his time with a plate of traditional roasted meats.

"You should try this." Kruger pushed the plate toward him.

"I'm good." He concentrated on his bowl of beans and corn the locals called *githeri*.

"You're missing out." Kruger stuffed another hunk of meat in his mouth. "You want a beer?"

He shook his head. "We should keep our heads clear."

"Good call."

They had the restaurant to themselves and with Kruger not sure what to say and Bishop not wanting to talk they ate in silence. Minutes passed until the shrill ring of Kruger's phone interrupted them. Bishop listened intently as the South African gave short responses to the person on the other end.

Taking a pen from his pocket Kruger jotted an address on a napkin. "That was Kogo, we're on," he said as he placed the phone in his pocket. "He wants us to help out with security on a boat transfer."

"Is Mamba going to be there?"

"He didn't say, but if they're shipping their ivory there's a pretty good chance he will be."

Bishop pushed his bowl aside. "What's the location?"

Kruger whistled the waitress over and asked her for a tourist map. She disappeared to find one. "Little town just to the north called Mtwapa. There's a boat ramp and a jetty. He wants us there." He checked his watch. "In a little over an hour."

The waitress returned with an ancient street directory. Kruger thanked her and flicked through the dog-eared pages. "Here it is." He spun it so Bishop could see. "Only about thirty minutes out of town. You can see the jetty marked near the main road."

"We need to get a move on if we're going to recce it," said Bishop rising from his chair.

Kruger tossed cash on the table and they hurried back to the hotel where the Mazda was parked. They loaded their bags and Kruger drove them through darkness at break-neck speed. It took barely fifteen minutes to reach the riverside town. When they arrived Kruger parked the car a few hundred yards uphill from the water and they went forward on foot armed only with their pistols. They found a cluster of trees that allowed them to observe the jetty but stay out of sight.

The rickety wooden structure reached out into the depths of a tidal channel. Beside it was an eatery that had closed for the evening. A single street light cast a dim glow over three vehicles parked on the road where the jetty met the shore. Bishop recognized one of them as the Land Cruiser Kogo used to take them poaching. At the end of the jetty a fishing trawler was moored. It sat high in the water with a gangplank running up the side.

"That looks like a cop car," said Kruger pointing at one of the vehicles, a blue and white pickup.

A group of men were gathered around the rear of the vehicle. They seemed to be arguing over something. Two wore blue uniforms with pistol belts; Kruger's assessment was correct. "You reckon it's a raid?" asked Bishop.

"More likely Mamba's paid for protection."

He watched as a tall figure appeared from the boat and walked down the wharf toward the group. In the dim light Bishop couldn't make out his facial features but from height and build he guessed it could be the elusive Mamba. "We should get down there."

"I'm not real sure about those cops, bro."

"You just said they'd been paid off."

"True, but I'm not sure how they're going to react to a couple of white boys crashing their party."

"Well, we're not going to find out up here."

They moved back to the car, checked their weapons, and drove down to the jetty. As they approached two men stepped onto the road and walked toward them. They were the police officers.

"This is probably far enough," said Kruger as he parked the Mazda and killed the headlights. "You sure about this?"

Bishop opened his door. "Yeah."

The police officers had stopped a dozen yards away and stood with their hands on their pistols. "This area is off-limits. You need to leave."

"It's OK, we work with Kogo," Bishop said holding his hands at shoulder height with the palms out.

The two cops turned to each other and talked before one returned to the jetty. A moment later he reappeared with the poacher.

"You guys took your time." Kogo waved them forward. "Come, Mamba is waiting."

Kruger locked the hatchback and they walked toward the other parked vehicles and the jetty. Bishop felt his muscles tense as he spotted Mamba at the back of a pickup. The light from the single streetlamp reflected off the sheen of sweat on the killer's face. He was attempting to manhandle a large wooden crate from the back of the truck and wore a snarl more befitting a wild animal.

"These are the men who saved me from the rangers," announced Kogo.

Mamba left the crate and gave them a once over. His gaze lingered on Bishop and for a split-second he thought the poacher had somehow recognized him. "So you're the great white hunters."

"And you're the snake of a poacher," snapped Bishop.

Their eyes met and Bishop held the gaze, his eyes boring into the other man's head. If thoughts alone could have killed, the Ugandan would have collapsed, his heart frozen by ice-cold rage.

Mamba glanced at Kruger. "I like these guys, they're hard-asses." He grinned. "Now, help us load these boxes onto the boat."

Bishop shook his head. "We want the cash for today first."

Mamba's forehead creased. "OK, I tell you what. I'll give you ten grand up front. But, you load the boxes and then you provide extra protection when we transfer our cargo."

"Transfer it to what?"

Mamba lowered his voice so the police couldn't hear. "A Chinese container ship."

Bishop glanced at the battered trawler. "In that tub?"

"It's not far, we're only sailing a few miles out."

He paused as if to contemplate the offer. Then he turned and shot a glance at the two police officers leaning against their pickup. "You don't trust these guys, do you?"

"No, but Kogo seems to think I can trust you."

He met Mamba's cold gaze and extended his hand. "OK, deal."

***

INDIAN OCEAN

Four nautical miles east of Mtwapa a Chinese freighter crept through the inky black waters at barely two knots. Rusted and worn, the *Zenhai* was not an impressive vessel. Classed as a feeder-ship, she was barely a quarter the size of the massive Panamax-class container ships dominating international trade routes. However, with two powerful cranes and a shallow draft, she was perfect for unloading and loading from underdeveloped seaports, an attribute that made her indispensable on the east coast of Africa. Owned by an influential Triad syndicate she frequently carried illicit cargo.

For that reason her crew, in particular the command team, were highly vigilant.

On the bridge the captain sipped tea from a china cup as he studied the radar screen.

"Can you see them?" asked an impatient voice from behind him.

He shook his head. "No, Kehua, the only contact is a tanker coming from the north." He turned to face the Triad gangster who had boarded his ship in Maputo. "If they do not appear within the hour we will press on. I will not risk the ship to pirates."

Kehua was a compact brute of a man with cruel features befitting his chosen occupation. Armed with a Chinese-made Type 81 assault rifle and dressed in black fatigues and an assault vest, he and his six men were responsible for securing the illicit cargo scheduled to have been loaded an hour ago. "Do not concern yourself with pirates. My men will deal with anyone who tries to board us. We will wait until the boat appears."

The captain nodded, not about to challenge the criminal. He had heard rumors of what happened when you failed to meet your contractual commitments to the Triads. More to the point, he would not risk the six hundred thousand yuan he'd been promised for delivering the shipment. He turned his attention back to the radar.

As the green beam swept around the scope a blip appeared to the west at the extent of the radar's range. A dozen more sweeps and he could see it was moving steadily toward them. "Contact, twenty five miles out."

Kehua stepped closer so he could see the radar. "Is it them?"

"I assume so. But, we will not know until they get closer." He glanced out through the freighter's windows and saw it was raining. That was good; rain reduced visibility making it harder for the Kenyan authorities to spot the transfer.

The gangster took a pair of binoculars from the ship's console and made his way to the port flying bridge. The captain watched him struggle to push the door open against the wind. Their contact was still fifteen to twenty minutes from visual range. But, who was he to tell the Triad lieutenant how to do his job. If Kehua wanted to stand outside in the cold that was fine with him. Glancing back at the scope he spotted another contact slightly to the right of the first. It appeared on the outer edge of the scope for a few revolutions of the beam then disappeared. He scratched at the scraggly beard adorning his chin and contemplated the anomaly. It could be a fishing boat, a rogue wave, or a false return. However, it could also be a pirate vessel or Kenyan security forces. He would keep an eye on it. Taking a handheld radio from the console he held it to his mouth and pressed the transmit button.

"First Mate, this is the Captain, I want you to prepare the cargo for loading."

The radio transmitted, "Net or hook?"

"Net."

"Yes, Captain."

He took another sip from his tea then returned his eyes to the scope. The first contact was closing steadily but the second anomaly had not reappeared. The smuggling vessel would be alongside within the hour and it would not take long for his crew to load the illicit cargo. Then he could give his undivided attention to transiting the pirate-laden waters off Somalia.

***

The dull throb of a diesel engine and the soft hiss of the ocean under the bow of the fishing boat was all Bishop heard as he scanned the darkness for any sign of the freighter. Kruger stood on the opposite side replicating his efforts. Mamba and Kogo were in the wheelhouse with the crew, staying out of the intermittent rain.

Bishop was waiting for an opportunity to slit Mamba's throat and toss him over the side. However, so far the poacher hadn't left the wheelhouse where the ship's crew surrounded him.

"Kogo tells me you know how to handle yourself in a gunfight."

The voice startled Bishop and he tightened his grip on his R5 as he turned. Mamba stood a few yards away with two members of the crew.

"We go alright," he said glancing across the deck at Kruger. The big man had left his post and stood off to the side, his rifle held ready.

Mamba sat on one of the crates stacked on the deck. "We could have used you the other day."

Bishop leant casually against the railing as he eased the weapon's safety off. "Rough gig?"

The poacher nodded. "We ran into some trouble in Zambia."

"Yeah, I heard about that. Rangers up at Luangwa got into a shootout trying to protect a black rhino."

"Word gets around fast."

He nodded. "It does when it comes to black rhinos. So what happened, they get the jump on you?"

"The exact opposite, we ambushed them, and killed at least two. Then the rangers came after us."

Bishop calculated he could gun Mamba and his colleagues down in half a second. Then he and Kruger could finish off the men in the wheelhouse and deep-six the bodies. Sailing the fishing boat back to Mtwapa wouldn't be difficult for the pair. He moved his finger to the trigger of the R5 and took up the slack.

The blast of a horn startled Bishop and he looked out to sea. Through the gloom he spotted the looming bulk of a cargo ship. Almost a football field in length, it dwarfed the trawler.

"Good, we're in business," said Mamba and he issued directions to the ship's crew.

"Ahoy!" a voice bellowed from above. Floodlights bathed the deck as the freighter nestled against tires the crew had lowered. Rubber screeched in protest and Bishop glanced across at Kruger. The South African jerked his head in the direction of the ship and mouthed, "On the way back."

He nodded in agreement.

"Lower the net!" Mamba yelled.

The boom of a crane appeared and with a whir and clank a large cargo net descended toward the fishing boat.

Bishop peered up at the side of the freighter. He spotted the silhouettes of a number of men wielding assault rifles. "Not a very advantageous position we're in here," he said to Mamba as they watched the net hit the deck. Their crew unhooked the bundle and laid it out flat.

"That's why you're here."

The crew quickly arranged the wooden crates full of ivory in the center of the net then reattached it to the cable from the ship's crane.

Over the noise of the engines Bishop thought he heard something else. He moved to the stern of the boat and searched the darkness.

"OK, lift it up," Mamba yelled.

A spotlight lanced out across the water from another vessel. "This is the police!" an amplified voice bellowed.

A rifle barked from the cargo ship above them and Bishop added a volley of well-aimed shots to the mix. Then he spun and ran for the cover of the wheelhouse. Machine gun fire erupted from the police launch and bullets thudded into the side of the freighter.

Bishop spotted the bundle of ivory rising off the deck. A figure clung to the side of the net. It was Mamba. The poacher had hedged his bets with the merchant ship.

The deck lurched beneath his feet as the fishing boat's engine roared. The skipper of the trawler had also decided to make his escape and they pulled away as more gunfire struck.

Bishop tossed his rifle aside, leaped to the top of the boat's rail, and launched himself into the air. For a split-second he thought he'd misjudged the gap but managed to snag the bottom of the net with one hand. Swinging wildly he reached frantically for another handhold. Finding one he set about climbing out from under the crates and up the side.

The bundle rose over the side rail of the freighter as the vessel gathered speed. Bishop clung to the net as they swung over a dark hold then dropped inside. The deep throb of the ship's engines blocked out the gunfire as the dimly lit floor approached. The cargo net touched down with a thump, the net went slack, and Bishop fell back with his limbs tangled. As he struggled free of the net he spotted Mamba disappearing through a doorway. Pulling a pistol from his vest he gave chase.

***

As they peeled away from the freighter Kruger caught a glimpse of her name high up on the stern. *Zenhai* was stenciled in fresh white paint, clearly visible as the searchlight from the police patrol boat danced along her side.

"Faster, faster!" screamed Kogo from the wheelhouse of the trawler.

With the police launch seemingly intent on tackling the cargo ship, Kruger concurred that they needed to slip away as fast as possible. Staying out of police custody was his highest priority, closely followed by recovering that crazy bastard Bishop from the *Zenhai.* He joined Kogo and the ship's skipper in the wheelhouse.

"Make the boat go faster!" Kogo screamed as he waved a pistol around his head.

"She's going as fast as she can," Kruger said.

A blinding light illuminated the wheelhouse. Kruger realized that the police crew had shifted target, aborting any attempt to board the massive freighter. The roar of turbocharged maritime diesels echoed off the water as they gave chase.

Kruger stepped outside and spotted the patrol boat hot on their tail. Kogo joined him and aimed his pistol. Before Kruger could stop him the poacher let off half a dozen shots.

He dropped to the deck as the police response caught Kogo flat-footed. High-velocity rounds tore through the Kenyan's body spraying blood and flesh. The poacher emitted a gurgling sound and toppled face down on the deck.

"Fuck me." Kruger raised his R1 and fired a volley. The spotlight exploded plunging them into darkness.

Tracer lanced out across the water like lasers, shredding the wooden superstructure. The fight was one-sided and Kruger knew exactly how it would end. He tossed the rifle overboard and vaulted over the railing.

The ocean was warm and he trod water as the trawler disappeared into the darkness with the police launch in hot pursuit. He stripped the magazines from his vest and let them sink. Emptying his water bottles he stuffed them back in the vest increasing his buoyancy. Checking the stars he orientated himself toward the coast, rolled onto his back, and started a powerful kicking rhythm he knew he could maintain for hours. By his estimates he was less than three hours from land. Once ashore he would contact Vance and try to find out where the *Zenhai* was heading and how he could get on board.

***

Bishop crept through the narrow corridors searching for Mamba. Only a minute earlier he'd seen the poacher disappear through a doorway deep into the bowels of the ship.

He paused in front of a fire hose and checked the emergency exit map stuck to the bulkhead. He was three levels below the bridge.

He checked his weapons again: a folding knife and a pistol. He wasn't equipped for anything more than a stealthy assassination and a swift exit. Which reminded him; he needed a way off the boat. Studying the map he located the lifeboats one level above. Moving cautiously up the ship's internal staircase he stopped when he heard voices. He slipped outside through a door, pulled it closed, and watched through the portal as two men dressed in coveralls made their way down, feet ringing on the metal stairs.

Once they passed he climbed up an external staircase to the next level and found the lifeboats. The bright orange craft sat on a chute aimed over the stern of the ship. He inspected the controls that would launch it toward the ocean thirty feet below. They looked simple enough.

Confirming his escape strategy he moved back to the door he'd closed. There was no sign of movement so he turned the locking mechanism and slipped inside.

If he were Mamba he would make for the bridge, use the ship's phone to contact someone ashore, and arrange a transfer. His other option would be to remain on board until they reached the next port. Considering they were probably bound for China that was unlikely.

With his pistol held ready he climbed the metal staircase until he reached the top. A heavy steel door blocked access to the bridge. He pressed against the wall to avoid being seen through the glass portal. Voices emanated from inside. Here, high above the ship's engines, he could hear Mamba's voice clearly.

Sliding across to the door he glanced through the round window. His pulse quickened as he spotted his target. The poacher was standing near one of the Chinese sailors. The white-uniformed Asian was perched in the captain's chair.

Bishop thumbed the safety off his pistol as he placed a hand on the door handle. He exhaled and readied himself. Two shots to the head and justice would be served. Then it was a short dash down to the lifeboat and freedom.

Pushing the lever down he shoved open the door and lifted his pistol.

"Stop!" a guttural voice ordered.

Bishop felt cold steel pressed against the back of his head. Very slowly he lifted his hands out to the side and dropped his gun.

"Step forward."

Inside Mamba had drawn his machete and was holding it ready to strike. Bishop looked him in the eye as he took a step.

"Turn around."

"Hey, it's OK, let's not get excited. I'm with Mamba," said Bishop as he turned slowly to face a pistol-wielding Chinese thug wearing a black uniform. Slightly shorter than Bishop, he sported cropped black hair and a wrestler's build. A tattoo of a snake peeked above the collar of his shirt. Two henchmen wearing similar black outfits and wielding assault rifles stood either side.

"It doesn't look that way. Say one more word and it will be your last." The man spoke near perfect English with a slight accent. "So, Mamba, is he yours?"

"Yes, but I'm not sure if he can be trusted."

Bishop assumed that the Chinese thug was a smuggler, possibly a Triad.

"He is one of yours but you cannot trust him? What sort of fool brings a man he doesn't trust to an illicit cargo transfer? Not to mention one who would try to kill him."

"Kehua, it's more complicated than that."

"Complicated? First the police boat and then an assassin on my ship. No doubt, he's an informant. My people will put a bullet in him and toss him over the side."

"No, I want to know who sent him," hissed Mamba.

Kehua glared at Bishop before speaking. "Fine, we'll throw him in the brig." He turned and barked an order in Mandarin. The Triads secured Bishop's hands with flexicuffs.

Mamba sheathed his machete. How that idiot Kogo had managed to recruit a police agent was beyond him. Unless he was already under surveillance.

"Do not leave the bridge. I will return shortly," Kehua said angrily as he recovered the white mercenary's pistol and followed his men.

Mamba watched as the Chinese gangsters marched the prisoner away. Once they were out of sight he turned to the ship's captain who had been silently watching the drama from his chair. "Where's the satellite phone?"

The man raised an eyebrow and pointed to the handset.

He grabbed it, punched in a number, and pressed it to his ear. As he waited for the call to connect he watched the digital speed displayed alongside the ship's wheel. It read twelve knots. "Can we go faster?" he asked.

The man shot him a frown. "This is fast enough."

Mamba turned his attention back to the phone, which had finally connected.

Zhou's voice came through in rapid-fire Mandarin.

"It's Mamba, the cargo is on board."

"Where are you calling from?"

"I'm on the ship. There was an unfortunate incident."

"What happened?"

"Kenyan Maritime Police. I lost my entire poaching crew. I expect to be reimbursed for my losses and I expect the ship to drop me off at Singapore." The Chinese smuggler didn't need to know about the South African mercenary.

"Once Kehua confirms the shipment you will be paid the agreed amount. The ship will not stop until it reaches Shanghai."

"Then what the hell am I supposed to do?"

"You should have thought of that before, like a rat, you snuck on board. The vessel is due in Shanghai in six days. I suggest you find a good book."

"What happens when I get to China?"

"I will make the necessary arrangements for papers and passports. I will purchase flights for you to return to Africa. Due to your losses I am happy to bear that expense myself."

"Very big of you, Zhou. How much will you make from this deal... ten million US?"

"Have an enjoyable cruise, Mamba. I look forward to finally meeting you in Shanghai. Have Kehua call me once he has confirmed the cargo."

"He can confirm the ivory but the rhino horn, I'll deliver myself. Think of it as insurance." As Mamba returned the satellite phone to its cradle the metal door swung open with a creak and Kehua strode in.

The gangster stared at the captain as he addressed him. "Where is the police boat?"

"Both contacts are three nautical miles behind us. The fishing vessel may have been boarded."

"And our cargo?"

"Safe in the hold."

"Good." Kehua turned to Mamba. "Your traitor is secure in the brig."

"I have contacted Zhou. He has requested that you confirm the ivory."

"We will do that together. Then you can question your friend." He directed Mamba to the door.

"There's no rush. I'll be with you till we reach Shanghai. Plenty of time to make him talk."

"I want him off my ship at the earliest opportunity."

***

The brig was a tiny cell on the same level as the ship's kitchen, dining area, gymnasium, and recreation facilities. The pile of cleaning supplies stacked in the corridor suggested it had not been used to secure a prisoner in some time.

When Kehua opened the steel door Mamba stepped in and met the angry gaze of the South African mercenary.

"Mamba. This is a serious misunderstanding–"

"Shut up." He stood over the prisoner who sat on the cold steel floor with his hands secured behind his back. A loop of chain connected his wrists to a steel eyelet on the wall.

"How long have you known this man?" asked Kehua.

"He joined us yesterday. Since his arrival the authorities have taken significant interest in my activities. First in Tsavo and then again tonight."

"Then he is a police informant."

The prisoner spat on the floor. "I'm no one's spy. Your man led us into those rangers at Tsavo and the cops you paid off probably sold you out for a cut of the profits."

Mamba paused in thought. "Why are you on this ship then? Hoping to track me down for the police? Assassinating me for the Kenyans?"

"No, I didn't want to get arrested. Getting sent to prison in Kenya is a death sentence, you know that."

Mamba looked intently at the South African. What he said sounded reasonable but something didn't add up. There had to be some other reason the former soldier had followed him onto the ship. Something drove him and it wasn't the fear of being incarcerated by the Kenyan police. Men like this were not intimidated by poorly trained and corrupt police officers.

"So, you going to let me out?"

"No." Mamba stepped out of the cell, switched off the light, and slammed the steel door shut.

"We should dispose of him," said Kehua as he locked the door.

"Not yet. I'm going to get something to eat and then I'm going to question him further. I want to know who helped him infiltrate my organization."

The gangster directed him toward the kitchen. "You have forty-eight hours. Then he is going over the side."

"He'll talk before then." Mamba opened the refrigerator and helped himself to a tray of cold meat. He took a six-inch butcher's knife from a magnetic strip fastened to the wall, tested the blade's sharpness with his thumb, and hacked off a sizable chunk of meat. "Plenty of time to find out everything he knows. Mamba stuffed the food into his mouth. "Is there anything to drink on this tub?" he said as he chewed.

Kehua gave him a hard stare. "You will not drink alcohol on this vessel." He snapped his fingers at one of the Chinese stewards. "Find him a cabin." Then he spun on his heel and strode out of the kitchen.

"Rude fuck," muttered Mamba at his back.

CHAPTER 10

MTWAPA, KENYA

Kruger's feet touched sand and he waded through the surf until he hit the beach. Dropping to his knees in the soft sand he checked his watch. It was a little after midnight. Pulling his phone from his vest he tried to power it up. Not surprisingly, it showed no sign of life.

Climbing to his feet, he staggered up the beach and into the tree line. He stripped his pistol and knife from his vest before dumping it in the bushes. Tucking the gun in his belt and the knife in his pocket he pushed through the scrub to a road that followed the coastline.

By his estimates he was at least three miles from Mtwapa, possibly more. What he knew for sure was that he needed to head south. He broke into a trot and followed the road. The moonlight revealed shacks and houses on either side. A dog barked as he slapped his way along the road, his wet clothing rubbing against his body. The undersides of his arms were raw from swimming and the inside of his thighs stung from chafing. It didn't slow him though. Every minute he delayed the *Zenhai* steamed away from the Kenyan coast and further out of reach. He focused on getting back to the car to use his satellite phone to contact the PRIMAL team.

A flash of headlights caught his attention and he glanced over his shoulder. He paused as a vehicle approached, and held up a thumb.

The car slowed to a halt but left its high beams on. He squinted, the doors opened, and he caught a glimpse of a uniformed figure.

"Hold it right there."

Kruger recognized the voice from earlier in the evening. The cop was one of the two Mamba had hired to protect the transfer to the boat.

"Where is Mamba?" the officer asked as his partner climbed out of the blue and white pickup.

"I don't know. Look, I fell overboard and swam ashore. I don't know what happened."

The two men spoke in hushed voices as Kruger waited in the headlights. He held his hands by his side and closed his eyes relying on his hearing to give him the location of the two men. He recognized the telltale click of a safety catch and dove into action. One hand lifted his shirt and the other snatched the pistol from his belt. His eyes snapped open and he fired two rounds through the open driver's door. One of the police officers grunted as the bullets shattered the window, hitting him.

He leaped sideways as the second policeman let off a burst from his AK stitching the road. He felt a round tug at his wet pants and he rolled firing again, this time at the man's exposed legs.

The cop screamed as he fell and Kruger clambered to his feet, finishing him with a double tap to the head.

He checked the first officer was dead before loading both bodies and the AKs into the back of the police pickup. Only then did he check his leg. The bullet had carved a groove along his calf that oozed blood; a flesh wound.

Jumping in the truck he took off down the road toward Mtwapa. When he reached the marina he skidded in the gravel and halted alongside the battered Mazda. It was exactly where he and Bishop had parked it a few hours earlier, alongside the bank of the tidal river.

Grabbing a rag from the trunk he wiped down his pistol and tossed it off the jetty into the water. Then he took a jerry can of fuel from the back of the police pickup and doused the bodies inside. As he waited for the truck's cigarette lighter to heat he took his satellite phone from the Mazda's glove box and dialed the emergency number for the PRIMAL headquarters in the UAE. Following the open line protocol he waited for someone to answer.

"Kruger, what's going on?" It was Vance.

"Listen up, I don't have much time. Bishop is being held on a Chinese freighter called the *Zenhai.* He boarded off the coast from Mombasa. I'll call back in an hour to explain the details. You guys need to track it and get some of the boys together for a boarding party."

He could hear Vance scribbling notes.

"OK, bud, we've got it. I'll stand by for your call."

Kruger hung up, reached in through the window of the police vehicle, and pulled out the cigarette lighter. He tossed it in the back of the truck and the fuel ignited with a soft thud. He watched it burn for a few seconds then climbed into the Mazda.

As he raced down the highway he called Toppie's number. The arms dealer answered after a few rings. "It's Kruger. Shit's gone south, I'm going to need your help."

"We going to war?" croaked Toppie.

"Yeah, we're going to war."

***

THE SANDPIT, ABU DHABI

Vance glanced over Frank's shoulder, checking the personnel tracker. A map of the globe was annotated with the location of all the PRIMAL personnel that had been stood down. Most of their assaulters, Kurtz, Pavel, and Miklos, had last checked in from Eastern Europe. Mitch, their tech support guru was in Israel. Only Mirza The black rhino stood with her calf in the shade cast by a camel thorn tree. The film crew that watched from less than a hundred yards away didn't in the least bit bother the majestic gray beast. She was familiar with the humans and their vehicles. As long as they kept their distance they caused her no concern.

Two cut-down safari trucks were parked to take advantage of the soft morning light. A cameraman and a sound technician stood in the back of one with a journalist in the other. Uniformed park rangers sat behind the wheel of each vehicle, ready to beat a hasty retreat if the rhino decided they had overstayed their welcome. The black rhino, unlike their cousins the white, were renowned for having a short temper, especially the mothers.

It was an instinct Afsaneh Ebadi could relate to. Four months pregnant, Saneh was already fiercely protective of the tiny life growing inside her. Although, not as protective as her partner. It had taken all her charms to convince Aden Bishop that she would be perfectly safe with the film crew and their ranger escort. A former Australian soldier, he wanted to wrap her in cotton wool and reinforce it with Kevlar.

The striking former Iranian intelligence operative had joined the group that morning, not willing to miss an opportunity to see the rhino calf. She sat in the front passenger seat of the truck that carried the journalist, dressed in the same khaki work shirt and shorts as the rangers.

In the opposite vehicle, Christina Munoz, a photographer and her close friend, shot stills of the rhino and film crew. She caught the eye of the petite brunette and flashed a grin. Christina smiled back and turned the camera on her.

Saneh tossed her long hair and pouted pretending it was a fashion shoot. With her Persian features, full lips, and mane of dark glossy hair, she was a natural in front of the camera. The photographer giggled and Saneh pressed a finger to her lips reminding her that they were still filming.

Christina poked out her tongue and directed her attention back to the rhinos.

She smiled contentedly. Luangwa National Park was a paradise for her. Almost completely untouched by tourism and protected from poaching it was one of Africa's few pristine wildlife reserves. She tipped her head to one side as she watched the rhino and her calf, listening to the words of the journalist.

"Behind me is Kitana the black rhino and her calf. This particular animal is important because she is one of only a handful of breeding females left in Zambia." The journalist was from the BBC and had a crisp British accent that reminded her of David Attenborough. "Reintroduced to the Luangwa National Park in 2003, the black rhinos are making a slow comeback. This young calf is the third to be born in as many years. She lives here under the watchful eye of the Luangwa Rangers, a local force trained by volunteers. But, while this is a good-news story for the future of black rhinos here in Luangwa, the same cannot be said across Africa. With less than four thousand animals remaining and a ferocious appetite on the black market for their horns, the rangers are fighting a losing battle. They simply do not have the resources to protect them all. So far this year, Kruger National Park in South Africa, only a thousand miles away, has lost a dozen rhinos to poachers. If this continues we can expect the black rhino to be extinct in less than ten years."

Saneh watched the noble beast and her calf with a heavy heart. The mother had two horns; the one at the end of her snout was long and curved, a lethal weapon with which to defend her offspring against lions and hyenas. Unfortunately it offered her no protection from poachers. The British journalist was on the money; her partner, Bishop, and the other volunteers were fighting a rearguard action. Every day endangered animals across Africa were slain for their horns or tusks. Why? So ignorant superstitious assholes in China and Vietnam could adorn their desks with carvings and pop pills containing the same chemical compound as their fingernails. The mere thought filled her with rage. She took a deep breath and tried to relax as the journalist wrapped up his monolog.

A faint noise caught her attention and she looked up. She spotted an electric drone circling above them and gave it a wave. Bishop was keeping an eye on her.

The PRIMAL operatives had been in Zambia for a little over a week. They'd flown in from Spain where builders were turning their tiny cottage into a family home. With PRIMAL off-line they had chosen to spend a few months working with Christina and her boyfriend Dominic Marks at the recently established Luangwa Anti-Poaching Academy.

Saneh and Bishop had met Dom only a few weeks earlier. They'd been visiting Christina at Kruger National Park and saved her from an attempted kidnapping. It was there that the Africa bug had bitten them both. Now they couldn't get enough of the exotic wildlife roaming the rolling savannah and lush floodplains.

"That's a wrap, people," announced the journalist. "Let's get back to camp for breakfast and a cup of tea."

Saneh gave the rhinos one last glance as the drivers started the vehicles. When the BBC team was ready they drove back to the track that led to base camp.

"So when will you broadcast your piece?" Saneh asked the journalist a mile into the journey.

"The crew will edit it and send it back to London tonight. Should be hitting the airwaves tomorrow morning."

"That soon?"

"The joys of technology. So how do you fit in here? Your partner works with Dom doesn't he?"

"Yes, we're friends of Christina. Taking the opportunity to see a bit of Africa while we can."

"I understand that. I can't get enough of the place."

"Yes, it does have that effect." She turned and took in the surroundings as they covered the last few miles through the bush.

As they pulled into the camp she spotted Bishop standing in front of the low-slung building that served as a training facility and headquarters. He was an unremarkable looking man. Medium height with an athletic build, he wore camouflage pants cut off at the knee, battered hiking boots, a short-sleeved khaki shirt, and a faded blue Yankees cap. The hat covered a mop of shaggy hair that matched the stubble on his face. Intelligent brown eyes and a lopsided grin greeted her as she jumped out of the truck, walked across, and flung her arms around him. "How are your little spy planes going?"

"Not great, we're getting some kind of interference on the signal. How was the trip out to see Kitana?"

"It was lovely. But, now I'm hungry."

Bishop touched her growing belly and kissed her. "You never stop eating. Come on then, let's find you something."

"Steak, Aden, I want a steak," she said as they walked to the camp kitchen.

"That kid's got to be a boy with the amount of red meat you've been craving. Oh, by the way, Kruger is heading up in the next few days. He's going to help us out for a week with some training." He referred to a South African former Recce operator who was one of PRIMAL's most capable warriors.

"How's he doing?" asked Saneh as she opened the refrigerator.

"He sounds a little bored."

She found a steak on a plate and pulled it out. "That's the biggest issue facing Vance and Chua. When they shut down operations they released an army of adrenaline junkies on the world." She referred to the leaders of PRIMAL, the vigilante organization that she and Bishop were part of.

Bishop took the plate and lit the grill. "Hey, some of us are doing just fine."

"Sure you are." She kissed him on the cheek.

***

SHANGHAI, CHINA

Wang Hejun's apartment was perched on the top floor of a residential tower overlooking Shanghai's business district. The beverage baron was one of the wealthiest men in China. With a net worth estimated at close to twelve billion dollars only a small number of Internet entrepreneurs sat higher on the Forbes China Rich List.

The apartment encompassed the entire penthouse level. Originally three separate residences, he had combined them into a single high-rise mansion. His study, formerly one of the master bedrooms, was where he spent most of his time now he was retired. Decorated in a garish interpretation of Italian baroque that included gilded mirrors and intricately carved furniture, it was where he hoarded his most prized possessions. Jade carvings, fine porcelain, and other works of art were displayed on either side of the room. In the far corner stood an illuminated glass cabinet with his prized collection of ivory, bone, and horn carvings. They represented trophies of exotic animals, with thousands of hours of work by master carvers to craft them into precious artifacts.

Hejun sat at his desk in a silk robe nursing a glass of Maotai as he stared at the gilded television on the wall. On screen a black rhino and her calf were standing in the shade of a tree. He didn't understand the journalist; he had never learned English. No doubt wailing about the animals' dwindling numbers or some such rhetoric, he thought. That was a weakness of the West. They did not seem to comprehend that nature was a resource to be exploited for the betterment of man.

His eyes never left the magnificent curved horn that adorned the beast's snout. The black rhino was one animal missing from his extensive collection. The Chinese government's ban on rhino horn had made it increasingly difficult and expensive to procure. Black rhino horn had become impossible to find. But here, on his television, was one of the finest examples he had ever seen. He hit a buzzer on the desk and a moment later the door opened and his assistant appeared.

"Yes, Mr. Wang." Fan Wei was in her mid-thirties with an attractive round face and high cheekbones. A tailored skirt and suit jacket emphasized her slender build.

He pointed to the screen where the journalist was still talking. "I want you to get me that horn," he croaked.

"Of course." Fluent in English, Fan read the tagline across the bottom of the screen. She committed the location of the animal to memory.

"Do you want it sent to a carver?"

He shook his head. "No, I want to see it first. Then I will decide what to do with it."

She bowed. "Very good, sir. Will that be all?"

"I want it now. Cost does not matter."

"I will contact our supplier immediately." She turned and left the room.

He continued watching the television until the segment about the rhino had finished. Then he turned it off, left the desk, and walked across to the ornate glass cabinet in the corner. The interior was lit showcasing the intricately carved horns and ivory inside. Opening it, he took out one of the horns and inspected it lovingly. The artwork was finely detailed; it would have taken a skilled artisan thousands of hours to work the delicate scrolls into the horn. The carvings represented power, longevity, and health, things he craved more than all else. This collection, along with his business empire, would be handed down for generations to come. It would be his legacy.

***

Fan had been to the Shanghai Greater Exports office on a number of occasions to collect packages for her master. Tucked away in the sprawling Shanghai docks, the office gave the impression of a legitimate business. Run by gangsters, it was a one-stop shop for anyone looking for access to the Chinese underground trafficking market. Illicit goods including endangered animals, military hardware, even slaves, were available for the right price.

She parked Hejun's Mercedes outside the office and introduced herself to the middle-aged woman behind the front desk. She was ushered through to see the man who controlled the gateway to illicit goods, Zhou. She didn't know the Triad's last name nor did she feel it necessary to enquire. She cared only that he could deliver the black rhino horn her master desired.

"Ah the pretty Fan Wei, back again to do the bidding of her wrinkled master." Zhou sat behind a large desk on which lay no less than a dozen cell phones, the tools of his trade.

She fought the urge to vomit as the gangster's eyes lingered on her. The man had a habit of licking his lips every few seconds. He reminded her of a bloated lizard she once saw at the Shanghai zoo. "Hejun would like you to procure something for him, something of great rarity."

"Of course, he desires only the finest ivory."

"He wants a black rhino horn."

Zhou sneered, "Of course he does but there are none to be had."

"There is one in Zambia, North Luangwa National Park."

He locked eyes with her. "How much is he willing to pay?"

"Whatever it costs."

Zhou's tongue circled his lips. "I'll see what can be done."

"He wants it as soon as possible."

"Then I will have an answer for you today."

"I will wait here."

"That is not necessary. I'll call you and confirm the price. Unless you wanted to stay for a different reason?" He licked his lips again and watched her stride out of the office. Maybe he would offer Hejun a discount for a night with her, he thought. He smirked; the old dog had probably already had his way with her. He reached for one of his phones and dialed a number. As it rang he imagined what Fan Wei would look like naked, bouncing on his lap.

***

MOMBASA, KENYA

Six thousand miles away in a rusted warehouse a battered phone rang. David 'Mamba' Mboya scowled from the stack of crates he was perched on. The leader of the poaching gang drank from a bottle of beer and let the phone ring a half-dozen more times before it finally got the better of him. He tossed the bottle and it shattered against the sheet iron wall. "Kogo, answer the damn phone!"

A moment later Julias Kogo appeared; lighter-skinned, slight of build, and with a shaved head. Kogo was Mamba's right hand man and errand boy. "Yes, Mamba." He used the former Ugandan paratrooper's nickname, a reference to the African snake renowned for its ferocity and speed. Grabbing the phone off the cradle he pressed it to his ear and listened before turning to his boss. "It's Zhou, says he has another job for us."

Mamba climbed off the crates, uncoiling his wiry frame to its full six-foot-five. Without a hint of fat, the ebony-skinned Ugandan was an imposing sight. His hair was clipped short, a testament to his time in the military. He wore a faded check shirt left unbuttoned, revealing a lean torso covered in scars. "I don't want to talk to that piece of shit. He ripped us off on the last shipment of tusks. Tell him I'm going to find a new buyer for this batch."

Kogo relayed the response to the Chinese gangster on the other end of the line. "He says he has something big this time."

"He always does." Mamba opened the refrigerator and pulled out another bottle of beer. He twisted the lid off using the crook of his bicep and downed half of it. "Give me the phone." Grabbing the handset he raised it to his ear. "Zhou, you crooked Chinese hyena, do you have the money you owe me?"

"I paid you the agreed amount."

"Yes, but then you doubled the price you sold it for."

"That's not true."

"I saw it on the internet, Zhou. You might think we're all monkeys you yellow bastard but we're smarter than that."

The gangster paused. "I will make it up to you on this next consignment."

"Tell me more."

"I have a buyer for a black rhino horn."

"That's great, Zhou, but I don't have a fucking death wish."

"You can name the price."

He took a swig from the beer.

"I'm talking big numbers, Mamba, two, three hundred thousand."

He smacked his lips. "Make it five." He could hear Zhou hissing through his teeth. "The black rhinos are protected by armed rangers. Not the usual deadbeats, I'm talking ex-military and police. I'll need men who are willing to take the risk and I'm going to have to find a rhino with a big enough horn. None of that comes cheap."

"Do you know North Luangwa National Park?"

"Do you know The Great Wall of China? Of course I know it, you idiot, it's in Zambia."

"There's a black rhino there."

"There are also rangers. Your number just became six hundred."

"Fine, but I am not paying you extra money for the elephant horns."

"They're called tusks and I've spent two weeks assembling the weight you ordered. I will include the black rhino horn for a total of eight hundred thousand, American dollars."

He could hear Zhou typing on the other end. "I have a ship due in at Mombasa on Friday. Can you have the entire shipment ready by then?"

Mamba drained the last of his beer. "Transfer a hundred grand into my account now and we'll go to work."

"You've never needed money up front before."

Mamba lobbed the bottle at the back of the warehouse where it shattered. "You haven't asked for a black rhino horn before, Zhou. Make it happen." He passed the phone back to Kogo who returned it to the cradle. "We're going to need at least five men."

"Any preference?"

"For this job, only the best, and I want one who knows Luangwa."

"OK, boss."

Mamba pulled another beer from the refrigerator. "And Kogo, make sure they're killers."

CHAPTER 1

NORTH LUANGWA NATIONAL PARK, ZAMBIA

Aden Bishop stood on the verandah of the raised bungalow he shared with Saneh, staring out at the rolling savannah. He ate from a bowl of oatmeal as he watched a family of warthogs foraging in the dry grass. PRIMAL seemed like a distant memory as he watched the sow and her two piglets digging for roots. There was something about Africa that soothed the soul. It was a harsh land with an underlying beauty that took your breath away.

"Good morning, handsome," Saneh purred from behind him. She wrapped her arms around his waist and he could feel the slight bulge of her belly against his back. Her pregnancy was beginning to show.

Bishop smiled as he spooned more oatmeal into his mouth. In a couple more months they would head to Sydney, Australia, to have the baby in his hometown. Then, after a few weeks, it would be back to their newly renovated home in Spain. That reminded him, he needed to check in with the builder.

Saneh rested her chin on his shoulder and spotted the hogs. "They're so cute."

"They have a certain repugnant appeal."

"You've got something in common." She laughed. "Hey, we got an update from Vance."

"Yeah, and how is the team doing?"

"Remarkably busy considering we're supposed to have stood down. Mitch is in Israel building spare parts for Ice, Mirza is working with Tariq delivering humanitarian aid, and the headquarters staff are still working the intel piece from Abu Dhabi. They're calling the new safe house the Sandpit."

"I knew they wouldn't be able to stay away from work. What games are they playing in their new play pen?"

"The usual, keeping an eye on things. Making sure the CIA isn't still trying to find PRIMAL." She kissed his neck. "Oh, and they're running a sweepstake."

"Yeah, and what are the odds?"

"Twenty to one."

"Let me guess, they're all betting we're going to have a girl."

"How did you know that?" She feigned surprise.

He chuckled. "Because, they all think I deserve a daughter."

"Come on, it wouldn't be so bad, would it? I mean, I've wrapped you around my little finger. Imagine what it would be like with two of us."

He shook his head. "That's not something I want to contemplate."

"So, what have you got planned for today?"

"I'm going to help Dom train the new guys in apprehension techniques."

"Sounds exciting."

"Hardly, but it's necessary."

"Christina is heading out this afternoon to take photos of one of the black rhinos."

"The one with the calf?" He took another mouthful of his breakfast.

"Yes, I want to go with her. Two of the rangers will accompany us, it will be perfectly safe."

Bishop put down his bowl and turned to face her. "I'm allowed to be a little protective of the woman I love and our unborn child."

She smiled. "Of course you are. But, nothing's going to happen. You know there hasn't been a poaching incident here in years."

"It's not the poachers I'm worried about. Those black rhinos are grumpy mothers."

"Oh please, Kitana is not aggressive at all. Plus, I won't leave the truck."

"I don't know why you're asking when you've already made up your mind. I'll see you later today. I've got to run, Dom's waiting for me." He kissed her on the forehead and entered the bungalow. As he dropped his bowl into the sink his phone rang. He glanced at the screen. It was Kruger, the South African PRIMAL operative. "Hey, brother, what's up?"

"I'm fucking bored, *ja*. What are you doing?"

Bishop laughed as he left the bungalow and walked across a dusty clearing to the training hall. "I'm still up at Luangwa. I thought you were going to drop in, plenty of work here to keep you busy. Where are you?"

"I'm in Zimbabwe, just north of Harare. Been spending some time with an old Recce mate. He's a family man now so he has to go to work and all that."

"You're not far away. Come on up, we're at the ranger school. I'll flick you the coordinates."

"Maybe tomorrow, *ja*."

Bishop could hear a dog barking in the background.

"Hey, I've got to go but I'll give you a call before I head up, OK?"

"Sounds good, mate."

Bishop ended the call as he entered the training room. Dom was standing in front of a bench lined with flexicuffs and lengths of rope.

"You running a detention lesson or an S and M workshop?"

Dom chuckled. "Morning, Aden, you ready to get started?"

"Yeah, how long do you have the lesson scheduled for?"

"An hour. What's up? You got a hot date with Saneh, bro?"

"No, I'm keen to work through the bugs in the drone and get it up again tonight." Bishop spotted the first of the rangers filing into the shed for the lesson.

"I've got nothing else planned for the day. We can mess about with the drones all afternoon." He grinned. "Use it to keep an eye on the girls."

"Sounds like a plan."

***

Mamba pulled a cold beer from the cooler in the back of his four-wheel drive and twisted the lid off on his bicep. It was midday and the sun beat down relentlessly on the Zambian bush. "Kogo, where the fuck is your boy, hey?" He glared at his second-in-command who was sitting in the shade of a tree with the other three members of the hunting party. They had waited for twenty minutes for the guide Kogo had arranged.

Less the absent guide, they were all poachers that Mamba trusted. The two black Ugandans were brothers recruited from his old Army unit. Reconnaissance specialists, they were the finest trackers in the business. The older white Zimbabwean, Colin, was a professional poacher who shot his first elephant when his country was still called Rhodesia. He was their shooter. Mamba had witnessed the gray-haired hunter drop a bull with a single bullet from over five hundred yards.

"He'll be here," Kogo said peering down the track.

Mamba took a swig from the beer. "He better."

The five men were armed with assault rifles and carried an assortment of backpacks. They wore a mixture of faded camouflage pants, khakis, and long-sleeved bush shirts. All except Mamba, who wore a black T-shirt with the sleeves torn off under a tan South African-style assault vest. The handle of a machete protruded from a scabbard secured to the back pouch between his broad shoulder blades.

The splutter of a motorcycle caught the poaching boss's attention and he turned to spot a scooter struggling along the sandy track. As it pulled up alongside them he scowled. Kogo's guide was a scrawny kid who didn't look a day over sixteen. "What the fuck is this?"

The barrel of the AK-47 slung over the teenager's bony shoulder stuck up above his head like a radio antenna.

"He was a ranger here," said Kogo as the youth parked his battered scooter under a bush by the side of the road.

"Why isn't he anymore?"

"Because he stole from his comrades."

"He's a fucking thief?"

Kogo shrugged. "Aren't we all?"

The youth eyed the five men suspiciously as he unslung his AK and held it across his body. "Who is Kogo?"

"That's me."

He held out his hand. "I want my money."

Mamba stepped forward, towering over the boy. "You'll have your money when I have my horn."

The youth made to reply but Mamba continued, "Now, are you going to lead us to the animal or are you wasting my time?"

The kid swallowed but looked up defiantly. "We have to leave the car here. We walk east to the Mwaleshi river. That is where the rhino will be. It is a hard walk but if we go now we will be there by nighttime."

"Why can't we drive in, eh?" asked Colin. "There's probably plenty of tracks through the park."

"No, the rangers patrol the tracks and there are tour operators. Between here and the river it is bush, no one goes there much. We will not be seen."

"Are there many camps near where the rhino is?" asked Mamba.

The former ranger nodded.

Mamba turned to Colin. "Needs to be a silent kill."

"I'll take the dart gun. More than enough cyanide to drop a big female. We'll take off her horn with machetes." He made a chopping gesture with his hand. "Real sharp, real quiet, then we get the fuck out of there."

Mamba nodded. "We're gone by the time they find the carcass." He raised his voice. "OK, get your gear ready. We're leaving in five." He turned to the teenager. "You'd better lead us to the rhino, boy." He finished his beer and tossed it into the bushes. "Because if we don't find her I'm going to hang you from a boab and skin you like an antelope." He laughed as he took a folding-stock AK assault rifle out of the four-wheel drive and cocked it.

***

Saneh found the men in the clearing behind the training hall. They had set up a table in the shade of a tree and were working on the delta-winged electric drone. There were laptops, a toolbox, and components strewn across the bench. "Have you boys eaten any dinner?" she asked as she approached.

"Huh?" Bishop glanced up from where he was inspecting the aircraft. "Yeah, we grabbed some sandwiches from the kitchen."

"Hi Saneh." Dom shot her a smile. "You and Chris off soon?"

"In a few minutes. How's the drone going?"

"Ask Aden, this stuff's all alien to me."

Saneh laughed. "I can see you're very busy. OK, boys, we'll see you when we get back." She gestured to the drone. "Or, if you ever get that thing working again, you'll see us out there."

"OK, babe, have fun."

Saneh shook her head as she walked back. "Boys and their toys." As she entered the lecture room she spotted Christina crouched over a backpack. "You all good?"

The photographer gave a smile. "Yep, the guys are already loaded and out the front." She zipped up the bag and hefted it over her shoulders. Loaded with camera gear, it was almost larger than her petite frame. "Let's go."

One of the stripped-down Land Cruisers was parked in front of the building with two rangers in the front seats. They greeted Saneh and Christina with broad smiles as the women climbed into the back.

"All right, boys, do we know where Kitana is?" asked Christina as she buckled in.

"One of the patrols spotted her up north," said Francis, the driver. "Near the Mwaleshi falls."

"Well, let's head up there and have a look. We've got about thirty minutes till sunset so we need to find her quickly." Christina unzipped her backpack and withdrew a camera with a telephoto lens. She slung it around her neck and cradled the body in her lap.

Francis started the engine with a clatter. "We'll find her. Kitana doesn't like to walk far with the baby."

"Who could blame her?" Saneh chuckled.

"Do rhinos get morning sickness?" asked Christina as they left the camp.

"I hope not, I wouldn't wish it on anyone."

They continued their banter as the Land Cruiser negotiated a sandy track through the bush. It followed the Mwaleshi River for five miles before they turned off and skidded down a steep bank. Francis slowed as they negotiated a rocky riverbed pock-marked with bath-sized pools of slimy green water.

"Is it this low all year round?" asked Saneh as they splashed through a stagnant pond.

"No, when the wet comes the river becomes a torrent. It's only really low during the dry months. Look, it's deeper over there," Christina said as she raised her camera. She aimed it at a group of hippos half-submerged in a lagoon on the opposite side of the river.

Saneh smiled as one of the massive beasts yawned opening its mouth to reveal a lethal array of yellow teeth. Behind them, on the bank, a herd of impala were making their way down to the river to drink.

Christina snapped a few shots. "They're smart, they know if there are hippos there won't be any crocodiles."

Francis stopped and waited for Christina to finish taking photos before continuing. "If we don't hurry, Miss Munoz, you will miss the light."

Christina laughed. "You're all over it, aren't you, Francis."

The two rangers in the front chatted in their native language as they drove through a shallow rivulet and back up the sandy bank. They continued to follow the river as it wound its way toward the falls.

"This is the best time to be out," said Christina as she snapped a photo of a giraffe and her calf drinking. The mother eyed them warily as they drove slowly past. "So many mothers out with their babies." She shot Saneh a smile. "That'll be you soon."

"I might avoid hippo and crocodile-infested waters. Aden wasn't exactly happy with me being out tonight." She glanced at the pump-action shotguns mounted between the front seats. Even though there had not been a poaching incident in nearly three years Dom insisted every patrol was armed.

"I've been meaning to ask," said Christina as they turned onto another track. "How did you two meet?"

"He caught my eye in a restaurant." Saneh wasn't about to explain that she had first crossed paths with Bishop when she was a covert operative in the Iranian intelligence service. Nor did Christina need to know that she had saved Bishop's life on the streets of Kiev while dressed in heels and a particularly revealing cocktail dress. It all seemed so long ago. A tear formed in the corner of her eye as she remembered her friend and former comrade, Aleks. She had met him the same day she met Bishop, but now he was dead.

"Are you OK?"

Christina's voice snapped her back to reality. "I'm fine."

"We're nearly there," interrupted Francis from the front of the truck. "One of the rangers saw Kitana around the next bend earlier today."

"Excellent, can we go slow so we don't spook her?" Christina asked before turning to Saneh. "The two of you are a great couple. He's going to make an awesome father."

She shook her head. "Yes, I know Aden's going to be a great dad. I just, well… Something reminded me of an old friend. Someone I cared about very much who passed away, that's all."

"Oh, I'm sorry." Christina reached inside her backpack, pulled out binoculars, and handed them to her. "But hey, I need your eyes tear-free and ready to spot a two thousand pound momma and her four hundred pound bubba."

"God, I hope I don't get that heavy." Saneh managed a smile as she hung the binoculars around her neck.

***

Mamba sat against a tree cradling his AK assault rifle. He sipped from a canteen as he watched the remaining members of his hunting party resting in the shade. They had walked for a half a day to reach the banks of the river. All were seasoned bushmen but the heat had made it hard going. The walk back in the cool of the night would be easier. He squinted and scanned the scrub for any sign of their young guide and one of the trackers. The pair had been sent forward to locate the rhino and check for rangers. "Kogo, where the hell is that little thief? He better not have sold us out."

Kogo lay in the shade half asleep. "He'll be back. The rangers can't pay him what we can."

"Maybe, but I still don't trust him. You know what they say, you can't buy a Zambian, you rent them."

Colin, the grizzled Rhodesian, laughed from where he was assembling his dart gun. The weapon resembled a hunting rifle complete with a scope and long barrel. In place of gunpowder it used compressed gas to propel a poisoned projectile out to a range of seventy yards. That meant the hunter had to stalk very close to the target and a rhino was not an animal you wanted to anger. It was a job requiring steely nerves and a crack shot; Colin was both.

A rustle in the bushes alerted the men. Safety catches clicked to fire. The thick grass parted and the young former ranger appeared with the tracker. Both were sweating heavily as they dropped in the shade.

"Well?" demanded Mamba.

"We found her," reported the tracker. "She and the calf are not far from here. They're sleeping in the shade of a big thorn tree."

"Good, we'll make the kill now and recover the horn." He glanced up at the darkening sky. "By the time we finish it will be nightfall."

"Solid plan." Colin slid a dart the size of a cigar tube into the gun and closed the bolt. "Ready when you are." The projectile contained nearly an ounce of pure cyanide, more than enough to kill a full-grown rhino. He had three more like it secured in his hunting vest.

Mamba tucked his water bottle back into a pouch. "Lead the way, little ranger boy."

The youth scowled and set off back into the bush with the others in tow. They followed a game trail along the riverbank to a thicket of saplings. The teenager held up his hand then pointed. Mamba knelt and peered through the branches. It took him a second to spot the massive animal. She resembled a granite boulder in the fading light.

"She's a big one, eh," whispered Colin as he cradled the dart gun. "Good thing I brought extra darts. Might not go down with just one."

"Just get it done."

Colin slid forward on his chest, tucked the weapon against his shoulder, and aimed through the scope.

Mamba crouched behind him watching the massive beast as she rested on her belly. He couldn't see the head but he had no doubt the horn was impressive.

The gun emitted a pop not unlike an air rifle and the dart struck the thick hide with a thud. A loud bellow reverberated as the rhino struggled to her feet and turned toward them, nostrils flaring.

Now Mamba could see the long curved horn as well as the sheer size of the fully-grown rhino. She bellowed again and he caught a glimpse of the calf cowering behind its mother. Mamba shouldered his assault rifle as the one-ton animal lowered her horn. He swore it was staring directly at him.

Colin had already reloaded the dart gun and fired once more hitting her square in the chest.

"Jesus Christ!" Mamba yelled as the rhino charged.

She halved the distance between them in under a second. As she was about to plow into the thicket where they hid she skidded to a halt and stood panting not a dozen feet away. Mamba raised his AK and aimed at her head.

"Steady." Colin pushed the barrel of the assault rifle down. "She's done."

The rhino wheezed and convulsed. Her eyes grew wide as her front legs crumpled and she dropped to her knees. It took mere seconds for the huge dose of cyanide to cripple her respiratory system. Her powerful heart was the next to go. It beat slower and slower before finally, as the flow of oxygen ceased, it stopped and she toppled over.

"Good work." Mamba pushed through the thicket and approached tentatively. He ran his hand over the horn. It was impressive measuring as long as his forearm. The animal lifted her head and gave one last bellow. The forlorn cry for help startled Mamba and he fell backward in the long grass.

"She was a beautiful animal," Colin said staring with sad eyes.

"Don't get all soppy on me, old man. You've killed more than most." Mamba scrambled to his feet and pulled the razor sharp machete from its scabbard. With deft blows he hacked at the flesh around the horn. A pathetic bleating sound interrupted his butchering and he turned to see the rhino calf standing a few yards away. It was as big as a large dog with a tiny horn the size of a golf ball.

"Can I shoot it?" asked the ex-ranger.

"No, you idiot. It will grow and then we come back for the horn."

As Mamba worked to hack the horn free the other men faced outward with their guns. The teenager, sulking, moved down to the riverbank.

Mamba sweated as he worked. His preferred method of removing horns and tusks was a chainsaw. However, with the threat of rangers he couldn't risk the noise. As he continued to hack at the base of the horn the kid called out.

"Hey, hey, can you hear that?" The teen scrambled through the tall grass back to the carcass.

He paused and listened. Over the bleating of the calf he could hear a faint noise. It took him a moment to identify it as the clatter of a diesel engine. "Fucking hell." He handed the machete to Kogo. "Finish this."

He gestured to the others as he unslung his AK. "We'll check it out." With the rifle held at the ready he patrolled through the thick grass until he could see down into the riverbed and across to the other bank.

A cut-down safari truck appeared a few hundred yards downstream on the opposite bank. He knelt and watched as it crept toward them. Whoever was in it was searching for something, probably the rhino and her calf. Mamba took a compact monocular from his vest and focused it on the vehicle. There were two green-uniformed rangers in the front seats. Shifting his focus he spotted two women in the back. One of them was holding a long-lensed camera. The other, a strikingly attractive brunette, had a pair of binoculars slung around her neck.

"What are we going to do?" the youth whispered as he caught up.

"Nothing, unless they see us," Mamba said as he flicked the safety off his AK.

***

The Land Cruiser slowed and came to a halt at the river. It gave the occupants a clear view of both the rocky riverbed and the opposite side.

Saneh looked up, searching the sky for Bishop's drone. Maybe he would spot the rhinos first, she thought.

"Was this where she was last seen?" asked Christina.

"Yes, it was a hot one today. She will stay close to water," replied Francis as he switched off the engine.

Saneh scanned the far bank with her binoculars. Searching the thick grass she caught a glimpse of what looked like a man crouched behind a clump of foliage. Beyond the figure a flash of movement caught her eye and a heart-wrenching bleat filled the air. "Oh my god, it's Kitana's calf."

The bark of an AK-47 sounded in the still air jolting her into action. "Get down!" She shoved Christina out of the vehicle and leaped after her. They landed in a heap as bullets thudded against the vehicle.

Her training kicked in and she assessed the situation. Realizing the only weapons were in the front of the vehicle she wrenched the driver's door open. Francis rolled out into the dust. His shirt was covered in blood, his face pale, eyes wide.

She fought the urge to check him for wounds. The only aid in a gunfight is self-aid, she reminded herself as she grabbed a pump-action shotgun from between the front seats. A quick glance told her the other ranger had been hit. He was slumped forward against the dash. Bullets slapped the bonnet of the truck as she pulled the weapon free and took cover with Christina.

"Are they poachers?" asked Christina.

"Yes, there are three shooters," Saneh said as she pumped the fore grip of the shotgun. "I need you to check Francis."

Christina was staring at her with her mouth open. "What… how?"

"Chris, focus. If we're going to get out of here we need to work together. I'm going to try to buy us some space. You need to look after Francis."

"I'm OK," the driver stammered from where he lay in the dust. "I think Melon is dead."

Saneh crab-walked to the front of the truck and peeked around the bumper. Spotting a muzzle flash she pulled back and took a deep breath. She knelt, grasped the shotgun firmly and leaned out sideways. The 12-gauge bucked in her shoulder as she fired two rounds where she had seen the flash. She heard a scream as she pulled back. "One down. Chris can you get to the radio?"

The bursts of gunfire intensified as she shuffled backward. Popping up over the front of the truck she searched for another target. Darkness was closing in and she could barely make out the opposite bank. She snapped off a single shot. The scrub exploded with muzzle flashes. Bullets snapped through the air and slammed into the side of the Land Cruiser. Saneh kept firing the shotgun until, as the trigger clicked on an empty chamber, she registered a flash of pain and felt herself falling. As she collapsed she realized her life was not the only one that could be lost. "I'm sorry, Aden," she whispered as she slipped into a black pool of nothingness. "I'm sorry."

***

Bishop swatted an insect the size of a fist away from his face as he squinted at the laptop screen. The sun had long dropped behind the horizon and the bugs were going nuts over the glow of his equipment.

"Aden, might be time to call it quits." Dom offered him a cold beer.

He glanced up and took the bottle. "Thanks, you might be right. I can't get the damn ground station to sync with the updated autopilot software. Keep getting the same error message." He slammed the laptop shut in frustration and took a swig from the beer.

"All good, we'll have another look tomorrow."

He nodded. "I know someone I can call. He's all over this sort of stuff."

"You've got a lot of interesting friends."

"Wait till you meet Kruger."

"The guy that's coming up tomorrow?"

"Yeah, former South African Recce. You two will get along just fine. Hell, you might be able to convince him to stay and help out."

"Could definitely use another hand."

Bishop packed the laptop and the compact drone inside a purpose-built case.

"Can you hear that?" Dom asked.

He tipped his head. There was a slight breeze that carried the sounds of the river. Faintly, in the background, he thought he could hear the sound of a car horn.

"Someone's in a hurry," added Dom.

The horn got louder and soon it blended with the roar of an engine.

“Yeah, sounds like one of our Land Cruisers.” Dom placed his beer down and ran toward the lecture rooms.

Bishop's heart was pounding before he even started sprinting. He passed the New Zealander, dashed through the building and out to the track. The safari truck roared toward him with the horn still blaring. He spotted Christina at the wheel as it skidded to a halt in a cloud of dust. Francis, the driver, was in the back cradling someone in his arms. It was Saneh. Bishop fought the panic welling up inside him. “Dom, we need a medevac.”

“Already on it.”

He took Saneh’s limp body from the truck and laid her gently on the ground. As he frantically checked her vitals Dom appeared with a medical kit and stretcher. She had a weak pulse. He tipped his ear to her mouth; she was breathing.

“Her head, her head, they shot her in the head,” Francis blurted.

A quick check found the wound above her right ear, beneath hair matted with blood. A bullet had creased her skull leaving a half-inch groove. “I need a bandage,” he yelled at Dom.

Bishop bound the wound and they transferred her to the stretcher wrapping a space blanket around her body. “Who did this?” he asked as he monitored her vitals.

Christina sobbed hysterically. “It was poachers. They shot the radio, we couldn’t call through.”

“They killed Melo,” added Francis.

Bishop clenched his jaw. “How long till the medevac arrives?”

“Thirty minutes,” said Dom.

He clutched Saneh's hand. “Hang in there, babe.”

CHAPTER 2

NORTH LUANGWA NATIONAL PARK, ZAMBIA

The hacking laugh of a hyena sent a ripple of fear down Mamba's spine. He knew the predators posed no immediate threat but still aimed his AK at the dark shapes that lingered at the edge of his vision. The pack had been tailing them through the bush for the last few hours. He knew they sensed a meal was coming. They could smell death and it excited them.

"How much further?" he asked the younger of the brothers.

"At least eight miles, we're moving very slowly."

"No shit." He glanced back at the two men carrying the makeshift stretcher; it was what had attracted the hyenas. Their guide, the young thief, had taken a shotgun blast to the stomach. Mamba wanted to ditch the casualty but Colin had convinced him otherwise and volunteered to help carry the boy. A body was evidence he'd argued; sign on a trail that might lead the authorities to his door.

The two stretcher-bearers, Colin and the other tracker, lowered the wounded boy to the ground as Mamba strode toward them. There was a half moon in the clear night sky and he could see the shine of sweat on their faces. "We're moving too slow."

"We're going as fast as we can," Colin said between catching his breath. He pulled a water bottle from his pack and took few measured sips.

"The thief is as good as dead. We'll leave him for the hyenas."

"The boy will live if we get him to help."

"And I suppose you'll drive him to the hospital?" Mamba hissed.

Colin nodded as he stowed the bottle. "If need be, he did his job. I won't leave him to die."

Mamba slid his finger to the trigger of his AK as he glared at the wounded teenager. It might be easier to put a bullet in both the boy and the old man. He thought better of it. Professional poachers were a tight-knit community and word would spread that he had killed one of their own. What's more, the Rhodesian was one of the best hunters in the business and quality ivory was getting harder and harder to find.

"Fine, but if we're not out of the park by dawn I'm going to leave you both here." Mamba turned and re-joined the tracker who was conversing with Kogo. "Let's get going."

The man glanced back at his brother and Colin. "What about them?"

"If they can't keep up we're going to leave the thief."

"OK, boss." The tracker rose and started off into the bush, his weapon held ready.

"We should leave the boy now. Save us some money," said Kogo.

"Do as you're fucking told."

Kogo shrugged and followed the tracker.

Mamba waited for the stretcher-bearers to pass him. Then he turned and peered into the darkness behind them. Despite the gunfight and the rangers escaping it looked like they were in the clear. No one but hyenas followed them.

***

CURE HOSPITAL, LUSAKA

The Special Emergency Services helicopter touched down at the CURE Hospital on the outskirts of Lusaka, the capital of Zambia. The crew rapidly offloaded the gurney carrying Saneh and pushed it across the helipad and inside the hospital. Funded by US and UK charities, the hospital was a beacon of professionalism in a region starved of medical services. Bishop followed the stretcher as far as the swinging doors to the emergency ward where a grandmotherly nurse stopped him.

"You can't go any further, dear. Come with me, I'll show you to the waiting room," she said guiding him through a separate door.

Bishop took a seat in the empty waiting area. There had been limited room on the helicopter; he was the only one who had accompanied Saneh. He stared at the wall, trying to contain his emotions. There was a war waging inside him, a battle between grief, rage, and guilt that left him numb. If he lost Saneh he... The truth was he didn't know what would happen if he lost her or their child. He didn't want to contemplate it. What he needed to do was get her the best medical attention possible.

He pulled out his phone and dialed a number.

"Hello," said the automated voice. "You've reached Telemetry Transport please enter your tracking number for an update on the progress of your shipment."

He punched in a five-digit code.

"Bish, that you?" The voice belonged to Frank, a member of PRIMAL, the vigilante organization that Saneh and Bishop were part of. His call had connected to their makeshift headquarters in Abu Dhabi where a bare-bones team was monitoring intelligence sources for any sign the organization had been compromised.

"Yeah, it's me. Is Vance there?"

"Sure is, I'll grab him."

A moment later the PRIMAL director's deep voice replaced Frank's. "Bish, what's up, buddy?"

"There's been an accident. Saneh has been shot. She's at the CURE hospital in Lusaka. I need you to coordinate a medical evacuation to Abu Dhabi so she can receive appropriate treatment."

"What?"

"Poachers ambushed her."

"Jesus Christ, OK, OK, we'll organize a medical evacuation for both of you. Tariq's people can arrange care here... Listen, buddy, are you OK?"

"I'm fine, just get Saneh the hell out of here." He terminated the call and glanced back at the nurse who was now manning the counter. Her friendly smile had turned into a frown.

"I'm sorry," said Bishop. "It's a lovely hospital."

"It's fine, dear. I know you must be very worried about your girlfriend but she's in good hands. Now, can I get you a cup of tea? It will make you feel better."

Bishop managed a nod as he slumped back into his chair. "She's in good hands," he murmured to himself. Panic welled up inside him and he fought the urge to scream.

"Here you are." The nurse appeared with a mug of tea.

"Thanks." Bishop took a sip of the hot, sweet liquid.

"Doctor Anderson is very good," she said once she'd returned to the counter. "He trained in America and is very experienced in trauma surgery."

Her words did little to comfort Bishop. However, as he sipped the tea reality dawned on him. There was nothing more he could do to help Saneh. He had taken her to the hospital and now her life was in the hands of the doctor. His skills were better applied at bringing justice to the men who had hurt her. Placing the tea down he reached in his pocket for his phone and made a call. "Kruger, it's Bishop. How far are you from Lusaka?"

***

It seemed like an eternity before Doctor Anderson finally reappeared through the swinging doors guarding the emergency ward. Bishop's heart lurched as he spotted the grim expression on the man's face. "Is she OK?" he asked softly when the doctor sat next to him.

"She's in a coma."

"And the baby?"

"At this stage the baby is fine."

Bishop's throat was dry and he fought the urge to cry. "Will she wake up?"

"It's hard to say. The bullet damaged part of her skull causing trauma to the brain. The bleeding has stopped but she is going to need additional surgery to remove fragments and check for damage. I'm not going to lie, the prognosis is not great. I've seen people recover from injuries like this but I've also had patients who simply never regain consciousness."

Tears welled in Bishop's eyes and the doctor put a hand on his shoulder. "Your friends have been in touch. There's a private jet flying in. We'll help prepare for her transfer tomorrow morning. She is going to have the best care available."

The words did little to comfort him. He put his head in his hands, closed his eyes, and attempted to bring his emotions under control.

"There's nothing more you can do here, Mr. Barnes," the doctor said using the name he had given. "You should get some rest. If you like, the duty nurse can organize a hotel and transport."

Bishop rose. "No thanks." He felt like a zombie as he walked out of the hospital into the crisp evening air. Glancing at his watch he calculated that only two hours had passed since Christina had driven the shot-up truck into the camp. Kruger was due to arrive at any moment and if they moved fast there was a chance they could track down the men who had shot her.

The clatter of a diesel engine caught his attention and he squinted as headlights swung into the parking lot.

A Nissan truck pulled up alongside him. "Get in," yelled an Afrikaans-accented voice.

He opened the door and climbed inside. The man at the wheel was what was commonly referred to in the military as a 'unit'. Kruger's spiked brown hair touched the roof of the shabby interior of the truck and his broad shoulders filled the cab.

"OK, here's the plan." Kruger wasn't one to mince words. "Old mate of mine has a light aircraft waiting at a strip nearby. He's got us weapons and transport to Luangwa and there's enough room for Princess."

"Who is Princess?"

Kruger turned to him with a frown. "Princess is a Rhodesian-Mastiff cross. She's the best hunting dog on the continent." He jerked his head over his shoulder. "They've got a bit of a head start but if you're keen we can track them down."

Bishop turned in his seat and spotted a pair of brown eyes and a wet black nose. "I want these bastards dead."

Kruger drove the truck out of the parking lot and accelerated down the dark road. "Dead we can do."

***

NORTH LUANGWA NATIONAL PARK, ZAMBIA

Thirty minutes later a Cessna Caravan touched down at the dark airstrip behind the ranger camp at Luangwa. Bishop jumped out of the cabin wearing a South African-style chest rig, carrying a worn R5 carbine. He strode across to the waiting Land Cruiser and climbed in the passenger side.

"Is she OK?" asked Dom from the driver's seat. He glanced at their weapons.

"No, she's in a coma."

"I'm so sorry, Aden."

Kruger climbed into the back of the vehicle and Princess followed, leaping in beside him. He was similarly equipped as Bishop but carried a heavier R1 rifle.

"Dom, this is Kruger."

The massive South African leaned forward and shook the New Zealander's hand.

Dom drove at high speed away from the airfield, through the camp, and out onto the track north toward Mwaleshi Falls.

"How is Christina?" yelled Bishop over the engine.

"Pretty shook up. They took her by ambulance to Lusaka." Dom weaved the two-ton truck through a thicket of trees with the finesse of a rally driver. "Look, I can't send my rangers with you. They're not trained or equipped to deal with people like this."

"That's OK. We've got it."

"I don't think you understand. We're talking military training and weapons. These guys are hard-core criminals. They'll gun you down in cold blood."

"Not if we get the drop on them," said Kruger.

"You're seriously going after them?"

"Yep," replied Bishop.

"Then I should come with you, you'll need an extra shooter."

Bishop shook his head. "Negative, we'll take care of it."

They drove in silence before he caught a glimpse of lights through the scrub. As they got closer he could see there were vehicles parked beside the riverbank.

"OK, we're here," said Dom as he skidded the truck to a halt.

"Princess, let's go." Kruger and the dog leaped out of the cab. The South African surveyed the scene with his weapon at the ready.

"They killed a black rhino on the other side of the river," said Dom. "Left her calf." He gestured to the four-wheel drives parked in the long grass. A team of rangers were clustered around the baby rhino, illuminated by the headlights of the vehicles. "Poor little bugger was hysterical. We're lucky we found him before the hyenas or the lions got to him."

"You said there were at least four, with one possible casualty?"

"Correct. And they've got at least an eight hour stomp before they're clear of the park."

"Alright, you stay and take care of Christina and the calf. Kruger and I will run with this." He stepped out of the truck and skidded down the riverbank into the water. It reached his knees as he waded across. Princess and Kruger were already on the other side. He scrambled up the bank pushing his way through the long grass. A flashlight flicked on and he could hear Kruger talking to the dog.

"What have you got?" Bishop asked as he caught up.

The light revealed the corpse of the rhino. Its head was drenched in blood. A hole had been hacked in its snout where the horn once was.

"Fucking bastards," Bishop said as he stared at the macabre remains.

There was a snuffle from the bushes and Kruger aimed the flashlight. Princess had her nose to the ground and was moving in circles sniffing frantically. "Find them, girl."

The stocky hound gave a loud snort and bounded off into the bush.

"She's got them. You ready to run all night?" Kruger said switching off the light.

"I'll chase them to the gates of hell if I have to."

"Well, that's exactly where we're going to send these pricks." Kruger slapped him on the shoulder. "Half moon, plenty of light. Let's hope we don't run up against anything that wants to eat us." He laughed heartily as he trotted off into the bush after his baying hound.

Bishop paused for a second, glanced up at the stars, and said a quick prayer for Saneh. Then he grasped the R5 with both hands and held it close to his chest as he ran after Kruger.

***

ABU DHABI INTERNATIONAL AIRPORT

The G450 Gulfstream was powered up and waiting on the tarmac when Vance strode out from the airport's VIP terminal. Bathed in floodlights, the green cross emblazoned on the aircraft was a poignant reminder of the mission at hand. He made a beeline to where a lone figure stood at the stairs of the jet.

Dressed in one of his signature Savile Row suits Tariq Ahmed waited with a grim expression. "Do we know any more?" he asked as he shook Vance's hand. Tariq, who was

PRIMAL's benefactor, had pulled out all stops to organize Saneh's evacuation. As the owner of Lascar Logistics, an airfreight company with a fleet of aircraft, sourcing the aeromedical jet had not been difficult. However his staff had also arranged the best neurosurgeon they could find to accompany Saneh, and had also convinced the world's foremost expert on coma treatment to fly in from the UK.

"There has been no change to her situation. She's stable but no sign of waking."

"And the child?"

Vance frowned. "How did you know she was pregnant? It was supposed to be a secret."

"Please, you think Mirza can keep a secret?"

"I would hope so, all things considered." Mirza Mansoor, Bishop's operational partner, was currently working for Tariq helping to coordinate humanitarian relief flights.

"Does he know about Saneh?"

Tariq shook his head. "No, I didn't want to tell him until he gets back. He's got enough on his plate for the moment. I take it you're not recalling everyone?"

"That's right. We're keeping this low key. Chua and I are concerned that if we spread the word the team is going to converge on Abu Dhabi. We can't afford that sort of visibility at the moment. It seems harsh but I think it's for the best."

A voice from the top of the stairs drew their attention. "Gentlemen, we'll be ready to go in a minute."

Vance gave the green-uniformed crewmember a nod and turned back to Tariq. "Thanks for pulling this all together."

"We're a family, Vance, and families take care of each other. Now go get our girl. I've got a coma specialist flying in from London and everything will be ready when you return." He gave Vance's hand a firm shake and walked toward the terminal.

Vance climbed the stairs into the sleek white interior of the jet. Along one side were two stretchers with a bank of state-of-the-art medical equipment attached to the wall. At the front of the cabin the medical team was already strapped into their seats. He took his place next to one of them as the door closed and the engines spooled up.

"Are you the father?" asked the middle-aged woman next to him.

He pulled his safety belt tight and gave her a grim smile. "Yeah, I guess you could say that."

"My name's Lynne. We'll get your daughter home safe and sound."

"Thanks." Vance glanced out the window as the jet rolled forward. While getting Saneh back to Abu Dhabi and world-class medical attention was his focus it wasn't the only thing weighing on his mind. Another concern was how badly Bishop was going to react to the situation. The PRIMAL operative already carried the weight of his parent's death along with dozens of innocent lives that he held himself responsible for. Saneh was his rock, his beacon of light in a very dark existence. With her life hanging by a thread it was possible he would go completely off the reservation. His only hope, that Kruger could talk some sense into him before he turned renegade.

***

NORTH LUANGWA NATIONAL PARK, ZAMBIA

Despite the cool night air Bishop's shirt was damp under his chest rig and his hair was matted with perspiration. He caught up with Kruger as the South African paused to inspect the ground with his flashlight.

"They're moving slowly." Kruger shone the light on an area of crushed grass. Ignoring the stiffness in his legs Bishop knelt and took a closer look.

"Stretcher?" he asked.

"*Ja.* You can see where they placed it down. Saneh definitely wounded one of them." The light revealed a patch of bloodstained grass. "Badly!"

He touched the grass; the blood was dry.

Kruger moved the beam behind the stretcher. There were fresh paw prints in the sand. "Princess isn't the only one following them."

"They're not her tracks?"

"No, hyenas. They can smell the blood."

A single bark penetrated the darkness reminding them Kruger's hound was still hot on the poachers' scent.

"Will they attack her?"

"Yes, we need to catch up. You good?"

His knees cracked as he rose. "Yeah." He cradled his R5 as Kruger secured his flashlight in a pouch and took a quick sip of water. The big man reminded Bishop of a lion stalking its prey through the dark savannah; alert, poised, and lethal.

"Let's go."

Princess barked again and they set off jogging in her direction.

***

Barely a mile away Mamba tilted his head and listened. He was moving at the rear of the column pushing the stretcher crew to move faster. Noise traveled far in the cool night air and he clearly heard the bark of a dog. The noise troubled him more than any hyena. It meant someone was hunting them. "Fuck!" He grabbed Colin by the shoulder. "We need to dump the kid."

The lack of a rebuke confirmed that Colin also heard the dog. The stretcher was lowered and he unslung his rifle. "The kid will have to take his chances with the rangers."

"No, he'll talk." Mamba slid the machete from the sheath between his shoulder blades.

"He won't," Colin said half-heartedly.

"You want to risk spending the rest of your life in a Zambian prison? You wouldn't last a week, old man."

The boy mumbled something from the stretcher. The sweat glazed across his face shone in the starlight.

"He's almost dead. I'm doing him a favor."

"You're a bloody animal, Mamba," Colin said as he turned and walked away.

Mamba knelt down and whispered in the boy's ear. "Nobody likes a thief."

The rhino's thick hide and horn had dulled the machete's edge. It smashed rather than sliced through the windpipe. A gurgling emitted from the boy's mouth and he feebly tried to raise his hands. Mamba drew back and swung harder. This time the blow almost severed the slight neck and blood sprayed. In a few seconds the gurgling ceased and the thief lay silent.

He wiped the blade on the dead youth's pants before returning it to the sheath. A hasty inspection of the corpse's pockets revealed a wallet and mobile phone. The hyenas would consume the rest leaving nothing to identify, he thought as he joined the other men.

"Now we move fast. If we're not at the trucks by dawn you all lose half."

"Boss, that's not—" whined Kogo.

"Shut up and run."

They ran through the scrub with the trackers in the lead and Colin bringing up the rear. Behind them the dog barked again, this time louder. Mamba's lip turned up in a snarl, which transitioned to a smile as he remembered the hyenas. Feasting on the corpse the savage predators would hopefully make short work of the dog. Without the hound there was no way the rangers could catch them.

CHAPTER 3

NORTH LUANGWA NATIONAL PARK, ZAMBIA

Bishop struggled to keep pace with the tall South African as he ran over the rugged terrain. The sandy soil had been replaced by loose rock that shifted under foot and thick patches of thorn-covered bushes. His legs were burning and his lungs screamed but the thought that the men who had attacked Saneh and Christina could get away drove him on.

He was falling behind when Kruger skidded to a halt alongside Princess. The dog's hackles were raised and she emitted a low, savage growl, sending a shiver up Bishop's spine. In the darkness ahead he spotted half a dozen canine-like shapes clustered around something on the ground. Moonlight reflected off white teeth and yellow eyes as the hyenas shifted their attention toward the dog.

"Fucking hyenas," said Kruger as he drew a suppressed pistol and fired a round at the ground in front of the animals.

With their hunched backs, flashing teeth, and a hackling snarl, the creatures reminded Bishop of something from a horror movie. He flicked off the safety on his R5 and prepared to follow Kruger's lead.

Princess stalked forward, her growl increasing in intensity.

"Hold." Kruger fired another round. "Get the fuck out of here!"

The hyenas were unwilling to give up their meal. The largest of the pack, the alpha, lunged forward snapping and snarling. Kruger shot it neatly through the head and it dropped to the ground.

Spurred on by her master's actions the Rhodesian-Mastiff cross leaped forward and the remainder of the Hyenas turned tail and fled.

He exhaled, releasing a breath he didn't realize he held.

"Didn't want to have to kill one, but they might have hurt Princess." Kruger strode past the dead pack leader and shone his flashlight at the object they had been feeding on. It was a body. "Christ."

Bishop grimaced as he inspected the mangled corpse. It was barely identifiable as human. Most of the clothing had been ripped off and the torso torn apart exposing the bloodied organs contained within. Most of the stomach, intestines, groin, and a leg were missing.

"This must be the one Saneh wounded, *ja.* He looks young."

"They left him for the hyenas?" Bishop said in disbelief.

Kruger aimed his light at the body's neck. It was almost fully severed. "They cut his throat first."

The chuckle of a hyena sounded from the bush and Princess growled. Standing a few yards away she stared into the darkness intently, teeth bared.

"The body's still warm," said Kruger drawing Bishop's attention to the steam rising off the gaping abdomen cavity. "They're not far away." He snapped an order in Afrikaans to the hound and she focused her attention back to their direction of travel.

Bishop spotted a glint of metal and bent down to find the corpse had a cord around what was left of its neck. Underneath the tattered and blood-soaked shirt hung a key. He ripped it off and stuffed it into his pocket.

"We'll catch these fuckers within an hour." Kruger switched off the flashlight.

Bishop's eyes adjusted back to the darkness as they stepped off after the dog. They weren't more than a dozen yards from the body when he heard it being ripped apart by the hyenas. He felt no compassion for the poacher; there was every chance he could be the one who shot Saneh. Before long he would be joined in hell by the rest of his gang.

***

Every poacher heard the excited bark of the dog when it rang through the night air. By Mamba's estimates it was only a few hundred yards away and gaining fast. He swore; they might not cover the final few miles before the rangers were on them. Fatigue was taking a toll and Kogo and Colin were lagging behind. Waiting till they reached a clearing he called out to halt. Once the men had gathered he spoke. "They're going to catch us. We need to ambush them."

"That's risky," Kogo managed to say between breaths. "We don't know how many there are."

"They're moving too fast to be a large team," said Colin. "One dog and three or four men at most. They'll be gathering a bigger party to come out at dawn."

"We can handle them," said the younger of the trackers.

He addressed the Ugandan brothers. "Both of you take care of it and I'll give you the thief's share right now."

The trackers glanced at each other and nodded. Mamba had appealed to the strongest of their desires, greed. "It's a deal."

Mamba reached into a pocket, took out a thick wad of bills, and handed half to each man.

"I'll stay as well," said Colin.

The elder of the brothers shook his head. "No, white man, we can handle this. You go with them to the trucks. Up ahead there's open ground and a ridge. We'll kill them there."

Mamba smiled. "Let's do this." He followed the two trackers into the bush. Both of them were experienced fighters as well as poachers. Recruited from his old Army unit they were experienced bush warriors that would make short work of the park rangers following them.

Less than a hundred yards further they reached a dry sandy riverbed. To one side a rocky outcrop of boulders offered excellent cover for an ambush.

"Follow this river all the way to the road," said the tracker.

"Yes, I remember," said Mamba.

The two brothers left them in the riverbed and climbed up to the rocky outcrop. A moment later they were hidden among the boulders. Mamba gave the exposed killing area one last scan then led Colin and Kogo along the dried waterway. The men following them would soon be dead. Even if they weren't the ambush would slow them enough for him to reach the vehicles and escape.

***

Bishop sensed something was wrong when Kruger slowed to a walk then paused behind a thorn bush. Following suit he peered through the branches at the dry riverbed illuminated by the soft glow from the half moon. He spotted Princess at the edge of the clearing. She was crouched low with her head canted in the direction of a rocky outcrop.

"They've doubled back and laid an ambush," whispered Kruger.

"How the hell do you know that?"

"Princess told me."

Bishop shook his head. He'd seen Military Working Dogs in action but never witnessed the level of communication Kruger shared with his hunting dog; it was uncanny.

"They're up there in the rocks." Kruger gestured with a gloved hand. "They expect the dog to follow the scent up the river but she's too smart for that shit, fucking amateurs. We're going to hit them from the flank."

"Got it." The adrenaline had already started to pump as Bishop eased the safety off on his R5 and they stalked into the darkness. When they reached the edge of the rocky outcrop Kruger gestured for him to move up alongside. They shouldered their weapons, Kruger gave a low whistle, and Princess started barking. Both men caught the slight movement ahead in the rocks and opened fire, their muzzle flashes lighting up the bush.

"Covering!" yelled Bishop as he took a knee and continued to shoot in the direction of the movement.

Kruger moved forward his weapon held ready. He dropped to a knee and they repeated the sequence. "Covering!"

The stench of cordite filled Bishop's nostrils as he flicked the empty magazine out of his rifle and inserted a fresh one. He kept one eye closed, only opening it between shots, an old trick an instructor had taught him to preserve his night vision. He spotted the flash of a muzzle as he dashed forward. A bullet ricocheted off a rock and Kruger retaliated with a half dozen well-aimed shots. One of the ambushers cried out and the firing ceased.

When Bishop reached the position they had seen movement he spotted a crumpled body. He felt zero remorse as he fired two rounds into the poacher then continued to scan ahead. Spotting a figure dash toward the creek he fired again. His bullets went wide as the man disappeared from view.

"Princess, hunt!" bellowed Kruger as he and the dog gave chase.

Bishop took a split-second to check the first poacher was dead before running in the direction of Princess's frantic barking. Stumbling on the loose rocks he slipped down the bank into the sandy riverbed.

"Son of a bitch."

Climbing to his feet he realized he'd rolled his ankle. The pain was sharp but bearable. He ignored it as he limped up the riverbed. As he rounded a bend a horrific scream reverberated through the air. Bishop forgot his ankle as he as he caught up with the others.

The poacher writhed on the ground screaming as he held an arm across his chest. Kruger stood over him, the long-barreled R1 aimed at the man's face. Princess crouched to one side, her teeth glinting in the moonlight as she emitted a savage growl.

Bishop knelt by poacher's head. "Do you speak English?" He took a glow stick from one of his pouches and cracked it. In the soft orange glow he inspected their captive.

The poacher looked young, mid-twenties, his face a mask of agony and his shirt drenched in blood. Princess had de-gloved the right arm from midway up his forearm. The skin had peeled back to his knuckles exposing bloodied muscle fibers and bone. He sucked air loudly through gritted teeth.

"Answer the man. Do you speak English?" Kruger barked.

"Yes, yes I speak English. Please, please keep that dog off me. I didn't shoot the rhino, I didn't shoot it."

"How many men were with you?" Bishop asked.

"Six, there were six."

Bishop glanced up at Kruger who nodded. They still had three more to hunt down. "Who's in charge? Who organized the job?"

"Mamba, Mamba Mboya. He's the boss man poacher in Kenya. If you go fast you can catch him."

"One more question," he hissed. "Did you fire at the women in the truck?"

The wounded man's pause was all the confirmation Bishop needed. He rose to his feet and held out his hand to Kruger. The South African passed him his suppressed pistol.

"I didn't shoot. I didn't, it was Mamba."

The snap of the pistol ended his cries as Bishop shot him through the face. He felt nothing as he handed the weapon back and started up the creek. "You heard him, we can still catch them."

"Princess, hunt," commanded Kruger and the dog raced off down the riverbed.

Bishop glanced up at the horizon to the east; already the stars had disappeared, replaced with the soft orange glow of a rapidly approaching dawn. He ignored the pain in his swollen ankle and started jogging. If he had his way the men who shot Saneh were not going to see another sunrise. The poacher known as Mamba Mboya was going to die badly.

***

"Come on, you slow shit." Mamba shoved Kogo in the back as the smaller man struggled to climb the riverbank. He pushed him over the ledge then scrambled up after him to where Colin waited. As he paused to catch his breath he heard the dog bark again. He had assumed the volley of gunfire had killed the rangers and their hound. Clearly he was wrong. "Those fucking idiots."

"They're dead now," grunted Colin.

"And we will be too if we don't run." Mamba pushed past the white poacher and sprinted through the bush. The dog would catch them before they reached the vehicles and he didn't want to be last. Kogo or Colin could battle it out with the rangers; they could be replaced. He managed a smile as he reached the track. His costs for the mission had been cut significantly.

In the soft pre-dawn glow he spotted the trucks a hundred yards away parked off the dirt road. Breathing hard he stumbled in the soft sand at the edge of the track. Behind him the dog barked excitedly. He glanced over his shoulder and saw Kogo and Colin hot on his heels. Grasping his rifle he turned and sprinted for his vehicle.

The dog was louder now, a deep angry bark that shook him as he reached the four-wheel drive. Wrenching open the driver's door he jumped in and tossed the AK on the passenger's seat. He pulled the keys from his vest and turned the ignition. It coughed once as the passenger door sprung open and Kogo scrambled in screaming. "The dog, the dog, go, go, go!"

The engine spluttered again. The rear door opened. A savage snarl filled the air and Colin cried out as he dove inside. Mamba glanced over his shoulder as he pumped the accelerator and turned the key again. A massive bull-headed mastiff had one of the poacher's legs clenched firmly in its mouth.

"Drive, drive!" screamed Colin as the engine finally kicked over.

Mamba jammed the truck into gear and stomped on the accelerator. Checking the wing mirror he spotted two figures crash out of the bush. They were silhouetted by the first fingernail of the orange sunrise. "Get down!"

Bullets smashed through the back window and out through the windshield showering Mamba in glass.

"Jesus Christ!" screamed Kogo as they accelerated up the dirt track.

He held the wheel steady as more rounds slammed against the four-wheel drive. They rocketed along the road until the gunfire ceased. He glanced up at the mirror; a cloud of dust obscured them from the attackers. There was no sign of the dog.

"Mamba, Mamba!" Kogo screamed from the passenger seat.

"Shut the hell up." He peered through what remained of the windshield as he drove the vehicle around a bend in the road.

"Colin's dead."

He glanced over his shoulder at the crumpled body. A bullet had punched through the old Rhodesian's skull and blood and gore were spread across the back seat.

Mamba grinned manically. "Do you want to split his share?"

***

Bishop lowered his rifle as the four-wheel drive disappeared in a cloud of thick dust. Searching frantically he spotted another truck parked among the bushes. Sprinting to the other vehicle he reached for the key he'd taken from the dead poacher. It didn't fit. "Fuck!" Then he saw the scooter dumped alongside the road. The key worked and the tiny engine spluttered to life. Twisting the throttle he lurched into the dust cloud behind the escaping vehicle.

The little bike hiccupped and coughed like a drunken smoker as it plowed through the soft sand. He squinted, struggling to maintain visual on the escaping truck. Dust stung his eyes and as the road turned his front tire slid. The bike was dumped on its side throwing him over the handlebars. Rolling in the dirt he leaped to his feet and shouldered his weapon. Dust filled the air blocking his view. He lowered the weapon. Mamba was gone and he had failed Saneh.

Princess appeared out of the haze. She walked slowly toward him with her tail between her legs.

"I know the feeling, girl." Bishop reached out and patted the dog's head.

Kruger jogged up behind him. "I'm sorry, Bish. I really thought we had them."

"Me too. But, we're not done yet. We're going to find Mr. Mamba Mboya and I'm going to kill him."

Kruger nodded as he took a satellite phone from his chest rig. "First we have to get out of here. You need to call Dom."

CHAPTER 4

NORTH LUANGWA NATIONAL PARK, ZAMBIA

Bishop handed Kruger back his satellite phone before collapsing against a tree. "It's going to be a few hours before they get here."

"*Ja*, best get some rest then." Kruger had removed his boots and lay in the grass using his assault vest as a pillow. Princess was sitting under a tree panting, having drunk her fill from water sloshed into the South African's bush hat.

He unlaced his boots, wincing as he freed his swollen ankle from the leather. The sprain wasn't severe but had already turned a dark shade of purple. He took a roll of medical tape from his vest and strapped it. Then he leaned against his gear hoping to get some rest.

The adrenalin was long gone from his system but his mind still raced. He looked over at Kruger who had his damp bush hat pulled low over his eyes.

"Kruger?"

"*Ja*."

"I should've been with her when it happened."

Kruger lifted the hat from his eyes. "First poaching incident in years, right?"

"Yeah."

"You couldn't have predicted that."

He shook his head. "You don't understand. She's pregnant and I let her put our child at risk. Two rangers with shotguns and a cheap shitty drone isn't security against gunned-up poachers."

An awkward silence passed before Kruger spoke. "Look, I know a guy in Mombasa that's got his ear to the ground. We'll deal with Mamba first, then Saneh will get better, and after that we'll talk to Vance about helping Dom and his boys out."

"Thanks, brother." Bishop closed his eyes.

The morning sun had crested the trees and was shining fiercely by the time one of the rangers picked them up. Once they'd piled into the safari truck, Kruger and Princess promptly fell asleep. The hound and her owner snored heavily as they drove along the pot-holed dirt road around the perimeter of the national park.

As exhausted as he was Bishop couldn't sleep. He stared out the window at the bush but his mind wasn't on the wilderness. All he could think about was Saneh. The image of her lying unconscious in the dust was a memory he would take to his grave, but not before he put Mamba in one of his own.

As they pulled into the camp Bishop spotted Dom at the entrance to the lecture hall. The New Zealander strode across to the truck as it slowed and yanked open the door.

"Are you guys OK?"

He climbed out and stretched his legs, testing his sprained ankle. "Yeah, we got four of them. The others escaped." As he spoke Christina appeared from the building. She looked haggard with dark bags under her eyes. "How are you feeling?" he asked, managing a half smile.

"I'm OK. I just spoke to the hospital."

"Any change?"

Tears formed in her eyes as she shook her head. She stepped forward and wrapped her arms around him. "I'm so sorry, Aden," she sobbed.

"Hey, it's not your fault." Bishop fought back tears of his own as he hugged her. He felt something brush against his leg and glanced down to see Kruger's dog leaning against him. "Hey, have you met Princess?"

The dog greeted Christina with a wet lick that brought a smile to her face and a flurry of pats in return. Bishop managed a smile as he watched the savage hound reveling in the attention. He glanced up at Dom who watched with a sad expression on his face. "Hey, bud, can we talk?"

The New Zealander nodded and led him into the lecture hall. Kruger joined them as Dom opened the refrigerator and offered them each a beer.

Bishop waved it away. "Does the name Mamba Mboya mean anything to you?"

Kruger took a beer and twisted the top off. "Tall black guy," he added.

Dom nodded. "Yeah, I've heard of him. He's a poacher out of Mombasa; ex-military with access to heavy-duty hardware. You think the boys who did this were his?"

"Not think, we know. Mamba was there, we just missed him."

"Jesus, that's not good."

"I need to find him. Kruger and I are heading to Mombasa."

Dom shook his head. "Maybe it's best to let it go, Aden. These people are killers."

Kruger snorted into his beer. "We're not exactly Boy Scouts."

Bishop shot a frown at the PRIMAL operative. "Dom, we need to bring this evil piece of shit to justice. He could have killed Chris and he may have killed Saneh."

"I've got some contacts down there in the anti-poaching community. They might be able to help." He picked up his beer and led them outside. "I want you to see something."

Bishop followed him out the back across the open area to where they had tested the drone. Behind the clearing the rangers had constructed a makeshift pen. Inside lay the baby rhino. The calf rested in the shade of a tree bleating pathetically for its dead mother.

"Poor little fella," said Bishop.

"His mother was one of three breeding-age females on Luangwa. Now, without her, the program is likely to fail. I can almost guarantee the black rhino will be extinct in Zambia within five years." He took a swig from his beer.

"Once Kruger and I are done, I can guarantee Mamba will be the one who ends up extinct," said Bishop.

"Let me know if there's anything I can do to help. I can take you down to Mombasa and introduce you to my anti-poaching contacts. You're going to need an extra set of hands."

He shook his head. "No, Kruger and I will take care of this. You need to stay here with Christina, she needs you."

"Yeah, and Saneh needs you."

"I can't do anything for her here. She would want me to hunt Mamba down." He placed his hand on Dom's broad shoulder. "I'm not putting anyone else's life at risk. Can you give us a lift to Lusaka?"

"Yeah, of course."

They walked to the front of the lecture room where Christina continued lavishing Princess with attention.

"Hey Dom, can I leave the hound here with you guys?" asked Kruger. "I'll come get her when all this is done."

"Sure, Chris will be happy with that."

"I'm going to grab some gear. I'll meet you back here in five." Bishop left the two men watching Christina with the dog and made his way across to the accommodation. He hadn't been back since the accident and the single room bungalow was exactly how he and Saneh had left it the previous morning. Their clothes were still strewn on the bed, dirty dishes in the sink. On the bedside table sat the only photo she traveled with, a picture of them at the beach. Stripping off his khaki ranger shirt and camouflage shorts he dressed in jeans and a plain T-shirt. Sitting on the edge of the bed he grabbed a backpack and stuffed some other clothes inside. As he finished packing his phone rang.

It was Vance. "Hey, buddy, how you doing?"

Bishop could tell from the background noise that the PRIMAL Director of Operations was calling him from an aircraft. "Yeah, I'm OK."

"Hey, I just wanted to let you know we'll be on the ground in Lusaka at 1330 hours local. We'll transfer Saneh direct to the medevac bird and get you both back to Abu Dhabi. You at the hospital now?"

"I'm not far away. I'll be there."

"OK, see you then."

Bishop terminated the call and grabbed his bag. He left the bungalow and strode across to where Dom and Kruger were waiting next to one of the camp's hardtop Land Cruisers. "They're going to transfer Saneh at 1330," he said tossing his bag in the four-wheel drive.

"We better get a move on if we're going to be there in time," said Dom as he climbed in with one of his rangers.

"You talk to Vance?" asked Kruger when the others were out of earshot.

"Yeah."

"You tell him we're going after Mamba?"

"No. He wants me to go back with Saneh."

"Do you think he'll authorize a mission?"

"Unlikely, not with PRIMAL on lock down. We leave now and Mamba's trail goes cold."

"Fuck that. You and me can have that prick wrapped up within a few days."

Bishop slapped him on the shoulder. "Means the world to me, Kruger."

"What can I say, you and Saneh are family... and no one messes with my family."

***

CURE HOSPITAL, LUSAKA

At 1305 hours the nurse led Bishop to Saneh's room. She lay perfectly still in the hospital bed. If it wasn't for the hoses running from her mouth and nose she could have been sleeping. He swallowed back his tears, turned to the bald African American seated in the corner of the room and gave him a nod. "Thanks for coming."

Vance pried his hulking frame from the plastic chair and gathered Bishop up in a bear hug.

"Hey steady on, old man, you're going to break a rib," he wheezed.

Vance released him and glanced at the bed. "I feel so helpless seeing her like this."

"Yeah, tell me about it."

A knock at the door caught their attention. Doctor Anderson walked in. Behind him a team of green-uniformed medical staff waited with a gurney.

"Gentlemen, we need to prepare the patient for transport. If I could ask you both to move to the waiting area."

"Saneh, her name's Saneh," said Bishop.

"That's a lovely name," said the doctor as he led the team of medical professionals into the room.

He felt Vance's hand on his shoulder and let the PRIMAL chief guide him out the door.

"She's in the best hands we could find, bud."

"Yeah, thanks, I appreciate it."

Kruger sat in the waiting room and greeted Vance with a handshake. "Hey, boss."

"I'm guessing you two have some idea of who's responsible for Saneh's condition?"

Bishop met his steely gaze. "We've got a few leads to chase down."

"I know you want vengeance, Bish, but now ain't the time. Saneh needs you. We'll mount an op to deal with these shit-kickers once we've got her safe and stable in the UAE."

"You'll do that? Even with the CIA after us?"

Vance nodded. "They messed with our family."

"Kruger and I can lay the groundwork," said Bishop.

"No, this can wait till we're ready. You roll now and you're on your own with no gear and no intel. I'll get Chua and Flash to dig up all the dirt and then we'll take 'em out together."

"Yeah, I guess you're right. Kruger and I will grab our gear and meet you at the airport. Are you OK to take care of things at this end?"

"Yeah." Vance's voice softened. "Do what you need to do, buddy."

***

KENNETH KAUNDA INTERNATIONAL AIRPORT, LUSAKA

Vance watched as Doctor Anderson and his staff handed over Saneh to the medical team he had brought from Abu Dhabi. She looked so delicate and frail strapped to a gurney with medical staff swarming around her; a dark contrast to the energetic PRIMAL operative he'd known for nearly five years. He still remembered the day she had joined the team. Bishop, in typical fashion, had rescued her from certain death at the hands of her Iranian masters. Vance admitted he'd been dubious about recruiting the beautiful intelligence operative into PRIMAL. However, his doubts had been laid to rest as Saneh had proven her mettle time and time again. She had quickly won over the team of former intelligence and military operatives and become an integral part of the family.

He waited as they lifted her inside the Gulfstream. The medevac aircraft was one of the most advanced air ambulances in the world. Had Tariq not owned the jet it would have cost close to half a million dollars to charter. A price Vance would have paid personally to ensure she received the best care available. He saw Saneh as a daughter and that meant the fragile life inside her was the closest thing to a grandchild he would ever have.

Satisfied she was safely inside, Vance scanned the airport for any sign of Bishop. He checked his watch; they were scheduled to take off within a few minutes.

"Sir, we are ready to go," the steward said sticking his head out the door.

"OK, buddy, I'll be right up."

As he pulled his phone out to call Bishop it vibrated with a text message.

Enroute to Mombasa. Objective is Mamba Mboya. Will report once target is neutralized. Have Sandpit identify follow-up targets.

He tried to call but the phone rang out. This was exactly what he was afraid of. Saneh was the only thing that had been keeping Bishop from coming undone. She was his anchor, and now with her life hanging in the balance he would let his rage consume him.

As Vance climbed the stairs he tried to ring Kruger.

"Sir, you're going to have to power your device down before take off," said the steward.

"Will do." He stared at the screen as the call rang out again.

"Sir, we need to secure the door."

"OK." Vance turned off the phone and took his seat at the front of the jet. As he strapped in he glanced over his shoulder at the medical staff preparing Saneh for takeoff. "Come on, girl," he whispered. "Come back to us before that man of yours gets himself killed."

***

MOMBASA, KENYA

Mamba threw his backpack on the bench and wrenched open the refrigerator. Pulling a beer from the shelf he twisted the lid off and poured the ice-cold amber liquid down his throat. "Twenty two hours in the back of that piece of shit pickup. That cheap chink Zhou better pony up the rest of the cash." He flung the empty bottle at the corner of the warehouse where it shattered.

He and Kogo had abandoned the shot-up four-wheel drive twenty miles from Luangwa where they had set fire to it burning their weapons and Colin's body. Kogo had haggled with a local farmer and purchased a battered single-cab truck with a missing passenger seat. Somehow the dilapidated vehicle had carried them the thousand miles across pot-holed highways back to Mombasa.

"My back is stiffer than a baboon's cock," said Mamba as he reached for another beer.

"I wouldn't mind one of those."

"What, a baboon's cock?" Mamba laughed as he tossed his assistant a bottle and slammed the refrigerator door. He put his own bottle on the bench and unzipped the backpack. Inside, wrapped in plastic, was the bloodied rhino horn. "There she is, seven hundred grand's worth of horn."

"It cost four men their lives," said Kogo.

Mamba snorted. "We can always get more men. Which reminds me, we've got a shipment due out in three days and we're short. You need to find some shooters and get us more ivory."

"There's not enough time."

"If we don't make weight it's coming out of your cut." Mamba flashed him a smile and took another swig from the beer.

"I'll find the men."

"Yeah, that's more like it." He inspected the horn before placing it on the bench. "Throw it in the safe. I'm going to go sleep. Don't wake me unless the place is burning down."

"Should we let the families know?"

"What fucking families?"

"Colin and the brothers."

Mamba spat on the floor. "You're an idiot, Kogo. What are you going to tell them? That they died poaching black rhino? If they don't report us to the police they'll come after us for their share of the loot. No, they can all go to hell. They knew the risks."

"OK, I will find more poachers."

Mamba pushed open the door to his office. "And get me a new four-wheel drive."

Kogo picked up the phone on the bench. "Yes, boss."

"Something nice."

***

ZAMBIA - TANZANIA BORDER

Bishop drove up to the checkpoint and handed their passports to the border guard. Both he and Kruger waited silently while the khaki-uniformed official inspected the documents. He watched another AK-wielding guard through the windshield as the man gave the battered Mazda hatchback the once over. Dom had helped them buy the car in Lusaka before driving Kruger's truck, with their weapons, back to the National Park.

"What will you be doing in Tanzania?" the guard asked.

"We're just passing through to Kenya."

"And what will you be doing there?"

"We're heading out to the game parks to take some photos."

He peered in through the back window. "Where's your camera gear?"

"Camera gear?"

Kruger leaned across. "Our bags were stolen in Zambia, *ja,* along with our hire car. Our insurance people have arranged for replacement equipment to meet us in Mombasa."

The guard handed back the two passports and directed them to drive through. Bishop gave him a nod of thanks, started the car, and they crossed into Tanzania.

"I should have thought more about our cover," he said as they accelerated along the highway.

"You've got a bit on your mind."

"We could have borrowed some gear from Christina."

"It's all good. My man in Mombasa, he can get us anything we need."

"Guns?"

"Guns, tanks, intel, choppers, he can provide anything for the right price."

"Good, we're going to need someone who can give us access to the underbelly of the town."

"My man will get us in." Kruger fished his phone from his pocket. It was vibrating and flashing. "It's Vance again, do you want me to answer?"

Bishop shook his head. “No, he's just going to try to talk us down. I'm not turning back now.

“In for a penny, in for a pound,” said Kruger as he terminated the call and switched off the handset. “We've got at least another fifteen hours of driving before we reach Mombasa. You sure you don't want me to take over?”

“I'll drive for a few more hours then we can swap.”

“OK.” Kruger laid his seat back and tipped his cap low. “Let me know when you want to change.”

A few minutes later the South African was snoring gently. Bishop stared intently at the road as they raced along the highway toward Kenya. He doubted he could sleep if he wanted to. He was driven by a thirst for revenge, a burning desire to make Mamba Mboya pay for the pain he had inflicted.

CHAPTER 5

BAREEN HOSPITAL, ABU DHABI

Vance paced the hospital corridor as he waited for the neurosurgeon to finish his initial assessment. To say he was uneasy was an understatement. There was every chance the specialist had bad news. A combat veteran, Vance had seen hard men felled with a blow to the head far less severe than Saneh's injury. At least the hospital itself reassured him. It was one of the most advanced medical facilities in the Middle East; funded by Emirati oil and equipped with cutting-edge technology. Tariq had arranged for a team of the brightest medical professionals available. He had gone so far as to dispatch a private jet to the UK to bring in a world authority on brain trauma and coma.

Vance turned as the door to Saneh's room opened and a nurse appeared. "You can go in now, sir."

He gave her a nod and stepped inside the pristine white room. A doctor stood next to Saneh's bed checking the readout attached to the wall. He looked to be comparing the information against the tablet in his hands.

"What's her status, doc?"

Doctor Edwards turned to Vance. "I'm sorry to keep you waiting."

"Is she going to live?"

Edwards frowned. "The question is not will she live. It is whether or not she will come out of her comatose state."

"That's what I meant."

He gestured to the seat in the corner of the room. "Would you like to sit down?"

Vance shook his head. "No, give it to me straight."

"OK." He paused. "Saneh suffered a highly traumatic head injury that inflicted significant bruising to her brain. The shock is what put her in a coma. There is a chance, once the bruising subsides, she could regain consciousness on her own. However, I want to warn you. I've seen a lot of cases where people never wake up."

Vance sighed. "And the child?"

"She is perfectly safe."

His eyebrows shot up. "It's a girl?"

"Yes, we had to do a detailed ultrasound."

Tears welled in his eyes. "She wants a girl."

"I'm not going to lie. The prognosis for Saneh is not great. I give her a thirty percent chance that she will come to of her own accord."

He swallowed and wiped a tear from the corner of his eye. "We can't improve those odds?"

"Yes, it's very expensive but we can significantly improve the odds."

"Money is not an issue," said an almost regal voice from behind them.

Tariq Ahmed strode in, impeccably dressed in a navy pinstripe suit with a crisp white shirt and a red tie. He held a huge bouquet of vibrant orange gerberas in one hand and had a book tucked under his arm. With his dark features and perfectly manicured beard he looked every part the modern Arab sheik. "Hello, Vance."

Vance gave him a nod. "Tariq."

The doctor extended his hand. "Mr. Ahmed, it's a pleasure."

Tariq shook the doctor's hand. "You were about to explain how we could improve Saneh's odds."

"Yes, I've been working on a new treatment that may significantly improve her chances of recovery. There's only one issue..."

"And that is?"

"The treatment may have adverse effects on the child."

Vance frowned. "What do you mean by adverse?"

"The drugs stimulate the body. They increase cognitive function but there is a chance it could terminate the pregnancy."

"So our choice is between the baby and Saneh?"

The doctor nodded. "My team still need to conduct some more tests but we should be able to start treatment within the next twenty-four hours. After that, every day you delay the choice the chances of saving her decrease." He paused. "Gentlemen, I realize this is a heavy decision. I'm going to leave you to discuss the options. If you need me to talk through any of the details I will be in my office."

Tariq thanked the doctor as he left the room. Vance stood by the bed and gazed at Saneh.

"Have you been able to contact Bishop?" asked Tariq.

"No, he and Kruger have gone after a poacher in Mombasa and we don't have comms."

"This is not a decision I am comfortable making without his consultation."

"Yeah, this is his decision to make," said Vance.

"However, if we cannot communicate with him then he cannot make it in a timely fashion. That in turn could cost Saneh her life."

"When he checks in he can make the decision."

"And if he doesn't?" Tariq said as he laid the flowers on a side table.

"We'll cross that hurdle when we get to it."

"Have you spoken to the rest of the team?" Tariq asked as he lowered himself into a chair.

Vance shook his head. "No, I came straight here."

"You should go. They will want to know how Saneh is faring and you need to get onto Bishop." He pulled a pair of wire-framed reading glasses from his suit and donned them. Then he opened his book and began reading to Saneh.

***

PRIMAL HEADQUARTERS (THE SANDPIT), ABU DHABI

PRIMAL had started life as a small team of former intelligence and special operations operatives. Initially based out of a hangar at Abu Dhabi International Airport, it soon grew into a sizable organization enabled with customized aircraft, advanced weaponry, and intelligence assets.

It had been Tariq Ahmed who found the vigilante organization a home on an isolated island in the South West Pacific. From there Vance and his team had waged a relentless war on injustice for five long years. But, like all good things, it had come to an end. A potential compromise by an element of the CIA had forced them to abandon their island lair and shut down operations. Most of the PRIMAL operatives were now on leave until further notice. With orders to maintain a low profile and avoid compromise, they had handed in their signature equipment: iPRIMAL secure smartphones and state-of-the-art military-grade weaponry.

Now, the only part of the organization that remained active was an intelligence monitoring post based in Abu Dhabi. Vance and three others had moved to a luxury villa in an island resort for the sole purpose of making sure no one was hunting them.

Vance dropped his backpack in the tiled hall, strode through the open-plan living area and up a staircase to where two bedrooms had been converted into offices. When he opened the door to the makeshift operations center there were two men sitting at the computer terminals.

"Hey boss, how's Saneh doing?" asked Frank, a former British paratrooper and one of PRIMAL's operations officers.

"Not good, bud."

"Is there anything we can do?" asked the other man in the room. James Castle, or Ice, was one of the original founders of PRIMAL. Tall and broad-shouldered with short blonde hair and a heavily scarred face, he had only recently re-joined the team. Presumed KIA on a mission in Afghanistan, the badly injured ex-CIA operative had been captured by US forces and spent four years in captivity. PRIMAL had rescued him from a CIA black site in Alaska and he'd spent the last few months regaining his strength and adapting to life with a prosthetic forearm and lower leg.

"Yeah, it's imperative that I talk to Bishop."

Frank shrugged. "Boss, there's nothing we can do. They're not answering their phones and since they're probably in Mombasa by now they'll be using a local number. We've got to wait for one of them to contact us."

"Damn it. I'm going to see what the intel guys can do." As Vance walked out Ice rose from his chair and followed him to the corridor. He moved with ease despite the fact that his right leg, from just below the knee, was carbon fiber and titanium.

"Hey, Vance, can I have a quick word?"

They stopped outside the door to the intel room. "What's up, brother?"

"If there's a job going downrange I want in."

"Don't know if there's going to be a gig, bud. We'll let the intel team do their thing and see if there are any targets worth hitting once Bishop's done."

"Yeah, but if there is a job."

"You think you're ready?"

Ice nodded. "The gear Mitch has hooked me up with is state-of-the-art. I can shoot and move as well as I ever could."

He had to admit that Ice's recovery was impressive. The former Marine was now physically more imposing than he remembered, and with the artificial limbs he resembled something from a Terminator movie. He made a mental note to find out what supplements he was using. "I'll keep it in mind."

"Thanks, bro."

Vance left him in the corridor and stepped into the room being used by their Chief of Intelligence, Chen Chua, and his offsider, Flash.

Chua, a lightly-built Chinese American looked up from his laptop. "How's Saneh?" he asked as Vance dropped into a spare seat.

He shook his head. "Doesn't look good. There's a new treatment that might help, but we could potentially lose either her or the baby."

Chua grimaced. "You're kidding."

"No, Bishop needs to make the decision, if we can get comms with him. What's Flash up to?"

"He's working up the intel on this poaching guy, Mamba."

"What've you got so far?"

"His real name is David Mboya, a former Ugandan military officer. Smart guy, trained by the Brits, and reported to have an exemplary service record."

Vance raised his eyebrows. "Not your average dirt-bag criminal then."

"I'm sure Bish and Kruger will have no trouble dealing with him. What Flash and I are working on is the Chinese angle. We're trying to find out who Mamba supplies."

"Good, can you also have him focus on establishing comms with Bish?"

"Not a problem. Flash has already pulled data off Kruger's sat phone."

"Yeah?"

"It's currently inactive but he last used it in Zambia the night Saneh was shot."

"And?"

"Looks like he and Bish followed up the poachers. Before they met you at the hospital they'd covered over thirty miles on foot."

Vance shook his head. "Why does that not surprise me. Let's hope that goddamn crazy Aussie finishes Mamba before it's too late."

Silence filled the room as Vance stared into space, his thoughts back with Saneh at the hospital.

"You doing alright, Vance?"

He shook his head. "No, when we started PRIMAL I always knew we would lose people. But, I thought as long as we're doing good in the world it would be a sacrifice worth making. I never thought we'd face a decision like this."

"What are we going to do if we can't raise Bishop?"

He sighed. "I don't know, bud. I really don't know."

***

MOMBASA, KENYA

"Not bad," said Bishop as he stood beside Kruger in the foyer of the New Palm Tree Hotel. The building looked well maintained and hospitable. He noticed the white walls had been freshly painted and the staff were dressed in clean, pressed uniforms.

"Don't get too excited, once we dump our gear we're going to head down to Mtongwe."

"Tong what?"

"Suburb a few miles south of the harbor. Total shit hole."

As they crossed a terracotta-tiled courtyard Bishop caught a whiff of frangipani and his heart lurched. The fragrant white flower was one of Saneh's favorites.

The room was cramped but clean with two single beds, a desk, and a wardrobe. An antique box TV sat on a stand in the corner. Bishop tossed his bag on a bed. "You good to go?"

Kruger shook his head. "No. You need a shower. You stink."

"I don't care. We need to get out there and find this Mamba fucker."

"Relax, Toppie is making some discreet inquiries."

"Your dodgy mate?"

"Yeah, Mamba won't be hard to find."

"What about weapons?"

"He can hook us up with everything we need. How much cash do you have on you?"

Bishop took out his wallet and handed over some notes. "I've got more in my backpack." He emptied his clothes out of the bag and used a knife to slice open the lining. He pulled out a thick wad of US dollars and tossed it to Kruger.

"This is a good start but we're going to need more. There's a bank around the corner. I'll see to it and get us a local phone to use. Get yourself cleaned up, *ja*."

"OK, I'll sort you out later."

Kruger shrugged. “I'll get Vance to cover it.” The big man tossed a room key on the bed. “I'll be half an hour at the most.” He disappeared through the door leaving Bishop alone with his pile of clothes.

For the first time since Saneh had been shot he felt tired. Checking his watch he saw it was only a little past midday. Laying back on the bed he contemplated calling Vance to check on Saneh. No, he needed to stay focused on the job at hand. He would take a five-minute nap then shower. As he drifted off his thoughts turned to killing the man called Mamba Mboya.

***

As Bishop slept, the man he wanted to kill sharpened his machete not more than two miles away. “What’s going on with my new poaching crew?” he asked as he tested the edge of the blade with his thumb. His eyes narrowed and he picked up his beer, took a swig, and dripped some of the amber liquid on the sharpening stone.

Kogo grimaced at the sound of the blade dragging across the stone. “I've put the word out.”

“I don't want any gang-banging scum. Get me ex-military guys. The cops are cracking down on poachers. I'm not taking chances with idiots.”

“That makes it harder, boss.”

He stopped sharpening and fixed Kogo with a glare. “You fuck this up and–”

The shrill ring of the phone on the bench interrupted him. He picked it up and held it to his ear. “What?”

“Have you got the horn?” Zhou asked.

“Yes, but it cost us.”

“How so?”

“We ran into trouble and lost four men.”

“But you will still be able to make the shipment, yes?”

“We're a few tusks short.” Mamba tucked the phone under his ear, picked up his assault vest from where it lay on the bench, and slid the machete back in its scabbard. "But, I have a plan. You'll get what you requested."

"I better, I have clients who will be less than impressed if we don't deliver."

"Don't threaten me, Zhou. I can find new buyers for the ivory and the horn."

"I've already paid a deposit."

"And like I said, it will all be there." Mamba slammed the phone back on the cradle. "Send that whining chink a photo of the horn." He stormed across to a battered SUV that was parked facing the warehouse doors and flung his vest on the back seat. Then he grabbed a compact chainsaw from the bench and placed it in with his equipment. "I'm heading up to Mbale for a couple of days to get more ivory. I want you to find new men and poach elephant at Tsavo."

"By myself?"

"No, you idiot. I said find new men. Take the recruits and use it as a test." He climbed in the driver's seat. "Now, open the fucking doors before I miss my flight."

Kogo slid the warehouse doors open and watched as the vehicle disappeared down the street. When the doors were shut he chained them and walked through to the office. The room was as run-down as the rest of the building. A single bare light bulb hung over a metal desk. Behind it sat an old bank safe. He unlocked it with a brass key and swung the heavy door open. Inside were two shelves, the bottom stacked with wads of US dollars. It was a mere morsel of the fortune Mamba had made poaching. On the top shelf lay the rhino horn wrapped in plastic. As he grabbed it the stench of rotting flesh made him gag.

He locked the safe and took the horn back into the warehouse. It was hard to believe someone was willing to pay hundreds of thousands of dollars for such an ugly object, he thought. Opening a drawer in the bench he took out a wire brush, scalpel, and a box knife. He'd become quite adept at removing flesh from elephant tusks and rhino horns. Not a pleasant job but it had its perks. Mamba gave him an extra hundred dollars per item. Once he'd prepared the horn he would take photos and email them to Zhou. Then he needed to find a new team and plan their mission to Tsavo.

***

SHANGHAI, CHINA

Fan Wei was overseeing the preparation of her master's dinner when the phone in her pocket vibrated. Rinsing her hands she left the chef to continue as she checked the message. Zhou had sent her photos of the horn. Walking into a tiny office she opened her email account and hit print on the photos. As the printer hummed she opened her favorite luxury goods website and checked the price on a bag she had her eye on. If the horn turned out to be exactly what Wang Hejun wanted her bonus would be significant. She might even be able to afford some new earrings as well. She collected the images from the printer, slipped them in a folder, and carried them through the penthouse apartment. At the door of Hejun's study she knocked and waited.

"Enter."

She pushed the door open and spotted the billionaire at his desk reading. "Sir, I have photos of the black rhino horn." She stepped forward and held them out.

Hejun raised his eyes from the book. "Only photos? Where is the horn?" He snatched the folder and emptied it on his desk.

"It is still in Africa. It will leave by ship on Friday and should arrive early next week."

He grunted as he adjusted his glasses and stared intently at the images. "It is a fine horn. What are we paying for it?"

"A little under 6 million yuan."

He nodded. "A fair price. When it arrives I will collect it in person."

"Very good, sir."

He pushed the photos to one side and refocused his attention on the book. "That is all." He dismissed her with a wave of his hand.

On her way back to the kitchen Fan smiled as she visualized the outfit that would match her new bag and earrings. Working for Hejun may be a chore but at least it paid well.

CHAPTER 6

KENYA

Bishop gazed out the window of the Mazda as Kruger drove them along the highway south from Mombasa. The road was lined with ramshackle tin-roofed stalls selling everything from local farm produce to nappies, plastic buckets, and flip-flops. The contrast between this area and Mombasa Island was stark. Once they had crossed on the ferry into the suburb of Likoni the hotels and resorts were replaced with a vast shantytown stretching as far as the eye could see.

Bishop spotted a sign advertising energy drinks and contemplated asking Kruger to pull over. The half-hour nap he'd inadvertently taken instead of showering had left him feeling worse for wear. What's more he still wore the same clothes and wouldn't have a chance to shower till they got back to the hotel later that evening.

"So the guy we're going to meet," Kruger said interrupting his thoughts. "Toppie, he's a bit strange, *ja*."

"How so?"

"He worked with me in the Recces back in the day."

"An operator?"

"No, company quartermaster before they kicked him out."

"What for?"

"Making a little on the side selling equipment."

"Right, so he's an entrepreneur."

"No, Toppie's a nut job. After they booted him from the Regiment he set up here in Kenya. Hooks people up with things they need."

"Like guns?"

"Of course. He's got a thing for Soviet-era kit, but if he likes you then he can get whatever you want. Not just weapons: intel, contacts, anything…"

"And if he doesn't like you?"

"Then you're proper fucked." Kruger laughed.

"Great." Bishop turned his attention back to the roadside. Patches of bush grew between the dilapidated shacks. Within a few miles the landscape turned to savannah with scrubby bushes and long grass.

Kruger turned them off the highway and the hatchback rattled and bounced along a rutted dirt road for a mile or two more before they reached a sandy track. A few hundred yards further and he brought them to a halt.

"What the hell is this?" Bishop stared at the fortress blocking their path in disbelief. It resembled something from a Mad Max movie. Thick steel plated gates towered over them. On either side an earthen bank was topped with coils of barbed wire. In front of the banks an eight-foot deep ditch was impassable to vehicles. "This guy really doesn't like house calls."

"Like I said, he's a bit strange." Kruger stepped out of the car.

He watched as Kruger picked up an old military wire phone bolted to the gate frame, spun the handle, and spoke into the handset. The gates gave a groan and swung slowly open revealing the road beyond.

"Bat shit crazy," said Kruger as he drove them up the driveway.

"Is he some kind of apocalypse survival prepper?" Bishop spotted no less than five sandbagged fighting positions as they followed the track through the scrub. As they came around a corner they passed another earthen bank. On the far side they approached a Soviet-era vehicle graveyard.

"BRDM, BTR, T-55." Bishop rattled off the names of the armored vehicles parked in the clearing. The better part of a Russian military museum lined either side of the track. "Is that an old An-2 Colt?" He pointed at the tail of an aircraft protruding from a curved corrugated iron hangar. Behind it a dirt airstrip stretched out into the bush.

"That's Annie, his pride and joy," Kruger replied as he parked the car in front of a pile of stacked shipping containers. "Don't get out of the car yet."

It took him a moment to realize the steel boxes had been welded together to form a building. There were windows, doors, vents, and a satellite dish perched on top.

A pack of dogs exploded around the corner barking furiously. "Shit!" The animals looked like clones of Kruger's dog, Princess; massive brown hunting hounds with lean muscular bodies and huge square heads filled with razor-sharp teeth. They jumped up against the car barking loudly and rocking the little Mazda.

A shrill whistle rang out and the dogs disappeared back in the direction they had come from.

"OK, now we're good."

As they alighted from the hatchback a short figure appeared from the hangar and strode purposefully toward them. "Kruger, that you, boy?"

The man walking toward them was almost as wide as he was tall with a long gray scruffy beard reaching to his belt. He wore jeans, cowboy boots, and a leather vest that would have been at home on one of the Village People. A pistol belt topped off his outfit and Bishop identified a modern FN Five-Seven on his hip.

"*Ja,* Toppie, it's me." Kruger took the quartermaster's hand and shook it.

"How's that hound of yours?"

"Princess, she's doing good."

Toppie turned to face Bishop and he felt the gray eyes giving him the once over. "This your friend? The one with the girlfriend who's sleeping because of that scum bag Mamba?"

"That's him."

Toppie stuck out his hand and Bishop grasped it. "Any friend of Kruger's is probably a fucking asshole." He grinned showing a set of yellow teeth. "But, aren't we all?"

Bishop forced a smile.

"Now, what do you need?"

"Weapons, ammo, and everything you know about Mamba and his operations," said Bishop.

Toppie sucked his gums as he contemplated the request. "Any chance you boys have already had a crack at Mamba?"

"Maybe. Why's that?"

"Because he's got this second-in-command, a Kenyan called Kogo, and the weaselly little prick is asking around for poachers. Rumor has it they got slapped around pretty bad down in Zambia."

Bishop shot Kruger a glance and he nodded. "Any chance you can arrange an introduction?"

"Depends?"

"On what?"

Toppie grinned again. "On how much cash you got."

"Money isn't a problem."

"Then I might know a guy. Now come and have a look at this." Toppie gestured for them to follow him to the hangar. As they approached the rusted shell Bishop spotted a number of shipping containers buried under a mound of dirt. Their scruffy host unlocked one of them, wrenched the doors open, and switched on a light.

"Sweet mother of Jesus," murmured Bishop.

The walls of the container were lined with weapons. Assault rifles, sniper rifles, sub-machine guns, pistols, rocket launchers, and machine guns, Toppie had them all.

The gray-bearded quartermaster turned to face them, his yellowed teeth exposed in a broad smile. "Welcome to Toppie's cave of carnage."

Bishop took an R5 off the wall and inspected it. "You got ammo and a couple of chest rigs, Toppie?"

"Do hippos shit in the river?"

"Yes they do." Bishop took a near mint-condition Browning High-Power pistol from the wall and checked the action. "They certainly do."

***

MBALE, UGANDA

Mamba paid the pilot with a wad of cash and opened the door of the Cessna light aircraft. Grabbing his gear from behind the seat he shrugged on his assault vest as he set off across the tarmac with the chainsaw in hand. A team of camouflage-uniformed men was waiting next to a white military Bell 412 helicopter.

"David, it is good to see you." The man who greeted Mamba by his Christian name wore the rank of a full colonel on the shoulders of his fatigues.

"You too." Mamba hugged his older brother and handed him a small bag filled with diamonds. "You've saved my skin with this one."

"Anything for family, David." The colonel turned to his aircrew as he slipped the bag into his pocket and gave them the signal to start the helicopter's engines. "Let's go hunting."

"Did you bring my gun?"

The colonel flashed a smile. "Of course I did."

Twenty minutes later the helicopter thundered over Mount Elgon National Park with the side doors open. Mamba sat in one of the side seats with a headset on and a M60 machine gun resting across his knees.

"We've only got an hour's flying time," said the colonel as they swept in low over a river and followed it north.

"It's getting dark, they'll move down to drink. We stay on the river."

"OK, but if we don't find any within thirty minutes we'll have to head back."

Mamba gave his brother thumbs-up as he scanned the banks of the river. He spotted a tour group and ignored their waves. A few miles further he found what he was searching for, a small herd of elephants on the floodplain. "Down there," he transmitted over the radio.

"Roger." The pilot banked the helicopter and circled around. The elephants raised their heads and ran from the noisy intruder.

"Come in low over the top." Mamba yanked back the cocking handle on the M60. The elephants seemed to know his intent and made a beeline for the trees. He smiled and aimed at a large bull as it turned and raised its trunk in a challenge.

The M60 roared and bucked against his shoulder as he sent a line of tracer into the bull. The elephant staggered falling behind from the rest of the pack. Mamba continued to fire, pumping round after round into the wounded beast. It dropped to its knees as he emptied the last of the one hundred round belt. "Take us down," he ordered as the weapon ran dry and smoke streamed off its barrel.

The pilot brought the helicopter down to a hover as Mamba reloaded the machine gun and slung his chainsaw over his shoulder. He dropped down onto the grass and moved cautiously toward the bull.

The groan of the dying animal was music to his ears. Setting the M60 on the ground he started the chainsaw. The sharp teeth ripped through the elephant's flesh as he cut through to the base of the tusks. When he'd exposed as much ivory as possible he sliced through the tusk and let it drop to the ground. Letting the saw idle he wiped sweat from his brow.

As he ripped into the other tusk an angry bellow caught his attention. Turning toward the noise he saw a massive elephant charging through the grass. "Holy shit." The tusks were lowered and he leaped to one side. It thundered past and he dropped the saw, diving for the machine gun. "Fuck." The weapon had been crushed under the charging beast's massive feet.

He spun toward the threat; it was a female elephant. She had turned to the corpse of her mate and prodded him with her trunk. Snorting in rage she looked up and charged again. As Mamba turned to run there was a burst of gunfire. He dropped to the ground and watched as his brother emptied an entire magazine into the skull of the animal. She died with a bellow hitting the ground with a thud.

The colonel offered his hand to Mamba and pulled him to his feet. "You're getting careless, David."

He dusted off his clothes and picked up the saw. "Maybe, but at least now I've got two sets of tusks."

"Always about the bottom dollar."

"Someone has to keep your wife in all her fancy clothes."

The colonel laughed and slapped him on the shoulder. "Just hurry up, the sun will set soon."

"Still scared of the dark, big brother?" Mamba asked as he went back to work on the first elephant.

"No, I'm scared of my pilots trying to fly in the dark."

He chopped the other tusk free from the bull, dumped it next to the crushed M60, and strode across to work on the cow. "I think you're afraid of missing dinner with your wife. She's got you by the balls." He grinned as he revved the chainsaw and sliced the dead female elephant's face open.

***

MOMBASA, KENYA

"This is the address," said Kruger as he pulled the Mazda into a poorly lit gravel parking lot.

The headlights lit up a half-dozen other vehicles including a police car. Behind the parking lot a corrugated fence topped with barbed wire was strung with colored party lights. From inside the car they could hear vibrant music.

"Looks inviting," Bishop said dryly as he double-checked the Browning pistol he'd purchased from Toppie, and tucked it into the waistband of his pants.

"Hey, it's not too bad by African standards."

"I'm not sure how comfortable I am leaving all our gear in the trunk." In addition to the pistol Toppie had sold them assault rifles, ammo, and chest rigs similar to what they had left in Zambia.

"They'll be fine." Kruger parked next to the police car.

They checked the gear was concealed in bags, locked the hatchback, and entered the drinking establishment through an open gate in the iron fence. What lay beyond surprised Bishop.

The fence hid a beer garden that looked far more inviting than the exterior suggested. Long wooden benches sat on a terracotta-tiled terrace with a web of vines forming a roof above them. The party lights illuminated the customers sitting on benches devouring plates of ribs. "You sure this is the right place? Toppie gave me the impression it was a shit hole."

"This is the address. We need to ask for a guy called Steve."

"Steve?"

Kruger shrugged as he strode to the bar. Made from polished hardwood it displayed an impressive collection of spirits on softly lit glass shelves. In an adjoining dining hall there were more benches and patrons enjoying dinner.

Bishop's stomach grumbled. "How about we grab some of those ribs?"

Kruger waved over the bartender, a middle-aged woman with an apron tied around her ample waist. "Can we order a couple of beers and some ribs?"

She smiled. "Sure thing, honey."

"Can you also tell Steve that Aden and Kruger are here to see him," added Bishop.

Her smile faded and she focused on pouring them two locally brewed ales.

"Seems Steve's not real popular around here," Bishop said as they took a seat. He took a sip of the beer and sighed. "God, I needed that."

"You also need a shower." Kruger took a swig of his own beer as a waitress appeared with a massive plate of pork ribs. "That was quick."

They ate with their hands devouring the meat in a matter of minutes. When they were done the waitress reappeared with a bowl of lemon-scented water and hand towels. "Mr. Hanna will see you now." She led them around the bar through a service door. The staff paid them no attention as they walked through the kitchen and out into a corridor. "Wait here." She knocked twice on a door before leaving.

Bishop rested his hand on the pistol concealed under his T-shirt.

The door opened and a tall middle-aged Caucasian with thick dark hair waved them inside. "Sorry to keep you waiting, gentlemen. I hope you enjoyed your dinner." He had a strong South African accent.

"Top notch," replied Kruger. "I assume you are Steve."

"That's correct. Please take a seat." He sat behind his desk. "I want to apologize in advance for this meeting being short. I have a lot of business to take care of tonight before I go home to see my children. Now, I understand from Toppie you're both ex-South African military and looking for work."

"*Ja*, we've got a bit of expertise in the bush, tracking and the like."

Steve scribbled something on a notepad. "Very good, those are skills I can sell."

"We'd like to make some real money," added Bishop with a South African accent of his own. "If you get what we mean."

"Oh, I think I do. Where are you staying?"

Bishop hesitated.

Steve smiled. "No, nothing sinister, I've got someone I want you to meet."

"We're at the New Palm Tree Hotel," said Kruger.

"Ah very nice, a friend of mine owns it. Make sure you mention my name when you check out, OK?"

"Sounds good."

Steve rose, reached out, and shook their hands. "It is very nice to meet friends of Toppie. Him and I go back a long way."

"He's a good man," said Kruger.

Steve laughed. "He's a lunatic. Anyway, I hope I can help you to find something. So you know, the deal will be I take twenty percent of everything you make."

"Fifteen," said Bishop.

"Twenty is customary."

"Maybe for criminals and petty thieves. We're neither."

Steve nodded. "OK, we've got a deal, fifteen percent. Gentlemen, it has been short but still a pleasure. Feel free to enjoy more food and drink. Have as much you wish, it's on the house." He gestured to the door.

Bishop and Kruger left the office and made their way back through the kitchen to the bar. Kruger ordered two more beers and another plate of ribs. They sat in a corner away from the other customers. "What do you think?" he asked Bishop.

"A lot more professional than I expected."

"Yeah, Toppie had me thinking we were meeting with a crime boss."

"I get the feeling Toppie lives on a different planet to everyone else."

"That's true."

"Let's finish up here and get back to the hotel. I want to take a shower and get my head down."

"Might be an idea to check in with Vance, *ja.*"

For the first time in the last few hours Bishop's thoughts turned to Saneh. He felt guilty that he'd lost himself in the mission and forgotten about her. "Yeah, maybe."

***

As Bishop and Kruger finished their beers Kogo ate takeout at the bench in the warehouse. His plans were not progressing well. So far he'd only recruited one new member to the team; a bush meat poacher living in the slums of Likoni. The man could hardly be called capable. His only virtue; he knew every inch of Tsavo. Two men were not enough but he was reluctant to postpone the mission. The idea of disappointing Mamba terrified him.

The phone on the bench rang, interrupting his meal. He snatched it from the cradle. "Hello."

"Kogo, is that you?"

"Yes, who is this?"

"It's Steve, I've got two men for you. Former South African military, they've got the skills you want, and they're clean."

"You sure?"

"Yes, they're not police informants. They come highly recommended from a source I trust."

"You sure?"

"The men are staying at the New Palm Tree Hotel. You can check them out for yourself. They're under the name Aden. Oh, and I get fifteen percent of whatever they make."

"You will have to discuss that with Mamba."

"I'm discussing it with you."

"Fine, if I use them you get fifteen percent."

"Deal. Let me know if you need anything else."

"A hundred pounds of ivory."

Steve laughed. "Your game, not mine." He hung up.

Kogo contemplated the offer then grabbed his keys. If these men were suitable his mission tomorrow could still go ahead.

***

Bishop struggled to stay awake as Kruger pulled the Mazda into a parking space at their hotel. He checked his watch; it was nearly midnight and they had been on the go for almost 72 hours.

"You look and smell like shit," said Kruger as he stepped out of the car. "If you don't take a shower soon I'm going to hose you down."

"Thanks mate, good to know you've got my back."

As they unloaded their bags of gear Bishop noticed a new model Toyota Land Cruiser parked nearby. The expensive truck was fully fitted out: roof racks, spare tires, jerry can holders, and spotlights. Not a common sight in Kenya.

"Aden?" someone said from the shadows.

Kruger dropped his bag and spun toward the voice with a pistol drawn. "Show yourself."

"It's OK, I'm a friend of Steve's." The man walked forward with his hands extended. Lightly built with a shaved head, his coffee-colored skin hinted at a mixed ethnicity. "Can we talk in your room?"

Kruger glanced at Bishop who nodded and they led the man from the parking lot.

"What's your name?" asked Bishop as Kruger opened the door to their room. He knew it wasn't Mamba.

"You can call me Kogo."

Kruger dumped his bags on the floor and gestured for the man to sit on a bed.

"It's late, Kogo, so feel free to get to the point," said Bishop as he pulled the door shut. "We already spoke to Mr. Hanna. Is this the second half of the job interview?"

"Yes, he vouched for you but I wanted to meet in person before I offer you work."

Bishop sat on his bed facing the poacher. "OK. So do you have any questions?"

"Have you hunted elephants before?"

"*Ja*," said Kruger. "We did some work in South Africa but things got a little hot. That's why we're here."

"There's a lot of anti-poaching organizations in South Africa," said Kogo.

"Not so many here," said Bishop. "Hey, let's talk money, we don't come cheap."

Kogo nodded. "The money is good. We'll give you a five percent cut each of the ivory."

"We, who is we?" asked Bishop.

"I work for someone, he authorizes all the details."

"And his name is?"

"You don't need that information at the moment." Kogo got up from the bed. "I will pick you up in the morning. Do you need equipment?"

"Don't bother, we don't work for people who don't have names," said Bishop.

Kogo's brow furrowed and he glanced around the room. "OK, OK, I work for a man called Mamba Mboya."

Bishop fought the urge to grab him by the throat. "Will he be coming with us?"

The poacher shook his head. "No, think of this as a trial. If you prove yourself to me then you will work with Mamba."

"Fair enough. So, we've got our own gear. Where are we going?"

“I'll give you the location in the morning.” Kogo offered Bishop his hand.

“We don't work like that.” Bishop ignored Kogo's attempted handshake. “You either tell us where we're going or you find someone else.”

Kogo glanced nervously at Kruger then back to Bishop. “Tsavo East National Park. Are you familiar with it?”

“No, but we'll do our research. See you in the morning.”

Kogo nodded. “4.30 am. I'll have another man with me who knows the park.”

Bishop opened the door. “See you then.” He waited for the poacher to leave before moving across to the window and watching him climb into the Land Cruiser.

“You looked like you were going to kill him,” said Kruger.

“Wanted to, that slimy prick was probably at Luangwa.” He left the window. “Can I use your local phone?”

“What's up?” Kruger handed him the device.

“I'm going to give Dom a call and see if he knows people at Tsavo. I for one will not be shooting any elephants.”

CHAPTER 7

TSAVO EAST NATIONAL PARK, KENYA

It was a few minutes past eight in the morning when Kogo stopped the Land Cruiser and killed the engine. He glanced in the rear vision mirror and made eye contact with Bishop. "This as far as we can drive."

"Better get cracking then, *ja*." He and Kruger alighted from the four-wheel drive and joined the third man at the back. He was their tracker; a lean bush-meat poacher familiar with Tsavo who spoke very little English. Bishop shrugged on his chest rig and inserted a magazine into his R5 assault rifle. Kruger carried a R1 and had a heavy-caliber double-barreled rifle slung over his shoulder.

"The tracker will lead us to the elephants. He says they will be near the lake a few miles from here." Kogo took a compact chainsaw from the trunk and locked the vehicle. "Kruger will make the kill. I cut the tusks and we leave as fast as we can."

"Is this area heavily patrolled?" asked Bishop as he checked his pouches. The South African-style vest he'd bought off Toppie contained the essentials including water, ammo, a compact pair of binoculars, and a medical kit.

Kogo turned to the tracker and asked him in Swahili.

The man shrugged and rattled off a few sentences.

"Not really," translated Kogo. "There are volunteers patrolling the park but it's big."

"So there's a chance we could bump into a patrol out there."

"It is possible, that's why you have been hired."

"I haven't seen any money yet, champ. I'm not about to go in there and get myself shot on the off-chance your mate here can find us an elephant. How about you cough up some cash up-front?"

Kogo shook his head. "I can't do that."

"Listen, fuckbag, you've dragged us all the way out here because you're desperate. I don't know why but you need tusks and you need them fast. The way I see it you need to pay up-front or cut us in for a bigger slice." Bishop locked eyes with the poacher.

"I can't make that decision."

"You've got a sat phone, call your boss."

Kogo looked to the tracker for support but the man shrugged. He wasn't about to challenge the heavily-armed former soldiers. "OK, fine, I will make the call." He took the satellite phone from his pocket and dialed.

Bishop watched him intently as he waited for the call to pickup. Turning his back Kogo talked in Swahili.

"Do you have a map?" Bishop asked the tracker.

The man shrugged again.

"Do you speak any English?"

The only response was another shrug.

"I guess not." He took the opportunity to check the surroundings. It was a lot like Luangwa: dry red earth, scrubby bushes, and tall thorn trees with sparse cover. It reminded him of Saneh, bloodied and wounded, lying in the dust next to the safari truck. Turning back to Kogo he saw the poacher had finished his call.

"I can't pay you now but we can offer you five thousand dollars each if we return with at least two tusks."

"And if we don't?"

"Then I can pay you a thousand each for your time."

Bishop glanced at Kruger who nodded.

"You've got a deal. But, if you try to screw us you're a dead man."

Kogo swallowed.

"Have you got a map of the area?"

The poacher reached inside his vest, pulled out a folded map, and handed it over. Bishop opened it on the bonnet of the four-wheel drive. "Ask your man where the elephants are."

Kogo spoke to the tracker who leaned over the map and pointed at a smudge of blue.

"The lake. It's a good start. Kruger, we need to plan our route so we avoid patrols."

Kruger pulled out a GPS and checked the map. "We're here." He stabbed a finger at the map. "We can use this creek line to minimize the risk of hitting a patrol. They'll be sticking to the vehicle tracks."

Bishop folded the map and slid it inside his shirt. "I like it. Let's get moving."

As the local tracker and Kogo led the way Kruger hung back, took out his own satellite phone, and sent a text message.

***

THE SANDPIT, ABU DHABI

"Vance, we've got a hit," Flash yelled from the top of the staircase inside PRIMAL's Abu Dhabi headquarters.

"Where is he?" Vance slammed the refrigerator shut and stormed out of the kitchen.

"Kruger just sent a text message over his sat phone. Looks like they're in Kenya."

"Do we have an open line of communications?"

"No, the phone's switched off now."

Vance climbed the stairs and followed Flash into the intel room. "What are they up to?"

Flash returned to his terminal and showed Vance the message. "Check this out. Kruger sent a grid reference to someone in vicinity of North Luangwa National Park. I bet it's the ranger Bishop was hanging out with, Dominic Marks. According to the message the boys are hunting elephants near the lake at Tsavo East National Park."

"And why would they be doing that?" asked Vance.

"It must have something to do with tracking down Mr. Mamba Mboya."

"Find out who Kruger messaged."

"Roger." Flash's fingers danced over the keyboard.

Vance glanced at his watch. "I'm going to head across to the hospital and replace Tariq." The two of them were taking turns watching over Saneh. "Keep me posted."

"Will do."

As he walked downstairs his phone vibrated with an incoming call. "Speak of the devil." It was Tariq.

"Good afternoon, Vance."

"Tariq, I'm on my way in now."

"Doctor Edwards wants to schedule a meeting with us this afternoon. We're running out of time."

Vance sighed. "OK, I'll be there within the hour." He stopped in the kitchen and contemplated pouring a scotch.

"Hey, what's up, big man?" Ice walked into the kitchen with a pistol holstered on his hip.

"I'm about to head to the hospital. How's the training going?" Ice had set up an airsoft range in one half of the villa's garage and had been spending hours practicing weapon manipulation with his robotic hand.

"Not bad, I was wondering if I could come to the hospital with you." He took off the pistol belt and placed it on the bench.

Vance shook his head. "We're trying to keep a low profile, brother. Better if you stayed here with the team."

"Yeah, OK, well if you need to talk I'm always here for you."

"For sure." Vance swallowed hard as he grabbed a set of keys from the bench and strode toward the door.

"Oh and Vance, when it comes time to pull Bishop out of the shit, I'm good to go."

"Let's hope it doesn't come to that. Knocking off a dirt-bag poacher shouldn't be too difficult for Bishop and Kruger."

"We both know what Bish is like."

He managed a smirk. "Yep, goddamn shit magnet."

***

BAREEN HOSPITAL, ABU DHABI

Vance walked slowly along the spotless white corridors as he searched for Doctor Edwards' office. He found it five doors down, exactly where a pretty young nurse had directed him. Pausing with his hand raised to knock on the door he contemplated turning and walking away; leaving the decision that needed to be made to Tariq. In all his years as a paramilitary operative then as the Director of Operations for PRIMAL he had never faced a dilemma like this. Life and death decisions were part of his day-to-day routine but that hadn't prepared him. His shoulders dropped as he knocked.

"Come in."

He pushed the door open and nodded to the man behind his desk. "Hey, Doc."

"Vance." Edwards directed him to take the seat next to Tariq.

The Arab rose and they shook hands.

"Tariq, good to see you, brother." Vance sat and placed his clenched fists on his thighs. "So what's the prognosis?" He didn't really need to ask. The grave expression on Doctor Edwards' face said it all.

"Gentlemen, Saneh's situation has begun to deteriorate. In the last twenty-four hours her brain activity has slowed. I'm afraid we're losing her."

Vance sighed. "What about the baby?"

"I've been consulting with a colleague of mine who is the hospital's leading obstetrician. We concur that as long as we keep Saneh's body alive the child could continue to develop normally. But, there will be an increased risk of complications."

"What kind of complications?" asked Tariq.

"The child could be either mentally or physically impaired. There is also an increased likelihood that Saneh's body might terminate the pregnancy."

"And the alternative?"

"We begin a revolutionary program to stimulate Saneh's brain."

"But there will be an impact on the child."

Doctor Edwards nodded. "The risk remains that, as a side effect of some of the drugs, her body will terminate the pregnancy. This is uncharted territory, I don't know of any other cases where–"

"Can't we use other drugs?" interrupted Vance.

"We can but the chance of recovery is significantly reduced." Edwards placed his hand on a document on the desk. "These are the release papers authorizing the treatment. I'm going to give you a few minutes to discuss the options." He rose and left Vance and Tariq in the office.

"I never thought I'd have to make a decision like this," said Vance.

"You still haven't been able to reach Bishop?"

He shook his head. "No, he's offline still."

"And we've run out of time."

"Yes, we both know what needs to be done."

Tariq's eyes were glassy as he rose from his chair. "We always knew there would be times like this."

"Seems to be a lot of them recently, bud."

Tariq placed a hand on his shoulder. "We're doing the right thing."

"I know."

***

TSAVO EAST NATIONAL PARK, KENYA

Bishop held up his hand signaling the hunting party to halt. Crouching in a thick patch of grass he surveyed the terrain ahead.

Five hundred yards away a meager herd of elephants foraged on a floodplain next to a shallow lake. Upwind, the majestic beasts were oblivious to their presence. Bishop grimaced as he spotted the massive tusks on the bull. Kogo would want them for sure.

He took binoculars from his vest and scanned the trees beyond the floodplain. There was no sign of human activity.

"What's the plan?" asked Kruger kneeling alongside.

He continued scanning the bush. "They should be here. Dom said he would pass on our message to the Kenyan rangers."

"Well they're not, so what are we going to do?"

The grass rustled behind them and Bishop glanced over his shoulder to see Kogo approach.

"What's going on?"

"We're waiting," said Bishop.

"What for? I can see the big bull. Shoot him, we cut off the tusks, and then we go."

"You can run out there if you want." Bishop fixed him with a glare. "Or we can wait and make sure we're not the only ones watching."

The poacher swallowed and gripped his weapon tight. "No, you're right. We should take our time."

Bishop wondered if Kogo had been there the night Saneh was shot. Had he been the man who escaped in the four-wheel drive with Mamba? He imagined dragging his knife across the poacher's throat. Instead he turned his attention back to his binoculars and the floodplain. After a few minutes he turned to Kruger. "How close do you need to get?"

"At least another three hundred yards."

He looked back at Kogo. "You and the tracker wait here. Once we make the kill come forward and take the tusks. Don't move until we shoot. Got it?"

"Yes, of course."

Kruger unslung the double-barreled hunting rifle and cracked open the breech. He checked both the high-powered cartridges and snapped it shut. Tucking the weapon under his arm he slung the R1. "I'm good to go."

"OK, you're on point. I'll hang back a few yards and cover you if needed."

They left the others at the edge of the floodplain and stalked through the grass toward the elephants. "Where the hell are they?" he whispered to himself.

"What are we doing, Bish?" Kruger hissed as he crouched behind a clump of grass only a few hundred yards from the herd, well within range.

A shout sounded from their flank startling the elephants. Bishop turned and spotted figures emerging from the far tree line. There were at least a dozen green-uniformed men swarming toward them. "Right on time." He flicked off the safety and fired a burst over the men. They disappeared as they dove to the ground.

"Let's get the hell out of here. Covering!" Bishop fired off a few more shots as Kruger dashed past him. Out the corner of his eye he saw the elephants fleeing from the gunshots. "Run, run, run," he murmured as he fired again. When Kruger's weapon barked he scrambled to his feet and dashed past. They repeated the process until they reached the spot where Kogo waited.

"What the fuck is going on?" The poacher cowered in the long grass clutching his weapon.

"Where's the tracker?" Bishop asked as he slid in next to him.

Gunfire crackled through the air as Kruger joined them.

"He ran... As soon as the firing started, he ran."

"Fucking chickenshit." Kruger fired off more rounds. "There's a crap load of these guys, *ja.* We need to keep moving." He gave Bishop a nod and grabbed Kogo by the shoulder. "We'll cover you, OK?"

The poacher's eyes were wide. "Yes, of course."

"Now go."

As Kogo took off through the bush Kruger turned and fired well-aimed shots either side of him. "Run you little cocksucker."

"Go, go, go!" Bishop yelled.

They sprinted through the bush after Kogo firing their weapons into the ground as they ran. Bishop was amazed at how fast the poacher moved. They covered half a mile in a matter of minutes.

"That's far enough," yelled Bishop as they skidded down a dry streambed. He glanced around; there was still no sign of the tracker.

"Are they going to catch us?" Kogo stammered. "If they hand us over to the Kenyan Wildlife Service we'll end up in jail."

"No one's going to get us," Bishop snapped. "We're almost at the car." He turned to Kruger who covered their rear. "Let's be careful, they may be staking it out."

"Roger, you take point. I'll bring up the rear."

Bishop led them through the scrub, his eyes peeled for any of the rangers. The Land Cruiser was where they had left it, parked off the road at the edge of the park.

"Get in, let's go." As Bishop yanked open the passenger door he heard the roar of an engine. "Shit." He stepped out onto the track and spotted an olive drab truck speeding toward them. "Kruger, you've got the wheel." He aimed at the approaching vehicle. Firing low he put five shots into the engine block. Steam and smoke exploded from under the hood.

Turning he ran back and leaped in the Land Cruiser. "Let's get the hell out of here!" He slammed the door shut as Kruger launched the four-wheel drive through the bushes and out onto the sandy track. They fish-tailed down the road, the big V8 roaring.

"Thank God," said Kogo from the back seat.

Bishop glanced over his shoulder to see the poacher staring out the rear window at the smoking truck.

"You're not going to back out of the cash are you, Kogo?"

The poacher turned and shook his head vigorously. "No, you'll get your money. You saved me from prison... or worse."

"Good, make sure you let Mamba know because we need more work."

"I will."

"Guys," Kruger interrupted. "Check this out."

Bishop squinted through the windshield and spotted a dark skinny figure running along the road in front of them; it was the tracker. "You want to pick him up, Kogo?"

“No, he ran like a startled gazelle. He can keep running, we have no need for him now.”

Bishop gave Kruger a slight nod and they sped past the man leaving him in a cloud of dust. “You're a ruthless bastard.”

“You haven't met Mamba yet.”

“When is he back in town?”

“He should be back now.”

“Will he have work for us?”

“Maybe later tonight. I’ll call you this afternoon with the details.”

“If you hand over the cash then we're keen, *ja*.” replied Bishop. “But, first we get the money, then we do the next job. We're not running a charity.”

“Yes of course, I'll talk to Mamba.”

“Good, I'm looking forward to meeting him.”

CHAPTER 8

THE SANDPIT, ABU DHABI

As Vance climbed the staircase to the upper levels of the villa, Chen Chua, PRIMAL's intelligence chief, called him into his workspace. Both Chua and Flash looked up from behind their computers as he walked in.

"OK, team, what's up?"

"Everything alright?" asked Chua.

"Yeah."

"How's Saneh?"

"No change," he grunted. "What have you got? Established comms with Bishop?"

"Not yet, but we'll come back to that. I spoke to Dominic Marks, the ranger who Kruger was communicating with."

"And?"

"According to Marks, Bish and Kruger were with a group of poachers in Tsavo national park. What's really interesting is they tipped off the local rangers. Marks thinks they're trying to infiltrate Mamba's poaching gang."

"Makes sense. Does Marks have a number for them other than the sat phone?"

"Yes, he gave us their Kenyan number. It's only a matter of time before they're back in range of the cell towers."

"Good work, bud. Let me know when they're online." Vance turned and left the room. He was halfway down the corridor when Chua caught up with him.

"Vance, what's going on with Saneh?"

"Like I said, no change."

Chua shook his head. "I know you're lying. Look, we're all family here and we deserve to know."

He exhaled. "They gave us a choice, Chen. Either we lose Saneh and try to save the child or we try to save Saneh and possibly lose the child."

"So that's why we need to get in contact with Bishop so urgently."

"Yeah, but we ran out of time. The decision had to be made today."

"And you and Tariq made it?"

Vance nodded.

"So what now?"

He shrugged. "We keep working the intel on the poachers and hope Bishop stays out of the shit."

"When we have comms what are you going to tell him?"

"Tell him? Tell him what? That we weighed the life of his unborn child against the life of his woman? How do you tell a man that, Chen? How do you tell him that because you couldn't reach him you had to make the hardest decision of his life for him? And what happens if he doesn't agree with the decision?"

"Bishop can't judge the decision you and Tariq made when he chose to chase vengeance rather than stand by Saneh. He'll live with it and he'll be grateful he didn't have to make it himself. You're a damn good man and a brave leader, don't you ever forget it."

He fought back tears and embraced Chua in a bear hug.

"Get some sleep, Vance. We'll have comms with Bishop in a matter of hours and the hospital will take care of Saneh."

***

MOMBASA, KENYA

Mamba swallowed another mouthful of beer as he gazed at the dial on the kitchen scales. The tusk on it weighed-in at nearly fifty pounds and there were another five like it on the bench. He grinned; his Ugandan expedition had exceeded his expectations and put him overweight on Zhou's order. It also meant that whatever Kogo had managed to scrounge in Tsavo was a bonus. Thoughts of his second-in-command brought a scowl to his face. Where was the lazy shit?

Finishing the beer he glared at the warehouse door. Where the fuck was Kogo? The shipment was due out tonight and he sure as hell wasn't going to load it by himself. His assistant was supposed to be arranging extra security. The local cops had recently hiked the price for their protection and there was a risk they would try to strong-arm him again. They needed extra muscle to keep them in line.

The rattle of the lock on the warehouse door caught his attention and he grabbed his AK from where it lay on the bench. The door slid open and Kogo stepped inside. "Where the hell have you been? I tried to call you twice."

"Sorry, Mamba, the battery went dead."

He placed the weapon back on the bench and walked to the refrigerator for another beer. "So, where the fuck's the ivory?" Twisting the cap from the bottle on his bicep, he stared at the Kenyan.

"There was a problem."

"Oh, yeah? You hire some local deadshits who couldn't find an elephant in a tent?"

Kogo shook his head. "No, we ran up against the KWS. They ambushed us up by the lake."

He frowned. "You got away OK then. What about the others? The greedy white guys who wanted their cash up front."

"They're the only reason I'm alive. They're proper badasses, Mamba. They shot the KWS up good and got us out of there fast. Saved my life."

Mamba's eyes narrowed as he took a pull of the beer. He opened the refrigerator, pulled another bottle out, and tossed it over. "So you think you can trust these guys?"

Kogo opened the beer and took a sip. "They're mercenaries. I think if we pay them then we can trust them."

"As long as no one else pays them more."

"No one has as much money as you, boss."

It was true, he thought, and if tonight's transfer went off without a hitch then he would be rich and living on a tropical island. Maybe he could run the business from there with Kogo and these mercenaries doing all the heavy lifting and taking the risks. "Bring your white mercenaries along tonight. Have them meet us at the jetty."

Kogo frowned. "You want them as well as the cops?"

"Do you trust the cops?"

He shook his head.

"But you trust these guys. So double the standard rate and get them to keep an eye on the crooked cops."

"They can help us load the boat."

"Always looking for value aren't you."

Kogo picked up one of the tusks on the bench. "You're not mad we didn't get any tusks?" he asked cautiously.

Mamba shrugged. "We have enough. But, of course your cut won't be as big." He grinned. "And I'm taking the money for the mercenaries out of your share."

The Kenyan placed the tusk down. "Yes, boss."

"So, before I get you to call up your white boys how about you tell me everything you know about them. Starting with who recommended them."

***

Bishop's stomach growled as he lay on his bed in the hotel room staring at the ceiling fan.

"You might be hungry, bro." Kruger laughed as he pulled on a clean T-shirt.

"Skipped breakfast and lunch, who would have thought?"

"There's a place I saw around the corner, looks OK."

"What level of dining does an African OK get you?" Bishop asked. "Is that the local equivalent of a Michelin Star?"

"It means you can eat there and not shit yourself within ten minutes."

"Ah, the shit-yourself scale; very popular measure of culinary standards in South East Asia." He sat up and pulled on his boots. As he tied them Kruger's local phone rang.

The South African frowned at the screen, answered the call, and listened. "It's Vance, he wants to talk to you."

Bishop's stomach lurched and his throat went dry. He swallowed and held out his hand for the device. "Hello."

"Buddy, this line is not secure so I'm going to keep this brief. Her situation hasn't improved. We needed to make a decision to authorize a new treatment that could save her."

"Of course."

"There's more, it's possible this new treatment could cause her body to terminate the pregnancy."

Bishop felt like a truck had hit him. The room spun and the phone dropped from his hand.

"Hey, you OK? Is Saneh OK?" Kruger asked as he picked up the phone.

"We could lose the baby," he murmured.

Kruger spoke into the phone but Bishop heard nothing. He collapsed back on the bed, his emotions in turmoil. Despite the gunshot wound Bishop had never doubted Saneh would recover from her injury and give birth to their child. Previously a feeling of helplessness had driven his need for revenge. In the last few seconds, that had changed. Now pure rage coursed through his veins. He vowed to slaughter Mamba, Kogo, and anyone else who stood in his way.

"Vance wants us to stand down." Kruger's persistent tone snapped him out of his thoughts. "He's going to recall the CAT and send them down here to help target Mamba and his network."

Bishop sat up and shook his head. "No, I'm going to kill Mamba and I'm going to do it tonight."

"OK." Kruger relayed the information to Vance. Then he turned back to Bishop. "He wants to talk to you again."

Bishop held out his hand and took the phone. Terminating the call he tossed it back on the bed. "You in or out, Kruger?"

"I'm in."

"Good, now we wait for Kogo's call."

"You still want some food?"

Bishop pushed his emotions deep inside and vowed to leave them there. "Yeah, I prefer to kill on a full stomach."

CHAPTER 9

MOMBASA, KENYA

Bishop didn't feel like eating but he knew if he didn't he would crash. It was past eight in the evening and he hadn't eaten all day. Food was vital; he would need his energy to kill Mamba and Kogo. The bean salad he'd chosen from the menu could have been filled with flavor but to him it was bland. He shoveled a spoonful into his mouth as Kruger took his time with a plate of traditional roasted meats.

"You should try this." Kruger pushed the plate toward him.

"I'm good." He concentrated on his bowl of beans and corn the locals called *githeri*.

"You're missing out." Kruger stuffed another hunk of meat in his mouth. "You want a beer?"

He shook his head. "We should keep our heads clear."

"Good call."

They had the restaurant to themselves and with Kruger not sure what to say and Bishop not wanting to talk they ate in silence. Minutes passed until the shrill ring of Kruger's phone interrupted them. Bishop listened intently as the South African gave short responses to the person on the other end.

Taking a pen from his pocket Kruger jotted an address on a napkin. "That was Kogo, we're on," he said as he placed the phone in his pocket. "He wants us to help out with security on a boat transfer."

"Is Mamba going to be there?"

"He didn't say, but if they're shipping their ivory there's a pretty good chance he will be."

Bishop pushed his bowl aside. "What's the location?"

Kruger whistled the waitress over and asked her for a tourist map. She disappeared to find one. "Little town just to the north called Mtwapa. There's a boat ramp and a jetty. He wants us there." He checked his watch. "In a little over an hour."

The waitress returned with an ancient street directory. Kruger thanked her and flicked through the dog-eared pages. "Here it is." He spun it so Bishop could see. "Only about thirty minutes out of town. You can see the jetty marked near the main road."

"We need to get a move on if we're going to recce it," said Bishop rising from his chair.

Kruger tossed cash on the table and they hurried back to the hotel where the Mazda was parked. They loaded their bags and Kruger drove them through the darkness at break-neck speed. It took barely fifteen minutes to reach the riverside town. When they arrived Kruger parked the car a few hundred yards uphill from the water and they went forward on foot armed only with their pistols. They found a cluster of trees that allowed them to observe the jetty but stay out of sight.

The rickety wooden structure reached out into the depths of a tidal channel. Beside it was an eatery that had closed for the evening. A single street light cast a dim glow over three vehicles parked on the road where the jetty met the shore. Bishop recognized one of them as the Land Cruiser Kogo used to take them poaching. At the end of the jetty a fishing trawler was moored. It sat high in the water with a gangplank running up the side.

"That looks like a cop car," said Kruger pointing at one of the vehicles, a blue and white pickup.

A group of men was gathered around the rear of the vehicle. They seemed to be arguing over something. Two wore blue uniforms with pistol belts; Kruger's assessment was correct. "You reckon it's a raid?" asked Bishop.

"More likely Mamba's paid for protection."

He watched as a tall figure appeared from the boat and walked down the wharf toward the group. In the dim light Bishop couldn't make out his facial features but from height and build he guessed it could be the elusive Mamba. "We should get down there."

"I'm not real sure about those cops, bro."

"You just said they'd been paid off."

"True, but I'm not sure how they're going to react to a couple of white boys crashing their party."

"Well, we're not going to find out up here."

They moved back to the car, checked their weapons, and drove down to the jetty. As they approached two men stepped onto the road and walked toward them. They were the police officers.

"This is probably far enough," said Kruger as he parked the Mazda and killed the headlights. "You sure about this?"

Bishop opened his door. "Yeah."

The police officers had stopped a dozen yards away and stood with their hands on their pistols. "This area is off-limits. You need to leave."

"It's OK, we work with Kogo," Bishop said holding his hands at shoulder height with the palms out.

The two cops turned to each other and talked before one returned to the jetty. A moment later he reappeared with the poacher.

"You guys took your time." Kogo waved them forward. "Come, Mamba is waiting."

Kruger locked the hatchback and they walked toward the other parked vehicles and the jetty. Bishop felt his muscles tense as he spotted Mamba at the back of a pickup. The light from the single streetlamp reflected off the sheen of sweat on the killer's face. He was attempting to manhandle a large wooden crate from the back of the truck and wore a snarl more befitting a wild animal.

"These are the men who saved me from the rangers," announced Kogo.

Mamba left the crate and gave them a once over. His gaze lingered on Bishop and for a split-second he thought the poacher had somehow recognized him. "So you're the great white hunters."

"And you're the snake of a poacher," snapped Bishop.

Their eyes met and Bishop held the gaze, his eyes boring into the other man's head. If thoughts alone could have killed, the Ugandan would have collapsed, his heart frozen by ice-cold rage.

Mamba glanced at Kruger. "I like these guys, they're hard-asses." He grinned. "Now, help us load these boxes onto the boat."

Bishop shook his head. "We want the cash for today first."

Mamba's forehead creased. "OK, I tell you what. I'll give you ten grand up front. But, you load the boxes and then you provide extra protection when we transfer our cargo."

"Transfer it to what?"

Mamba lowered his voice so the police couldn't hear. "A Chinese container ship."

Bishop glanced at the battered trawler. "In that tub?"

"It's not far, we're only sailing a few miles out."

He paused as if to contemplate the offer. Then he turned and shot a glance at the two police officers leaning against their pickup. "You don't trust these guys, do you?"

"No, but Kogo seems to think I can trust you."

He met Mamba's cold gaze and extended his hand. "OK, deal."

***

INDIAN OCEAN

Four nautical miles east of Mtwapa a Chinese freighter crept through the inky black waters at barely two knots. Rusted and worn, the *Zenhai* was not an impressive vessel. Classed as a feeder-ship, she was barely a quarter the size of the massive Panamax-class container ships dominating international trade routes. However, with two powerful cranes and a shallow draft, she was perfect for unloading and loading from underdeveloped seaports, an attribute that made her indispensable on the east coast of Africa. Owned by an influential Triad syndicate she frequently carried illicit cargo.

For that reason her crew, in particular the command team, were highly vigilant.

On the bridge the captain sipped tea from a china cup as he studied the radar screen.

"Can you see them?" asked an impatient voice from behind him.

He shook his head. "No, Kehua, the only contact is a tanker coming from the north." He turned to face the Triad gangster who had boarded his ship in Maputo. "If they do not appear within the hour we will press on. I will not risk the ship to pirates."

Kehua was a compact brute of a man with cruel features befitting his chosen occupation. Armed with a Chinese-made Type 81 assault rifle and dressed in black fatigues and an assault vest, he and his six men were responsible for securing the illicit cargo scheduled to have been loaded an hour ago. "Do not concern yourself with pirates. My men will deal with anyone who tries to board us. We will wait until the boat appears."

The captain nodded, not about to challenge the criminal. He had heard rumors of what happened when you failed to meet your contractual commitments to the Triads. More to the point, he would not risk the six hundred thousand yuan he'd been promised for delivering the shipment. He turned his attention back to the radar.

As the green beam swept around the scope a blip appeared to the west at the extent of the radar's range. A dozen more sweeps and he could see it was moving steadily toward them. "Contact, twenty five miles out."

Kehua stepped closer so he could see the radar. "Is it them?"

"I assume so. But, we will not know until they get closer." He glanced out through the freighter's windows and saw it was raining. That was good; rain reduced visibility making it harder for the Kenyan authorities to spot the transfer.

The gangster took a pair of binoculars from the ship's console and made his way to the port flying bridge. The captain watched him struggle to push the door open against the wind. Their contact was still fifteen to twenty minutes from visual range. But, who was he to tell the Triad lieutenant how to do his job. If Kehua wanted to stand outside in the cold that was fine with him. Glancing back at the scope he spotted another contact slightly to the right of the first. It appeared on the outer edge of the scope for a few revolutions of the beam then disappeared. He scratched at the scraggly beard adorning his chin and contemplated the anomaly. It could be a fishing boat, a rogue wave, or a false return. However, it could also be a pirate vessel or Kenyan security forces. He would keep an eye on it. Taking a handheld radio from the console he held it to his mouth and pressed the transmit button.

"First Mate, this is the Captain, I want you to prepare the cargo for loading."

The radio transmitted, "Net or hook?"

"Net."

"Yes, Captain."

He took another sip from his tea then returned his eyes to the scope. The first contact was closing steadily but the second anomaly had not reappeared. The smuggling vessel would be alongside within the hour and it would not take long for his crew to load the illicit cargo. Then he could give his undivided attention to transiting the pirate-laden waters off Somalia.

***

The dull throb of a diesel engine and the soft hiss of the ocean under the bow of the fishing boat was all Bishop heard as he scanned the darkness for any sign of the freighter. Kruger stood on the opposite side replicating his efforts. Mamba and Kogo were in the wheelhouse with the crew, staying out of the intermittent rain.

Bishop was waiting for an opportunity to slit Mamba's throat and toss him over the side. However, so far the poacher hadn't left the wheelhouse where the ship's crew surrounded him.

"Kogo tells me you know how to handle yourself in a gunfight."

The voice startled Bishop and he tightened his grip on his R5 as he turned. Mamba stood a few yards away with two members of the crew.

"We go alright," he said glancing across the deck at Kruger. The big man had left his post and stood off to the side, his rifle held ready.

Mamba sat on one of the crates stacked on the deck. "We could have used you the other day."

Bishop leaned casually against the railing as he eased the weapon's safety off. "Rough gig?"

The poacher nodded. "We ran into some trouble in Zambia."

"Yeah, I heard about that. Rangers up at Luangwa got into a shootout trying to protect a black rhino."

"Word gets around fast."

He nodded. "It does when it comes to black rhinos. So what happened, they get the jump on you?"

"The exact opposite. We ambushed them, and killed at least two. Then the rangers came after us."

Bishop calculated he could gun Mamba and his colleagues down in half a second. Then he and Kruger could finish off the men in the wheelhouse and deep-six the bodies. Sailing the fishing boat back to Mtwapa wouldn't be difficult for the pair. He moved his finger to the trigger of the R5 and took up the slack.

The blast of a horn startled Bishop and he looked out to sea. Through the gloom he spotted the looming bulk of a cargo ship. Almost a football field in length, it dwarfed the trawler.

"Good, we're in business," said Mamba and he issued directions to the ship's crew.

"Ahoy!" a voice bellowed from above. Floodlights bathed the deck as the freighter nestled against tires the crew had lowered. Rubber screeched in protest and Bishop glanced across at Kruger. The South African jerked his head in the direction of the ship and mouthed, "On the way back."

He nodded in agreement.

"Lower the net!" Mamba yelled.

The boom of a crane appeared and with a whir and clank a large cargo net descended toward the fishing boat.

Bishop peered up at the side of the freighter. He spotted the silhouettes of a number of men wielding assault rifles. "Not a very advantageous position we're in here," he said to Mamba as they watched the net hit the deck. Their crew unhooked the bundle and laid it out flat.

"That's why you're here."

The crew quickly arranged the wooden crates full of ivory in the center of the net then reattached it to the cable from the ship's crane.

Over the noise of the engines Bishop thought he heard something else. He moved to the stern of the boat and searched the darkness.

"OK, lift it up," Mamba yelled.

A spotlight lanced out across the water from another vessel. "This is the police!" an amplified voice bellowed.

A rifle barked from the cargo ship above them and Bishop added a volley of well-aimed shots to the mix. Then he spun and ran for the cover of the wheelhouse. Machine gun fire erupted from the police launch and bullets thudded into the side of the freighter.

Bishop spotted the bundle of ivory rising off the deck. A figure clung to the side of the net. It was Mamba. The poacher had hedged his bets with the merchant ship.

The deck lurched beneath his feet as the fishing boat's engine roared. The skipper of the trawler had also decided to make his escape and they pulled away as more gunfire struck.

Bishop tossed his rifle aside, leaped to the top of the boat's rail, and launched himself into the air. For a split-second he thought he'd misjudged the gap but managed to snag the bottom of the net with one hand. Swinging wildly he reached frantically for another handhold. Finding one he set about climbing out from under the crates and up the side.

The bundle rose over the side rail of the freighter as the vessel gathered speed. Bishop clung to the net as they swung over a dark hold then dropped inside. The deep throb of the ship's engines blocked out the gunfire as the dimly lit floor approached. The cargo net touched down with a thump, the net went slack, and Bishop fell back with his limbs tangled. As he struggled free of the net he spotted Mamba disappearing through a doorway. Pulling a pistol from his vest he gave chase.

***

As they peeled away from the freighter Kruger caught a glimpse of her name high up on the stern. *Zenhai* was stenciled in fresh white paint, clearly visible as the searchlight from the police patrol boat danced along her side.

"Faster, faster!" screamed Kogo from the wheelhouse of the trawler.

With the police launch seemingly intent on tackling the cargo ship, Kruger concurred that they needed to slip away as fast as possible. Staying out of police custody was his highest priority, closely followed by recovering that crazy bastard Bishop from the *Zenhai.* He joined Kogo and the ship's skipper in the wheelhouse.

"Make the boat go faster!" Kogo screamed as he waved a pistol around his head.

"She's going as fast as she can," Kruger said.

A blinding light illuminated the wheelhouse. Kruger realized that the police crew had shifted target, aborting any attempt to board the massive freighter. The roar of turbocharged maritime diesels echoed off the water as they gave chase.

Kruger stepped outside and spotted the patrol boat hot on their tail. Kogo joined him and aimed his pistol. Before Kruger could stop him the poacher let off half a dozen shots.

He dropped to the deck as the police response caught Kogo flat-footed. High-velocity rounds tore through the Kenyan's body spraying blood and flesh. The poacher emitted a gurgling sound and toppled face down on the deck.

"Fuck me." Kruger raised his R1 and fired a volley. The spotlight exploded plunging them into darkness.

Tracer lanced out across the water like lasers, shredding the wooden superstructure. The fight was one-sided and Kruger knew exactly how it would end. He tossed the rifle overboard and vaulted over the railing.

The ocean was warm and he trod water as the trawler disappeared into the darkness with the police launch in hot pursuit. He stripped the magazines from his vest and let them sink. Emptying his water bottles he stuffed them back in the vest increasing his buoyancy. Checking the stars he orientated himself toward the coast, rolled onto his back, and started a powerful kicking rhythm he knew he could maintain for hours. He knew he was less than three hours from land. Once ashore he would contact Vance and try to find out where the *Zenhai* was heading and how he could get on board.

***

Bishop crept through the narrow corridors searching for Mamba. Only a minute earlier he'd seen the poacher disappear through a doorway deep into the bowels of the ship.

He paused in front of a fire hose and checked the emergency exit map stuck to the bulkhead. He was three levels below the bridge.

He checked his weapons again: a folding knife and a pistol. He wasn't equipped for anything more than a stealthy assassination and a swift exit. Which reminded him; he needed a way off the boat. Studying the map he located the lifeboats one level above. Moving cautiously up the ship's internal staircase he stopped when he heard voices. He slipped outside through a door, pulled it closed, and watched through the portal as two men dressed in coveralls made their way down, feet ringing on the metal stairs.

Once they passed he climbed up an external staircase to the next level and found the lifeboats. The bright orange craft sat on a chute aimed over the stern of the ship. He inspected the controls that would launch it toward the ocean thirty feet below. They looked simple enough.

Confirming his escape strategy he moved back to the door he'd closed. There was no sign of movement so he turned the locking mechanism and slipped inside.

If he were Mamba he would make for the bridge, use the ship's phone to contact someone ashore, and arrange a transfer. His other option would be to remain on board until they reached the next port. Considering they were probably bound for China that was unlikely.

With his pistol held ready he climbed the metal staircase until he reached the top. A heavy steel door blocked access to the bridge. He pressed against the wall to avoid being seen through the glass portal. Voices emanated from inside. Here, high above the ship's engines, he could hear Mamba's voice clearly.

Sliding across to the door he glanced through the round window. His pulse quickened as he spotted his target. The poacher was standing near one of the Chinese sailors. The white-uniformed Asian was perched in the captain's chair.

Bishop thumbed the safety off his pistol as he placed a hand on the door handle. He exhaled and readied himself. Two shots to the head and justice would be served. Then it was a short dash down to the lifeboat and freedom.

Pushing the lever down he shoved open the door and lifted his pistol.

"Stop!" a guttural voice ordered.

Bishop felt cold steel pressed against the back of his head. Very slowly he lifted his hands out to the side and dropped his gun.

"Step forward."

Inside Mamba had drawn his machete and was holding it ready to strike. Bishop looked him in the eye as he took a step.

"Turn around."

"Hey, it's OK, let's not get excited. I'm with Mamba," said Bishop as he turned slowly to face a pistol-wielding Chinese thug wearing a black uniform. Slightly shorter than Bishop, he sported cropped black hair and a wrestler's build. A tattoo of a snake peeked above the collar of his shirt. Two henchmen wearing similar black outfits and wielding assault rifles stood either side.

"It doesn't look that way. Say one more word and it will be your last." The man spoke near perfect English with a slight accent. "So, Mamba, is he yours?"

"Yes, but I'm not sure if he can be trusted."

Bishop assumed that the Chinese thug was a smuggler, possibly a Triad.

"He is one of yours but you cannot trust him? What sort of fool brings a man he doesn't trust to an illicit cargo transfer? Not to mention one who would try to kill him."

"Kehua, it's more complicated than that."

"Complicated? First the police boat and then an assassin on my ship. No doubt, he's an informant. My people will put a bullet in him and toss him over the side."

"No, I want to know who sent him," hissed Mamba.

Kehua glared at Bishop before speaking. "Fine, we'll throw him in the brig." He turned and barked an order in Mandarin. The Triads secured Bishop's hands with flexicuffs.

Mamba sheathed his machete. How that idiot Kogo had managed to recruit a police agent was beyond him. Unless he was already under surveillance.

"Do not leave the bridge. I will return shortly," Kehua said angrily as he recovered the white mercenary's pistol and followed his men.

Mamba watched as the Chinese gangsters marched the prisoner away. Once they were out of sight he turned to the ship's captain who had been silently watching the drama from his chair. "Where's the satellite phone?"

The man raised an eyebrow and pointed to the handset.

He grabbed it, punched in a number, and pressed it to his ear. As he waited for the call to connect he watched the digital speed displayed alongside the ship's wheel. It read twelve knots. "Can we go faster?" he asked.

The man shot him a frown. "This is fast enough."

Mamba turned his attention back to the phone, which had finally connected.

Zhou's voice came through in rapid-fire Mandarin.

"It's Mamba, the cargo is on board."

"Where are you calling from?"

"I'm on the ship. There was an unfortunate incident."

"What happened?"

"Kenyan Maritime Police. I lost my entire poaching crew. I expect to be reimbursed for my losses and I expect the ship to drop me off at Singapore." The Chinese smuggler didn't need to know about the South African mercenary.

"Once Kehua confirms the shipment you will be paid the agreed amount. The ship will not stop until it reaches Shanghai."

"Then what the hell am I supposed to do?"

"You should have thought of that before, like a rat, you snuck on board. The vessel is due in Shanghai in six days. I suggest you find a good book."

"What happens when I get to China?"

"I will make the necessary arrangements for papers and passports. I will purchase flights for you to return to Africa. Due to your losses I am happy to bear that expense myself."

"Very big of you, Zhou. How much will you make from this deal... ten million US?"

"Have an enjoyable cruise, Mamba. I look forward to finally meeting you in Shanghai. Have Kehua call me once he has confirmed the cargo."

"He can confirm the ivory but the rhino horn, I'll deliver myself. Think of it as insurance." As Mamba returned the satellite phone to its cradle the metal door swung open with a creak and Kehua strode in.

The gangster stared at the captain as he addressed him. "Where is the police boat?"

"Both contacts are three nautical miles behind us. The fishing vessel may have been boarded."

"And our cargo?"

"Safe in the hold."

"Good." Kehua turned to Mamba. "Your traitor is secure in the brig."

"I have contacted Zhou. He has requested that you confirm the ivory."

"We will do that together. Then you can question your friend." He directed Mamba to the door.

"There's no rush. I'll be with you till we reach Shanghai. Plenty of time to make him talk."

"I want him off my ship at the earliest opportunity."

***

The brig was a tiny cell on the same level as the ship's kitchen, dining area, gymnasium, and recreation facilities. The pile of cleaning supplies stacked in the corridor suggested it had not been used to secure a prisoner in some time.

When Kehua opened the steel door Mamba stepped in and met the angry gaze of the South African mercenary.

"Mamba. This is a serious misunderstanding–"

"Shut up." He stood over the prisoner who sat on the cold steel floor with his hands secured behind his back. A loop of chain connected his wrists to a steel eyelet on the wall.

"How long have you known this man?" asked Kehua.

"He joined us yesterday. Since his arrival the authorities have taken significant interest in my activities. First in Tsavo and then again tonight."

"Then he is a police informant."

The prisoner spat on the floor. "I'm no one's spy. Your man led us into those rangers at Tsavo and the cops you paid off probably sold you out for a cut of the profits."

Mamba paused in thought. "Why are you on this ship then? Hoping to track me down for the police? Assassinating me for the Kenyans?"

"No, I didn't want to get arrested. Getting sent to prison in Kenya is a death sentence, you know that."

Mamba looked intently at the South African. What he said sounded reasonable but something didn't add up. There had to be some other reason the former soldier had followed him onto the ship. Something drove him and it wasn't the fear of being incarcerated by the Kenyan police. Men like this were not intimidated by poorly trained and corrupt police officers.

"So, you going to let me out?"

"No." Mamba stepped out of the cell, switched off the light, and slammed the steel door shut.

"We should dispose of him," said Kehua as he locked the door.

"Not yet. I'm going to get something to eat and then I'm going to question him further. I want to know who helped him infiltrate my organization."

The gangster directed him toward the kitchen. "You have forty-eight hours. Then he is going over the side."

"He'll talk before then." Mamba opened the refrigerator and helped himself to a tray of cold meat. He took a six-inch butcher's knife from a magnetic strip fastened to the wall, tested the blade's sharpness with his thumb, and hacked off a sizable chunk of meat. "Plenty of time to find out everything he knows. Mamba stuffed the food into his mouth. "Is there anything to drink on this tub?" he said as he chewed.

Kehua gave him a hard stare. "You will not drink alcohol on this vessel." He snapped his fingers at one of the Chinese stewards. "Find him a cabin." Then he spun on his heel and strode out of the kitchen.

"Rude fuck," muttered Mamba at his back.

CHAPTER 10

MTWAPA, KENYA

Kruger's feet touched sand and he waded through the surf until he hit the beach. Dropping to his knees in the soft sand he checked his watch. It was a little after midnight. Pulling his phone from his vest he tried to power it up. Not surprisingly, it showed no sign of life.

Climbing to his feet, he staggered up the beach and into the tree line. He stripped his pistol and knife from his vest before dumping it in the bushes. Tucking the gun in his belt and the knife in his pocket he pushed through the scrub to a road that followed the coastline.

By his estimate he was at least three miles from Mtwapa, possibly more. What he knew for sure was that he needed to head south. He broke into a trot and followed the road. The moonlight revealed shacks and houses on either side. A dog barked as he slapped his way along the road, his wet clothing rubbing against his body. The undersides of his arms were raw from swimming and the inside of his thighs stung from chafing. It didn't slow him though. Every minute he delayed the *Zenhai* steamed away from the Kenyan coast and further out of reach. He focused on getting back to the car to use his satellite phone to contact the PRIMAL team.

A flash of headlights caught his attention and he glanced over his shoulder. He paused as a vehicle approached, and held up a thumb.

The car slowed to a halt but left its high beams on. He squinted, the doors opened, and he caught a glimpse of a uniformed figure.

"Hold it right there."

Kruger recognized the voice from earlier in the evening. The cop was one of the two Mamba had hired to protect the transfer to the boat.

"Where is Mamba?" the officer asked as his partner climbed out of the blue and white pickup.

"I don't know. Look, I fell overboard and swam ashore. I don't know what happened."

The two men spoke in hushed voices as Kruger waited in the headlights. He held his hands by his side and closed his eyes relying on his hearing to give him the location of the two men. He recognized the telltale click of a safety catch and dove into action. One hand lifted his shirt and the other snatched the pistol from his belt. His eyes snapped open and he fired two rounds through the open driver's door. One of the police officers grunted as the bullets shattered the window, hitting him.

He leaped sideways as the second policeman let off a burst from his AK stitching the road. He felt a round tug at his wet pants and he rolled firing again, this time at the man's exposed legs.

The cop screamed as he fell and Kruger clambered to his feet, finishing him with a double tap to the head.

He checked the first officer was dead before loading both bodies and the AKs into the back of the police pickup. Only then did he check his leg. The bullet had carved a groove along his calf that oozed blood; a flesh wound.

Jumping in the truck he took off down the road toward Mtwapa. When he reached the marina he skidded in the gravel and halted alongside the battered Mazda. It was exactly where he and Bishop had parked it a few hours earlier, alongside the bank of the tidal river.

Grabbing a rag from the trunk he wiped down his pistol and tossed it off the jetty into the water. Then he took a jerry can of fuel from the back of the police pickup and doused the bodies inside. As he waited for the truck's cigarette lighter to heat he took his satellite phone from the Mazda's glove box and dialed the emergency number for the PRIMAL headquarters in the UAE. Following the open line protocol he waited for someone to answer.

"Kruger, what's going on?" It was Vance.

"Listen up, I don't have much time. Bishop is being held on a Chinese freighter called the *Zenhai.* He boarded off the coast from Mombasa. I'll call back in an hour to explain the details. You guys need to track it and get some of the boys together for a boarding party."

He could hear Vance scribbling notes.

"OK, bud, we've got it. I'll stand by for your call."

Kruger hung up, reached in through the window of the police vehicle, and pulled out the cigarette lighter. He tossed it in the back of the truck and the fuel ignited with a soft thud. He watched it burn for a few seconds then climbed into the Mazda.

As he raced down the highway he called Toppie's number. The arms dealer answered after a few rings. "It's Kruger. Shit's gone south, I'm going to need your help."

"We going to war?" croaked Toppie.

"Yeah, we're going to war."

***

THE SANDPIT, ABU DHABI

Vance glanced over Frank's shoulder, checking the personnel tracker. A map of the globe was annotated with the location of all the PRIMAL personnel that had been stood down. Most of their assaulters, Kurtz, Pavel, and Miklos, had last checked in from Eastern Europe. Mitch, their tech support guru was in Israel. Only Mirza Mansoor was operational, flying humanitarian missions for Priority Movements Airlift, their cover organization. His icon flashed in Irbil, Kurdistan. "Do we have anyone close enough to respond in time?"

Frank shook his head. "No, does Tariq have any guys we can use?"

"Not that we can trust."

"We've got enough shooters here." The voice from the doorway belonged to Ice.

Vance turned to face him. Ice had been training relentlessly since he'd been rescued. His shoulders were broad and he stood confidently on his prosthetic limb. The scarring on the side of the face had transformed him from a handsome soldier into a lethal terminator. "We don't know who's on the ship, Ice."

"No, but we've got you, me and Chua. Plus Kruger who is already on the ground. Frank can run the back end with Flash. We move fast and we get Bishop off that ship before they know what's hit them. We've got all the gear we need at the hangar. We just need a chopper to put us on the ship."

"That's the main issue," said Frank. "We can get on board but without helicopters it'll be a challenge to get back to shore."

"We could take over the ship," said Vance. His eyes were still fixed on Ice.

"Not in those waters, boss. The anti-piracy task force will be all over us in minutes," added Frank. "A helicopter is our best option."

"If she's still within range of a shore-based helicopter," said Vance.

"She is." Chua appeared in the doorway behind Ice. "Flash found her on the marine traffic website. She's making twelve knots two hundred nautical miles south of Mogadishu. We also downloaded a copy of her schematics."

"She's still broadcasting her location?" asked Vance.

"Yes and on her current heading she's going to be in range of Mogadishu for the next eight hours. If we want to make a move I recommend launching now."

Frank raised his hand in the air. "Hey guys, I've got Kruger on the line."

"Put him on speaker."

Frank hit a key and Kruger's thick Afrikaans accent filled the operations room. "Vance, I'm just outside of Mombasa with a mate of mine, *ja.* He's got friends in Somalia; we can get up there and organize a helicopter to get on the ship. I need you to grab our gear and bring the boys to Mogadishu, OK."

Vance shot Chua a questioning glance and was rewarded with a nod.

"Roger, that's workable, but timings will be tight. You'll need to have the chopper turning and burning."

"Will do, boss." Kruger could be heard talking to someone else on his end. "Oh, and you need to bring lots of cash. Make sure it's US and high denomination."

"How much?" Vance asked.

"Couple of mill, *ja*. Hey, I've got to go. I'll see you in the Mog."

The phone went dead and the room fell silent as the PRIMAL team looked at each other with a combination of raised eyebrows and concerned expressions.

Vance broke the silence. "Ice, you and I are going to head to the hangar and sort out gear. We leave in five minutes. Frank, you're holding the fort here with Flash. I want you to contact Tariq's people and get us a Lascar jet ready to go in an hour."

"Sleek is fully serviced she should be good to go," said Frank referring to the highly modified Gulfstream jet PRIMAL used for many of its covert operations.

Vance shook his head. "No, I don't want to mess with Mitch's gear when he's not around. Get us something basic and unmarked with a long range." He turned to Chua. "We need all the intel we can get. Have Flash pull everything he can on the ship. I want the schematics loaded on the iPRIMAL network with real-time location updates. Meet us at the hangar as soon as you've got it worked up."

"Will do," said Chua.

"You want me to recall Mirza and the boys?" asked Frank.

Vance shook his head. "No, they'll arrive too late and we can't afford to bare our asses at the moment. The CIA could still be sniffing around so we need to keep this low-key."

Chua laughed. "We're talking about Bishop, nothing he ever does is low-key."

"Yeah, that's for sure. OK people, let's get moving."

***

INDIAN OCEAN

Bishop spat a mouthful of blood on the deck and glared at Mamba as the poacher flexed his fingers. "I don't know how many times I have to tell you, I'm not a goddamn cop." With his hands secured behind him he had no way of protecting himself from the onslaught of blows.

"Then who the hell are you?" Mamba balled a fist and made to strike again.

Bishop tensed in anticipation.

"What the fuck is wrong with you?" hissed Mamba. "You know, I think you're telling the truth. No cop would go this far for someone like me." He sat on a foldout bed and clicked his tongue against the roof of his mouth. "No, there is something else going on here. If you're not a cop, who do you work for?"

Bishop strained against the flexicuffs securing his wrists behind his back. "I'm a poacher just like you."

"Tell me how you got to Kogo. Who facilitated the introduction?" Mamba picked up his machete from where he'd laid it on the bed and tested the edge with his thumb. "We've got all the time in the world. If you don't talk I can make you hurt like you've never hurt before."

The bed creaked as Mamba rose. Stepping forward he leaned over and scraped the machete against the stubble on Bishop's jaw. "Tell me who you work for, or I'm going to start cutting you. I'm going to peel back your skin and watch you bleed."

Bishop flinched away from the blade and grunted as he fought against his bonds. The plastic cuffs cut deep into his wrists.

"Fine, it's your decision." Mamba reversed the blade and ran it down Bishop's cheek. The razor sharp edge parted the flesh from his cheekbone to his jaw leaving an angry red wound that quickly filled with blood.

He stared his captor in the eye as warm liquid ran down his face. “You want to know who I am, Mamba?”

The poacher nodded.

“I'm the man who is going to kill you. You took something from me and you’re going to pay the price.”

Mamba frowned. “Did I kill your favorite elephant? What are you, some kind of insane anti-poaching vigilante?”

Bishop saw the moment of realization on his face.

“The women at Luangwa.” He smiled proudly. “One of them was your woman and you blame me for killing her.”

Mamba watched Bishop’s expression intently. “I’m right, aren’t I? I didn't shoot her, you fool, one of the others did.” He leaned closer, their noses almost touching. “Those men are dead now.”

Bishop could smell the stench of his breath. “I know, I killed them.”

Mamba pulled back in surprise. “No shit, you and the big man were the devils chasing us through the park. You know, you nearly got us. But hey, I should be thanking you. You saved me a lot of money. Four greedy men all dead before I had to pay them and I still got the horn.” He sat back on the bed, relaxed now he knew Bishop wasn't an undercover policeman. “I respect you for coming to avenge your woman. I’d do the same. We're very alike you and I.”

“You've got more in common with a baboon’s asshole than me.”

Mamba laughed. “You're resourceful and tough. The sort of man I could make very, very, very rich. Your friend is probably in a Kenyan prison now. We could get him out, I could pay you for your loss, and then we could go to work.”

He struggled to control the rage boiling inside. Ignoring the searing pain from the gash on his cheek he gritted his teeth and stared at Mamba.

“She was just a woman, you know. There are plenty more out there. I could give you two or three.” Mamba chuckled waiting for a response.

He continued to stare.

"But you're not the forgiving type, are you?" The corners of Mamba's mouth turned up in a sickly smile. "If you tell me who put you on to Kogo I'll make your death quick." He paused. "How about you think it over?" He rose from the bed and tapped the machete on the door. "I mean, it's not like we don't have time."

Mamba opened the door, switched off the light, then slammed the door shut behind him.

Bishop was left in the dark with nothing but the throb of the ship's engines for company. He let his head slump forward. Tears filled his eyes and ran down the open cheek wound but he barely registered the stinging pain. His thoughts were preoccupied with Saneh and their child; he had failed them both.

CHAPTER 11

MOGADISHU, SOMALIA

Kruger clenched the sides of the metal copilot's seat with white knuckles as they circled Mogadishu airport. Toppie was at the controls, perched beside him on a padded box, peering out the filthy windshield. The arms dealer's feet barely reached the foot pedals as he threw the Soviet-era An-2 biplane around in a tight bank and lined it up with the runway.

"Don't you need to radio in?"

Toppie shrugged. "I don't have a radio."

He shook his head in disbelief. "We flew all the way from Mombasa at night without a radio?"

"Yep, what the hell do I need a radio for? Next thing you'll be telling me I need lights." He chuckled as he eased off the throttle and hauled back on the yoke.

Kruger squinted through the windshield at the rapidly approaching runway. The sun had just risen over the ocean and his sunglasses were in the cargo hold. He wasn't game to undo his frayed harness and grab them. "Toppie, what the fuck is that?" He pointed at the four-engine aircraft at the far end of the runway, facing them.

"Don't worry, he'll wait."

He stared wide-eyed as the aircraft grew larger. He swore there was black smoke billowing out behind its engines. "Toppie, he's coming right at us."

The pilot adjusted his glasses. "*Ja,* you might be right."

Kruger clutched his seat as the aircraft raced toward them. He whispered a prayer as they dove toward the asphalt and the airliner lifted off. The roar of the four turboprop engines washed over them as the aircraft's underside filled half the windshield and the runway filled the other.

"You crazy son of a bitch!" he bellowed as the biplane shuddered in the downwash.

They hit the tarmac with a thud and within a few hundred feet came to an almost complete halt.

"That was exciting wasn't it?" Toppie said as he steered onto a dirt taxiway on the opposite side to the terminal. He parked in front of a wire-fenced compound and killed the engine.

Kruger glanced out the side window and spotted a row of white helicopters embossed with UN in black lettering. "Please don't tell me we're going to be begging for a chopper from the blue hats."

"All is not as it seems," responded Toppie as he folded his glasses away and scrambled through to the cargo hold. He opened the side door and jumped down onto the dust. Kruger followed, squeezing his shoulders through the narrow hatch.

A tall man dressed in grubby blue coveralls met them. His hair was pulled back in a topknot and he wore a week's growth on his face. "Toppie, my old comrade. So good to see you. Did you bring me anything?" he said with a Russian accent.

Toppie smiled broadly. "*Ja,* Vanko, of course." He gestured to Kruger.

Kruger grabbed two cases of beer from under the Antonov's seats along with his gear bag. Sliding them across the floor to the door he climbed out again, slung the bag, and carried a case under each arm.

Vanko smiled broadly when he spotted the alcohol. "Good beer is so hard to get here in Mogashitu."

"There's another four cases in there if you help us out," said Kruger.

"Of course I can. I understand that you need a long-range helicopter."

"That's right."

"I have exactly what you need, follow me." He led them past a security checkpoint manned by armed contractors, and inside the fenced compound. They crossed a large square of cracked concrete and walked between two white UN helicopters into a maintenance hangar. Under the rusted tin roof sat another of the aircraft.

The Russian-built Mi-8 was a medium-lift helicopter designed for moving cargo and personnel. Powered by two turbines it was renowned for its reliability and strength. This particular airframe had been fitted with long-range tanks mounted on extensions attached to the side of the body. They reminded Kruger of the stubby wings usually affixed to attack helicopters.

"I didn't know the Mi-8 came with long-range tanks," he said as he placed the cartons of beer on a workbench covered in greasy tools and parts.

"The older ones don't. We salvaged the hard points from an Mi-17 that crash-landed here a few years ago. The fuel tanks are from a Hind gunship. The UN wanted to fly food further north and offered to pay lots more to get it there. So we adapt and we make more cash."

He nodded; the helicopter was exactly what the PRIMAL team needed. "How much to hire her?"

"Fifty thousand dollars. If you want crew, another fifty thousand. That doesn't include fuel."

He walked up to the aircraft and ran his hand over the Perspex nose and peered in at the cockpit. Unlike many of the Russian aircraft he had flown in over the years, including Toppie's An-2, the helicopter looked to be in good working order. "OK, you've got a deal. But, only if you let Toppie and I borrow a car for a few hours."

The Russian shrugged. "Of course. When do you need the chopper ready?"

Kruger glanced at his watch. According to the text message he had received from Frank, the PRIMAL team was due in two hours. "Twelve o'clock, we'll be back by then."

The Russian reached into his pocket and tossed Kruger a set of keys. "It will be ready. Try not to get yourself killed out there, it's a rough town."

"Maybe for commie pussies," scoffed Toppie.

"Have you got a phone number, Vanko?" asked Kruger.

"*Da,* of course."

"Good, give me the number. When my people arrive they will call you. Have someone meet them." He unzipped his backpack and pulled out a roll of US dollars secured with a rubber band. "There's five grand here." He handed it over. "That's for you for helping us out. The rest of the cash will arrive with my people."

Vanko smiled as he took the money. "*Spasibo.*" It disappeared into his pocket, replaced in his fingers with a grease-stained business card.

Kruger texted the details to Frank who would in turn pass them to the team in the aircraft. "OK, Toppie, we need to get rolling if we're going to make it on time."

They jumped in the mechanic's pickup that was parked behind the hangar. Kruger drove them past another security checkpoint and out through the perimeter of the airport. A sandbagged machine gun post and concrete T-walls barricaded the security contractors from the outside world. "So where are we heading?" Kruger asked as he drove between rows of shipping containers and out onto a main road.

"We head north. The Pirate King lives on the outskirts of the city."

"That's what we're going to call him, the Pirate King?"

"You can call him by his other name if you want."

"And that is?"

"Al-Mumit, the bringer of death."

"Pirate King it is."

***

THE SANDPIT, ABU DHABI

Flash was so engrossed in his work that he didn't hear the door of the intelligence cell open. The first he knew of Frank's presence was when the former British paratrooper placed a cold can of caffeine-enhanced energy drink on the desk next to him.

"You know if Chua catches you drinking those he's going to wig out," he said as he grabbed the can and cracked it.

"Pfft, you think he's going to point the finger at me? Everyone knows you're the one who raids his stash."

"Dude, you know that's bullshit."

Frank laughed. "It's all good, I've got my own supply." He dropped into a spare seat. "What are you working on?"

Flash took a gulp and placed the can on the desk. "I've hacked the TRAFFIC servers. Trying to find out if there's any dirt on the *Zenhai*," he said, referring to the wildlife trade monitoring organization.

"You're going after the whole network? Even though they don't pose a direct threat to us?"

"Correct, poachers and smugglers are scumbags. We should unleash everything we have on those pieces of shit."

"Because they hurt Saneh?"

"Yeah, but they're also stripping the planet of wildlife for a profit. Makes me so damn angry when I think that in the near future rhinos could be extinct because of greed, pure, filthy greed."

"Not going to get any disagreement from me. So what have you got?"

"There are a dozen reports linking Chinese shipping to the illicit wildlife trade. Not just in Somalia and Kenya but all the way down the east coast to South Africa."

"Any of them the *Zenhai*?"

"That's just it. The *Zenhai* isn't directly associated with any illicit activity but the description of four of the ships match her perfectly. The *Leikun*, *Guangheng*, *Leixun*, and *Guangjia* fit the exact same profile, and are all involved in Chinese smuggling. So I ran them through an international ship register search and guess what?"

"None of them are registered?"

"Not a single one. However, a little Wikipedia research revealed all the ship's names are from the Guangdong Fleet, the smallest of China's late 19th century fleets."

"The Chinese aren't known for their creativity."

"So I ran a search for every other name I could find and got a hit. The *Haichangqing* was a flat iron gunboat that served in the Guangdong fleet following construction in 1877. She's also a fifteen thousand ton cargo ship registered to a corporation in Shanghai. The same company has the *Zenhai* on their books."

"Two ships or just a single vessel with two names?"

"Sneakier than that. They've got a single ship with two legitimate identities and another four illegitimate ones."

"Crafty little bastards, so what's the next step?"

"Finding out exactly who the corporation is and then exposing their filthy underbelly." Flash downed the rest of his can, crushed it, and tossed it in a trash basket. "How long till the team hits the ground in Mogadishu?"

"Within the hour. How's the *Zenhai* tracking?"

"Still on course. I'm pushing her location over the iPRIMAL network. The ship's transponder is pinging her location every ten seconds."

"Good stuff." Frank rose from the chair and turned for the door. "Hey, Flash."

"Yeah?"

"Make sure you keep the hacking stuff low-key, yeah. Chua would be pretty pissed if we brought the CIA down on us again."

Flash nodded. "Keeping it real tight, buddy."

***

MOGADISHU, SOMALIA

Mogadishu wasn't quite what Kruger expected. He had never visited the capital of Somalia but he'd seen documentaries and images of the war-torn city splashed across television and the internet. Yes, many of the buildings were pockmarked with the scars of civil war and armed men stood on some street corners but he also sensed an air of hope. The people of the city were rebuilding and evidence of the rebirth surrounded them. Cranes towered over partially repaired office buildings. Donkey carts transported construction materials and children played among the rubble.

"Welcome to the Mog," said Toppie from the passenger seat of the pickup.

"Doesn't look too bad."

"Things have changed. The African Union pushed Al-Shabaab out of the city and fighting has stopped."

"Can't be good for your business."

Toppie shrugged. "I don't supply arms to terrorists."

"Regular fucking altruist, aren't you."

"No, I just don't like bastards who don't pay their bills." Toppie flashed him a yellow-toothed grin.

Kruger laughed.

They drove for another twenty minutes through the hustle and bustle of the city to the outskirts. Here the scars of the civil war were more evident. They past abandoned homes and shops whose owners had fled or been massacred. The rusted hulks of destroyed armored vehicles and burnt-out cars lined the road. Kruger noted some damage looked recent. They passed through an African Union checkpoint where heavily armed and alert Kenyan soldiers eyed them suspiciously.

"It's a different story out here. The bloody Islamists still raid the outlying settlements. The only things keeping them at bay are the warlords. This is the Bad Lands, my boy. Out here, unfortunately, business is booming."

"So what's the low-down on this Al-Mumit guy?"

"Used to be a fisherman but now he's the biggest of the pirate bosses."

"I thought the Task Force put an end to piracy off Somalia."

"Almost, the smaller gangs are gone now but Al-Mumit remains. His people manage to avoid the navy and still hijack the odd ship."

"Bit of a nutter then?"

"Not at all, he's a businessman. He runs his operation like a finely tuned machine." The arms dealer pointed to a side street. "You need to turn right. We go through that gate."

He followed the directions and pulled the truck up outside a high-walled compound. With sandbagged fighting positions on the corners and a pair of heavy steel doors it resembled a fortress. Toppie climbed out and yelled up at the men manning the battlement. A moment later the gates rattled open and he climbed back inside the truck.

Kruger parked beside a pickup sporting a 14.5mm KPV heavy machine gun. "One of yours?"

Toppie grunted and led them across the gravel parking lot to a large single-story cinder-block building. A throng of Somalis sat on crates under the eaves. They looked like a hard bunch, dressed in motley fatigues and military-style webbing. The only uniformity among them was the folding stock AKMs they all carried; more of the arms dealer's wares.

The roar of a crowd echoed from inside the building as they paused at the doorway. One of the men gave Toppie a nod and they proceeded inside.

As Kruger's eyes adjusted to the dim light a scene straight from an apocalyptic movie confronted him. Under a rusted iron roof a group of men had formed a rough circle around two fighters. Clad only in pants the bare-chested fighters looked exhausted, covered in blood and sweat. He watched as they struggled to throw punches. One of them managed to connect a blow to the jaw and his opponent went down like a sack of sand. Kruger winced as his face bounced off the concrete floor. The room erupted with cheering as the winner's supporters gathered their earnings from the backers of the downed man.

"Come on," Toppie said leading him toward a doorway at the back of the room.

They skirted the crowd and Kruger thought he glimpsed a hyena chained in the far corner. Ducking into a long corridor that stank of alcohol and urine Toppie strode to the other end. At an ornate wooden door a guard stood post dressed in full combat rig complete with a chrome Vietnam-style GI helmet and a bandolier of ammunition.

"We're here to see the King," barked Toppie.

“Wait here.” The guard opened the door and spoke to someone. Then he pushed it open and gestured for them to enter.

If the fight in the foyer was straight out of a movie then the next scene only added to the spectacle. As they entered the air-conditioned room their eyes were drawn to a wooden throne on a raised stage. Scantily clad ebony-skinned women lounged on silver cushions around it. Beneath, rows of desks topped with computers were manned by youths who wouldn't have been out of place in a programming class. Sitting on the throne was a middle-aged Somali dressed in a well-tailored three-piece suit.

“Toppie, how is my favorite arms-dealing geriatric midget on this fine day?”

Kruger suppressed a smile.

“Very well, Mr. King,” Toppie said approaching the throne.

“What wonderful weapons and means of destruction have you brought me from the far away town of Mombasa?” The man had a rich bass voice and spoke with a hint of a British accent.

Toppie shook his head. “Not weapons today, Mr. King. Today I've brought you some lucrative business.” He gestured to Kruger who stepped forward.

“Oh I see.”

The man they called Al-Mumit rose from his throne and strode down to greet Kruger. He flashed a charming smile filled with straight white teeth and thrust out his hand. “What kind of business do you have to offer, Mr....?”

“Kruger.” He accepted the firm grip and shook hands. It felt as if he had been weighed and measured all in a split-second. “There's a ship steaming off the coast of Somalia and I need you to attack it.”

Al-Mumit nodded thoughtfully then walked around the row of computer operators and stood behind one of them. “And what is the name of this ship?”

“The *Zenhai.*”

“Chinese-flagged?”

"Yes."

He placed his hand on the computer operator's shoulder and watched as the youth typed. "Yes, here she is. Only eighty miles away and tracking closer." He looked at Kruger. "And why, may I ask, do you need this particular ship attacked?"

"Because I have a good friend who's on board."

"Ah, so you want my people to provide a diversion."

Kruger nodded. Al-Mumit certainly wasn't stupid. "I don't need you to board the vessel, I just need you to keep them occupied for a while."

"Whilst you helicopter aboard, no doubt."

"That bit is my problem."

"True, well you are leaving this to the last minute, aren't you? The *Zenhai* will be long gone by this evening."

Kruger glanced at his watch and did a quick calculation. "Can you do it at 1230?"

"Anything is possible, for the right price." Al-Mumit pointed at the computer operator's screen. "You see this icon here? That's a destroyer from the Anti-Piracy Task Force. We don't mess with them."

"How much will it cost?"

The Pirate King's eyes narrowed and once more Kruger got the feeling he was being measured.

"A million US."

Kruger had anticipated a high number. "250 grand is all I have."

Al-Mumit shrugged. "Then, sir, we don't have a deal."

"OK, OK, I can go as high as 350."

"No, the price is one million. With that destroyer in the area there is significant risk. The price is fair."

As Kruger contemplated the deal Toppie spoke.

"How about you put Kruger up against your best fighter. If he wins you do the job for 250K."

Al-Mumit considered the offer before breaking into a broad smile. "Oh a wager, now this makes it far more exciting. Very well, but what do I get if he loses?"

"I'll give you the armored personnel carrier you're always asking for."

The Pirate King nodded. "A good deal." He reached out and shook Toppie's hand. "Your fighter up against my champion."

"Hang on a second." Kruger raised his hand.

Al-Mumit's expression changed from a pleasant smile to an icy stare. "Win or lose, a fight is the only way you're getting out of here alive." He turned and returned to his throne. "Now if you don't mind I have a business to run. I'll see you ringside."

Kruger turned to Toppie who smiled broadly. "What the fuck have you gotten me in to?"

The arms dealer patted him on the shoulder. "Come on, you were the Regiment's best boxer. You'll take this guy apart."

"And what if I don't?"

"Then I'll buy you a bag of ice on the way back to the airport."

CHAPTER 12

MOGADISHU, SOMALIA

Vance stood beside the Lascar Logistics business jet with a black backpack slung over his shoulder and a phone pressed to his ear. He'd dialed the number Kruger had sent him twice and no one answered. There was no sign of the South African. He was considering ringing the airport staff when a horn honked from behind and he turned to see a UN-marked truck crossing the runway toward him. It pulled up and a figure dressed in blue coveralls jumped down from the cab.

"Sorry about the phone. Network here is shit."

Vance offered his hand. "You must be Vanko. I'm Vance."

"*Da*, your friend said you might need a truck for your gear. We have nearly finished preparing the helicopter."

"Where is Kruger?"

"The big guy? He went to town with Toppie to do something. Said he would be back by lunchtime. You can wait over in the hangar." He nodded at a line of white helicopters parked in front of a maintenance facility.

Ice and Chua made their way down the jet's stairs and stacked their bags in the bed of the truck. Vance climbed into the cab with Vanko while the others sat in the back with the equipment. They drove across the runway, through a checkpoint, and into the maintenance hangar. The Russian parked alongside an Mi-8 utility helicopter painted white with UN lettering. A pair of coverall-clad mechanics were working on the fuel tanks attached to its stubby pylons.

"This is my helicopter," said Vanko. "Do you have the agreed amount?"

Vance opened his backpack and withdrew a folded orange manila envelope. "It's all here." He nodded to the other two PRIMAL operatives and they inspected the helicopter. Ice circled it before approaching Vanko. "Can you take the rear doors off?"

Vanko stared at the scars that marked one side of the operative's face. "*Da*, of course, but why?"

Ice strode across to the truck and grabbed a bulky black duffel bag. Dumping it on the floor he unzipped it and pulled what resembled a thick green python from inside. "So we can attach this to the winching lug and fast rope onto a moving ship."

The Russian pursed his lips. "We can do it in an hour. But, it's going to cost another five grand."

"Make it half an hour and I'll give you ten," said Vance.

"Deal."

Vanko turned to make a phone call while the team unloaded black weapon cases from the truck.

They piled their equipment behind the helicopter, laying out their individual rigs. Each had a set of carbon nanotube armor, a full-faced helmet, and their personal weapons. Chua and Vance were carrying suppressed Tavors chambered in 300 Blackout while Ice had a MK48 with a collapsible stock slung across his broad shoulders.

Vance noticed Ice easily using the artificial hand that had replaced the one he lost in Afghanistan. "How's the robot hand holding up?"

Ice extended the hand. "Care to shake?"

He took the hand and squeezed it hard. Ice raised his eyebrows and closed the grip. Vance felt the pressure increase and clenched in response.

"That all you got, old man?" said Ice as he squeezed.

Vance's hand was almost crushed by the vice-like mechanical grip. "OK, OK, you've made your point."

Ice relaxed the hand and jiggled the fingers gently against Vance's palm. "Plenty of dexterity too."

He tore his hand away. "You're a creep."

Ice laughed and turned his attention back to the gear. He checked his backpack; it contained a comprehensive trauma kit, spare belts of ammunition, and breaching charges. On the outside were pouches for additional grenades. Satisfied, he laid out a duplicate set of armor and weaponry for Kruger including another MK48 machine gun. Not a typical choice for a ship interdiction mission, the belt-fed weapon was a favorite of both he and Kruger.

Vance strode across to Chua. The intel officer had a backpack unzipped and was checking his specialist equipment. A compact drone, spare battery packs, hard drives, and a tablet were all packed in laser-cut foam.

"Chen, what's the go with the *Zenhai*? Is she still tracking north?"

Chua had been monitoring the ship's movements via Flash in the Sandpit. From Abu Dhabi the electronic intelligence specialist had added the ship's transponder data to the iPRIMAL personnel tracker. He glanced at the smartphone-sized device strapped to his wrist. "No change. She's still tracking north and still within range of the chopper. However, our window is closing. We need to be wheels up in forty minutes at the latest."

He checked his watch, it was twenty minutes past midday and still there was no sign of Kruger. At this rate they were going to have to launch the mission without him. Turning back to the helicopter he caught Vanko staring at the men and equipment. Catching Vance's eye he looked away. "Vanko, can you get your aircrew over here? I want to brief them on the mission."

The Russian smiled as he wiped his hands on a greasy rag. "That's easy because you're talking to him already."

"You're flying?"

"This is correct. You're lucky because I'm the best pilot we have."

"How many pilots do you have, Vanko?"

"Three, but the other two are drunks."

"Don't you need a copilot at least?"

The Russian shrugged. "Copilots are like seat belts and life jackets. Nice to have but not necessary. But, I think Toppie is going to help."

"Toppie?"

"Kruger's friend, the arms dealer."

Vance rolled his eyes. "And if he's not here?"

"We can go without him."

He checked his watch again. "Let's go over the plan, boys. If Kruger isn't here in the next forty minutes we're leaving without him."

***

"So what are the rules?" Kruger asked Toppie as they were led them out to the amphitheater beneath the rusted roof.

The arms dealer snorted. "There are no rules. You fight until the other man cannot stand. That's it."

"Doesn't sound very sporting."

"That's because it isn't."

The crowd surrounding the fighting pit had doubled in size and now included women and children. They were packed in tightly and Kruger was forced to push his way through. People jeered and hurled abuse at the tall South African.

"You're a bit of a novelty. They don't get many white people here."

"You don't say," replied Kruger as he wiped spit from his face.

When he reached the center of the ring Kruger searched for his opponent. When no one stepped forward he shrugged and turned to Toppie. "What's going on?"

At that moment the crowd erupted into wild screaming and shrieking. A chant started and it took a moment for Kruger to identify what it was they were saying. "Toppie, what does *jazzer* mean?"

"It's another word for gentle."

"Really?"

The arms dealer smirked. "No, it means butcher."

"Oh shit."

The crowd parted and Kruger found himself staring at possibly the most intimidating human he had ever laid eyes on.

Jazzer stood at least six-foot-eight with arms like a gorilla's and a head the size of a bowling ball. His eyes were wide set and he had beaded braids of greasy hair hanging almost to his waist. His ebony skin barely contained the muscles straining underneath. Stripped to the waist with his hands wrapped in tape, he looked ready for the fight, with a crooked grin on his massive face.

"I'll hold your things," Toppie offered.

"That's big of you," Kruger snapped, taking off his shirt and handing it over along with his pistol, phone, and knife.

Jazzer, the Somali gorilla, entered the ring and Al-Mumit appeared from behind him. The immaculately-dressed Pirate King smiled. "This is my champion fighter, Jazzer. He has never been defeated."

"Good to know. Now if you don't mind I'm late for my next meeting." Kruger took up a fighting stance and the crowd booed.

Jazzer grinned and lifted his fists in a guard. He shuffled forward with his head bent low, gaze fixed on Kruger, growling like a bear.

"You're shitting me," mumbled Kruger. "I'm going toe to toe with a rock ape."

The two fighters circled each other before Jazzer sprung into action. He lunged, firing a volley of punches. Kruger covered up and wore the sledgehammer blows on the forearms. One slipped through his guard sending him reeling.

The crowd roared as he staggered backward to escape from the onslaught.

Kruger had boxed throughout high school and into his military career but never faced blows like these. If he didn't go on the offensive he knew the fight would end imminently.

Fortunately Jazzer didn't feel the need to press the attack. He raised his hands in the air, enjoying the attention from the crowd. Kruger sprung forward and delivered a powerful front kick to the giant's stomach. Jazzer dropped his guard and Kruger dove forward hammer-fisting the temple before spinning his elbow into his brow.

In Krav Maga the method was known as chaining; delivering a sequence of savage blows drawing on every tool in the fighter's arsenal. An accomplished proponent of the art, Kruger had used it to devastating effect in lethal combat.

The assault shook Jazzer but apart from splitting open his eyebrow the effect seemed to be minimal. He stepped back, wiped the blood from his brow, and licked it from his hand. Roaring he charged across the ring with his arms wide.

Kruger launched a lightning fast combo as he attempted to sidestep the onslaught. Widespread arms caught his sweaty torso and lifted him off the ground. Kruger drove his elbow down on the top of his skull. Pain shot up his arm but the Somali giant continued to squeeze depriving him of oxygen. He smashed a fist into the behemoth's temple with absolutely zero effect.

The crowd went wild and he looked down at the grinning face of his opponent. A sickening crunch emitted from his rib cage, like the noise a roast chicken made as you pulled it apart. He bellowed in pain as he reached down, grasped Jazzer's face, and drove his thumbs into the eye sockets.

Al-Mumit's fighter reacted swiftly tossing Kruger aside. He sailed through the air and collided with the spectators sending them sprawling.

Kruger gasped for air as he untangled himself from the mass of limbs. He felt a hand grasp him by the ankle and Jazzer dragged him back into the ring. The giant let go of his leg and knelt over him, grabbing his throat with both hands. Kruger thrust skyward with his hips and pushed his assailant sideways as he clawed free from the chokehold. Rolling away he leaped to his feet.

Jazzer was a brawler; powerful with lightning fast hands, he relied on long reach and brutal blows to overwhelm his opponent. He had never practiced the finer art of ground fighting or the skills to recover from the deck. Kruger launched a sidekick as Jazzer slowly rose to his feet. His boot smashed into the fighter's jaw with all the force he could muster. Bone shattered and Jazzer toppled sideways, hitting the dusty concrete floor with a thud.

The room went quiet as Kruger struggled to catch his breath. A slow clap broke the silence as Al-Mumit stepped forward.

"Well done!" The Pirate King smiled. "I never thought I'd see the day someone defeated Jazzer."

Kruger rose shakily to his feet and winced as he clutched his ribs. "Do we have a deal?" he said curtly.

"Of course, I'm a man of my word." He pulled a pocket watch from his suit and checked the time. "I'll make the call and my people will be in position within the hour."

"And the money?"

"Give it to Toppie. I'll place a new order in a few days."

The arms dealer handed Kruger his shirt and pistol. "No problem, Mr. King. Pleasure doing business."

The pirate disappeared back to his throne room leaving Kruger and Toppie in a ring filled with semi-hostile Jazzer fans and disgruntled gamblers.

"Let's get out of here before they tear you apart," said Toppie as he led him to the door.

Kruger staggered after him squinting as they emerged into bright sunlight. He knew he was going to have a hell of a headache. "Toppie, where is my phone?" he asked as he stuffed his pistol back in his belt.

The arms dealer climbed into the passenger seat. "I don't remember a phone."

"And my knife? One of these pirate whores took them." He shook his head. "That bastard Mumit better come through with what he promised." Kruger turned the ignition, jammed the truck into gear, and spun the wheels as he aimed for the steel doors. The gate rumbled open and he accelerated out onto the highway.

***

Vance strode to the hangar door and checked the compound's security checkpoint. Still no sign of Kruger. He glanced at his watch as boots rang on the concrete behind him.

"We're running out of time," said Chua checking his iPRIMAL. The wrist-mounted device was streaming the *Zenhai's* position. "The target vessel has increased her speed to 20 knots. Every minute she gets further away, limiting the helicopter's loiter time. We push it too far and we might get stuck on board."

"Yeah, yeah I know." He sighed. "OK, let's get the bird turning and burning."

"Roger."

Vance waited at the doorway a moment longer before joining Ice and Chua in the cargo hold of the helicopter. All three were clad in their black-armored assault rigs, with helmets and weapons laid out on the bench seating. The rear clamshell doors of the Mi-8 had been removed and Ice had attached a thick rope to a fastener on the ceiling, coiling it on the floor.

"Kruger's kit is over there," Ice yelled as the twin turbines spooled up to an ear-splitting whine. He gestured to the black gear bag strapped to the side seating.

Vance shot him thumbs-up and the helicopter jolted forward as the ground crew towed it out of the hangar.

Once in the open it took a moment for the crew to detach the towing tractor then Vanko engaged the gearbox and the blades started turning. Fifteen seconds later they lurched off the ground and climbed skyward. Vance slipped his full-face helmet on and powered up the integrated iPRIMAL system. As he did he glanced out the back and spotted a white pickup racing across the taxiway.

"That might be Kruger," Ice transmitted over the radio.

Vance strode into the cockpit and tapped Vanko on the shoulder.

The Russian glanced back and his eyes grew wide at the sight of the space-age helmet.

Vance pulled the helmet off. "Take us down, our man's arrived."

"OK, but we're burning fuel."

A moment later the helicopter touched down and Kruger leaped into the back followed by a scruffy bearded man wearing a leather vest and pistol belt. Vance greeted the PRIMAL operative with a handshake and frowned when he spotted the swollen lump growing on the side of his head. "What the hell happened to you?" he bellowed over the turbines.

Kruger shook his head. "Don't ask. Vance, this is an old friend, Toppie."

The grizzled South African shook his hand then hurried through to the cockpit of the helicopter.

"Is he good to go?" asked Vance.

"Yeah, damn fine pilot."

As the helicopter climbed skyward Vance grasped Kruger's shoulder and directed him to his gear. Kruger slipped the armor over his shirt and strapped it in place with a grunt. Vance saw him wince as he slid the full-face helmet over the expanding bruise on the side of his head. "You going to be OK?"

"Yeah, bit sore is all," Kruger replied as he strapped an iPRIMAL to his forearm and checked his MK48 machine gun. With a loadout similar to Ice, and an equally impressive stature, they could almost pass for twins. Once they had their fully-enclosed helmets on only Ice's bionic hand and prosthetic leg would set them apart.

Vance opened a communications channel to the entire team. "Alright, Kruger, give us what you know."

"Boys, sorry about the lack of information but I've been jumping through my ass to try and get things organized to get on the damn ship."

"We understand, brother," said Vance. "Do we know how many hostiles are embarked?"

"At least four shooters. I saw three men on the railing when Bishop got on board. With Mamba that makes four."

"And Mamba is Bishop's target?' asked Chua.

"Correct, we were loading ivory onto the ship when a police launch attacked us. Mamba escaped to the cargo ship and Bishop went after him."

"So Bishop could be a hostage, could be hiding, or may have jumped overboard."

"We have to assume he's still on board because we've heard nothing."

The helicopter finished its climb and tilted forward on a heading out to sea. The heads-up display in Vance's helmet told him the *Zenhai* was a little over a forty nautical miles away.

"Let's roll with the worse-case scenario, that he's a hostage," said Vance. "Now, I've never hit a ship before. Ice, you did this all the time in the Marines, so you're running the show."

A schematic of the *Zenhai* appeared in their helmets courtesy of Chua.

"If they're light on men they're going to post their security around the superstructure at the aft," said Ice.

"If things go to plan the security personnel will be occupied," added Kruger.

"With what?" asked Chua.

"Pirates, they're scheduled to attack at 1230 hours. That's what I was doing in Mogadishu."

The time indicated in their helmets was 1207. ETA on target was 1240.

"Cutting it fine. What if they request assistance from the anti-piracy fleet?" asked Chua.

"If they're smuggling ivory and have Bishop detained I'm guessing they won't."

"Ice, what's the best way to do this?" asked Vance.

"We fast rope down to the bow. If we're forward of the rigging and containers it will make us harder to hit. We work in pairs, one either side of the ship, and fight our way to the superstructure then search for Bishop."

"Roger," Chua said. "And once we get close we should be able to track him via his implant."

"Wait, we've got tracking implants now?" asked Ice. "So we'll know exactly where he is?"

"It only has a short range, dozen yards at best, and no not everyone has one," replied Chua. "Just the high-risk individuals."

"OK, that will make the search easier. Vance, you'll work with me. Kruger, you've got Chua."

"*Ja,* no problems." The broad-shouldered South African pointed at his designated partner. "Stay out of the way, little man. Uncle Kruger is going to bring the hurt." He slapped the side of his MK48 machine gun.

"Try not shoot down my drone when you're blazing away, Rambo," quipped the intel chief.

"We're ten minutes out," said Ice.

Vance checked over his equipment and racked the action on his Tavor. Scrolling through the menus on his iPRIMAL heads-up display he confirmed all systems were green. Then he turned to his battle buddy, Ice, and checked his rig.

"Just like the old days," said Ice. "Except the kit's a bit better."

"Gear or no gear, I'm too old for this shit."

"What's wrong, old man? Knees getting sore? You could always get Mitch to whip you up some new joints."

He grasped the bigger man's shoulder. "The terminator look suits you better, bud. Now let's go get Bishop out of the shit."

"Like I said, just like the old days!"

CHAPTER 13

INDIAN OCEAN

Bishop sat in darkness listening to the dull throb of the ship's engines as he contemplated his fate. The Chinese Triads, he assumed that's who they were, had taken all his equipment including his watch when they locked him in the brig. Lapsing in and out of consciousness he'd lost track of time. Sleep would have been a welcome relief but chained to the wall all he could manage was few minutes slumped forward before the pain in his shoulders became unbearable.

Doubt and fear assailed him as he fought the urge to scream with rage. He should have listened to Vance and waited for PRIMAL to launch a full-scale operation. Now, his only hope was that Mamba or the Chinese made a mistake that he could capitalize on. It was far more likely that they would torture him to a point where he was incapable of escape.

Apart from the initial visit from Mamba the only other person he'd had contact with was an assault rifle-wielding guard who had given him a box of juice with a straw. The juice was long gone and Bishop's mouth parched.

Despair washed over him as his thoughts turned to Saneh and their baby. He didn't even know if they were alive. Choking back tears he channeled his emotion into a ball of rage. If he failed to kill Mamba there would be no justice for either of them.

The creak of the door's locking mechanism snapped him back to reality and he squinted as light streamed into the cell. A figure stood for a moment in the doorway before the light switched on and the door slammed shut. It was Mamba.

"Are you ready to talk?"

Bishop struggled to stay silent. He knew that as soon as he gave up the information Mamba wanted the game would be up. His usefulness would expire and he'd be tossed overboard.

The poacher sat on the bed laying his machete beside him. Bishop noticed he held a rhino horn wrapped in plastic.

"Don't want to talk? That's OK, you'll talk soon enough. Now, I wanted to show you this." He unwrapped the horn and held it up to the light.

Bishop struggled to keep his rage under control as he realized it was the horn cut from the snout of the black rhino at Luangwa.

"This is what it's all about. This is what makes me money."

He could feel Mamba's eyes on him, studying how he reacted to the horn and his words.

"I need you to understand that this is only business. It was unfortunate your woman was killed. But, it happened and soon you will be joining her. It's up to you if we make it quick, or slow and painful."

Bishop strained against the ties securing his wrists. Every fiber of his being wanted to break free of the bonds, take the horn, and kill Mamba with it. That would be justice.

The poacher smiled as he wrapped the horn and stowed it in a thigh pocket of his cargo pants. "So now I need you to talk, and make things easier for yourself."

He clenched his jaw.

"No?" Mamba stood and unsheathed the machete.

He braced himself as Mamba leaned forward testing the edge of the blade with his thumb. With his hands tied to the wall he was helpless; death was inevitable. As Mamba's lip curled into a sinister smirk a dull thud shook the deck.

"What the fuck was that?" The poacher stood straight, turned, and pushed open the door. He pointed his machete at Bishop. "This has bought you minutes, that's all."

The door shut with a slam leaving Bishop alone in the dark. Despite the blood weeping from his raw wrists he started work on his flexicuffs, rubbing them frantically against the steel chain.

Mamba sprinted for his cabin located half way up the superstructure. Over the hum of the air-conditioning he could hear more gunfire. He pushed open the cabin door and grabbed a Type 81 rifle, borrowed from the Triads, and his assault vest. Stowing his machete in its sheath he shrugged on the vest and dashed along a corridor. Climbing up a stairwell he almost collided with Kehua running down with one of his men. They were also carrying rifles.

"What's going on?" he asked.

"Pirates!" said the gangster as he ran past.

Mamba climbed the final flight of stairs and burst into the bridge where he found the captain hunkered behind the ship's console.

"More of your friends?" the captain snarled.

Mamba stormed out to the port side wing and surveyed the situation. Less than a mile away three Somali skiffs were in pursuit. He spotted a puff of smoke as a RPG launched from the lead boat. The rocket streaked toward them and slammed against a stack of containers with a muffled explosion. The other boats began pouring machine gun fire into the ship. Heavy-caliber rounds peppered the steel containers and superstructure. Mamba ducked as a fusillade of bullets ripped through the bridge shattering the windows. Below him weapons barked as Kehua and his men returned fire. A moment later the rattle of a machine gun joined the rifles; the Triads had broken out their own heavy weapons.

Mamba beat a hasty retreat inside as more rounds slapped against the ship's steel walls. He hunkered low beside the captain behind the console. "Can they get on board?"

"At this speed, I doubt it. They'd have to disable us and the only way they could do that is to hit the rudder or the engines."

"Then what the hell are they doing?"

"I don't know. I've tried hailing them but no one has responded."

Outside the gunfight was growing in intensity.

"I know someone who will." Mamba retrieved his phone from a pouch and scrolled through his contacts. Hunching he made his way across to the ship's satellite phone and grabbed the handset. Dialing a number he held the receiver to his ear.

When the call connected he yelled, "Get me Al-Mumit! Tell him it's Mamba."

Seconds past and another round smashed through the glass showering him with shards.

"Mr. Mboya, to what do I owe the pleasure?"

"No pleasure, are your people attacking the *Zenhai*?"

There was a pause. "Possibly, why?"

"Because I'm on the fucking ship!"

"Really, well I do believe we have a conflict of interest then."

"Call them off, you're not going to get on board."

"They don't need to. Well, I hope you enjoy your little cruise, Mamba."

"Fuck you, I've been good to you and this is how you repay me?"

The Pirate King sighed. "I suppose one good turn deserves another. If I were you I'd find somewhere to hide. There is a very large white man with a bad temper about to come aboard your ship. It might pay to give him what he wants." The line went dead.

"What the fuck does that mean?" Mamba threw the handset. It reached the end of its spring cable and retracted with the speed of a striking cobra, smashing into the console.

He flinched and the captain snorted with laughter.

Mamba turned to him. "Where the fuck are the crew?"

"In the safe room."

"Where is it?"

"Behind the engine room. You can join them if you like."

"And hide like a dog?" He picked up his rifle and caught a glimpse of movement out the window. Staying low he pushed open the side door and slipped outside. He squinted, spotting a white helicopter. It was a couple of miles out, flying in the same direction they were traveling and banking toward them. The large white man with the bad temper was coming. He turned and charged back into the bridge. "Do you have radio communications with Kehua?"

The captain nodded holding up his radio.

"Tell him we're about to be boarded."

"By who?"

"By a fucking helicopter." Mamba sprinted out of the bridge and down the stairwell. He needed to find Kehua fast.

***

Ice braced himself against the inside of the helicopter, his machine gun slung across his chest. His robotic hand held the thick rope in a death grip as they descended over the bow of the *Zenhai*. He stared through the missing rear doors across the ship's cargo of containers to the superstructure a few hundred yards away. Out to his left he could see the three pirate skiffs. One of them burned fiercely and another had withdrawn from the battle. Glancing down he made sure the foredeck thirty feet below was clear of obstacles. "Hold her steady, Vanko." As he transmitted he spotted a dark figure crouched alongside a container aiming a weapon. "Shooter!"

Next to him Kruger unleashed an automatic burst as bullets struck the chopper punching holes in the aluminum tail boom.

"Break away, break away!"

Ice grabbed Kruger by the shoulder as the helicopter nosed down in front of the ship. "You get him?"

"Negative."

"Fast rope is not an option," Ice transmitted to Vanko. "Can you go wheels down on the foredeck?"

"I can hover in front. You crazy Cossacks can jump."

"Good, man, let's do this. People, we're going to jump. Kruger and I will cover you."

The team now faced the looming bow of the Chinese freighter as Vanko kept them hovering a dozen feet above the water in front of it. The churning wave thrown up by the bow looked as if it was bearing down on them.

"OK, take her up." Ice crouched with his MK48 held ready.

Vanko hauled up on the collective and they climbed above the ship's railing. Kruger and Ice didn't take any chances. They laid down a withering hail of fire with their machine guns as the Russian pilot hovered a few feet above the ship's railing.

"Go, go, go!" yelled Kruger.

Chua was first to jump. He leaped out the back, hit the deck, rolled, and found cover behind one of the rusted windlasses used to raise the anchors.

Vance was a split-second behind him and moved to the opposite side.

Before Ice and Kruger could jump the chopper lurched away from the ship. "I'm having problems holding her steady. It's the updraft coming off her front," reported Vanko.

"Bring her down," transmitted Ice as he readied himself. He could see Vance and Chua covering from their positions on the deck. The shooter who'd engaged them earlier was nowhere to be seen. The helicopter dropped abruptly, hitting the ship's railing.

"Power on!" Ice yelled as Kruger dropped to the deck. The chopper's engines screamed and it soared skyward as he leaped clear, landing heavily on his prosthetic leg. The inbuilt shock-absorbers dissipated the energy and he recovered, shouldering the machine gun as he moved to Vance. Behind him the UN-marked helicopter climbed away.

"You guys better be quick and find me somewhere to put this thirsty bitch down," transmitted Vanko over the radio.

"Will do. Keep us informed on your fuel state," replied Ice. Using the iPRIMAL attached to his wrist he silenced the channel to the pilot. "OK, team, is everyone ready?"

"I'm good," reported Vance.

"Team one is good to go," replied Kruger from his position with Chua on the opposite side of the ship.

"Drone is up." Chua had tossed the compact quadcopter skyward and it buzzed a few dozen feet above them.

Ice shouldered his machine gun as the video from the frisbee-sized aircraft appeared in his helmet. "OK, let's roll." He rose and advanced swiftly down the side of the containers stacked on the deck.

***

Kehua watched intently as a rocket streaked toward the last of the pirate skiffs still engaging the merchant vessel. The high-explosive warhead detonated amidships and the craft exploded in a ball of flame. As the smoke cleared all that remained of the wooden boat was burning wreckage. He turned to the two men manning the Type 98 rocket launcher. "Well done."

The Triads were lined up on the side of the ship's superstructure with their weapons aimed at the fleeing pirates. At the first sign of the attack he'd ordered them to deploy their heavy weapons. Two machine guns and the Type 98 had quickly turned the fight in his favor.

"They're coming!"

The yell caught his attention and he turned to see Mamba sprinting up the stairs from the ship's deck. "They're on board and they're coming."

"Who?"

"Demons," Mamba managed between breaths. "Black-armored demons. They landed in the helicopter up front."

The Chinese gangster had spotted the UN helicopter but he'd assumed it was from the anti-piracy fleet. "How many?"

"No more than six. I shot at their helicopter."

Kehua changed the magazine on his assault rifle and gave Mamba a look of contempt. "This is the second time you've brought trouble to this vessel. You're lucky I don't hand you to these men. Now, stay out of my way, I'm going to kill them." He snapped out orders to his men and they leaped into action. The machine guns were orientated toward the new threat and the lower doors accessing the superstructure were secured.

His plan was simple; ambush the intruders as they tried to gain access to the superstructure. If they made it through the kill zone then they would have to cut their way through the steel doors, that's if they had the equipment. In the time it took them to breach Kehua and his men would pull back and wait in the stairwells.

Kehua used his radio to check his fire teams were ready then turned to Mamba. "Go and get the rhino horn. It will be safer with me."

"Zhou will get it when I see him and not before. Your job is to protect this ship and the cargo. That's me and the horn." He turned and disappeared inside.

The gangster cursed in Mandarin.

The gunner next to him unleashed a long burst, startling him. He turned and scanned the length of the ship. Spotting a figure duck behind a container he fired his own weapon and waited for the target to appear again. He smiled; the open deck in front of the bridge was a perfect killing ground.

***

Ice spotted the muzzle flash of the machine gun high up on the superstructure. He laid down suppressive fire from behind a ventilation stack as bullets sparked off the deck.

"Vance, you OK?" His battle buddy had been advancing along the deck when they were hit.

"Yeah, I'm good but those motherfuckers got me dancing like Fred Astaire on speed."

Ice suppressed a laugh as he viewed the drone feed in his heads-up display. Two machine guns were firing from the near the ship's bridge, one aimed at him and Vance and the other at Kruger and Chua. "How's the port side tracking?"

"Taking cover, same as you guys. So much for the Pirate King," reported Kruger.

Ice glanced out at the ocean and spotted the burning remains of a wooden skiff. The other two vessels were nowhere to be seen. "The pirates may have come off second best," he said.

"As will we if we don't get off this deck."

Ice had to admit the situation was less than optimal. Using the feed from the drone he held the MK48 out from cover and squeezed the trigger. In his HUD he could see the rounds striking the superstructure where he had spotted the flash from the machine gun. His efforts were met with a long burst forcing him to pull the gun back in.

"We can't stay here," Vance transmitted.

Ice spotted a crane jutting out between a gap in the containers. "Vance, you remember that time in Kosovo?"

"Gotta be more specific, bud."

"Never mind, I'm going to pop smoke, they're going to blast it, and then I'm going to move to the gap in the containers. Once I'm in place you bump forward."

"Got it."

Ice took a smoke grenade from his vest, tore out the pin, and lobbed it past Vance. It bounced once and clattered to a halt a dozen yards ahead of them where it began belching thick pink smoke.

"Pink, haven't seen that before," Vance said as the gunfire from the ship's defenders focused on the smokescreen. "You get it specially made?"

"Couldn't help yourself could you." Ice activated his helmet's thermal sensors while waiting for the gunfire to pause. "I know you swapped them out, Vance. I checked them back at the Sandpit."

"I thought you'd like it. I mean, you've always been in touch with your feminine side. Think of it as a welcome back gift."

"Thanks, bro, nice to know you care." Ice ducked out from behind cover and sprinted along the walkway. As he slid into the gap between the containers a machine gun started firing again.

"They don't let up do they," said Vance.

"You're next."

"Woo hoo," Vance said dryly.

When the firing paused Vance rushed forward and joined Ice.

The space between the shipping containers housed a massive derrick used to hoist containers when ports lacked the necessary infrastructure.

The clatter of another machine gun announced the arrival of Chua. He appeared from the other side and a moment later Kruger joined him.

"How the fuck are we going to get inside?" spat the South African. "Pricks have got the bridge sealed up tighter than a nun's–"

"Listen, I've got an idea," Ice interrupted. "Does anyone know how to operate a crane?"

"Yeah," said Chua.

Vance turned to the intelligence officer. "Where the hell did you learn how to use a crane?"

"Before I switched to intel I was an army engineer."

"You've kept that quiet."

"So what exactly are we going to do, Ice?" asked Chua. "We're running out of time."

"According to our drone feed their defenses are focused on denying access to the superstructure and the bridge. The crane is going to get me around that."

***

Thirty-eight nautical miles north east of the Chinese freighter a sleek gray warship knifed through Somali waters on a patrol of the primary shipping lanes. The *USS Roosevelt* was a nine thousand ton Arleigh Burke-class destroyer assigned to Combined Task Force 151, the international anti-piracy fleet. For the past month she had been patrolling the waters off Somalia with little in the way of action. Boarding attempts by the pirates had all but ceased since the Task Force commenced operations.

The ship's captain sat perched on his command chair flicking through a copy of the latest intelligence reports from CTF headquarters. It made for some pretty dry reading. So much so he welcomed the interruption from the officer of the deck.

"Sir, we've got a distress signal from a Chinese-flagged merchant ship forty nautical miles south," reported the dark-haired female Lieutenant. "They claim she is under attack from pirates and..."

"And?"

"And a UN-marked helicopter."

The captain raised his eyebrows. "A UN chopper? Sounds like the Chinese are a little confused." The only piracy incident they'd responded to in the last month had been a false alarm, a fishing boat that had strayed near a cruise ship.

"Sir, the Captain of the *Zenhai* sounds calm and his English is good. Perhaps the pirates have managed to steal one of the UN helicopters?"

The captain gave her a hard stare.

"Or maybe the Russian contractors are outsourcing their services."

He sighed. "What's the status on our helos?"

"One bird is down for maintenance. The other is refueling and can be in the air within 30 minutes."

The captain looked out through the bridge windows. "I want a SEAL team on board that ship. Have them airborne in the next twenty."

"Aye, sir."

"Helmsman, bring us about. I want to close with the vessel at full ahead." He rose and tossed the intelligence file on his chair. Bracing against one of the bridge consoles he felt the deck slant as they adjusted course. As unlikely as the Chinese captain's report was it was his responsibility to respond to all distress calls. He smirked as the ship came around; helicopter-borne pirates verged on the ridiculous. Still, at least it added a little excitement to an otherwise monotonous day.

CHAPTER 14

INDIAN OCEAN

Kehua knelt next to one of his machine gunners, scanning the approaches to the superstructure. "Watch the containers, they could try to come over the top," he said in Mandarin. His men had managed to stop the black-armored figures from advancing but now they had disappeared behind billowing smoke. With the walkways either side of the shipping containers denied he anticipated they would come over the top of the containers and attempt to suppress his positions. Surprise was the only advantage available to the attackers and now they had lost it the battle was all but won.

He spotted a tiny drone hovering in the air and aimed his assault rifle. Four shots later and the flying robot had dropped out of the sky, bounced off the ship, and fallen into the ocean.

He smiled. Now the attackers were without both surprise and knowledge. It was only a matter of time before they made their move and his men gunned them down. Thumbing the empty magazine from his weapon he caught a glimpse of movement on the port side walkway. "Get ready, here they come," he said ramming home a fresh magazine.

Kehua frowned as he realized the movement he had spotted was of objects not people. More smoke grenades bounced over the stack of containers and down the walkways. With a hiss they spewed thick pink smoke across the ship. "Fire, fire!" he bellowed as he blasted at the top of the containers.

Gunfire assaulted his eardrums as bullets snapped through the billowing smoke and punched into the steel superstructure. The gunman next to Kehua cried out as return fire clipped his arm. "Ready with grenades," he ordered as he waited for figures to appear through the smoke. The thick cloud had already started to dissipate as it wafted toward them. Soon the breeze created by the forward motion of the ship would render the smokescreen useless.

"Up there!" the yell came from one of his men.

Kehua glanced skyward and spotted a figure sailing through the air. He raised his rifle but bullets sang on the steel railing in front of him and he ducked for cover. Beside him he heard a wet slap followed by a thud. Turning he saw his machine gunner lying face down on the deck, shot through the head. "An intruder is on the bridge," he transmitted over the radio.

High above the defenders, hanging from the crane, Ice swung through the air. The steel hook looped through the drag handle on the back of his armor, allowing him to concentrate on firing his MK48. He hammered the lower levels of the superstructure as he soared toward the bridge. The crane jolted to a halt only six feet from the bridge wing. Momentum swung him forward and he reached out with one hand for the steel weather shield. Falling short he swung back.

"I can't extend the boom any further," transmitted Chua.

"Pull me back. Turn it as fast as you can and feed out the cable," Ice replied between firing bursts from his machine gun.

"Roger". Chua swung the crane back then forward again. As Ice sailed through the air and reached the furthest point of the boom he released the cable.

Ice soared toward the wing and managed to grab the edge of the bridge railing. The weight of the cable jolted him back. With his MK48 hanging from its sling, he used one hand to draw his knife, reach over his shoulder, and slice through the nylon strap cutting the hook free. He sheathed the knife and hauled himself over the weather shield. Hitting the steel decking with a thud he clambered to his feet, weapon ready.

Through the glass he could see a single figure hunkered down behind the bridge console. Wrenching open the door he stormed in and the uniformed man screamed with fright.

"You speak English?"

The terrified Asian nodded frantically. "Yes, yes I speak English." He wore the gold bars of a ship's captain.

"Good, how many armed men are there?" Ice checked the captain for weapons and secured his hands with flexicuffs.

"Seven... eight if you count the black man."

Ice's eyes darted toward the access door on the opposite side; it was partially ajar.

His MK48 spat lead, the 7.62mm rounds punching through the metal. He heard a cry and gave it another burst for good measure. Transferring the machine gun to his back Ice drew his Glock and pulled a teargas-laced concussion grenade from his vest. Dropping it through the shattered window in the middle of the door he braced himself against the wall.

The explosion threw the door open and Ice charged in, pistol ready.

Gunfire echoed off the steel walls and he felt a round glance off his armor. The thermal sensors in his helmet gave him near perfect vision through the gas and he shot the gunman in the chest as he stepped over a body. Readying another grenade he dropped it further down the stairwell. It clattered as it bounced down the stairs and exploded with a heart-stopping boom.

Stepping quietly down the stairs he heard coughing a level below. Taking a Taser from one of his pouches he held it ready under his pistol. In the confined corridor the CS gas hung thick. Despite the filters in his helmet he could taste the metallic tang. Reaching the landing he spotted the thermal signature of a man fumbling for the door handle.

The Taser's barbed electrodes shot into the gunman's back and he convulsed dropping his rifle. It clattered to the deck and Ice released the trigger on the Taser before smashing the butt of his Glock down on the man's skull. He collapsed to the ground, out cold.

"I'm on the same level as the gunners," Ice reported over the communications link.

"Roger, we've taken out the port side. We can't get a bead on the starboard weapon," replied Vance.

The staccato hammering of a machine gun confirmed he was in position to deal with the remaining weapons team. He waited for the gun to fire again and shoved open the door.

The gunner spotted him and turned. Ice rushed forward and grabbed the smoldering barrel with his robotic hand. With the other he shoved the pistol against the man's forehead. "Hands in the air."

The Chinese gunman let go of the weapon.

"Kneel."

He dropped to his knees next to the body of one of his comrades. Ice secured his hands and feet leaving him lying beside the corpse.

"Second gun is down," he reported.

"Roger, heading to the superstructure."

He checked the port side landing and confirmed the men there were neutralized before moving down the stairs. At the next level he unlocked the door that led outside. Pushing it open revealed the smoking barrel of Kruger's machine gun. It was the rest of the team.

"Love your work, bro." Kruger bumped knuckles with Ice as he stepped inside.

"I've cleared from the bridge down. The Captain is detained along with two shooters. There are four KIA."

"Copy," said Vance. "Now we clear the rest of the ship and find Bishop. Then we get our asses off this rust bucket."

"Has anyone contacted Vanko?" asked Ice.

"Yes, he's putting the bird down on the forward containers," replied Chua as he unslung his backpack and removed a device resembling a satellite phone. He turned it on, extended a thick black antenna, and it immediately began emitting a beeping sound. "OK, I suggest we start at the bridge and work our way down."

Vance turned to Ice. "Alright, big man, lead the way."

***

Mamba wiped the tears from his eyes as he struggled to catch his breath. He'd been in the bottom of the stairwell when the first gas-concussion grenades had exploded. His ears were still ringing. One glimpse of the black-clad assassins slaying the Triads was all he needed to prompt his retreat into the bowels of the ship. He had the rhino horn tucked into his vest and planned to hide until the intruders had departed. They'd come by helicopter so he assumed they would leave the same way.

Clutching his assault rifle he followed the stairs down to a door with a glass portal. He glanced inside and spotted machinery in the gloom; the engine compartment. Pushing open the door the noise and heat from the massive diesel engines hit him. The room stank of oil fumes and the walkway was slippery with grease and grime. Looking around he searched for somewhere to hide. The captain had mentioned a safe room but he couldn't see any other doorways in the dark recesses. Carefully navigating the steel gantry above the rows of engines and generators, he spotted a coverall-wearing figure standing at a console below. He slung his rifle, climbed down a ladder, and approached.

The man threw his hands in the air, a mask of terror on his face.

"Where's the safe room?" asked Mamba.

The elderly engineer shook his head and mumbled.

"Fucking hell." Mamba shoved the man aside, unslung his weapon, and followed the walkway deeper into the shadows.

***

Bishop had no way of knowing what was going on outside his tiny cell. He'd heard what could be gunfire and explosions but it was difficult to discern over the throb of the ship's engines. At one stage he thought he felt an explosion reverberate through the steel floor and swore the air coming through the vent above him was tainted with tear gas. A far as he knew it could all be his imagination. He'd finally lost track of time, having drifted off into a fitful sleep.

The blood on his cheek had coagulated so he knew it had been at least half an hour, possibly more, since Mamba had last come to see him. His wrists were raw but he'd come no closer to breaking the plastic cuffs that bound his hands behind his back. Helplessness washed over him as he realized the severity of his situation. If Kruger was dead or in prison then no one in PRIMAL could know he was on the ship. Unable to break the ties on his wrist he would inevitably end up the same way. If he still had tears they would have flowed freely.

In his mind he could see Saneh lying in a hospital bed with wires and tubes running from her body into banks of machines. He imagined the moment the doctor turned them off, dropped his head, and sobbed.

The door creaked and he lifted his eyes, squinting as he waited for the light to flash on. It didn't. Instead a figure stood in the doorway and called out.

"It's him. I've found Bishop."

The voice sounded synthetic and harsh. It took him a moment to identify it as human.

"Who, who is it?"

"Bish, it's me, Chua."

Relief flooded his body as the figure entered the room and pulled off its helmet. A light snapped on and Bishop looked up to see a second hulking black-clad operative. "Kruger?"

"*Ja,* it's me."

"Saneh," he said frantically. "Saneh and the baby."

"They're still alive. She's hanging in there," replied Chua as he used a combat knife to cut the flexicuffs. "Damn it, buddy, they made a real mess of you," he murmured examining his face.

"Did you find Mamba?" Bishop croaked as he staggered to his feet. The blood rushed back into his shoulders and hands as he clenched and unclenched his fists.

"Not yet."

"We've searched the entire superstructure. There's no sign of the rat," added Kruger.

"Give me a weapon," he said gesturing to Chua.

The intelligence chief drew his Glock and handed it to Bishop along with a spare magazine. "Vance is up on the bridge with the prisoners. There's a chopper at the bow ready to take us back to Mogadishu."

"I'm not going anywhere till Mamba is dead."

"Bish, we need to get out of here."

He walked stiffly for the door. "This won't take long. That bastard will be hiding in a dark hole somewhere. I'll find him."

Kruger blocked his exit from the room. "I'll come with you."

He reached out and plucked a concussion grenade from the South African's chest. "Stay the hell out of my way, this is personal." He stormed out the door and down the corridor.

"You better follow him," said Chua.

"*Ja,* I know." Kruger turned and jogged after the renegade operative.

***

Bishop knew Mamba would have fled, leaving the defense of the ship to the Chinese gangsters. The poacher must have found somewhere to hide. The team had already cleared the superstructure so he wasn't in one of the cabins. That left the cargo hold and engineering compartment. Mamba wouldn't risk being caught with the ivory stowed below, which narrowed it further.

He found the staircase leading down and as he reached the bottom a door opened. A Chinese man wearing coveralls stepped out and seeing Bishop, flung his hands in the air, eyes wide with fear.

"English?" Bishop lowered the Glock.

The grease-covered man shook his head. "Bad, bad, bad," the engineer said pointing back through the door he had emerged from.

"Thanks, mate." Bishop stepped past him his pistol held ready.

The multi-level space was dark and stank of fuel. The throb of the diesel engines added to the pounding in his head; a symptom of dehydration. He exhaled in an attempt to clear the pain and focus on finding Mamba. Walking along the gantry linking the entry point to a ladder he surveyed the compartment. Half way across he felt the frame rock slightly and he looked back. A dark figure stood at the entrance to the catwalk, Kruger.

He scowled and gestured back toward the door.

The South African extended a gloved hand and raised his middle finger.

Bishop shook his head and turned his attention back to hunting Mamba. He wouldn't tell the South African but it felt good to know he had his back. He tucked the Glock under his chin and slid down the ladder to the grated floor. Returning the pistol to his grip he moved forward cautiously past a workbench littered with tools.

The noise of the engines was deafening and the heat oppressive. Checking between the engine blocks and an exhaust system he began to doubt Mamba was there. Sweat ran from his forehead into the wound on his cheek and he clenched his jaw as it stung. As he dragged his forearm across his brow, he glimpsed movement ahead. He fired as he leaped sideways, into a nook between two pieces of machinery. A blast of automatic fire swept the walkway as an entire magazine was unleashed. Bullets ricocheted off metal, smashed lights, and punched holes in equipment as Bishop hunkered down.

When the firing ceased he leaned out and snapped off a series of rapid shots. Where the hell was the covering fire from Kruger? Glancing over his shoulder he spotted a figure collapsed on the overhead walkway. The South African was hit.

Bishop heard the telltale noise of a weapon being cocked over the clatter of the engines. He turned back in time to see Mamba's distinctive silhouette but only managed to fire two rounds before being forced to ducked back. Again the gunfire was thunderous but this time the poacher kept the bursts tight and controlled.

"I wasn't going to throw you overboard," the poacher yelled.

Bishop fired at the voice. "Screw you, Mamba."

"We can cut a deal." Bullets sparked off a generator opposite his head.

"Then why are you shooting?"

He was answered by another burst of automatic fire.

"If you stop I will," yelled Mamba. "I've got information on other poachers."

"Gutless bastard," murmured Bishop as he wiped more sweat from his face. His hand came away wet with blood. The wound on his cheek had split open but he was oblivious to the pain. He was completely focused on destroying the man who had put Saneh in a coma. Peering out he spotted the barrel of an assault rifle. It was aimed up at Kruger lying on the walkway.

Pulling out the concussion grenade Bishop popped the pin and tossed it. He closed his eyes, cupped his hands over his ears, and opened his mouth. The shock wave hit him like a punch to the gut as the toilet roll-sized tube detonated. He scrambled to his feet and dashed forward, pistol ready.

The rifle lay on the floor beneath a haze of smoke. There was a guttural scream from above and he glanced up to see Mamba leap from atop the generator, machete held high.

Bishop fired the Glock twice before a boot hit his chest. His bullets went wide, the slide locking back on an empty magazine. Twisting sideways, he narrowly avoided the machete and it sparked on the steel floor. As he staggered back he flicked the magazine clear and reached into his pocket for the spare.

Mamba came after him swinging the machete like a deranged gardener attacking a wayward hedge. "Fucking die, you white piece of shit."

Bishop was forced to use the empty Glock to block the blade. Slammed by the machete he lost his grip on the magazine and it clattered across the floor.

Mamba's blade had snagged on the rear sight of the pistol driving back the slide as he forced down on it. The blow tore it from Bishop's grip and the blade narrowly missed his shoulder. He twisted past the lean poacher, driving his forearm into his nose.

Mamba screamed in pain as Bishop scrambled across the greasy floor searching frantically for a weapon.

Remembering the workbench he skidded around the generator and grabbed a steel wrench.

Mamba was on him as he turned. The machete flashed down and Bishop blocked it with the foot-long tool. Steel flashed on steel and the machete's razor sharp blade chipped.

Bishop managed a grim smile. The machete was made from cheap steel where the spanner was high grade. "Come on, what are you waiting for," he goaded. "Or do you only attack women?"

"Fuck you," snarled Mamba as he raised the machete and swung it in an arc.

Bishop parried with a blow of his own and blade met wrench with a clang. The machete snapped at the hilt and Mamba was left swinging an empty handle.

Seizing the opportunity Bishop reversed his swing and jabbed the heavy tool into the poacher's stomach.

His blow met the resistance of a rock hard abdomen and Mamba smashed him in the jaw with the machete handle. Rocked by the blow Bishop staggered backward, the wrench slipping from his grasp. Mamba charged, slamming into his torso and driving him up against one of the pulsating engines.

Trapped between the hot engine and the enraged poacher Bishop grabbed hold of the man's vest and made to throw him sideways. His hand hit something hard and sharp protruding from a pouch, the rhino horn.

Mamba shifted his weight pressing his forearm against Bishop's throat.

He grasped the horn and wrenched it free. Fighting for breath he smashed it against the side of the poacher's head. Mamba grunted and Bishop struck him again, harder.

The weight eased off and he shoved Mamba away before hitting him a third time. The poacher staggered back staring at the horn in disbelief. It was the last thing he ever saw as Bishop used both hands to drive the sharp point through his eyeball into his brain.

Mamba stood for a split-second convulsing. Blood dribbled from his nostrils and mouth before he toppled over and hit the deck with a clang.

Bishop took a moment to regain his breath. Placing a boot on the dead man's throat he wrenched the horn free. He wiped the blood off on Mamba's shirt then tucked the horn into the waistband of his jeans.

A creak from the walkway above reminded him about Kruger. He looked up to see the South African staggering to his feet. "You OK?" he yelled over the noise of the engines.

Kruger gave thumbs-up as he braced himself against the handrail.

He climbed the ladder and checked on the South African. Up close he spotted a rent in the ballistic visor of his helmet. Kruger had taken a bullet directly to the face.

"Fucker caught me cold," Kruger grunted as he pried off his headgear.

"I got him," Bishop said. "We can go now."

CHAPTER 15

INDIAN OCEAN

While Bishop dealt with Mamba, Chua and Ice set about extracting information from one of their prisoners. They established themselves in the ship's galley where Ice had fastened the leader of the Triads to a chair using a roll of thick tape.

"Who do you work for?" Chua asked. Through the fully enclosed helmet his voice sounded sinister.

"Santa Claus." The gangster laughed and spat on his visor.

Ice stood alongside him, reached down with a gloved hand, and grabbed the man's face. "Show some respect, dirt bag."

The gangster rolled his eyes and went silent.

"He's not going to talk," said Chua.

Ice stepped back and gestured for Chua to join him at the bench directly behind their prisoner. "I can make him talk." He shrugged off his backpack and removed a comprehensive medical kit. Unzipping it on the bench he revealed a set of syringes. "When I was a guest of the CIA at Gitmo I was introduced to some pretty nasty techniques. There was this little worm by the name of Aaron Small. He taught me a trick that cracks most hard men."

Ice took a canister of pepper spray from his rig and flicked off the safety bail. He sprayed a tiny amount in the lid and sucked it inside a syringe. Then he pulled out a morphine injector. "You want to hold his head or should I?"

"I'll do it."

Chua gripped the gangster's face with both hands.

"What are you doing?" he demanded as Ice presented the syringe.

"Oh, now you want to talk, hey."

The captive stared at the needle.

"What I'm going to do is inject pepper spray into your eyeball." He tapped the syringe's chamber. "The pain is going to be more intense than anything you have ever experienced. If you don't start talking then you don't get the morphine in syringe number two. Now, let's get started." He grasped his jaw and aimed the point of the needle at his left eye.

The gangster tried to twist his head away, his eyes wide with fear. "NOOO!"

"Then tell us who you work for," snapped Chua as he struggled to hold him still.

"I work for Zhou, I work for Zhou."

"What's his full name?"

"Just Zhou, that's all I know. Shanghai Greater Exports, that's the name of the company. They own the ship, I work for them every now and then."

Ice backed off with the syringe. "A good start, now keep talking."

"Where is the Shanghai Greater Exports head office?" asked Chua. "I want names, I want addresses, and I want phone numbers."

Vance's voice interrupted through his helmet. "Team, we've got an anti-piracy chopper inbound. We need to exfil, ASAP."

"Roger, we'll finish up here. Any news on Bishop?" Chua transmitted after muting the external speakers on his helmet.

"Yeah, he and Kruger are on their way up to the bridge. Get your butts up here now."

"On our way."

Chua turned his attention back to their prisoner. "You've got one minute to tell me everything you know about Shanghai Greater Exports. If I'm not happy with your answer then... well, we all know what happens then."

Ice held up the syringe.

"Get talking."

***

Twenty-five nautical miles away on the bridge of the *USS Roosevelt* the captain turned to the officer of the deck. "Time to target?"

She checked her battle management console. "The Seahawk is three minutes out. We're still an hour from the *Zenhai*."

"Excellent, have you heard anything more from the ship's captain?"

"I have communications now." She held one hand to her headset and paused to listen. "Sir, someone is hailing from the *Zenhai*, but I don't think it's the captain. He sounds American and wants to speak to you."

"Very well." He reached for the handset on the control panel in front of him. The Lieutenant gave him a nod to let him know it was connected.

"This is the captain of the *USS Roosevelt*, to whom am I speaking?"

There was a pause.

"Hello, Captain, my name is not important. What is important is that you understand you are potentially about to compromise an Agency operation." The voice sounded deep and distinctly American. "I need you to order your helicopter to stand off and not interfere with activities on the *Zenhai*."

The captain frowned. "You are currently operating within CTF-151's battlespace. We have every right to board that vessel and I intend to do just that."

"That would be a serious mistake, Captain Edwards."

Edwards turned to the officer of the deck with his eyebrows raised. His name wasn't public information. "Listen punk, I'm not some UN official you can strong arm with your secret squirrel shit. A SEAL team will be landing on the *Zenhai* and you can explain in person what exactly it is you're doing on that ship." Edwards slammed the handset down in its cradle. "Arrogant cocksucker."

"Sir, the Seahawk has eyes on the target vessel and can confirm there is a UN helicopter positioned on the bow. Additionally the vessel shows signs of damage from heavy weapons."

"Acknowledged, give the SEAL team leader authority to board."

"Aye, sir."

***

Bishop and Kruger met Chua and Ice at the door that led out to the deck and the waiting UN helicopter. Bishop had the rhino horn tucked under his arm. His was face swollen and covered in blood with a wicked gash on his cheek.

"Hey, Bish, we need to leave that behind," said Chua pointing to the bloodied horn.

Bishop handed it to him. "I'm done with it now."

Chua took the horn as Vance appeared on the staircase from the bridge. "Team, we ready to roll?"

"Give me twenty seconds." Chua ran up the stairs to the messing hall. He placed the horn on the kitchen bench then checked on their prisoner. Their interrogation victim was still attached to the chair.

"Chua, hurry the hell up!" yelled Vance. "We've got a US Navy chopper up top and they're not here to deliver pizza."

Chua ran back down the stairs and joined the rest of the team at the door.

"OK, let's get moving," said Vance as he shoved open the door. The downwash of a hovering helicopter buffeted them. "Shit, they're directly overhead." He ducked back pulling the door half shut.

"We can't stay here," said Ice. "They'll rope onto the bridge then work their way down. We need to move now."

***

The MH-60 Seahawk hovered over the *Zenhai*, a thick rope hanging from its side door trailing to the port-side bridge wing. The first member of the SEAL boarding party slid down and hit the deck. A second later another assaulter landed and the pair stormed inside.

"US Navy, hands where I can see them!" yelled the lead assaulter aiming his MK18 Carbine at the figure behind the helm.

"Not again," said the captain as he turned his back to the intruder to show his hands were still secured.

The rest of the six-man team gathered on the bridge before the helicopter peeled away. SEALs covered all the entry points as the team leader reported in. "*USS Roosevelt*, this is Team One, we've secured the bridge."

The response was instantaneous. "Acknowledged, Team One. Any sign of hostiles?"

"Negative, just the UN chopper."

"We are standing by."

The team leader turned to the captain. "Hey, bud, you speak English?"

The Chinese man nodded.

"Good, where are the bad guys?"

He pointed toward the door two of the commandos had covered. "They just left. If you run you might catch them."

The SEAL snapped into action. "Harrison, you're on the wing. If they try to escape you are weapons free."

"Copy that." A barrel-chested SEAL carrying an MK46 machine gun made for the side door.

"The rest of us are going down, let's move."

The lead assaulters pulled open the door and entered the stairwell, weapons held ready.

***

Kruger heard the clatter of boots at the top of the stairwell. "They've made entry," he transmitted to the rest of the team.

"Roger, let's roll," replied Ice from where he waited behind the door to the deck. He had consolidated all their remaining smoke grenades in a dump pouch attached to his belt. He tossed the first grenade out onto the walkway that ran the length of the ship.

It hissed and spluttered spewing a thick cloud of smoke down the side of the vessel. Ice led the team out to the deck and down the walkway. With his thermal imaging activated he could see clearly. He tossed another grenade as they made their way toward the bow.

A machine gun barked and rounds hit the containers above him. “Keep moving,” he bellowed as he skidded to a halt and turned aiming his MK48 at the bridge.

The thermal imager in his helmet identified the glowing barrel of the shooter. He stitched the wing with suppressive fire as the others ran past.

“Last man,” said Kruger as he sprinted to cover. He took up a firing position and yelled, “Go, go, go!”

Ice gave the bridge one last burst, turned, and ran past Kruger to the base of the containers on which the chopper was perched. He gave Bishop a leg up then they helped Vance.

“Jesus, what've you been eating,” yelled Bishop as he hauled the PRIMAL director up alongside him.

“It's the gear,” grunted Vance.

“It’s the donuts.”

They repeated the process with Chua then Kruger. Ice was last to climb up the container to the waiting helicopter. While Kruger worked his machine gun Ice leaped into the cargo hold and the Mi-8 powered skyward.

Ice strode through to the cockpit and spotted a gray US Navy Seahawk through the windshield. It hovered sideways with a machine gunner aiming directly at them.

“US Navy helicopter this is a UN-flagged airframe operating in international waters. If you do not move we're going to collide,” yelled Vanko over the radio.

Ice used his iPRIMAL to tune to the frequency and listen in.

“UN aircraft this is the US Navy, you will land immediately or we will be forced to fire.”

“Fuck you, comrade!” Vanko hauled up on the collective and the Soviet-era helicopter launched itself toward the Seahawk.

Ice flinched as the gray helicopter loomed in the windshield before it peeled off to avoid a collision.

"Yankee pussy," the bearded South African copilot said as Vanko sent the chopper thundering across the ocean.

Both men burst out laughing as Ice turned back to the team sitting in the cargo hold. He could see the ship and helicopter shrinking through the open back of the chopper. Without air-to-air missiles there was no way the Seahawk could intercept them.

"Where did you find these cowboys, Kruger?" he transmitted over the PRIMAL team channel.

"Mogadishu, where you will never find a more wretched hive of scum and villainy."

"Yeah, well they're trying to beat the record for the Kessel run."

"Will you ladies stop quoting Star Wars and take a look at the slash on Bishop's face," snapped Vance. "This mission ain't over till we get back to the Sandpit."

***

MOGADISHU, SOMALIA

The Mi-8 touched down at Mogadishu airport with less than fifteen minutes worth of fuel remaining. Vanko taxied in front of his hangar and parked next to Toppie's battered biplane. The team disembarked and filed into the shed to strip down their equipment and pack it away.

Vance left the group and using his iPRIMAL contacted Frank in the Sandpit. "What's the news on Saneh?"

"I spoke to Tariq an hour ago. Her brain activity has increased. The doctor thinks she might be coming back to us. Mirza arrived this morning and he's been in with her all day."

Mirza was Bishop's closest friend and more times than not his battle buddy. The former Indian Special Forces operative was also close to Saneh; she had asked him to be their child's godfather.

"That's good news. We've got Bishop and we'll be back later tonight."

"Yeah, Chua gave an update in his message. We're chasing down all the leads on the intel he picked up."

Vance frowned. "Keep a close handle on Flash, I don't want him hacking any government databases and tipping off the CIA. It's bad enough we've been exposed to the Navy."

"We haven't seen any indicators of a compromise. I'll warn Flash to keep it real low-key."

"Good stuff, we'll see you soon. Vance out."

As he walked back he made eye contact with Bishop who walked stiffly toward him. The wound on his cheek had been sewn shut but he still looked like someone who'd gone twelve rounds with Mike Tyson.

"Vance, I'm sorry about all this," Bishop said quietly.

The PRIMAL director nodded. "You fucked up, Bish. You should have waited for the team. Kruger is the only reason you're alive."

"I know."

Vance grasped his shoulder. "No more renegade ops."

"OK, boss." He sighed. "Is there any news on Saneh?"

"Yeah, good news. The doctors think she's improving."

"And the baby?"

"Too early to tell, bud. You can talk to the doctors when we get back to Abu Dhabi. We'll be airborne soon. Try to get some rest, you look like shit."

Bishop managed a grimace. "Thanks. Hey, can you make sure the guys who helped out Kruger are looked after."

"Will do."

It didn't take the team long to load their gear into Vanko's truck and he drove them across the runway to where the Lascar Logistics business jet waited.

Vance watched as Bishop, Chua, and Ice thanked Toppie and Vanko. Once they had disappeared inside the jet he stepped forward with Kruger and opened an aluminum suitcase on the stairs revealing wads of crisp US currency.

"OK, Vanko, how much more do we owe you?"

The pilot licked his lips. "A hundred thousand, plus eighty thousand for fuel."

"That's not what you quoted," said Kruger as he folded his arms.

The Russian grinned sheepishly. "All right, a hundred covers it."

Vance took two bundles from the suitcase and handed them to the mechanic come pilot. "Here's a hundred. I'm guessing I don't need to tell you that if anyone asks..."

"*Da,* we never met. This never happened." The Russian's eyes didn't leave the cash as he flicked the bundles. Stuffing them in his coveralls he turned to Toppie. "I'll wait for you in the truck."

When the Russian had left Vance reached out and shook the grubby little South African's hand. "You really came through for my people, Toppie." He handed over a stack of cash. "If there is anything I can do for you, just ask Kruger."

Toppie bowed his head as he accepted the bundle of notes. "Thank you, this should cover what we owe Al-Mumit, *ja.*"

Vance glanced at Kruger, who nodded. He took another wad of cash from the case. "This is for your help."

"No, that wouldn't be right. Helping out my old Recce mate was enough."

Kruger's eyes narrowed. "You do want something though, don't you, Toppie?"

The grizzled old quartermaster shrugged. "You know me too well." He gestured at the ancient biplane sitting in the distance. "Annie is getting a little old and..."

"I'll get my people on it," interrupted Vance.

Toppie flashed his yellow teeth. "Thanks." He turned and joined Vanko in the truck, leaving Vance with Kruger.

"You're not coming with us?"

"No boss, Toppie's going to fly me back to Luangwa. My dog's up there with Bishop's friends."

He offered the South African operative his hand. "Thanks for looking out for Bish."

"That's what family does, *ja*. Plus, I need the excitement. Things have been pretty boring since we shut up shop."

Vance shook his head. "It hasn't even been two months."

"Exactly, any longer and I would have gone insane. Keep me posted on any work."

"Will do." He climbed the stairs to the aircraft and secured the door. Most of the team was already reclined and fast asleep.

The pilot's voice came through over the intercom as they began to roll forward. "Welcome back to Priority Movements Airlift, team. Help yourself to refreshments and make yourself comfortable. Next stop, Abu Dhabi International Airport."

CHAPTER 16

ABU DHABI

The doors to Bareen Hospital slid open and Bishop spotted Mirza waiting for him in the well-lit foyer.

The bearded Indian managed a weary smile and stepped forward. "I'm sorry I didn't come earlier."

"It's all right, mate."

Mirza reached forward and grasped Bishop's shoulders. "She's awake."

His heart lurched. "When?"

"Three hours ago."

"Take me to her." He strode toward the elevator. "Where is she?"

Mirza caught up as the elevator doors opened. "Level three, ward echo. Look, Bish, she's pretty disorientated, you need to take it easy."

He waited for Mirza to step inside, hit the corresponding button, and watched the floor numbers as they climbed. Once the doors opened he raced into the ward, heart pounding. It was late at night and no one manned the nurse's station.

"This way." Mirza directed him down a corridor. "Room 304."

He spotted the number on the door from a dozen feet away. Stopping he tentatively glanced back. Mirza gave him a solemn nod. Taking a deep breath he approached and pushed open the door.

Saneh lay on a bed surrounded by vibrant flowers. Without the tubes and machines attached to her she looked asleep. As he shut the door her eyes opened and he nearly burst into tears. Struggling to speak he managed to blurt out a few words. "I thought I lost you."

She blinked away her own tears as he bent down and wrapped his arms around her.

He felt her body shudder as she sobbed burying her face in his neck. "Where have you been? We lost her, Aden. We lost her."

The words hit him like a bullet to the chest. Tears flowed as he wept holding her tightly. Their baby had been a girl and she had never even made it into the world.

"It's going to be OK," he croaked. "It's going to be OK."

He held her until a nurse came and explained they needed to sedate her. She was still far too weak to deal with the emotion of losing the child. Bishop pulled a chair close and held her hand as the drug took effect and her eyes closed.

Mirza entered the room silently and put his hand on his best friend's shoulder. "I'm so sorry for your loss."

Bishop stared at Saneh sleeping. "I went after the man who did this, Mirza. I went after him and I killed him. What did it achieve? Nothing. I should have protected her that night. I should have been by her side."

Mirza shook his head and took a seat. "You can't beat yourself up over this. You brought justice to the man responsible, that's all Saneh could ask. You need to be thankful you didn't lose her as well."

"I started building a home for us in Spain, on my parent's land."

"It can still be your home. She loves you, Bish, nothing is going to change that."

He wiped his eyes. "You're right. I need to make sure it's ready for when she leaves hospital."

They sat in silence as Bishop held her hand. "So what has Tariq had you working on?"

"I've been doing some flying for the real Priority Movements Airlift."

Bishop managed a smile. "Giving more legitimacy to the cover firm, that's a pretty smart move on Tariq's behalf."

Mirza nodded. "We've been delivering humanitarian aid to refugee camps in Syria and Kurdistan. Not exactly taking down bad guys but it fills the void until PRIMAL is back online."

"I think I'm done with PRIMAL. I can't stand the idea of losing her. Not after everything that's happened."

"You're not a machine, Bish. No one expects you to keep fighting."

He turned to Mirza with tears in his eyes. "Good, because I can't."

***

Vance pushed open the door to the intelligence cell and dropped into an empty chair. "Saneh is awake but they lost the baby," he said quietly to Chua and Flash.

"Oh no," whispered Flash from where he sat behind his terminal.

"Are they OK?" asked Chua.

"Mirza's in with them now. Saneh is still recovering from the treatment. Bishop's doing as good as can be expected. He wants to take her back to Spain as soon as she's released."

"Yeah, that's probably for the best. I'll arrange clean passports for both of them," said Chua.

"Do you think they'll ever work on the team again?" asked Flash.

Vance shrugged. "I don't know, bud. I do know we still need to lay low. Our little run-in with the Navy might trigger a response."

Chua shook his head. "No, we've seen nothing to suggest they're on to us. I think your little CIA charade had them spooked, they kept the incident reporting in-house."

He frowned. "It's not like you to talk the threat down." He studied his counterpart's face for a moment. "OK, I get it. What have you two got in mind? I'm guessing you want to go after the guys responsible for the ivory on board the *Zenhai*?"

"Correct." Chua gestured to a screen on the wall. Displayed was a link analysis chart, an intricate web of lines joining events, locations, and personalities. "Flash started with the ship and he's tracked every link back through to a number of dummy corporations to a Triad syndicate based in Shanghai.

They've got a front man, Zhou. He handles all the smuggling. Our gangster on the *Zenhai* reported directly to him."

"And you want to take him down."

"Yes, this is a cause Saneh and Bishop both believe strongly in. It might help them deal with their loss and it's a just cause in its own right."

Vance sighed. "OK, so what's your plan?"

"It's simple. The *Zenhai* isn't set to reach Shanghai for another five days. I want to make sure the Chinese authorities are ready and waiting."

"And, let me guess, you can't do it without hitting the ground?"

"I need to make sure the authorities action it. I can't guarantee that if I only send them a tipoff."

"Right, and you just so happen to have a contact on the inside willing to help you get to the right people."

"I want to go in posing as a member of TRAFFIC. I'm fluent in Mandarin and I'm not going to pop up on anyone's radar. I can be in Shanghai within eight hours."

Vance frowned. "There's more isn't there?"

"Yes, I want to take a media team with me."

"Definitely not."

"Listen, Bishop mentioned there was a BBC team working in Luangwa when Saneh was injured. I've tracked down the journalist and I want to take him with me to China to capture the moment when the criminals are apprehended. The media component of this is just as important as the arrest."

"You think the Chinese will go for it?"

"They will when he tells them he has evidence that a Chinese corporation has been backing the poaching of black rhino. They want to be seen doing the right thing when it comes to the illicit wildlife trade."

Vance let out a sigh. "OK, make it happen." He glanced at his watch; it was three in the morning. "I'm going to bed. Don't stay up too late." As he made for the door he realized the order had fallen on deaf ears. Both men were hard at work at their terminals. He shook his head; these intel guys were like a dog with a bone.

***

Bishop had never been to the Hotel La Capiard but he knew the history behind the luxurious residence. It was where Vance had confronted Tariq and set the events in motion that led to the forming of PRIMAL. Hallowed ground as far as Vance was concerned and it didn't surprise Bishop when the Director of Operations wanted to meet him there. The hotel wasn't far from the hospital and Saneh was resting.

He spotted Vance sitting at a table when he entered the restaurant. The big man wore his standard attire, a garish Hawaiian shirt and linen slacks.

"Hey Vance," said Bishop.

The hulking African American rose and embraced him in a bear hug. "So sorry to hear about the loss."

"Thanks, look I know I owe you for saving Saneh. If you hadn't come and got her I might have lost them both."

"You're family, bud."

They sat at the table and Vance waved the waiter over. "You want some coffee?"

"That would be great."

Vance ordered two black coffees. "Whatever you and Saneh need, the team is here for you."

"Yeah, I know. You've all been amazing." He took a deep breath. "Hey, when PRIMAL starts up ops again, I'm not sure you're going to be able to count me in."

Vance nodded as their coffees arrived. When the waiter disappeared he spoke. "Bish, no one expects anything from you."

He took a sip of the sweet black coffee. "I feel like I'm letting you guys down."

Vance scowled into his own beverage then looked up. "You've taken more risks than anyone else. You've put more on the line and, well you've lost more than most. No one is going to feel let down."

"Doesn't make it any easier."

"Listen, bud, I remember the day I recruited an angry young man who wanted nothing more than to avenge the death of his parents. You've come a long way since then."

"Really, I don't think so. I went after Mamba instead of staying by Saneh's side. I let her down when she needed me most. Not to mention that I put the entire team at risk."

"What can I say, you always run hot when it comes to justice."

"Not anymore."

Vance nodded and inspected the menu. "So, can I buy you breakfast? The pastries here are divine. Ice loves the chocolate croissants," he said with a chuckle.

Bishop managed to smile. "Sure is good to see him back on the team."

"Nothing seems to hold him back."

He lowered his eyes to the menu. Ice had lost limbs and four years of his life and he still wanted to be part of PRIMAL.

"Shit, I didn't mean it like that."

Bishop sighed. "How about we get some of those pastries, yeah."

They shared small talk as they ate breakfast. Once done Bishop shook Vance's hand and walked across town to the hospital.

By the time he reached the entrance sweat drenched his shirt. As he composed himself in the air-conditioned foyer Mirza emerged from the elevator. The look on his friend's face told him something was wrong. "Is she awake?" he asked.

"She's gone, Bish."

"How? No, they told me she was doing well."

Mirza grasped his shoulder. "No, I mean she's gone, checked herself out of the hospital." He handed Bishop a folded piece of paper. "She left this for you."

Bishop took the note. The delicate writing on the front, spelling his name, was hers. He unfolded it and began to read.

Aden,

I pray that you will not think less of me for what I have to do. I can't bear to see you at the moment and I can't go back to Spain. When I woke and I was alone, I realized the life we had planned was over. I need to come to terms with this loss by myself. Please don't try to find me. I do love you and may return one day, I just don't know when.

S

Bishop fought back tears as he finished reading. "She's gone." He took a deep breath and started for the exit.

Mirza jogged after him. "What are you going to do?" he asked as he caught him at the doors.

"What can I do, Mirza? She's right. I should have been by her side. She doesn't want me to find her and God knows I probably couldn't." He clenched his jaw. "She needs time and time is what I'm going to give her."

He paused at the hospital doors unsure of what to do or where to go.

"What about you, Bish?" asked Mirza.

"I guess I could go back to Spain."

"And do what, mope around till she returns?"

"Well, what do you recommend? Hang around here and bother Vance for a job he's not going to give me? We're on cease-ops once Chua wraps up his loose ends in Shanghai."

"I was thinking something a little lower key. My crew could use another loadmaster on the runs into Syria and Kurdistan."

"You need help delivering humanitarian aid?"

Mirza smiled. "If you can promise not to go looking for trouble."

"Trouble, me? You're confusing me with someone else, mate." He swallowed hard and forced his emotions deep inside. "Sounds good, count me in."

CHAPTER 17

JARJANAZ, SYRIA

The ramp of the Priority Movements Airlift C-130 transporter dropped with a whine and Bishop shielded his eyes from the sand that whipped inside the cargo hold. He pulled on goggles and lifted his shemagh to cover his nose and mouth as he peered out over the ramp.

"Bish, can you chock the wheels? This wind is trying to push us back to the Emirates," transmitted the pilot through his headphones.

"Roger." Bishop unhooked the blocks of plastic joined by rope, yanked out his headset cable, and strode down the ramp to the dirt airstrip.

He glanced around. There wasn't much to see. Thick red dust hung in the air and in the distance a massive cloud of sand crept slowly toward them. He quickly shoved the blocks against the aircraft's wheels before returning up the ramp and plugging back in.

"No sign of our reception party yet," he transmitted.

"What do you think, Mirza?" the pilot asked his copilot over the intercom.

"We'll give them ten minutes. If they don't turn up we should take off, get clear of this sandstorm, and head across to Baghdad."

"Sounds like a plan."

Bishop stood on the ramp peering into gloom. Dark shapes grew in size until he could make out that they were vehicles. "We've got movement."

A convoy of five four-wheel drives appeared from the sandstorm and parked in a line perpendicular to the aircraft's ramp. "Five vehicles, Red Crescent markings," he reported as men stepped out of the four-wheel drives. "At least eight guys."

"Acknowledged, I'm coming back now," replied Mirza.

The men strode forward unarmed with their faces wrapped in keffiyehs, traditional Arabic scarves. One of them stopped at the ramp and lifted his hand in greeting. "*As-salaam alaykum*," he offered dropping the scarf to reveal a thin narrow face with a protruding chin and scraggly beard. "My name is Salim."

Mirza appeared from behind the crates of supplies secured in the cargo hold. "*Wa alaykum salaam,* Salim, it's a pleasure to meet you. My name is Mirza and this is Aden."

"The pleasure is all mine." He gestured to the crates. "Are all of these for us?" The aircraft was stacked with large wooden boxes stamped with World Health Organization markings.

Bishop nodded. "Yes and we need to get them offloaded as quickly as we can."

"Of course, you wish to beat the storm. We will hurry." He turned and snapped an order to his men. They formed a line as Bishop unfastened the straps holding the supplies in place.

The first pair of men lifted one of the wooden crates and struggled down the ramp with it. They were immediately replaced by another pair who lifted the next box clear.

He watched as they rapidly unloaded the stores from the back of the four-engine transporter and piled them on the sand-covered runway. Once all the boxes were stacked in front of the vehicles Bishop recovered the chocks and ducked back inside.

Mirza shook hands with Salim and the Syrian strode out of the cargo hold and down the ramp.

Bishop looked beyond him at the looming sandstorm as Mirza headed back to the cockpit. "Pedal to the metal, guys, we need to get the hell out of here."

"On it," replied the pilot.

The C-130's engines roared at full thrust adding more sand and wind to the mix. Bishop hit the ramp controls as he watched the workers struggle to stop the stack of supplies from blowing away. One crate toppled over and another splintered open tossing its contents across the sand. As the ramp closed

Bishop caught a glimpse of dark green tubing among the broken wood.

When the ramp thumped shut he pulled off his goggles and scarf and secured himself in the loadmaster's seat. He felt the aircraft gather speed, bounce, and lurch into the sky. The onslaught of the oncoming storm hit them hard and the airframe shuddered sideways.

"Hold on, this is going to be rough," transmitted Mirza in a tense voice.

"That's what she said," managed Bishop as he braced himself. The violent turbulence tossed him about in his seat as the pilot struggled to find smooth air in front of the storm.

After five minutes of clinging to his seat they leveled out and he unclipped his safety belt. As he walked toward the cockpit a glance out the side window revealed clear blue skies.

Bishop climbed the short ladder to the cockpit and opened the door. "Mirza, can I have a quick word?

"What was in the boxes?" he asked once they were back in the cargo hold.

"You know what is in those boxes, medical supplies."

He shook his head. "That's not what I saw."

"What did you see?"

"Goddamn TOW missiles."

Mirza frowned. "You sure?"

"I know what a bloody TOW looks like. Tariq has some explaining to do."

"He might not even know this is happening. Lascar is supplying the aircraft but the UAE government has organized the payload."

"Then he's being used or he is using us. We have no idea where those missiles will end up."

Mirza nodded. "We've got another shipment out in two days."

"We'll use it to find out exactly what is going on."

Mirza returned to the cockpit leaving Bishop alone in the empty cargo hold. He walked across to the aircraft's side door and peered through the window at the desert landscape below.

His thoughts turned to Saneh. She was probably in South East Asia by now, or so he hoped, turning to meditation and yoga to come to terms with the loss of their child. She had her way of dealing with loss and he had his. He would find out who was using Priority Movements Airlift to smuggle sophisticated weapons into a civil war rife with rogue militias and religious extremists. He had a new mission; one close to his heart. Poachers may have taken his child but it was an arms dealer who had cost him his parents.

***

SHANGHAI, CHINA

Rain drizzled from dark clouds as Zhou stood on a massive concrete wharf holding an umbrella. To his front the rusted flanks of the *Zenhai* reached up toward the night sky. The ship had docked half an hour earlier and already Chinese officials were on the bridge checking her paperwork and manifest. The Triad smuggler watched as a uniformed officer strode down the gangplank and avoided the puddles as he approached.

"I take it everything is in order." He handed the man an envelope thick with cash.

"Yes, there are no problems here." The official took the money, tucked it inside his green military jacket, and set off down the wharf to the next freighter.

Another figure approached from the gangplank. He recognized the stocky build and watched intently as Kehua presented a wooden box.

"Where is Mamba?" he asked.

"We had a disagreement and he took a swim," his lieutenant replied opening the box. The rhino horn looked dull and unimpressive.

"What about the ivory?"

"It is safe in the hold."

Zhou licked his lips. "Then I guess delaying his payment was a wise move." He took the box and tucked it under his arm. "You've done well, Kehua. A bonus is in order. Once you deliver the ivory to the warehouse come and see me in my office."

The gangster bobbed his head in appreciation and turned back to the ship.

As he shuffled between the shipping containers Zhou smirked. The deal had gone even better than he could have hoped. Without Mamba he was saved considerable expense.

He reached his BMW and handed the waiting driver his umbrella. Climbing into the back of the sedan he dialed Fan. Hejun's pretty assistant had been hassling him for updates on the horn. "I have it," he reported.

"We're waiting at your office," she said and terminated the call.

"Rude bitch." Zhou pocketed his phone and turned his attention back to the box and its contents. The horn felt cold and its surface rougher than expected. It was a fine specimen, however, heavy and in good condition with no cracks or chips visible on its surface. Hejun would be satisfied.

He glanced out the window as his driver guided them to the parking lot in front of Shanghai Greater Exports. The beverage tycoon's black Mercedes was parked at the entrance. Fan waited under an umbrella alongside the car.

His driver parked, stepped out, and opened his door with the umbrella held ready. Zhou returned the horn to the box and closed it. He licked his lips in anticipation of the payment he would soon receive.

Less than two hundred yards away Chen Chua watched the scene on a monitor in the rear of an unmarked police van. An adhesive label stuck to the front of his jacket announced in Chinese characters that he was an 'observer'. The other three people in the van were a BBC journalist, his cameraman, and their Chinese police minder.

"When will they make their move?" asked the journalist in his crisp English accent.

"Any second now," replied the policeman.

"Make sure you get this," the journalist said to his offsider who had a camera aimed at the image on the screen.

"We will make the footage available to you," said the officer. "China wants the world to see what we are doing to combat poaching." He had already delivered this party line a dozen times.

Chua smiled as his assessment of the situation had proven accurate. The Chinese government had jumped on the opportunity to portray their anti-poaching activities in a positive light. The information he'd presented them regarding Zhou and his syndicate had prompted a large-scale police operation.

"OK, they are going in now." The police officer pushed opened the door at the back of the van as police sirens wailed and tires screeched.

The BBC team leaped from the van and dashed across the road to where police officers were hauling people out of two cars and cuffing them.

Chua watched the screen from the van as Zhou and his two clients, one an attractive young woman and the other an elderly man, were shoved into a police car. "Justice is served," he whispered as he tore the sticker from his jacket and scrunched it into a ball. Stepping out of the van he walked a dozen yards to a busy street and flagged a cab.

EPILOGUE

NORTH LUANGWA NATIONAL PARK, ZAMBIA

Kruger brought the Polaris all-terrain vehicle to a halt and studied the screen bolted to the dashboard. He and his co-driver, a ranger named Francis, had driven the ATV deep into the bush under the cover of a starless night.

"What have we got?" the South African asked.

He saw Francis shake his head in the soft glow from the screen.

"We've lost them."

The image was being beamed down from a silent electric drone lurking in the dark sky. Its infrared camera had been tracking a group of suspected poachers who'd been spotted at the edge of the park. Kruger and Francis were on patrol nearby so were the first to respond. Other teams had been scrambled from the base camp.

"Springbok this is All-Black, what have you guys got out there?" Dominic Marks' distinctly New Zealand accent came over the headset Kruger wore underneath his helmet. The headgear was plugged into the high-powered radio mounted next to the tablet.

"Nothing, the drone has lost them." Kruger reached across and brushed his glove across the screen swiping from the drone feed to a map displaying the location of the other teams, the drone, and the previous location of the suspects.

The ATV and its high-tech fit-out was one of five anonymously donated to Dom's organization along with drones, non-lethal weaponry, radios, and night vision devices. It hadn't taken much to convince Kruger to stay and help train the rangers on how to use the new equipment. Within a matter of weeks they had deployed the systems and apprehended no less than five separate poaching parties.

"Springbok," continued Dom. "If we lose these guys there's every chance they could get through and kill Kassala. We haven't been able to locate her since her tracking chip went down." Dom referred to the last remaining female black rhino in the park. Recently confirmed to be pregnant, her GPS tracker had been working intermittently making it difficult for the team to protect her from the constant threat of poachers.

"Got it." Kruger examined the terrain around where the drone had first located the party of five. Numerous dense patches of trees could have been the reason the aircraft's sensors couldn't see the men. He swiped back to the drone feed, reached up, and flicked the pair of night vision goggles on his helmet down over his eyes. "Hang on, Francis, we're going to head in for a closer look."

The two-seater ATV accelerated with a high-revving roar as he pressed the pedal to the floor. With a stealthy hybrid-electric engine and capable of accelerating to 40 miles an hour in four seconds the nimble Polaris was the perfect vehicle for chasing down poachers. With Kruger at the wheel they darted between trees and bounced over rocky outcrops.

He followed a game trail that snaked through the bush toward the trees he'd spotted on the screen. Branches and thorns scraped the side rails of the ATV as they closed in.

"Springbok this is All-Black, we got a hit on Kassala, she's only a few clicks to the west," reported Dom over the radio.

"Roger," Kruger transmitted. He glanced across at Francis. "That's the direction these pricks were heading."

"If they get to her before we find them they'll kill her," Francis said frantically.

"That's not going to happen." Kruger sent them barreling through a thicket of bushes.

"I see them!" yelled Francis as they burst out the other side.

"Where?" Kruger stomped on the brakes and they skidded to a halt. He scanned the terrain through his night vision goggles.

"From the sky." Francis pointed at the tablet screen. On it a cluster of heat signatures was moving from the trees in the direction of Kassala.

Kruger glanced down under his goggles at the screen then scanned the terrain ahead. The forest was a thick dark mass that blocked their way. "We can't go through there." Spinning the wheel he skirted the trees searching for a way through.

"Springbok, we're not going to get to them in time. It's up to you," Dom's voice came through over the headset.

He hit the radio transmit button as they bounced over a log hidden in the long grass. His helmet slammed against the roll bar dislodging his night vision goggles. Stomping on the brakes he sent the ATV skidding sideways before it dove nose first down a slope into a dry creek bed. It rolled sideways completing a full rotation before landing back on its wheels.

"Springbok, you hear me?" transmitted Dom.

He secured his goggles and adjusted the racing harness that held him secure in the vehicle. After confirming Francis wasn't injured he replied, "*Ja*, we're on it." He checked the tablet and saw the creek would take them roughly in the direction of the suspects.

Amazingly the Polaris still ran; testament to its durability. It belted along the dry riverbed at top speed, Kruger weaving it around dead trees and large boulders like a seasoned rally pro.

"There's a track up ahead," yelled Francis. "The poachers are using it. They're getting closer to Kassala."

Kruger spotted tire marks in the sand. Backing off the throttle he skidded the ATV pointing the nose up the bank. They crested the rise and drove slowly through tall grass in the wheel ruts left by a safari tour. Glancing at the tablet he confirmed the poaching party's presence only a few hundred yards away. "You ready?"

Francis had taken one of the pump-action shotguns from the rack between the seats and held it across his knees. "I'm ready," he said adjusting his headset.

"Then let's do this." Kruger shifted the ATV's hybrid engine into electric mode to mask their approach. Up ahead he caught a glimpse of an armed figure walking alongside the road. As they rolled closer they saw all five men of the hunting party, armed with rifles and bush knives. Most likely they were dirt-poor farmers forced to poach to put food on the table.

He flicked open a red cover on the dash and held his finger over a button as they closed in. When the rearmost man turned toward them he stabbed the button with a gloved finger.

Above the roll cage a bank of xenon lights turned night to day, dazzling the poachers. Behind the lights a speaker screamed with an ultrasonic beam.

Wearing active-hearing headsets and sitting below the focused acoustic beam, Kruger and Francis were unaffected by the sonic weapon. The poachers were not and they dropped to the ground with hands over their ears, screaming and vomiting.

At the edge of the group a poacher raised his rifle. Francis fired the shotgun launching an XREP Taser. The high-tech projectile hit him square in the chest and he collapsed into the grass with five hundred volts coursing through his shuddering body.

They leaped out of the Polaris and easily disarmed and restrained the poachers. Only then did Kruger terminate the frequency emitter and contact Dom. "All-Black this is Springbok, we've intercepted and detained five suspects."

"Good work. We'll be in your location within the next thirty minutes to pick them up," replied Dom.

"Take your time, these guys aren't going anywhere. Springbok out."

An hour and a half later the five poachers were being loaded into a Zambian police truck back at base camp.

Kruger sat in the newly constructed command center with a tablet on his lap. He was filling out the forms the rangers submitted to assist the police in prosecuting the poachers. A bottle of cold beer sat at arm's length dripping condensation on the bench. Princess, his hound, lay at his feet under the desk, snoring gently.

"Enough excitement for you?"

Kruger glanced up as Dom walked across and took the seat next to him. The office was a recent addition to the anti-poaching facility. With its screens, radios, and laptops it reminded him a little of PRIMAL's old headquarters, the Bunker. "I live for the post-op paperwork," he replied sarcastically as he took a swig from the beer.

The New Zealander grunted in agreement. "Yeah I hate it too but it's probably the most important piece. Without it those guys will be back in the park within a week. The legal system here is flimsy to say the least. If we can get a prosecution then we can make them talk and cut a deal."

"To sell out the big wigs?"

"That's right. I mean let's face it, bro, most of the poachers are trying to make ends meet. We get some leverage on them and they give up the ringleaders pretty quick smart."

Kruger finished with the tablet, dropped it on the desk, and turned his attention to his beer. "So when do we get to go after them?"

"We already are. The ATVs, drones, and gear were only a small part of the donation that our anonymous," he used his fingers to emphasize the word, "benefactor made to the fight on poaching. TRAFFIC received enough money to hire permanent intelligence staff and lawyers to track and prosecute the smuggling rings. They're plugged into law enforcement agencies across the continent. But hey, you wouldn't know anything about where the money came from, would you?"

He shrugged. "Like you said, the benefactor's anonymous."

Dom shook his head and reached down to fondle the dog's ears. "You heard anything from Bishop or Saneh? Christina keeps asking after them."

"Bishop's working with a humanitarian aid organization and I haven't heard anything from Saneh."

"They're a good match those two. I really hope they sort things out and get back together."

"It'll happen, it might just take a while."

Dom rose from the chair. "Well, bro, another good day's work. You and Francis did a great job out there today." He gripped the big man's shoulder. "Thanks again for everything you've done."

"No problems at all."

The New Zealander left the office and Kruger reached down to give Princess a pat. "How do you feel about hanging out here for a few more months?"

The hound lifted her broad head and stared at him, licking her nose.

"Yeah, I thought as much. Don't count on having me around for too long though. It's only a matter of time till Bishop gets himself in the shit again. Although, with all the attention Christina gives you I don't think you'll miss me much, hey girl."

The dog grunted and Kruger laughed. "Yeah, I thought so." As he drank his beer he glanced up at the screen showing the feed from one of the drones. A handful of the autonomous electric aircraft now constantly patrolled the park pushing their video feed via the web to vetted volunteer observers all over the world. It had been Christina's idea to crowdsource the surveillance and it worked well. Literally hundreds of eyes didn't miss much.

As he downed the last of his beer a message pinged and a dozen alerts popped up on the side menu of the screen. Sure enough the image revealed three heat signatures well within the confines of the park.

His radio crackled to life. "Mr. Kruger, do you see the screen?" It was Francis. Since the ambush that had killed Melo and wounded Saneh the ranger had been obsessed with taking down poachers.

Snatching it from the desk he responded. "Don't you ever sleep?"

"I can sleep when the park is safe."

Kruger tossed the empty bottle in the trash. "Right, I'll meet you at the buggy."

As he rose and made for the door, a low whine emitted from under the desk. Princess raised her head.

"OK, you can come." He grabbed a tan vest from a hook on the wall and snapped it over her stocky frame. The K9 vest had been included in the last 'anonymous' donation. It offered the dog ballistic protection and allowed Kruger to track her in the scrub.

As he pushed open the door, Princess gave a sharp bark and dashed out into the darkness. He smiled; at least he wasn't going to get bored while he waited for the PRIMAL team to drum up some work. As he threw on his own assault vest, his cell phone rang. Striding outside he checked the screen. It was Toppie. "Hey, old man, if this is about your new wings you need to contact the service provider."

"No, the bird is beautiful. I've got a job offer for you."

"*Ja*, what is it?" Kruger directed Princess into the back of the ATV; Francis already sat in his seat, shotgun held ready.

"Our friend the Pirate King wants your help."

"Is that so? I don't work for criminals."

"It's against Al-Shabaab, they've kidnapped a bunch of women from a village he is responsible for."

"OK, you've got my attention. Tell me more." Kruger strapped in and checked the drone feed on the dashboard-mounted tablet.

"He needs brains. He asked specifically for you and he'll pay top dollar. I'll supply the weapons, you train and lead the muscle. We can get some of the old regiment boys in."

"I'll need to talk to some people about it. I'll get back to you, ASAP." Terminating the call he turned to Francis. "When it rains it pours, bro. Now, let's take down these poachers."

AUTHOR'S FINAL WORDS

Many of you are already aware that I'm working a number of projects outside of the PRIMAL series. Specifically PRIMAL 2055, my near future sci-fi project and SEAL of Approval, an action-comedy-romance. Before you all start sending the hate mail I want you to know that the traditional PRIMAL series continues with PRIMAL Deception. In fact you can read on for a sneak peek of both Deception and SEAL of Approval.

Once again I want to thank you for supporting me on my journey as both a storyteller and a writer. You guys are the only reason I can do this for a living so keep reading and feel free to reach out at anytime.

P.S. Don't forget to sign up for team PRIMAL on the website so I can let you know when my latest books and PRIMAL gear is available.

BOOKS BY JACK SILKSTONE

PRIMAL Inception
PRIMAL Mirza
PRIMAL Origin
PRIMAL Unleashed
PRIMAL Vengeance
PRIMAL Fury
PRIMAL Reckoning
PRIMAL Nemesis
PRIMAL Redemption
PRIMAL Compendium
PRIMAL Renegade
SEAL of Approval

ABOUT THE AUTHOR

Jack Silkstone grew up on a steady diet of Tom Clancy, James Bond, Jason Bourne, Commando comics, and the original first-person shooters, Wolfenstein and Doom. His background includes a career in military intelligence and special operations, working alongside some of the world's most elite units. His love of action-adventure stories, his military background, and his real-world experiences combined to inspire the no-holds-barred PRIMAL series.

jacksilkstone@primalunleashed.com
www.primalunleashed.com
www.twitter.com/jsilkstone
www.facebook.com/primalunleashed

CPSIA information can be obtained
at www.ICGtesting.com
Printed in the USA
BVHW050728201218
536072BV00014B/461/P

9 781533 62926